Born of
Proud Blood

by

Roberta C. M. DeCaprio

Between the Rifle and the Spear,
Book 4

Born of Proud Blood

Contact Information: info@thewildrosepress.com

Cover Art by *Arial Burnz*

The Wild Rose Press, Inc.
PO Box 708
Adams Basin, NY 14410-0708
Visit us at www.thewildrosepress.com

Publishing History
First English Tea Rose Edition, 2012
Print ISBN 978-1-61217-544-7
Digital ISBN 978-1-61217-545-4

Between the Rifle and the Spear, Book 4
Published in the United States of America

At the top of the hill he spotted her, pacing with a limp beneath the tree.

"Riley." Gabriel waited for her to turn and face him. In spite of her injured knee, she ran to him, meeting him half way.

Long, ginger curls spilled from the man's hat she wore, flowing over her shoulders and waving behind her in the chilled morning breeze. Tears of relief welled in her eyes as he caught her in his embrace, lifting her from the ground with a hand beneath her knees and one on her back. He drew her close, tight against his heart where his beat in unison with hers.

"I feared for you," she whispered against his throat, as she buried her face beneath his chin and wrapped her arms around his neck.

"I am here now," he reassured her.

Pulling back to look at him, she searched his face. Tears trickled down her soot-stained cheeks, streaking her flesh. "Never worry me so again."

His eyes focused on her lips, lush and moist...so near to his own. Did he dare kiss her? Did he have the right?

And then she decided for him. "I would welcome your kiss," she boldly stated.

He arched a brow and smiled, strangely flattered by her declaration. "Then I will not have to steal one of my own?"

Dedication

To the memory of my uncle, Raymond Doyle,
whose desk I sat at to write this book.
And thanks to his daughters,
Joan, Kathy, and Judi,
for gifting me with such a priceless family heirloom.

~~

Also to the memory of Artful Dodger,
my beloved rabbit....
and to my newly rescued kitten, Mikko.
Her spirit and determination to survive
has shown me hope always awaits us.

~~

Lastly, to my editor, Allison Byers.
Thanks for understanding my creativity.

Chapter One

London, England
Fall of 1894

Tattered, dirty clothes hung from reeking flesh. Hunger featured upon sunken-cheeked faces. Destitute and homeless, London's *toshers* scoured the sewers for pieces of tin, rags, bones, teeth, whatever they could find of any value to sell.

Riley Flanders knew them well. She was once a *tosher* herself.

As she past London's west end, the beautiful homes and stately mansions faded into wooden shanties and hovels of poverty. No longer could she spot women wearing the latest fashions, brocaded or silk dresses and hats with plumes. The disgusting odor rising from the Thames contaminated the air, making it too vulgar to inhale as she walked down dark and sordid alleyways.

Riley had grown up in such distaste. This side of London was a humankind junkyard, where the lower-classed individuals were tossed away like trash and left to live not much better than animals.

They were forgotten souls, scorned by society and resistant to all of life's developments. If Lady Lucinda Collins hadn't rescued her from the ugly and sinister realm of vermin and vice, by this time Riley could have very well sank in its smut or become a product of its crime.

Compassion for those still living in the face of scarcity continued to draw her back. Anything she might do to help was better than doing nothing at

1

all.

Making her way down the dank ally, arms loaded with blankets, she shivered. Though still early fall, the dampness seeped into her bones. Some nights, even burrowed beneath a heavy quilt, her flesh would take forever to warm. She often thought her body had stored the cold from all the bygone years she was made to endure it.

"Ye shouldn't be 'ere, miss, gettin' a chill like this," her very observant and caring attendant warned as she placed a chubby hand upon Riley's arm. "Ye will catch yer death, and then what will Lady Collins do without ye? 'Specially now, since 'er age 'as left 'er ailin'."

"I will be perfectly fine, so worry not," Riley assured. "My duties toward Auntie Cinda are of importance to me as well."

"I'm just statin' the truth o' the matter, miss. Catchin' yer death isn't somethin' any o' us want to grieve over."

She frowned. "I'm not used to hearing such doom and gloom from your lips. And I must say, Jane, I much prefer your usual cheery demeanor."

The stocky blonde, with her great sense of humor, balanced Riley's personality, which at times was too serious and straightforward for her own good. She contributed it to a reflex action from all the years she cared for her mother...had to be the responsible one in the face of her only parent's illness. But now with Jane around, Riley relaxed, actually found herself having fun.

"My cheer is back at Collins Stead, miss, where it belongs."

"Well, muster up a bit of it to shine on this ally, aye? I could use a change of spirit, especially since I am not quite sure of what I stepped in a few paces back that now clings to my boot. And from the corner of my eye, I'm sure I saw something scurry past that pile of garbage against the wall to your right."

"Ooooh, nay miss," Jane screeched, searching the garbage heap with wide eyes and moving closer to Riley. "I do 'ate coomin' 'ere with ye, but I know ye would coome alone if I didn't."

She swiped aside a lock of hair from her forehead and walked on, the sound of their footsteps echoing eerily through the ally. "Just keep your eyes out for Top Hat Tom so I can give him these blankets. The sooner we accomplish our task, the sooner we'll be back at Collins Stead."

"And 'ow do ye know this chap ain't goin' sell the blankets for a mug o' ale?"

She came to Tom's defense. "Top Hat's not like that. When I was a child living in the burrows with my mother, he looked after us." Tom's large gray eyes and toothless smile was a part of her world for as far back as she could remember. He thought of himself as a *dapper gent*, wearing a discarded, faded tux and a worn out top hat he found, to do his bidding in...thus giving him his name. "If it weren't for Top Hat Tom, most nights Mother and I wouldn't have eaten." She sighed. "I trust him to pass these blankets out to those who need them."

Jane glanced behind her, biting her bottom lip. "Charles sits alone with the carriage, miss. 'ope 'e doesn't get beat up while were waitin' on this other chap."

Riley suspected Jane and Charles were attracted to one another. However, her handmaiden's concern brought to light the fact the two shared a deeper attachment then she believed. "Most of these folks aren't the violent sort. They'll steal things so they can sell them, but they don't want to harm anyone."

"Ye know if any o' these *toshers* tries to rob Charles, 'e'll put up a good fight. Any one o' them could get 'urt then. Besides, miss, ye don't know all

3

o' them that dwell in these conditions anymore."

She frowned again, knowing Jane's words rang true. It had been almost twelve years since Anita Flanders died, asking on her death bed for her dear friend, Lady Lucinda Collins, to take Riley on as her ward. "Just keep your eyes out for Tom. He said he'd meet us at the sewer entrance by half past two."

With her free hand, Jane pulled a pocket watch from her pouch and flipped its cover. "I believe 'tis already near to that time now, miss."

"Hush, Jane, don't become a whiner. Top Hat promised to meet me, and I trust he will be along momentarily."

Jane replaced the watch and gripped Riley's arm tighter. "I 'ope ye're right, miss."

"I am, Jane. Tom has never broken his word to me, and I don't think he'll start now. He knows how important my help is to these folks." She sighed. "And then I promise you, as soon as we give him the blankets, we can go home."

Just as those words escaped her lips, Tom made his way to them. He was stooped over and walked with a cane. His once jet-black hair was now silver. "I didn't keep ye ladies waitin' too long now, did I?"

"A second is too long in this place," Jane mumbled.

Riley shot her a stern look, silencing Jane from commenting further. Turning a smile upon her old friend, she handed him the blankets. "I hope they go to those who need them."

Tom cast a sardonic smile to her remark. "We could all use them, Flandie," he said, using the endearing name he had dubbed her.

"Then I will rephrase and say, to those who need them the most."

Tom nodded, then put his fingers to his toothless mouth and whistled. A woman by the name of Naomi emerged from the shadows. "I can't carry things while usin' the cane, and I don't get far these days without one, which I was lucky enough to find while scavengin' around one night. So I asked Naomi to 'elp out today."

Riley knew Naomi from her childhood. Abandoned by her husband, she took to selling herself on the streets for money. Her homelessness brought her in acquaintance with Tom, who in turn introduced her to Anita. At the age of twenty-five, Naomi looked good in her bones. Long, blonde hair hung to her waist, large blue eyes twinkled with spirit, and her smile was enchanting. Now, over a decade later, the pale hair was dull and uncombed, the sparkling eyes tired and drab, and her teeth were badly rotted.

"I met a chap lookin' for ye, Flandie," Naomi said, taking the blankets. "Nice lookin' bloke in 'is forties, askin' all sorts o' questions about ye."

Riley frowned. "Who would be looking for me after all these years?"

"Ye can leave the gutter, mite, but the gutter never leaves ye." Naomi adjusted a hold on the blankets and narrowed her eyes. "So don't ye ever be thinkin' ye're better than us just because ye live in a fancy 'ouse and wear the latest fashions."

"Hush, Naomi." Top Hat hissed. "Flandie never was like us. Aye, she lived in a one room shanty on the poor side o' town, but I knew 'er Mum well, and she came from good stock. Anita worked 'ard for 'er wages, taught Flandie to be 'onest. Besides, yer sharp tongue is not necessary 'ere. Flandie's never flaunted 'er good fortune. If anythin', she's used 'er new found position to 'elp us...bringin' blankets and food." Tom turned his attention to Riley. "Ye were born of proud blood, mite, always remember that. Just because yer Mum fell on 'ard times, it doesn't mean ye're not as good as the rest o' them walkin' around London."

"'e said 'e was yer pa." Naomi brought the conversation back to the man she had met.

Her frown deepened. "He's a liar then. My father would be in his late seventies, isn't that right, Tom?"

Tom sighed, moving to lean his fragile frame against the brick wall. "That isn't quite the truth, Flandie."

"What are you saying, Tom?"

"I'm sayin' ye need to go 'ome and talk to Lady Collins. There's some things ye need to know, and 'tis only 'er place to tell ye." He motioned to the stack of blankets Naomi held. "And I thank ye for the blankets."

She turned her attention on Naomi. "Do you know how to find this man again?"

"Aye, 'twon't be 'ard."

"I will get to the bottom of all of this, and when I do, I will return. Then, I want you to introduce me to this man who claims to be my father."

Naomi nodded. "I ain't goin' anywhere, Flandie. When ye're ready, I'll be 'ere. Send me word through Top Hat, and I'll meet ye anywhere ye say."

She nodded and then gave Tom a quick hug before turning on her heels and making her way to the carriage.

Chapter Two

Gabriel Golden Eagle helped his sister into a chair. "Sunny, if you do not give birth to that babe soon, you will truly burst."

Sunny rested a hand upon her swollen belly. "I cannot believe how huge my tiny waist has become. Ah well, just a few weeks to go." She arched a brow. "My mother-in-law swears by the fact I carry twins, says there are double births in the family. My husband's paternal grandmother was a twin."

He chuckled. "And how does your husband feel at the prospect of having such a large family all at once?"

She shrugged. "What choice does he...does either of us have?"

He chuckled again. "True, it is too late for second thoughts."

Sunny looped a golden tendril of loose hair behind an ear. "Both Raven and I seem to be running a race as to who delivers her baby first. But with this being our sister's second child, I would say she will have a quicker time of it than I will."

He moved to the chair opposite hers and took her hand. "I pray you both have a quick and easy time. I could not bear to lose either of you, as I..." He clipped his tongue as the memory of his wife flooded his thoughts.

She looked into his eyes with sapphire orbs that matched his. "Not all women die in childbirth, my brother." She reached out to affectionately stroke his cheek. "These years after Fire Star's death have not been easy for you."

He swallowed hard, the emotion burning the back of his throat. "When she died trying to give life to our son, it took the very spirit from me as well."

His sister's eyes welled with unshed tears. "Now that I am going to be a mother, I have empathy for what you went through, losing them both as you did. And I have a better understanding of what you have overcome."

"And yet, through all the hurt I regret nothing. I am happy to have the time I did with Fire Star," he confessed.

Sunny cleared the sentiment from her throat. "I had hoped when you left our Apache village to escort Raven and me to England, the distance from the things you and Fire Star shared would help some?"

He nodded. "In some ways not being able to visit the familiar places or having the constant reminders of our days together lessened the pain. And then other times, I feel so lost because I cannot connect her with anything here in England. I do not want to forget her face or live as though she never existed."

"That will never happen, my brother. But life goes on, and you must go on with it. Have you not enjoyed meeting other women while in England, like Riley Flanders?"

He smiled and added. "Or Collette Halston, while we were aboard the ship."

She frowned. "I cannot believe you are still pursuing *that* woman."

He shrugged. "She fascinates me."

Sunny's frown deepened. "And I can only imagine what parts of her fascinate you the most."

"Well, then *dayden*," he teased, as brothers did to sisters, by using the Apache word for little girl, "do not imagine so much."

She rubbed her swollen belly and raised a defiant chin. "I am hardly a little girl anymore, Gabriel."

"You will always be to me," he said softly.

Instantly Sunny melted, and her kind heart once again was in his favor. "I wish for you to experience what Raven and I have...someone special to love, a family, grandchildren when you are old."

Gabriel stood and made his way to the large bay windows of the solarium. "I wish for those things, too."

"Mother always said, sometimes true love has been right beneath your nose all the time." She cocked her head sideways. "It could be you just need to open your eyes and really look, instead of just see. Your woman might only be an arm's length away."

He nodded, thinking how much Sunny reminded him of Golden Lady, with the same pale hair, the sapphire eyes, and the diplomatic way they were able to get exactly what they wanted from the fathers, brothers, sons, and husbands who loved them.

"Well, you are not going be able to truly look for the right woman if you continue to court Collette," Sunny added.

He looked out at Bentwood's lush front lawn. Since coming to Brighton, he had turned the Bentley family mansion he and his sisters had inherited from his maternal side of the family into a health resort with sweat baths, lodging accommodations, and even a boutique. Sunny and her husband, Rafe Cavendish, helped him run the place. "It is no news how you feel about Collette."

"I have no ill feelings toward her. She and I are friends, and I admire her independence. I also love listening to her tell stories of all her adventures."

He turned toward her. "Then why do you discredit her so?"

"Because she does not want the same things you want, my brother. And deep down you know that fact to be true."

Gabriel arched a brow. "Do you not remember your husband's attitude toward commitment?" He did not wait for an answer. "If I remember right, I warned you not to lose your heart to him because he had many hearts in his pocket. But it did not stop you."

"And if I remember right, Rafe came to me of his own accord," she countered. "He asked me to marry him. And I accepted because of the love I feel for him."

"Well, then maybe that is the problem. I have never proposed to Collette, so I cannot say what her answer would be."

"For two years now, the two of you have been..." Her cheeks reddened. "...intimate," she whispered. "How is it marriage never came up in conversation?"

He combed fingers through his hair. "Because I feared she would..."

"Refuse the idea," Sunny interrupted.

He nodded.

"And if she were so in love with you, why do you think she would do that?"

He reclaimed his seat and rested his head back, closing his eyes. "Point taken."

Her voice softened. "I cannot tell you how much I hate being right about this. But I knew from the start Collette Halston is a woman who lives like a man. She wants no binds, loves adventure in different countries, and will not be tied down to a family. Children are something she would detest. Is that the sort of mate you deserve?"

He opened his eyes to search her sapphire orbs. "We do not always get what we deserve."

"You speak the truth, but in this case you already know the outcome, so why put yourself through more pain?"

He leaned forward in his seat. "I have only surmised the outcome because I have been influenced by what you and others see and say about Collette. Perhaps I should let Collette speak for herself."

Sunny frowned. "Then you plan on asking her to marry you?"

"It seems I have waited too long already," he said.

She sighed. "Well then, when do you plan to leave for London?"

He stood, hope welling in his heart. "The first thing tomorrow, on the morning train."

Chapter Three

On the ride back to her residence in Glenshire Sussex, the lovely hamlet about three quarters of an hour from London, Riley Flanders' thoughts raced. What had Lady Collins kept from her all these years that Top Hat Tom had privilege to?

Once at Collins Stead, she escaped to her room, a sanctuary at the rear of the mansion, decorated in a soft rose shade with cream accents. A tranquil chamber which was perfect to sort out the sullen and confused mood she harbored.

Her gaze drifted to the vase of flowers that rested beside her toilet table. For a moment the weekly cornucopia of fresh roses, arranged painstakingly by Betsy, had her thinking. How pertinent was it to have a fresh bouquet each day when the money could be better spent helping others? Yet this arrangement became the several important trivialities that made up the sum of the upstairs maid's day.

When Jane entered the room, she helped to remove Riley's dress and clicked her tongue in reproach. "Look 'ere now, miss, traipsin' around the seedy side o' town's dirtied the 'em o' yer dress." The attendant forced a smile. "But never fear; there's not a stain around that I can't wipe out."

"I'm sorry to drag you along with me on these outings. I know how much you hate going to that part of town." She sighed, sitting on the edge of the bed clad in only a chemise. "But I made a promise to myself that if and when I ever made it out of the tunnels and had the means to help the others still there, I would. And since Auntie Cinda forbids me to wander around town unescorted, I have no choice but to have you accompany me."

"Ye're not one o' them. Ye 'eard what Tom said; ye were born o' proud blood."

"My mother is the reason for the proud blood that courses through my veins. Not from whence she comes."

"But 'er father was the 'onorable Judge Forester Noble," Jane said.

"And how much of an upstanding man did he turn out to be? He disinherited his daughter because she followed her heart? He had no qualms about letting her and the child she bore starve for a matter of principle. Then upon his death bed, he wills all his money to charity...helping feed strangers, instead of his own flesh and blood."

"Power makes some do strange things. I coome from poor folks myself, but I thank the sweet Lord I was more fortunate then the poor souls livin' in the gutter."

"Society has forgotten them. They're treated less than human."

"No one should be 'urt in such a way. But 'tis not yer responsibility to 'elp them all." Jane readied Riley's toilettes for a bath.

Riley took another audible breath. "I know I can't help them all, but I can help some, and I won't stop until I make a difference...even if it's in a small way. Do you hear me, Jane?"

"Aye, I 'ear ye." Jane placed a chubby hand on Riley's cheek. "Now, off with yer chemise and into the tub with ye." She covered Riley's nakedness with a silk robe. "At least I can wash away the grime o' that place from yer flesh, even if I can't wash it from yer 'eart."

"I won't take such a long soak tonight. I want to speak with Auntie Cinda before she has her dinner and retires for the evening. It's about time I found out the truth, and I'm determined not to walk away without it."

****

Riley found her aunt propped up on the library divan reading a book, legs covered with a quilt, shoulders wrapped in a shawl, a fire burning in the fireplace.

"Are you feeling any better this evening?" She sat in a nearby chair.

Lucinda looked out from atop the rim of her spectacles, a small smile curving her thin lips. "At the age of seventy, my dear, one is happy to just be able to move their bowels. And since I accomplished that task quite successfully today, then I am much better off this evening then I was the last."

She giggled at her aunt's humor. Lady Lucinda Collins was an outspoken woman, holding back none of what she thought and little of what she felt on most occasions. Tonight Riley would challenge that forth-righteousness.

She sat back in her seat and took an audible breath. "Do you remember, once I hit the teen years, all the questions I'd ask?"

Lady Collins chuckled. "You were a well-spring of curiosity, if I recollect."

"Most times you answered them quite to my satisfaction," she confessed.

"I am pleased to hear that, my dear."

"But there was one you were completely vague about explaining, and I believe it is time for you to indulge me with the details." Riley sat forward.

Lady Collin's smile fell, and her mouth tensed. The wrinkles framing her lips puckered like material pulled taunt by a threaded needle. "I should be happy to, if I can."

"There are certain facts about my mother's age in prospective to my birth that doesn't make sense."

14

Lucinda's expression grew stern, reminding Riley of the times she was about to be chastised and disciplined for being disobedient. Though her aunt doled out punishments with a fair and considerate hand, the outcome was never pleasant to endure.

Not waiting for a reply, she continued to speak her mind. "Correct me, my lady, if I am wrong, but wasn't my mother your childhood friend?"

"Aye, there were three of us girls who were very close, Anita Noble, Amelia Bentley, and myself." She chuckled. "We were as tight as herrings in a barrel."

"And you were all the same age?"

"Nay, I was the eldest, five years older than Anita and a year older than Amelia," Lucinda explained. She marked the page of the book by creasing a corner, before closing the cover, then slipped off her specs and frowned. "What troubles you, Riley?"

She returned the frown. "I was just thinking if Anita ran away at the age of twenty-two to marry the gardener's son, Eugene Flanders, as I am told, she would have had to live twenty more years as his wife before I was born. Why would a man, so many years married and loving the same woman, decide to abandon her when she finally becomes expectant with his child?"

Lucinda fidgeted with her shawl before answering. "You did know your father was several years older than your mother?"

"Aye, twelve years her senior, I've been told."

Lucinda nodded. "I believe, after so many years childless, the stress of a newborn at the age of fifty-two was too much for Eugene. He wasn't a skilled man in anything but gardening, and his love for a mug of ale made his work ethics unreliable, thus the household was running on debt at it was. A drunk is bad enough to cope with, but an overwhelmed drunk is impossible."

"So he becomes overwhelmed, and instead of working with my mother to make the household solvent, he decides to abandon his wife and daughter?"

"Aye, that's the way of it. As I said, he was a drunk. There is no reasoning to what they will or won't do. And Anita, after a decade of cleaning mansions and taking in laundry to keep food on the table, grew too old and ill herself for such strenuous work. You were eleven at the time she died, thus becoming my ward, at her request."

"As I calculate the math, Eugene would have to be going into his seventy-fifth year of life at this point in time...truly an old man."

"Aye, if he were still alive." Lucinda shook her head. "But a man who drank as much as Eugene did is probably long dead by now."

"Then what I learned today, while taking Top Hat Tom blankets, is truly strange."

Lucinda frowned. "You know I don't like you hanging about in that part of town."

"Putting that aside, I am much more troubled about what Naomi said."

Lucinda gave a sardonic laugh. "That little twit. She was always making trouble for your mother. Why would you take stock in anything she had to say?"

"Because her words were quite compelling," she admitted.

"I find it difficult to believe anything compelling could come from Naomi's mouth," Lucinda retorted.

"Well then, I'll let you be the judge. Naomi said she met a man who claims to be my father. The strange thing is, Auntie, he is just entering his forties. Something doesn't figure correctly here," Riley said. "And I think it's time I get to the bottom of it all immediately. Tom suggested I talk with you on the matter first."

"He did, did he?"

Riley nodded.

Lucinda placed a hand on her chest. "Must we go through this all now, my dear?"

"Aye, right now," she said.

"Well then, since you are that determined to wake a sleeping dog..."

"I am very determined," she interrupted.

Lucinda folded her bony white hands in her lap. "Eugene Flanders isn't your father. The truth is," she said, clearing her throat, "Anita isn't your mother either."

Riley drew a deep breath punctuated with several gasps and forbade her body to tremble. Meeting Lucinda's gaze, she answered in a rush of words. "I woke this morning Riley Gretchen Flanders, and by this evening I am not sure who I am."

"You are Riley Gretchen Flanders Delaney," was Lucinda's soft reply.

Defiance as well as a subtle challenge laced Riley's tone. "And who the bloody hell are my parents?"

Lucinda seemed startled by Riley's harsh response. Yet, she uttered no rebuttal or objection. Instead, a hand reached out to draw Riley near.

She shifted to sit on the edge of the divan, gripping the elder woman's hand like it was a lifeline. "Tell me the truth."

"Aye, I would say it is about time for you to know your birthright," Lucinda whispered, suddenly looking more frail than when the conversation began. "Your mathematical calculations are accurate." She laughed sardonically. "My fault, I suppose, for insisting you become accomplished in your schoolwork."

"Please, go on," she prodded, her patience hanging by a thin thread.

Lady Collins cleared her throat. "Anita Noble did indeed run off with the gardener's son, Eugene Flanders. She was twenty, and he was thirty-two. But that is where the truth ends."

"Then tell me where it continues," she demanded.

"Anita became with child within a matter of months after her elopement but had a miscarriage. Then, about five years later she gave birth to another babe, a daughter, given the name Mavis. Anita loved her deeply, wanting all the best life could offer the child. But that wasn't to be. With Eugene losing every job due to his drinking, the couple became more and more destitute. And then, when Mavis was only three years old, Eugene abandoned his family and was never heard from again."

"Did Anita's family really disown her?" Riley probed.

"Aye, cut her off from their love as well as their money," Lucinda said. "I did what I could for her, when I could. But my father, a friend himself of Judge Noble, didn't want to get in the middle of their family's affairs. So, he forbade my donations to Anita. Since I never liked going against my father, my contributions soon became far and few between."

"Definitely not enough to really sustain them," she added.

Lucinda shook her head. "It then became necessary for Anita to seek her own employment, thus her cleaning and laundry business began."

"And what of Mavis?" she said.

"The child, with a rich crop of auburn curls upon her head, was smart and resourceful," Lucinda explained. "But unfortunately, she was left way too much to her own devices, due to her mother needing to work. At the tender age of fourteen, Mavis cavorted with a young chap who came by way of a town called Limerick in Ireland. His name was Kevin Delaney. By the time Mavis was fifteen, she bore him a daughter."

"And she named the babe Riley Gretchen," Riley added.

"Aye, that she did," Lucinda confirmed.

Her voice shook with emotion. "Where is Mavis now, my lady?"

Lucinda paused. "She is dead."

She stood and made her way to the fireplace, looking down at the flames burning the logs. It wasn't the cool autumn evening that chilled her bones. "How did she die?"

"Giving life to you," Lady Collins said.

She turned to face her aunt. "And what happened to Kevin Delaney?"

"He brought you to Anita after Mavis died, told her he needed to travel to Ireland's shores to look for work. He asked that she care for you until he could get on his feet financially, and she didn't deny him."

"Then he planned on returning for me?"

"Aye, I think that was his honest intention since he wrote to Anita throughout the first year of your childhood, sending money he earned while working as a chimney-sweep. Then one day, the letters and funds ceased, and Kevin Delaney was never heard from again. Years passed; you grew older...so did Anita. And well, you know the rest."

"So Anita Flanders is my grandmother," Riley mumbled.

Lady Collins nodded.

"And this chap Naomi claims is looking for me could very well be my father," she added with a slight frown.

"Aye, but then again, as I've said previously, it is hard to believe anything Naomi says," Lucinda confirmed.

"I believe this time Naomi is telling the truth."

"I suppose it is your right to meet him."

She lifted her chin. "Aye, I would reproach myself forever if I didn't take this opportunity. Besides, he has much to explain."

"Very well, but you will take along Jane and Charles," Lucinda demanded.

"Aye, you have my word," Riley agreed.

"I'm sorry I didn't tell you all this sooner. But it was your grandmother's request upon her deathbed that you never learn of your illegitimate birth," Lucinda said.

"Who else knows I'm not Anita's daughter?"

"As far as I know, only the man you call Top Hat Tom. But I would assume he's confided in Naomi, since she's brought this to your attention," Lucinda said.

"If he did, then he had good reason as Tom would never do anything to hurt me."

Lucinda nodded. "He stuck by Anita through all her trials. And thank the good Lord he did, as I was unable to do much for her."

"Tom always brought us food just when we needed it," she remembered. "This is the reason I won't let him down. I truly want to help him and all the others he tries to help. There isn't a selfish bone in that man's body."

Lucinda frowned. "I still don't like you in that part of town."

"I know, and I'm sorry to worry you. But Tom was there for me, and I won't forget that."

Lucinda reluctantly nodded. "Then are we settled on this matter, my dear? Am I forgiven for hiding the truth from you all these years?"

Riley smiled. "All is well between us, Auntie Cinda. Besides, I can't be too harsh on you now, can I?"

Lucinda chuckled. "I'm hoping you can't."

"You were only keeping a death bed promise to

your dearest friend. I cannot fault you for that." She made her way to the divan, laid her aunt's book and spectacles on a nearby table, and pushed aside the quilt. Riley grasped the elder woman's hand. "Now, let me help you in to dinner."

Chapter Four

Gabriel should have headed back to Brighton on the next available train once he had left Collette's mansion. But his unexpected visit found her preparing to leave for Egypt with a shady looking character by the name of Jackson Hodge. The whole episode upset him so much that he had the carriage driver drop him in town. With a knapsack across one shoulder, he walked into a pub and ordered a mug of ale. Sitting alone at a corner table, sipping the cold brew, he mentally rehashed his conversation with Collette.

She did not hesitate to tell him exactly what he meant, or in this case what he did not mean to her. Perhaps he should have spoken of love?

Yes, how foolish of me. One does not propose marriage without mentioning love. But deep inside he had a strong inkling words of love would have only made the situation worse. And he was ashamed to admit, he had none to speak.

Could it be that deep down I also realized, as did Collette, the bond we shared was only a physical one, and not strong enough for marriage?

Embarrassed for his lustful actions void of the marriage vows, he pushed aside a lock of hair from his forehead before taking another swig of the ale.

"And so, who have we here," a familiar voice boomed.

Gabriel glanced up to see Captain Simon Canvendish, Sunny's brother-in-law, standing over him with a wide grin.

Simon looked around the pub. "Is my brother

with you?"

Gabriel shook his head and laughed. "You could not pry Rafe from my sister's side. Every move she makes, every groan she utters, he believes the baby comes."

The captain joined in on his mirth and took the seat beside him. "I was the same with Fiona when she carried our first child."

"I was as well," he whispered, remembering when Fire Star carried his child. He looked down at his mug, desperately wishing to bury the memory. "It is hard not to worry that something will go wrong." Then glancing up, he added, "And then when it does..."

"Sunny will be fine." Simon placed a hand on Gabriel's shoulder.

He gave a taunt nod. "I pray you are right, for both of my sisters' sakes."

"Aye, that's right, you're to be an uncle twice over."

"Three times, to be exact, as Raven already has a son," he corrected.

"What a fortunate man you are," was the captain's reply as he raised a hand to signal a server. Upon his mug's arrival, he raised it in salutation. "Shall we have a toast then, to the good health of both mothers and their babes?"

Gabriel agreed, raising his mug to click against the other man's and declaring, "To life."

"And to love," the captain said with a chuckle. "For there would be no life without it, aye?"

"Aye," Gabriel mimicked. "We must not forget about love."

****

After the evening meal, Riley took a message for Top Hat Tom to Addie, Collins Stead's resident cook. Addie's nephew, Oliver Mills, knew Tom as well as anyone, for the old *tosher* was a prominent fixture.

Oliver was a helpful young man in his seventeenth year of life, with large dark eyes and hair to match. He'd come to live with Addie at Collins Stead when he was ten, after his mother had died. In a way he was like a younger brother to Riley. Agreeable and congenial, he did many odd jobs around Collins Stead, had a good sense of humor, and never minded running a message to Tom's part of town whenever she needed. Though her note this evening was really for Naomi, she would address it to Tom to pass along, since Anita had taught him to read. Hopefully she'd have an answer by mid-day on the morrow so Riley could get on with the business of meeting the man who claimed to be her father.

With the events of the day racing through her mind, she lay wide awake in her bed, staring at the ceiling as she imagined what the man Naomi met looked like. How did he sound when he spoke? What would his first words to her be? Would he shake her hand or embrace her?

With such musings eluding sleep, she took an audible breath and slipped from beneath the warmth of the quilt to light a nearby lantern. Then, reaching for her robe, she donned the wrap and tied the sash about her waist. Taking the lantern in hand, she tip-toed down the stairs to the library. Outside of her own bedchamber, it was her favorite place in the mansion.

Being almost midnight, a fire barely burned in the fireplace. Its dying embers were the only speck of light in the cozy room. Setting the lantern upon the mantel, she placed another log on the grill, stoked it a bit, and watched it burn.

The library warmed, and the tranquility of the room enveloped her like a cocoon. She reveled in the heat, remembering the cold nights she had endured as a child. The small kiln that had heated the one room shanty she once called home barely did its job. It became unbearable to rise from the bed she had shared with Anita in the middle of the night to do her business. She'd hurry to the chamber pot, her bared feet swiftly growing cold as they ran along the unheated floorboards, her body shivering when bared bum met the pot's chilled seat.

Afterward, hours passed before her body stopped shaking, even when Anita would reach out to entwine her in a warm embrace. Her memories of being encompassed within the arms of the woman she had thought was her mother filled her with love. She wasn't allowed to dwell on such fond memories very long before a sharp knock at the front door interrupted them. She frowned.

Who would dare call at such a late hour?

Again with lantern in hand, she proceeded to the foyer to wait on Regis, the butler. Surely he would come to see about the disturbance. Another rap sounded; this time much harder and louder, and still she stood alone in the foyer.

Her frown deepened. *Perhaps this was the night Regis spent with his sister.*

Leaning against the door she inquired, "Who goes there?"

"Captain Simon Cavendish," the deep voice responded from the opposite side of the door.

Captain Cavendish was Sunny's brother-in-law. But why would the man, whom she had no more than a casual acquaintance with, be knocking at Collins Stead's door in the middle of the night...unless something happened to Sunny? Sunny was due to give birth at any time, and perhaps...

Biting her lip, Riley laid aside the lantern and threw open the door. "What news do you have of Sunny?"

The captain smiled. "Only that she's most likely sleeping soundly beside her husband in a warm bed."

He chuckled, his broad chest vibrating with his mirth. "And that is exactly what I should be doing, beside my beloved, Fiona."

She frowned. "Then what keeps you, Captain?"

"He does." Simon pointed to Gabriel Eagle, who leaned against the outside banister.

Her eyes widened. "Is he ill?"

"Nay, not at the moment, but come morning..." his words trailed off.

"Then he is drunk," she snapped.

"Aye, somewhat," the captain agreed.

She frowned again. "Why have you brought him here?"

"It is where he asked to come." Simon arched a brow. "Is he not the rightful heir to Collins Stead?"

"Aye, he is, but..."

"My good woman might we come in from this brisk autumn night so I can set him down someplace to rest before you question me further?"

She nodded and opened the door wide.

The captain threw Gabriel's knapsack into the foyer before he helped him over the threshold.

"With Regis not around to lend a hand, I fear climbing the stairs to the bedchamber Mr. Eagle occupies while here might prove unwise for the both of you to tackle," she commented, reaching for the bag.

"Your assessment is duly noted, Miss Flanders." What other solution do you have?"

"I suggest taking him into the library. A fire has just been stoked, and there sits a longer divan, much more suited to Mr. Eagle's physical conformation."

The captain chuckled again. "Aye, he is a tall chap at that."

As well as broad shouldered and extremely handsome.

Running ahead of the two men, she placed the knapsack beside the divan and the lantern on a table before she gathered an accent pillow from a nearby chair.

Mr. Eagle stumbled a bit, as the captain directed him to the settee. After helping the inebriated man to place his head upon the pillow, Captain Cavendish brought Mr. Eagle's feet up to rest at the other end.

She glanced down at the large American, then over at the captain. "And how was it you came by Mr. Eagle in this condition?"

"I was attending business on my father-in-law, Lord Wade's, behalf. And of course after the deal was struck, we ended up at the pub."

"Doesn't most men's business just happen to end up at the pub?" She raised her brow.

The captain's broad smile again brightened his face. "Aye, any successful venture, at least."

"And was yours successful?"

"Aye, that it was. And had I not encountered Mr. Eagle, I'd be long ago home with my wife, enjoying a successful night with her. But as it was, staying to keep an eye out for this chap, I fear I will be in dire straits with Fiona when I finally do walk through the door," the captain explained.

She placed hands on hips. "I'm somewhat perplexed as to why Mr. Eagle was out enjoying a drink alone. Usually when he's in London, it is to stay with Collette Halston. I am rather shocked to hear he asked to be brought to Collins Stead."

Simon Cavendish leaned against the mantel. "Aye, well, as I hear it, Miss Halston handed him a rejection tonight, the reason the poor chap was driven to indulge in so many mugs of ale."

Riley arched a brow. "You mean she's through with him?"

The captain nodded. "Sounds that way from what he says. It seems Miss Halston has decided to go off to Egypt with another chap."

She frowned. "That woman was not for him anyway."

The captain chuckled. "And do you propose to know what sort of woman Mr. Eagle needs?"

Her face heated. "I just know it isn't Collette Halston."

"Aye, well, maybe that's so, but if I don't get myself home, I'm going to be the next bloke to need a room at Collins Stead." The captain gestured in Mr. Eagle's direction. "I'm sure he'll just sleep now and shouldn't be too much of a bother."

"Mr. Eagle could never be a bother," she muttered.

Simon Cavendish cleared his throat. "And do I detect a bit of..."

"You detect nothing but concern for a member of Lady Collins' family." She reached for the lantern and walked the captain to the foyer. "Thank you for your help and consideration."

The captain inclined his head. "It was my pleasure. I bid you a good night."

Upon returning to Mr. Eagle, she slipped off his boots and removed his cravat. As she unfastened the first three buttons of his shirt, her fingers brushed against his hairless chest. Bronzed and hard, the smooth skin against her own sent currents of heat through her body...warmth that had nothing to do with a blazing fire.

English men wore beards and mustaches, but the handsome American's face was whiskerless. Once she asked Sunny why this was, and her friend explained the custom of an Apache ceremony performed to eliminate body hair on the tribe's men.

Riley liked the way a man looked void of chest and facial hair. Smiling, she wondered if Mr. Eagle was also void of hair below the belt. Clearing her throat, she shook the scandalous thought from her mind, muttering, "You are a wicked girl, Riley

Flanders."

Mr. Eagle's blue eyes opened, and he smiled at her. "And why do you scold yourself?" He reached out to wrap a long strand of her hair around a finger. "You should wear your hair free more often." He searched her face, his smile broadening. "It becomes you."

She stepped back. "You are drunker than a skunk at Christmas, Mr. Eagle."

He arched a brow. "Those critters drink a lot around here during the holidays?"

She burst out laughing. "Just how many mugs of ale did you have?"

"Enough, it would seem." He squeezed his temples with his fingers.

"If you think your head aches now, wait 'til the morn," she warned.

He shut his eyes. "I dare not think about it."

Riley reached for his hands and brought them down to his side. "Then don't; just rest now, Mr. Eagle."

He nodded, and then his body relaxed into a deep sleep.

She covered him with a throw that had been tossed across the back of the divan and pushed aside the gold streak of hair that curled upon his forehead. "The Collins mark," she whispered, glancing up at the portrait above the mantel.

There hung a framed memory of Lord Sherman Collins and his brother Silas, forever immortalized in oils for generations to come. Lucinda Collins had thought she was the last of the Collins linage, until Gabriel Eagle and Sunny arrived in London. Then, while discussing Silas Collins' travels to America, it was discovered he had married a woman of the Apache tribe and lived out his life with her people, having a daughter of his own. As it turned out, Silas Collins is Gabriel Eagle's great-grandfather, the two sharing the same streak of gold in their hair.

Riley sat down for a moment and compared the two. Besides the hair being the same, Lord Silas and Mr. Eagle's eye color and jaw line were similar. But the American was much taller and muscular.

Gabriel Eagle had captured her heart the moment she had set eyes on him. Now, sitting this close to him, watching him sleep, and enjoying every feature of his handsome face was like dwelling in a small compartment of heaven. And although her heart went out to him for his sorrows tonight, a part of her was pleased his time with Collette Halston had lastly, and quite abruptly, come to an end.

She sympathized with the hurt of such a shock. The few gentlemen callers who had courted Riley in the past had also ended tersely. Since her debut she had not exactly been deluged with romantic prospects, but the few young men who did attempt to call upon her were excellent prospects...gallant charmers with honorable backgrounds of both academic and family linage. They faded from her life as quickly as they came, after learning the circumstances she had lived before she became Lucinda's ward. She was hurt at first over their rejection, but lately she ceased to care, as her suitors were all snobbish and self-centered.

Now, at twenty-one she was quite accepting of the fact she'd probably be a spinster for the duration of her life, until she became acquainted with Gabriel Eagle. Those other males were but a poor figure in comparison to him, and for a tad bit of time, her heart was restored in the hope for love and marriage. But then they were again dashed when the handsome Mr. Eagle set his sights on Collette Halston.

But now the ungrateful wench is through with you. Her gaze wandered over his full lips. *Dare I begin to hope you might notice me?*

She smiled as she twirled a lock of her hair around her finger, much as Mr. Eagle had done only moments ago.

Perhaps you've begun to notice already.

Chapter Five

It had been a while since Gabriel woke with a mouth as dry as the desert floor. The pounding in his head reminded him of tribal drums during an Apache ceremony, and his stomach was not so stable either. All he experienced was the horrible aftermath of drinking the white man's fire water. Revisiting such distress came back to him in volumes, taking him to a time just after his wife's death. Getting drunk was the only way he could fall asleep, but it came at a price. Was he ready to pay that price again?

He groaned, disgusted with himself. The pain of just opening his eyes and having them grow accustomed to the brightness of the room was too much to bear. Once his lids did pry open, he found himself lying on the floor, enveloped with morning light streaming in from three large windows. His head was propped upon his knapsack, and his great-grandfather, Lord Silas Collins, peered down on him with disconcerting eyes. He could be no other place, then, but the Collins Stead library.

He covered his face with his hands to block the portrait's stare. Even that slight movement caused pain to cut through his head like a shard of glass. He moaned again, putting to use his Apache training. To override pain a warrior was taught to use mind over matter. He swallowed hard and set his focus on conjuring up the dark, sultry eyes of the woman who brought him to these dire straits in the first place. But it was not Collette Halston's provocative gaze that came to mind.

Instead he pulled from his memory another's glance, the genuine and concerned look of Riley Flander's emerald orbs. He remembered how they set upon him while he entwined a lock of her hair around his finger. And with great pleasure, everything about her penetrated his thoughts with an overpowering sentiment of awe.

"By Jove, sir," a voice from above boomed, the sound vibrating through his skull. "What have we here, you lying about like this upon the floor?"

Gabriel pried his eyes open once again to find the butler standing over him. Regis Tyrone was a man of middle-age, small build, and average height, with a strong-cut jaw and graying hairs at his temples. Outside of a moustache, also sprinkled with gray, he was otherwise clean-shaven. Well spoken, his speech was quite articulate. The man could be opinionated and doubled as a gentleman's gentlemen when Gabriel was at Collins Stead.

"Good morning, Regis," he croaked with a raspy voice.

The butler frowned and pinched his lips, giving his average, yet pleasant features, a constipated visage. Most of the English toted this expression. Gabriel blamed it on all the tea they consumed. The exact reason he had curbed his own intake of the bitter brew. It seemed to have just such an effect on his system as well.

"How is it you can utter such a travesty, sir, after spending the night sleeping upon the floor?" Regis probed further.

"I believe I started out sleeping on the sofa. But with it being so narrow, no doubt one turn landed me where I now lay." With great difficulty he pulled himself to a sitting position. "Not a problem, though. I have slept in worse places." His response opened a floodgate of memories. How many times, while working as a scout for the white man, had he slept upon the cold, hard ground, far from the warmth of the camp's fire and getting eaten alive by insects? Sleeping upon the library's floor was a significant upgrade in perspective to other places he had endured. "Have you any idea how I got to Collins Stead?"

"Miss Riley said she received you late last night. You were brought here by Captain Simon Cavendish," Regis explained.

He yawned and stretched. "Ah, it all comes back to me."

Regis inclined his head politely. "I'm sorry I wasn't at your disposal. But you see I was visiting my sister until early this morning, or I would have tended to you myself."

"No apology is necessary."

"I've drawn you a bath. And Addie will have breakfast waiting for you when you're ready." Regis arched a brow. "That is, if you have an appetite."

"Perhaps just coffee will do, and served very black."

"Very good, sir," Regis mumbled. Half the time Gabriel had a hard time understanding what the man said. Actually, that seemed to be the case with most of the folks in England, although deciphering the words was growing easier. "I'm at your service."

Usually he hated the fuss Regis went to on his behalf. Gabriel was quite capable of taking care of himself. But today, especially, he welcomed the other man's aid. Forcing a smile, he voiced his appreciation. "*Ashoge*, thank you, Regis."

The butler nodded and extended his hand. "Up you go then."

Gabriel accepted his help and stumbled to his feet, swaying a bit before catching his balance. Feeling his face heat with shame over his present condition, he cleared his throat and straightened his wrinkled waistcoat. "Is Miss Riley up and about yet?"

"The lady is awake. I know this to be a fact because I was summoned to her room upon my own arrival. That's when she explained your late entry. But she's far from ready to make her own appearance." Regis smiled. "Nay a worry. We'll have you cleaned up and looking dapper long before Miss Riley decides to come downstairs."

He nodded and reached for his knapsack, mimicking a phrase he heard the Brits use many times. "Then carry on."

"Very good," Regis replied, leading the way to the staircase.

****

Gabriel was not only disgusted with himself but ashamed for his behavior. And not knowing what sort of explanation Simon gave Riley for his condition, he thought it would be best to make it down to the dining room first. He needed to show her he was responsible and reliable to go on with his day, in spite of his actions the previous night.

When he entered the empty room, he could only chalk up his good fortune to the incredible amount of preparations a woman endures from the time she downs the night garb, to the moment she actually is pulled together enough to leave the bedchamber. Sunny educated him on a woman's ritual, clothes, and proper protocol it takes to be a lady in England. And when his sister completed her tutorial, he was even more blessed to have been born a man.

He sat for a few moments, drinking the black coffee Addie brought him, taking in the fine furnishings of the room. Done in light greens and gold, the dining room was filled with the bright light that shone through a large, bay window. The woodwork was a rich, dark mahogany which contrasted well against the room's color scheme. Cherry wood table, set of chairs, a large china hutch filled with bone white china, and a buffet table all matched. Above the fireplace hung a tapestry depicting a hunt, men on horseback chased a frightened fox into a thicket, and an oriental rug of deep green covered the hardwood floor.

When Riley joined him for the morning meal, Gabriel was working on his second cup of coffee. And as he glanced at her, he could not help but think the time she had taken to get herself ready for the day was not wasted. She literally took his breath away.

The fine lace collar gracing her neckline, entwined with peachy ribbons, brought a delicate bloom to her satin skin. As she made her way past him to the buffet to pour a cup of tea, the aromatic scent of lavender wafted from the frill of the full, cambric skirt just touching her ankles. Long, ginger curls cascaded down her back and ended just above a nicely-shaped backside. He smiled at how, from this angle, her well-rounded hips pleased him immensely.

She revealed her tender voice. "Do you like?"

Her unexpected question caused him to flush miserably. *How could she read my mind, know my thoughts?*

He cleared his throat, buying some time as how to answer.

She turned from the buffet, with cup in hand, not waiting for a reply. "My hair. I have decided to wear it loose, as you suggested last night. Do you like?"

He let out the breath he did not realize he was holding and smiled. "Yes, I do, very much."

The splendor of her return smile warmed him through and through. "I am glad."

"What else did I suggest last night? I hope I did not say anything to offend you. If that be the case, then I beg your forgiveness."

She took a seat beside him at the table. "Your

manners were, as always, in good conduct, Mr. Eagle."

"Then I am happy to learn I am still welcome at Collins Stead."

As she reached for a scone, he noticed a long, ragged scar atop her dainty hand. The red, raised mark was a stark contrast to her porcelain skin. The old wound bothered him, as he wondered about the circumstance by which she had received it. She was hardly the tomboy type. Truth be told, Riley was as gentle as he was rugged, her flesh as fair as he was tanned. They were two complete opposites, and yet there was something similar about them. He had not a clue what their comparable quality was, but he could sense it hanging in the balance.

"You are heir to Collins Stead, Mr. Eagle. So there isn't much chance you'd ever be kept from entering its doors," she said as she buttered the scone.

"Well, allowed to enter and being welcome are two different things."

She reached over and gave his hand a reassuring pat. "Not to worry, you are still in good standing with me. But I hear that isn't the case between you and Collette Halston."

He took an audible breath. "How much did Captain Cavendish tell you?"

"Only that Collette has decided to run off with another chap to Egypt," she said, before popping the scone into her mouth.

He nodded. "That is the truth of it."

She sipped her tea, washing down her food before speaking again. "I'm sorry, Mr. Eagle. I know she was...well," she hesitated, her voice softening, "rather special to you."

"Apparently I was not as special to her," he confessed, sipping his cold coffee.

"I don't think that was it at all. I think the two

of you want something different out of life."

"You sound like my sister. She never believed Collette was the woman for me either," he said.

"And deep down, what do you believe, Mr. Eagle?"

He combed his fingers through his hair. "I think you and Sunny are right. But how could the two of you know this before me?"

She arched a brow. "If I was a betting woman, and I'm not," she quickly added, "I'd say you knew exactly what you were getting into, but you were too taken...your senses clouded by other observations."

He chuckled. "And what observations do you speak of?"

"Why, Collette's ample outer endowments of course, and the way they all came together so perfectly for your pleasure and amusement."

His eyes widened at her bold and accurate summery. "Well, certainly no one can chastise you for sparing words."

She giggled. "Did you think you were being discreet?"

"Let us just say I had hoped I was not so obvious."

"Aye, well, you are only a man, after all," she said, dabbing her full, bowed lips with a napkin.

"And does the fact I am only a man excuse such behavior for you?"

"Nay, there's never an excuse for a man's indiscretion. But it does explain it," she added, as she reached for a second scone.

Leaning back in his chair, he studied her with curiosity. An air of efficiency about her fascinated him. Something in her manner, both soothing and yet with a hint of maddening arrogance, radiated a vitality that drew him like a moth to a flame. Why had he not seen this woman for the intelligent, vibrant, and stunning being she was?

Because I was lusting after Collette.

A sudden pain squeezed his heart for the way Collette had dismissed him, but perhaps he deserved what he got. In all the time he had spent knowing every crevice and curve of the woman's body, he never once looked upon her as he was now doing to Riley. In a sense he had wronged Collette in his refusal to see her in the proper manner a gentleman courts a lady. Could it be she felt his indifference and put up a shield of defense?

No, others knew she was not the settling-down type. And he did not listen to those wagging tongues. Or did he? Could it be somewhere in the back of his mind he stashed away what was said and given Collette an unfair advantage?

But I was ready to propose marriage to the woman.

Perhaps because he knew she would decline, and he would have the weight of doing the proper thing off his shoulders. His drunken binge last night was wounded pride, not a broken heart.

And now, sitting in the dining room of Collins Stead with Riley Flanders, it was almost like the scales had fallen from his eyes and from around his heart. He was no longer blind to his attraction for the lovely lady before him.

He saw the heart rendering tenderness in her eyes. From them he felt an eager affection, genuine and pure. Her whole being seemed to be filled with anticipation. It was almost like she had a glimpse of how good the two of them could be together, and through those emerald orbs, she showed him what could be if only he would take a leap of faith.

He tried to throttle the dizzying current racing through him. How could he be attracted to another woman when his pride still stung from the first? Certainly no one would take him seriously. He wondered himself at the inconsistency. Yet the idea of her wrapped in his embrace made his spirit soar the way it did when he first set eyes on his late wife. The feelings he experienced had nothing whatsoever to do with reason.

And he felt there was a deeper significance to their visual interchange on Riley's part as well, for the longing in her eyes wrapped around him with invisible warmth, soothing the ache that had burned deep within him for so very long. His insides jangled with excitement at the idea of her eagerness, her interest, and attention.

Caught up in the moment, he opened his mouth to confess the tangible bond he felt between them, only to have his words silenced when Addie entered the dining room.

"Got a message 'ere for ye, miss." Addie handed a folded piece of paper to Riley. "I believe 'tis the one ye 'ave been waitin' for."

"Thank you, Addie," Riley said, breaking eye contact to read the note.

At first he bristled at Addie's interruption, but then, as the heated and charged moment between them cooled, he became relieved his words never made it to Riley's ears. On a second glance, he had no right to gather her hopes to him, or his to her. Last night in the pub he had decided, after both his sisters gave birth to their babies, he would return to America and help care for his tribe. He was a wealthy man and could make a difference in the Apache people's lives. No more would they be under the white agent's rule. But his obligation to Collins Stead was the only problem standing in his way. That is why he proposed a deal to Simon Cavendish before the fire water blurred his senses.

Riley stood, her expression turning from ease to concern, and crushed the note in a fist at her side. "I'm sorry, but I've just had an appointment confirmed in London."

He frowned. "Is all well, Riley?"

"Aye, for now at least."

The uncertain tremble in her voice worried him. "Are you sure?"

"It's just my past catching up with me, Mr. Eagle, and naught for anyone to worry." She stuffed the crumbled note into her skirt's pocket. "And I know you've heard all about where I grew up." She cast a glance at her shoes. "Not exactly something to boast about."

He stood and neared her, placing a hand on her shoulder. "Never be ashamed of who you are."

She raised her eyes to meet his. "That is easy for you to say. Your lifestyle has not been frowned upon and scorned by all of London."

"No, not by the people in London, but by the Americans. In my homeland the Apache are thought of as the lowest of low. The white man took our land and put a halt to our traditions. Because my mother is white and my father is an Apache, my sisters and I have been labeled *half-breeds*. To the white men living in my country, a *half-breed* is almost as bad as the plague."

"And how do you bear it?"

"One day at a time and never do I forget I am born of proud blood."

She smiled. "My friend, Top Hat Tom always says the same."

He returned the smile. "Then this Top Hat Tom is a wise man."

"Aye, he is at that," she whispered.

He removed his hand from her warm shoulder. "I will not keep you further, but tell me you do not go alone."

She bit her bottom lip and looked away. "Lady Lucinda does not allow me to travel about without at least Jane to accompany me."

"She is wise as well," he said.

She cleared her throat and stepped back. "I'm sorry I will be leaving you without a carriage for the afternoon. Perhaps if you have business in London as well and plan to leave immediately, I can have Charles drop you to your destination on the way to mine."

"Truthfully, I do have business this afternoon, but I plan to carry it out at Collins Stead."

"Then you will remain another day?" she said, finally meeting his gaze.

He nodded.

Her face brightened. "Can I count on you to share the evening meal with me, Mr. Eagle?"

He smiled. "Only on one condition."

She frowned. "And what might that be?"

"That from this time on you start calling me Gabriel."

"That would be most inappropriate."

"But it would please me greatly," he said, enjoying the blush that crept into her beautiful face.

She cleared her throat and repeated her earlier statement, using his first name this time. "Can I count on you to share the evening meal with me, Gabriel?"

He nodded. "You have my word."

****

Riley hated lies, telling them and being lied to. But this morning she told an untruth, trading one lie for another. All her life she believed her parents were Anita and Eugene Flanders. And although her childhood was not made up of frills and comforts, Riley loved the woman she had known to be her mother, trusting every word she spoke. Now at twenty-one, discovering Anita was her grandmother and Kevin Delaney her father set her emotions in a spin. All this time she had been lied to...obviously for her own good, but nevertheless her birthright had been kept a secret. Lady Lucinda and Top Hat Tom, the two people who knew the truth, were not exactly eager to explain the situation. She wondered if Kevin Delaney hadn't returned to England and met up with Naomi, if they would have ever bothered to tell her at all.

As for her own lies, this morning she told a few to three people she cared for and respected. Her first fib was to Gabriel Eagle, then to Charles, and lastly her handmaiden, Jane. The note she received earlier instructed her to travel alone to London because Kevin Delaney was a wanted man. Naomi couldn't read nor write, and although Tom could do both, his penmanship resembled chicken scratches. The note she received was written in an even, legible script, so it had to be Kevin Delaney who composed it. As she read on, she was disappointed to learn he was only passing through England on his way to America where he hoped to start a new life. If she were accompanied by anyone, Kevin would refuse to meet her.

The whole situation nagged at her common sense. First, why was Kevin Delaney wanted by the authorities? What had he done? Had he been, all this time, locked away in an Irish prison? Could that be why his letters to Anita ceased? How did he escape his jailers? And if he were on the run, why would he stop to look her up after all these years? Was it for sentimental reasons, or did he hope to coerce from her the necessary funds for his travels? *Most likely it was the latter he had come for.*

And at a second glance, Jane and Charles posed nay a threat, so why was it necessary for her to meet Kevin alone? Riley prided herself at being level-headed, weighing every issue and coming out with the best laid plans after thoughtful examination. How was it she now cast caution to the wind?

Because I want...nay I need to set eyes upon my father. If he runs from the law to America, this might

43

be the first and last time I have a chance to do that.

Her lies were easy to carry out. She gave Jane and Charles, who were happy to have time together, a day off. Instructed them to take the carriage and enjoy themselves. She didn't, however, plan on Gabriel staying at Collins Stead and was extremely relieved when she heard Regis talking to Addie about Captain Cavendish coming to the mansion on business. Gabriel would be staying close to Collins Stead, and she merely called a bluff by offering him a ride into London, knowing full well he'd decline. Thinking Jane and Charles were with her, he'd be none the wiser of her plan to escape to London alone.

With the hood of her cape draped over her head to hide her identity as well as keep the chilled autumn breeze from stinging her face, Riley sat on the worn, wooden seat of the wagon driven by Addie's nephew. Once in London, Oliver would drop her off at the ally where she always met Tom. From that point she'd be taken to her father. She had one hour to ask Kevin Delaney decades of questions, but she would have to make the best of it. She shivered, pulling the hood tighter around her cold face.

"Are ye all right, miss?" Oliver turned a concerned glance her way.

"I'm fine, Oliver."

"Sorry the ride's so bumpy and there's not some sort o' an enclosure to keep the cold from yer bones," he said, pushing a dark curl aside from his forehead.

"All is fine," she repeated.

"I think not 'cause ye are shiverin', and so quiet."

"I'm just doing a bit of praying," she said.

"About what?" Oliver probed.

"That I learn the truth to questions concerning my life, Oliver." She gripped the wagon's armrest to keep her balance. "And hopefully, by the time you return for me, I'll have the answers."

Chapter Six

Gabriel found Lady Collins sitting on the sofa in the library, drinking none other than a cup of tea.

He smiled and seated himself opposite her. "Good morning, my lady."

She returned the smile. "Heard you slept here last night." She patted the sofa cushion beside her.

His face heated. "You heard correctly."

"Humph," she said, taking another sip of tea.

"I'm sorry. I meant no disrespect to you or this household."

Lucinda waved a dismissive hand in the air. "Aye, well, these things happen at times, especially when life becomes more imperfect than usual." She leaned forward. "Did I ever tell you about the time my father came home inebriated beyond belief?"

Lucinda Collins was a storyteller, had told a fair share of them in the time he had known her. For sure she would have gotten along famously with the Apache people. "No, I haven't heard that one as of yet."

"Well, one night after a fight with my mum, Lord Sherman Collins storms out of the mansion and walks himself to a small pub that existed a few blocks from Collins Stead." She frowned. "It has since burned down, but it was the favorite of many of the local men. Anyway," she said, getting the story back on track, "Papa heads to this pub on foot and gets himself so liquored-up he comes home minus his pants."

Gabriel arched a brow. "You mean to say he was actually..."

"Aye, naked from the waist down. He managed to confiscate a tablecloth a neighbor had drying on a clothes line, but it was for a small table and didn't cover much. So his backside was as bare as a newborn babe, and all else he was about commenced to flap in the breeze."

He threw his head back and laughed. "And what explanation did he give to your mother?"

Lucinda joined in on his mirth. "He told my mum he was robbed. Since his wallet was attached to his belt by a chain, and in his drunken state he was unable to release the hook, the robber had him remove his pants." She laughed harder. "Sometimes, the day before laundry day, he'd run out of clean underwear."

"And so it happened that day was just such a day?"

"Aye, that it was. So when he removed his trousers, he was left naked from the waist down."

"Did your mother believe him?"

Lucinda arched a brow. "Well, now you figure that one out...seeing he was drunker than a skunk during the holidays and coming home without pants certainly didn't set her in a good mood."

He chuckled again. "No, I would imagine not."

Lucinda patted the sofa cushion again. "Come to think of it, Papa slept here that night as well."

It was then he heard the distinct sound of a carriage approaching. He went to the window and noted Captain Simon Cavendish's vehicle coming to a halt in front of the mansion.

Lady Lucinda joined him. "Quite an elegant *chaise* Lord Wade has provided for his son-in-law's travels."

"I agree," he said, admiring the attractive vehicle. "It looks very comfortable. Far different than the way most Americans travel."

"And how is that?" Lucinda probed.

"A saddled horse usually suffices for a cowboy or scout. And a modest, plank-wood wagon similar to what Oliver drives is preferred by the women."

"Well, most of England's upper crust is rather particular about their mode of travel. Sometimes, how they choose their carriage becomes an art form."

He frowned. "In what way?"

"Well, for example, open carriages are used for shorter jaunts, as they're not as stuffy as their enclosed counterparts. Another quaint transport is the low *phaeton*, pulled only by a pair of ponies," she explained. "Now, a more serious vehicle is a four-wheeled *phaeton*, which is pulled by four horses. And then there are those that are pulled by eight horses. But those are unusual to find and only owned by the very wealthy."

He arched a brow. "Impractical for only needing a ride into town."

"Aye, but those of great financial means care more about their image. However, even the very wealthy face the drawbacks for their elaborate choices."

"And what would that be?" he said.

"*Gigs* and two-wheeled *curricles* are only built to be pulled by a pair of horses instead of a single beast. This leaves the owner faced with the difficult task and immense expense of finding an equally well-matched pair of horses ranking in quality."

"And what vehicle has the best speed?" he inquired further.

"The *curricle* could easily pass a carriage. However, it can only seat two at a time and is open to dust, wind, and rain. The *barouche*, on the other hand, can accommodate a party of six. And with its top up, affords some protection against the elements."

At that point Regis entered the room. "Begging your pardon, my lady, but a Captain Simon

Cavendish is here to see Mr. Eagle."

"Show him in, Regis." She made her way to the door. "It's been a good conversation we've had, Gabriel. But now I will leave you to your business."

"I wish for you to stay as it concerns you and Collins Stead as well," he said.

She frowned. "Is there a problem, Gabriel?"

"I do not believe there has to be." He gave her a reassuring smile.

"Very well, then. I will hear you two chaps out," she agreed, taking a seat once again upon the sofa.

Simon entered the room. With a broad smile, he greeted them both and then glanced from the Collins brother's portrait hanging above the mantel to Gabriel. "By Jove, the resemblance is uncanny."

"Aye, almost eerie," Lucinda agreed. "The day Gabriel first walked through my door, I almost believed it was my dear Uncle Silas home again. If not for the fact my uncle was much shorter, he and Gabriel could be twins." She sighed. "As the last living Collins, I feared Collins Stead would fall into the hands of strangers after my death." Lucinda smiled at Gabriel. "But now, with discovering Gabriel and his sisters are of the Collins' bloodline, I can go in peace when the grim one decides to take me."

Gabriel motioned for Simon to take a seat. "That is why I have asked the captain here today. I would like him to help me maintain Collins Stead when it is time for me to take it over."

Her brows arched. "Oh?"

"Aye, my lady," Simon replied. "But first let me explain a bit of back story."

Lucinda folded her frail hands in her lap. "I'm listening."

"As you know my dear wife Fiona is the daughter of Lord Morgan Wade."

"Aye, I am aware of that," she said.

Simon continued. "Then you must also know after the two of us wed, we took up residence at Wade's Landing."

Lucinda nodded. "I am aware of that as well." She smiled. "I've been to the mansion a time or two. It is a lovely place, so grand."

Simon took an audible breath. "Aye, well, even though Fiona and I dwell in a wing of the estate all of our own, the place is not grand enough."

Lucinda frowned. "How can that be, Captain Cavendish?"

Gabriel chuckled sardonically. "How can that not be, when you add my Aunt Kaylena to the group?"

Lucinda's lips curled into a grin. "Ah, I have forgotten. Kaylena Bentley is Lord Wade's wife and lives at Wade's Landing as well."

"And I do not believe an entire island would be big enough for anyone to live on with her along," Gabriel remarked.

Simon tried to be polite. "She's a nice enough person most of the time, and I don't think she actually means to cause hard feelings but..."

"Bah. I've known Kaylena all of her life. She is the younger sister of my dear friend, Amelia Bentley." She glanced over at Gabriel and added, "Your grandmother."

He nodded.

"And she's a stubborn, rigid, and frigid woman if ever I met one," Lucinda concluded.

"You tell me nothing new," Gabriel chimed in. "Do not forget my sister and I lived with her for a time when we first arrived in England. At that time, Kaylena heavily drank fire water and threatened to discipline my sister with the same shameful sort of beatings she had received from her father." He folded his arms across his chest. "I would have none of it. That is why I brought Sunny here to stay with you."

"I believe my father-in-law has changed Kaylena's outlook and attitude somewhat with his love and devotion," Simon reflected. "But she still has the tendency to take control and has voiced her opinions on child-rearing to my wife beyond all appropriateness."

"And I take it your wife is growing upset over the whole situation," Lucinda assumed.

"Aye, that is the way of it," Simon agreed. He ran fingers through his hair. "And I am quite at a loss as to know what to do. I haven't saved enough to buy Fiona a home she would feel comfortable in, and yet we dare not stay much longer living at Wade's Landing and still remain civil. Fiona has bitten her tongue more than I can count as not to cause trouble for her father, but it is wearing on her nerves. Soon, my wife will become so distraught she will say something she will forever regret or take to her bed with some sort of breakdown."

Lucinda frowned. "I sympathize with your predicament, but I fail to see how I can come up with a solution."

"If you permit me, I think I might have an answer," Gabriel chimed in.

Lucinda inclined her head politely. "Enlighten me."

"On my many visits to Collins Stead, I have taken time to walk the grounds, getting myself familiar with the many acres that make up the property and checking each dwelling. I have particularly taken an interest in the smaller manor house that sits opposite the gardens, at the south end."

Lucinda nodded. "That was the first Collins Stead, built in the early 1700s when my great, great grandfather purchased the property. He and his wife had fourteen children, three sets of twins, and outgrew the house's six bedrooms within a decade. That was why this mansion was built. Unfortunately only three of those children lived to adulthood."

"I have toured the house, and although it needs some work, I believe it can be made livable again in no time and for little cost. With six bedrooms, a fairly good-sized dining room, parlor, kitchen, and the third floor accommodations ready to turn into staff quarters, I think it would fit Simon and Fiona's needs perfectly."

"Our household staff is small, consisting of Fiona's handmaiden, a nanny, a cook, a maid, and my gentleman's gentleman, who is also the butler," Simon added.

Lucinda arched a brow. "And how would Kaylena feel if the staff left with you?"

"She's hired a whole new crew, wanting these few loyal folks gone. But Fiona has known them since she was a child and feels them to be more like family," the captain explained. "And I would be more than willing to pay for any renovations needed."

Lucinda waved a hand casually in the air. "That is the least of my worries. I am not concerned with the cost."

"Then what does concern you?" Gabriel said.

Lady Collins took an audible breath. "Do you recall when you first arrived at Collins Stead, asking me what would become of Riley after my death if you were to inherit the property?"

Gabriel nodded. "You said Riley would be more than compensated for."

"Aye, and the smaller manor home is her compensation. As well as the three acres surrounding the dwelling and a yearly stipend that will keep Riley independent of any man...of any person, for the rest of her life." Lucinda paused. "I have set up a fund with my barrister, a man I've known for years and trust, for the money to be invested...giving Riley dividends throughout her life to sustain a comfortable lifestyle. Upon my barrister's death, as he is getting on in years as well, his son will preside over the clause so Riley will always have council in her favor. If she should marry one day, there is a stipulation in my will stating she will be the only person able to control the funds. In this way my girl will never be homeless again."

"I want nothing taken away from Riley," Gabriel reassured her. "In fact, as long as I am alive I will also see to it she is properly cared for, as is my duty to Collins Stead. The two will always go hand in hand. But she is not planning on moving into the smaller home while you are still alive."

Lucinda chuckled. "Haven't you noticed, my dear man, I am not getting any younger? Only the good Lord knows how much time I have left." She frowned. "If I allow Captain Cavendish and his family to take over the smaller house, and in a few months I should pass away, where is Riley to live?"

"Where you have planned for her all along," Gabriel said. "Only now the house will be in an immediately live-in condition."

Lucinda's frown deepened. "Then where would the captain and his family live?"

"Here, in the main mansion."

Lucinda's lips thinned. "And where then, would you live?"

He took a deep breath. "I have been thinking strongly about returning to America. I believe I am needed there by my people."

"And what of your people here?" Lucinda asked.

"I only agreed to come to England long enough to safely escort my sisters. Now, both are married and have their husbands to care for them. As soon as Sunny and Raven give birth to the babes they carry, which is within a month's time, and I know all is well with them, I am leaving England."

"I am not quite sure of this plan, Gabriel."

"I am only making Simon caretaker of the estate in my absence," Gabriel confirmed. "He is to keep in contact with me, as well as Sunny and Raven, about the affairs here. And he will only abide by our advice and requests."

"Aye, my lady," Simon added. "It is only the Eagle family's wishes that I would adhere to in the running and care of Collins Stead. And my respect and loyalty hold true toward Miss Flanders as well."

"And we would still be the sole owners. I know you wanted the property to stay in the Collins bloodline," Gabriel assured her.

"What happens when Mr. Cavendish decides to purchase property of his own?" She glanced over at Simon. "I am assuming this is something you are eventually planning to do."

"Aye, my lady, it is," Simon agreed.

Lucinda brought her gaze back to Gabriel. "Obviously Sunny has her hands full with Bentwood Manor in Brighton, and Raven is settled in Ireland. With Captain Cavendish moving into his own estate one day, how is Collins Stead to be cared for?"

"When that time arrives, I will return to England," Gabriel said. "I just need a few years to get my people on their feet. I wish to buy land of my own in America so I can build homes for the tribe. I must keep them safe from further eviction and invasion. Then I will take back my duties here until one of Sunny's children is old enough to continue in my place."

Lucinda arched a brow. "The poor girl hasn't given birth to one babe yet. And besides, that child will be in line for Bentwood Manor."

He smiled. "Sunny's mother-in-law believes she will give birth to twins."

Simon laughed. "And my mother is rarely wrong about such things."

"If that is the case or not, I am sure Rafe and Sunny are planning on having more children in the future," Gabriel added. "Between Sunny, Raven, and hopefully my own offspring, there will be enough heirs in the coming years to take over Collins Stead."

"Aye, you make a valid point," Lucinda agreed. She took an audible breath and relaxed further back into her seat. "And your wife Fiona won't mind leaving her father? I know she takes comfort in his nearby presence when you are off at sea."

"I am only captain of my father-in-law's cargo ship twice during the year, and I travel only to Ireland and back. Besides, Glenshire Sussex is only three quarters of an hour from London. If Fiona wishes, she can make the trip easily enough by carriage, as well as Lord Wade. And she will have you and Riley about the property if she is in dire need of anything."

Lucinda nodded. "True, we will be here for sure and would be more than happy to lend her a hand in any way needed." She smiled. "And it might be nice having a babe around."

"You won't regret your decision, my lady," Simon added.

"Very well, Captain, if you, your family, and staff wish to inhabit the smaller manor house, you have my permission to do so."

Simon stood and took one of Lucinda's hands in his. "I promise to help you run Collins Stead in Gabriel's absence so you will not be burdened by as many dealings as you have been."

She smiled up into Simon's eyes. "And for that I am grateful as I am growing too tired for so many responsibilities, Captain."

"Please, call me Simon," he requested.

"If you will call me Lucinda."

Simon inclined his head politely. "I shall be honored."

"I would say, in the long run, this decision is for the best. With you already moved in, I will have the chance to school you well in what needs to be done, for when the time comes I am no longer around."

"And we all pray that is not for a very long time," Gabriel said.

"I agree," Simon added.

Lucinda chuckled lightly. "Aye, well, it's all up to the good Lord. But the transition will be easier on Riley if she's used to you and your family beforehand, and then has your help and support when the time comes for her to take over the smaller home."

Simon nodded. "And I will do whatever I can, Fiona as well, to make sure Riley receives all you have set aside for her."

"As will I and the heirs to come," Gabriel said.

"Then I will summon my barrister in the morning so the appropriate papers can be drawn up and signed," Lucinda said. Then, casting a glance at Gabriel, her eyes moistened. "I shall miss you, my dear, more then you know."

He smiled. "I am not gone yet and have months of plans to complete until I am."

Lucinda nodded and opened her mouth to respond when a ruckus in the foyer halted her words.

Gabriel stood and made his way to the door. Upon opening it, he spotted Jane in a confrontation with Regis. "What goes on here?"

"Sorry and all to bother ye, sir, but Regis 'ere tells me Miss Riley isn't at 'ome...'asn't been all afternoon. It seems she was supposed to 'ave been with me. But that's news to my ears." Jane cast a glance at her feet, her face turning crimson as she spoke her next words. "Ye see, Miss Riley gave Charles and myself time off today. So we could be together a bit and all."

Gabriel frowned, making his way further into the foyer. "I was under the same impression. Riley received a note this morning confirming an appointment in London. I remember asking her if she planned on going alone, and she distinctly said you would be accompanying her as Lucinda does not allow her to go out unescorted."

"And that's the truth of it," Lucinda said.

He turned around to find the elderly woman standing in the doorframe.

Lucinda's lips thinned. "What's this about Riley receiving a note?"

"Addie brought it to her during the morning meal," Gabriel said.

"And do you have any idea what this note said?" Lucinda prodded.

He shook his head. "But she seemed troubled while reading it."

Lucinda glanced at Jane. "See if Riley left the note in her chamber."

"Aye, my lady," Jane said, taking her leave.

"She did not. I saw her stuff it into the pocket of her skirt," he said. "But perhaps Addie will know something more."

Lucinda addressed Jane again, her eyes widening. "Find Addie."

"Aye, my lady," Jane said, taking off to complete the task when another ruckus broke out.

All of them followed the commotion through the kitchen and out the side door. There Addie's nephew, Oliver was tending to an elderly man lying wounded in his wagon. The older fellow was dressed in a faded tuxedo, his shirt stained with blood that seeped from a large gash in his chest.

"Top Hat Tom." Lucinda approached the wagon. "What has happened?"

The old man coughed and choked for air.

"I found 'im bleedin' in the ally when I returned

for Miss Riley," Oliver explained.

"And what ally is this?"

Oliver flushed. "The one I dropped 'er off at, my lady."

"Damn fool girl went to meet him alone," Lucinda said.

"Who was this man she was meeting?" Gabriel suddenly felt an unexplained jealous rage rush through his veins.

"One who claimed to be her father," Lucinda explained.

Gabriel's angry glance went to Oliver. "And you had no thought of the danger Riley could be in traveling alone, that you failed to tell me what she was up to?"

Oliver raised a defiant chin. "She weren't travelin' alone, sir. I was with 'er."

Gabriel frowned. "And did you stay with her?"

Oliver cast his eyes to his feet. "Nay, sir."

Addie pinched her nephew's arm. "And where is Miss Riley now?"

"I dunno. All I found was Tom crawlin' from the ally, bleedin' from 'is chest."

"And after seeing Tom injured, you didn't bother to search for Riley?" his voice thundered.

"I couldn't think of nothin' but gettin' 'elp for ole Tom," Oliver blurted, his voice rough with anxiety.

"'Tis a child's way ye think, so 'tis a child's discipline ye'll get." Addie grabbed Oliver by the ear. "'Tis to the stables with ye now, for a good birchin' across yer bared bum."

Oliver's face turned a deep shade of red as he twisted out of her grasp. "I'm too old for ye to be still doin' that, Auntie."

"If anything has happened to Riley, I'll beat you myself."

"Let's all calm down and see what this elder chap can tell us," Simon advised.

Both Simon and Gabriel helped Tom from the wagon and brought him into the library, laying him down upon the sofa while Jane ran for clean cloths and a basin of water.

Opening Tom's shirt revealed a deep wound. If it weren't for the wallet hidden in a vest pocket taking the brunt of the attack, it could have been fatal. Jane pulled it free, handing the sliced billfold to Gabriel.

He opened the wallet to discover a wad of money and the real owner's identification. Arching a brow at Tom, he placed the wallet aside.

"One's got to eat," Tom said, coming to his own defense. "And I ain't as agile as I used to be, so my meals aren't all that regular."

"Well, this time your skills, agile or not, seem to have saved your life," Lucinda commented. "Although it's obvious you're going to need stitches to close that wound." She motioned to Regis, who stood behind the sofa looking down at Tom. "Have Charles bring the doctor."

Regis inclined his head politely. "Aye, my lady."

After Tom's wound was cleaned and bandaged to the best of Jane's ability, she propped a pillow behind his head and gave him a sip of wine.

Gabriel then questioned the elderly man. "What happened in the ally, Tom?"

"'Tis all my fault Miss Riley is gone," Top Hat groaned.

"I doubt that, Tom," Lucinda comforted, taking a seat on a nearby chair. "You've done nothing but care for and protect Riley."

"But I let my guard down, trusted Naomi, needed 'er 'elp since I've been ailin'. The trouble makin' twit found a letter I've been savin' all these years," he said, reaching into his pants pocket with a shaky, blood-stained hand. He passed the wrinkled correspondence to Lucinda. "I wasn't too worried because Naomi can't read, but she must 'ave found someone who could do the job for 'er. I believe she took the letter from me one night while I was asleep." He looked away ashamed. "After a night in the pub, I sleep quite soundly."

Lucinda opened the letter, her eyes squinting for lack of her glasses, and read it. "It's the last letter Anita received from Kevin Delaney."

"And this Kevin Delaney is the one who claims to be Riley's father?" Gabriel said.

"Not claimin' to be...'e *is* Riley's father." Tom took another sip of wine from a glass Jane held to his lips. "And that bit o' truth was only known by Lady Lucinda and me. But since I've been ailin' and Naomi 'as been 'elpin' me now and then, she discovered the letter."

"And then she conveniently came up with the story of meeting a man who is looking for Riley and claiming to be her father," Lucinda concluded.

"Aye, that's the way of it, my lady," Tom said. "I should 'ave seen through Naomi's words, but then again I thought what could she gain by lyin'?"

"Did you happen to have a chance to read the note Naomi sent to Riley this morning?" Gabriel inquired.

Tom coughed and cleared his throat. "I did, sir. Like I said, Naomi can't read, so I read it for her, and somethin' did strike an uneven cord. The handwrittin' on the note didn't match Kevin Delaney's last letter to Anita."

"Then why, in God's name, did you allow Naomi to send the note to Riley?" Lucinda admonished.

"Well, for one thing I didn't know if 'twas Kevin Delaney who wrote all the letters 'e sent Anita in the first place. And on a second thought, if 'e was runnin' from the law and headin' for America after 'e met with Riley, like the note said, I figured Riley 'ad a right to see 'im one last time. So, I went along with the whole thing. But then I got worried. Thought 'e might be seein' if 'e could ask Riley for money or 'elp, or somethin' such as that. So as soon as I discovered where Naomi was plannin' on meetin' Riley, I followed 'er."

Lucinda frowned. "What could Naomi have gained by tricking Riley?"

"We'll never know the truth o' that because Naomi ain't gonna be able to tell us even if she wanted to. Fact is, she ain't gonna be able to tell anyone anythin' ever again." Tom coughed once more. "They killed Naomi, ran a knife through 'er heart. Then they did the same to me. Didn't want any witnesses, thought they left me for dead, except I'm too stubborn to die. Then they took Riley," he choked out.

Gabriel's nerves tensed, and his heart sunk to his toes. "Who has done this? Who has taken Riley?"

Tom gasped for breath. "The men in the red jackets...the scoundrels who take all the young women." Tom groaned.

Lucinda leaned forward and placed a hand on Tom's arm. "What men in red jackets, Tom? I don't understand what you are talking..."

"I do," the captain interrupted.

Everyone turned to look at him.

Simon's mouth twisted in disdain. "I know who the red-jackets are. I even have an idea what sort of deal Naomi struck with them." He took an audible breath. "And if what I am thinking is correct, it isn't going to be easy getting Riley back...not easy at all."

Gabriel squared his shoulders. "I have accomplished *not easy* before."

"Let me re-phrase that, then." Simon arched a brow. "How are you at accomplishing the impossible?"

"I will not know that until I have tried. And make no mistake about it; I do not plan on failing."

Chapter Seven

The floor's dampness seeped through Riley's cape, chilling her back and shoulders. She shivered and slowly opened her eyes. A shock of pain sliced through the center of her head, straight through to the back of her skull. Her ears buzzed, and her stomach lurched. She rolled onto her side and wretched. Warm liquid dripped from her nose, the red splotches pooling in her vomit.

My nose is bleeding!

When she raised a hand to wipe the blood away, she discovered both were bound together by rope. The tight knot cut into her wrists. She wiggled her fingers, now turning numb, and scooted away from the foul-smelling mess. Forcing herself into a sitting position, she focused on her surroundings.

Her vision spun but then stilled on a stream of light coming from a small window. The tiny portal's glass was shattered, and part of it was boarded up with a cracked plank of wood. The small opening was too high off the ground, almost reaching to the ceiling, and too tiny to escape through, but light from it helped her assess her whereabouts. She glanced at the brick wall, and as she watched a roach slip through the fractured mortar to whatever lay on the other side, she realized she had stared at the same scene once before.

Riley swallowed the panic rising in her throat and took a calming breath...well, as calm as she could take after finding herself bound and bleeding. But she was still clear-headed enough to know she would do herself nay a shred of good if she surrendered to the fear creeping around the edges of her demeanor.

Think, Riley. What is this place and when have you been here before?

She sniffed. Smells always triggered the memory the most. The heavy scent of mildew and lye soap lingering in the air set the wheels in motion. She inhaled again, allowing the stale aroma to take her back to a time when she stood naked and wet in this very room.

She was all but six years old at the time. Her mother, or rather her grandmother, as she recently learned was her relationship to Anita Flanders, worked as the laundresses for The Hotel Van Devere. The large Victorian mansion was an exclusive twenty-bedroom facility that catered to the discreet elite. Better known as the place where married men kept their mistresses.

With Anita clutching her hand, the two would walk past floral-scented rooms where the occupants spent most of their time. Women dressed in lacy under garments would smile at Riley and say she was a sweet child. Sometimes they'd gift her with peppermint sticks, pastries, and ribbons for her hair, as she and Anita made their way down the hall and to the basement laundry room.

On Thursday mornings Anita would heat up an extra basin of water, strip Riley of her dirty garments, and give her a bath. She'd fidget and fuss as the lye soap stung her tender flesh. Anita would scold her at first, but usually Riley didn't stop her antics until a sharp slap was administered to her wet bum. Anita had work to do, and there was little time to spend bathing Riley, so tears and protests were ignored and the scrubbing continued until all the filth and grime that settled on her body was washed away.

After her weekly cleansing, she stood, naked

and cold, while Anita dried her with a towel. Other laundresses stood working and chatting around her, so there was no room for privacy. Her face would heat with shame, and she'd cast a glance to the worn wooden floor to escape those who watched, as Anita rubbed her flesh dry.

She then had to sit wrapped in the towel for the remainder of the day, on a wooden table, bare feet curled beneath her, while her only pinafore and blouse were also being washed and dried.

She hated the inconvenience of being poor. To have a bath, get the chance to eat a warm meal, or find a bed to sleep in was always at the mercy of others. Anita took what she could, when she could, for the two of them, and if that meant being bathed in the basement laundry room of a hotel, filled with watching eyes, then so be it. She was taken care of the best that could be, under the circumstances. Though her clothes were worn and torn, most of the time they were clean. Though her shoes had holes in the soles, they fit her feet. The coat she wore, a three-quarter length *pelisse* that buttoned down the front, might have been decades old in fashion and in need of great alterations to fit her child's size, but it served its purpose. And sometimes she went hungry, but she never starved. It was Top Hat Tom who always made sure of that.

Oh, Tom, I watched them stab you and Naomi to death.

The scene of them lying in a pool of their own blood wrenched her heart. Tears welled in her eyes and overflowed down her cheeks as she mourned them both, even though Naomi set her up to believe Kevin Delaney came back to town and wished to see her. The woman she knew all her life was a traitor and had been promised payment to hand her over to a man in a red jacket. But the capture wasn't as quick and easy as Naomi obviously anticipated.

The man played a double-cross of his own, and the only payment Naomi received was a knife to the heart. Top Hat, who had come along to the meeting, looked uneasy while they waited for the man who claimed to be her father to arrive. Riley refused to believe Tom was in on the scheme, as he did his best to attack the kidnapper once chaos broke out. But being old and ill, Top Hat was no match for the other man and met the same fate as Naomi.

Riley wanted to run, but her feet would not move. She wanted to scream, but her voice caught in her throat. So she just stood frozen, watching those she loved bleeding on the ally's cold ground. Then the assailant turned on her, grabbed a fist full of her hair, and punched her in the face. It was the last thing she remembered before everything went black.

The sound of men's voices brought her back to the present. She would have to put her grief on hold for those who died today, as she needed instead to set her focus on getting free. Whoever her capturer was, he destroyed two lives in a blink of an eye and now held her fate as well. She forced her wobbly legs to stand and leaned against the door to listen to the conversation taking place on the opposite side.

"Did you get rid of the blonde wench, the one called Naomi?" the first man asked.

"Aye, Captain," the second man responded. "I stabbed her through the heart with my blade. The old man they call Top Hat Tom as well. Both are dead. Their lips sealed for good."

She flinched at the cavalier way her friend's lives had been snuffed out by this man.

"Splendid, splendid," the first man said. "Last thing I need are witnesses."

"I don't think you had much to worry about, Captain. Nay a person with any sense is going to listen to anything a couple of *toshers* would have to say against your word," the second man replied.

"The reason I am a success at what I do, Lieutenant, is because I am careful to cover my steps, leave nothing to chance and foresee the inevitable," the first man said.

"Well, if that be the case, Captain, have you anticipated Lieutenant Gray's reaction when he finds out the Naomi twit is dead? He enjoyed that one, said she had a tight arse and loved it when he put his..."

"That's quite enough, Lieutenant. I haven't time to discuss Addison Gray's sexual romps right now," the first man interrupted.

Riley closed her eyes, a mixture of sadness and disgust filling her heart. Naomi not only set her up but had been intimate with the third man in on her capture.

"Now, is our new guest here?" the first man continued.

"Aye, she lies unconscious just beyond that door," the second man explained. "I had to punch her senseless."

The first man took an audible breath. "Was it really necessary to use brute force?"

"Aye, it was the only way I could quietly get her to the wagon," was the second man's trembling reply. "I forgot the sleeping powder."

The first man's voice deepened. "And dare I hope you didn't mark the merchandise to ghastly proportions in the process?"

"Nay, just a bluddy nose." Then the second man added. "And it doesn't appear broken."

"You'd better hope it's not," the first man warned. "Our client wants a flawless face, young and beautiful and her virtue intact. Although I happen to know this one grew up on the streets, and that is to be a fact we do not divulge to the client," he added. "She was taken in by money at an early age, so in view of that, I tend to believe she is still untouched."

"By the time we get her to the island, her nose will be healed, and as far as her virtue," the second man chuckled, "I haven't yet checked."

Riley swallowed hard the fear rising to her throat and locked her trembling knees together.

"And you won't," the first man informed him. "This one can fetch us a pretty purse left just the way she is."

The second man chuckled again, his cackle more sinister then before, and chills raced down her spine. "And after our client's through, I've got first claims on her."

"We'll talk about that later," the first man said.

The second man's voice sharpened now. "You promised if I was able to pull this capture off, I could have her after the client's finished with her."

"I believe what I said was if the client was satisfied with her when all was said and done, then you could have her next," the first man disputed.

"Oh, he'll be satisfied all right," the second man boasted. "I took a bit of a look at her while she lay unconscious. She's slender and slight, but far from scrawny like the others were. And her breasts are full and firm, not to make light of a well-rounded arse and long, shapely legs."

Riley's face heated, and suddenly she felt dirty and used at the thought of her lying vulnerable to this man's eyes. She swallowed hard the humiliation and degradation that soured in her mouth.

"But the little twit has to be compliable, and that's not always an easy thing to do when beating and starving her into submission isn't probable."

"Aye, right, she's got to be flawless," the second man reflected. "I hope this venture isn't going to be impossible. I mean, I've gone to great lengths, and I really want this one."

"Ah, now old chap, quit your worrying. Something improbable isn't necessarily impossible," the first man said. "There's always her family we can threaten her with."

Riley's heart skipped a beat with a mixture of fear and rage.

"Aye, we know who she is and where she lives," the second man agreed.

The first man's tone turned diabolical. "And we will kill each and every one of those that dwell at Collins Stead if she's uncooperative. On that she has my promise."

She covered her mouth with hands stained from her dried blood to keep from crying out. Already she lost Tom, but to think of Lucinda, Jane, all the others dead, was unbearable. And Gabriel, how could she go on in the aftermath of his murder? She loved him the moment she first set eyes on him, yearning...dreaming for the moment when the two of them could come together. For a time while he courted Collette Halston, her hopes were dashed. But now the other woman was gone, no longer in the picture, and after spending time together at the morning meal, she felt a connection with him. Her heart soared when he asked her to call him by his first name. Then another thought, not so pleasing, struck her with velocity.

After these men are through with me, I may not be around either.

The second man's wicked laughter, again chilling her bones, brought her back to the present. "Then she'd better be a good little miss and do everything she's told."

"Aye, I have no doubts whatsoever she'll be at our disposal," the first man reassured him. He cleared his throat. "Now, shall we have a better look at our little gem?"

"Aye," the second man eagerly agreed. "I've been waiting for this all afternoon."

The bolt was swept aside, and the door opened.

She stepped away from the heavy portal just as two men dressed in red jackets, black trousers, and knee-high boots entered the basement chamber. Raising a defiant chin, she squared her shoulders and met the first man's gaze.

He was a tall man of slender build but solid in the shoulders and chest. His blond hair fell into his eyes as he bowed politely and addressed her. "Good afternoon, Miss Flanders. It's so nice to finally make your acquaintance."

The second man was portly, actually pear-shaped with dark hair, skin tone, and eyes. He had a round face with hanging jowls and a very large nose.

As the blond man neared her, she stepped back, her hips coming into contact with the same table she sat upon as a child. Though they were troubled and rough times, she'd gladly trade them for the present.

"Stay away from me," she choked out.

"Now, now," he continued with false comfort and calm, "there's nay a need for you to be frightened."

She cast a quick glance at the second man, who came up beside her, rubbing his hands together like he were about to sit down to a mouth-watering meal.

"All will go smoothly if you remain cooperative," the blond man said. She looked into his light gray-blue eyes and fear coursed through every fiber of her being. His gaze darkened as his eyes roamed the length of her and lips curled into a slow, leering smile. "And I think in time you'll find we might even become friends."

"I think not," she sputtered, the thought of him...of either of them touching her was even more nauseating.

"I think so." He raised a bushy blond brow. "I am willing to bet eventually we'll even be intimate friends at that."

Chapter Eight

"If you know who these scoundrels are, why are we not calling the authorities?" Gabriel snapped.

"Because in a sense, they are the authorities," Simon returned.

He frowned. "The constables do not wear red jackets."

"I'm not referring to England's law enforcement," the captain explained.

Frustrated to the tips of his toes, Gabriel took an audible breath. "Then who do you refer to, Simon?"

Simon arched a brow. "The Sea Patrol."

Those words paralyzed his insides as thoughts of how close the Sea Patrol came to hurting one of his family surfaced. Originally it had been two sisters, Raven and Sunny, he had accompanied to England. After he was sure his siblings were settled in their cabins, he made up the excuse his luggage never came aboard. With that fabrication he could get a fast drink at a shore-line cantina they had passed on the way to their ship. But he had stayed too long, and his sisters discovered he had lied. That was when Raven left the England-bound ship to search for him. And when she did not find him, she hurried back to the vessel she believed was the one she left. With the twilight of day and the fog setting in, her perspective was clouded. She accidentally boarded the wrong craft, a cargo ship going to Ireland.

His sister's illegal passage, if such a status was discovered by the Sea Patrol, could have caused her to be arrested and taken to prison. If not for the kindness of the Lord of Limerick, the ship's owner, Braiton Shannon, agreeing to say the vows of matrimony with Raven to rescue her from such a horrible plight, she would have been lost forever instead of now being happily wed and living in Ireland.

"They don't normally have jurisdiction on land," Simon added, breaking through his thoughts. "But they've volunteered to clean up London's prostitute problem when not at sea."

"And using the girls for their own purpose, no doubt," Lucinda said.

"No doubt at all," the captain agreed. "And I would say that's the deal this Naomi woman made with them using Miss Flanders."

"Aye, 'tis," Tom admitted. "If I'd known for sure the wench was a traitor, I'd 'ave stopped 'er in some way."

"Then we must go to the police and tell them what has been going on," Gabriel suggested.

Simon let out an audible breath. "We'd only be laughed at and sent away like a hound with his tail between his legs."

He frowned. "I fail to see why."

"Think about it, Gabriel," Simon continued. "The only proof we have is the word of a *tosher*?" He glanced at Tom. "I don't mean any disrespect or offense, old chap."

"None takin', Captain," Tom choked out hoarsely.

"That is not true," Gabriel challenged. "They have kidnapped Riley and have her with them. When they are caught, her presence will be proof enough of their doings, as well as the note she carries."

"Nay, it will not," Lucinda said. "Riley was born a *tosher* as well. Folks have seen her on the streets as a child...still see her now and then when she brings food and blankets to Tom. The Sea Patrol could merely say they thought she was a street-walker. As far as the note goes, it could almost make matters worse, proving she was meeting someone wanted by the law. I'm afraid London's social class is a hard society to breech. They look way too often down their nose at those who do not live up to their standards."

Lucinda's assessment brought to Gabriel's mind the way the white agents treat his people. The Apache are considered the lowest of lows. America, as well as England, holds prejudice toward others. Except the English folk discriminate with a bit more manners.

"'Tis for that very reason, so far only street-walkers have been taken, that I've not been able to tell all I know to the authorities," Tom pulled Gabriel back to the situation.

"And what do you know?" he prodded.

"I know they take the women to the Van Devere Hotel, which 'as long been abandoned, and lock them in the basement until they can move them to the next location. But I think we might 'ave caught a break 'ere."

Gabriel's frown deepened. "How is that, Tom?"

"I think the red-jackets must 'ave decided to raise their sights from the usual street-walkers they've been tradin'," Top Hat said. "I 'eard around town Lord Wellington's daughter, Suzanna 'as been missin' for a few days."

"Aye, I read of her disappearance in yesterday morning's public chronicle," Lucinda said. "Good heavens, do you think the same men who have taken Riley have Lady Wellington as well?"

"Aye, there's a better than good chance of it, my lady," Tom said. "And I think Naomi was also in on that kidnappin'."

"What draws you to that conclusion?"

"I found out on the eve before last Naomi was 'ired to do laundry for the Wellingtons. She'd been at the job a few weeks." For a moment Tom closed his eyes with his pain, cleared his throat, and continued. "The young society women, especially one still virtuous, can bring a larger bounty than a street wench. These scoundrels must 'ave propositioned Naomi, since she was workin' for a prominent 'ousehold. Paid 'er to get Lady Wellington in a position whereby they could snatch 'er."

"And then Naomi's greed brought her to think of Riley," Lucinda said.

"Aye, that's the way of it," Tom agreed.

"So these men can move around freely, unsuspected because they appear to be cleaning up prostitution, when in truth, they're just making it *their* business now," Lucinda reflected in disgust.

"And a very lucrative one at that," Simon added. "But I think Tom's on to something. If the Sea Patrol has widened their scope to kidnapping society women for an increase in money, then finding Lady Wellington in their clutches would be the proof we would need to put them out of business for good."

"You said they lock the women in the hotel basement until they can be moved to another location."

"Aye," Tom said.

"Do you know where they take them from that point?"

"I think I 'ave an idea," Tom offered.

"Well tell us and be quick about it."

"Aye, every minute that passes is another they get farther away with Miss Flanders," the captain agreed.

"They can take away the street-walkers without question, but with the society ladies they must take more precautions," Tom explained.

"What precautions?" He prayed the old man did

not pass out from the blood he was losing before he answered the questions.

Jane, who still tended to Top Hat's wound, reiterated the same sentiments. "I wish the physician would get 'ere soon."

Tom coughed. "I'll be fine, miss."

"Where does the Sea Patrol take the women when they leave the hotel?" Gabriel coaxed.

"To the River Thames where they board one o' their special small steamers and sail on the English Channel to Lands End. Nay a soul questions them, as they think they're just doin' their job."

"And then the women are held at Lands End," Gabriel said.

"Aye, that's where they stay 'til they are transported to the Isle o' Wight."

"How did you come by this information, Tom?" Lucinda said.

"I drink with a few sailors and on occasion some *mud-larks*, who 'ear things," Tom said. "A drunken tongue will tell ye many secrets."

Gabriel remembered when he first arrived in England, his sister's husband, Rafe Cavendish explaining *mud-larks* were people who skimmed the Thames River for coal and other items to sell. "What happens then, Tom?" he implored, this time almost afraid to hear the truth.

"A ship arrives from the West Indies, mostly Santa Domingo, but there is a vessel from Egypt as well, and the women are sold."

A cold knot formed in his stomach. "Who are the women sold to?"

"Sometimes Sultans and Princes, then..." Tom hesitated, swallowed hard, and cleared his throat. "Then they are turned into concubines or slaves. They prefer the young women, in fact the younger the better. 'Tis easier to change the young females into concubines, their obedience and adjustments are faster. Soon they are actually embracin' their new lives. 'Tis then that they are truly lost forever to their families."

With a gasp, Jane and Lucinda muttered "Mercy" in unison.

"No mercy would be more accurate." The knot in Gabriel's stomach tightened along with every other muscle in his body.

Lucinda's voice broke with emotion. "What is there for us to do if we can't go to the authorities?"

"I will go after Riley," Gabriel said. "I will need to find Suzanna Wellington as well, so this all ends now."

"I will join you, since I know the English Channel, where to get a small craft, and the uncharted island," Simon offered.

"Count me in," Oliver offered, "since I know where the hotel is and some o' the *mud-larks* who might be o' 'elp to us."

"Nay, ye won't, mite," Addie protested. "When yer mum passed, I promised 'er I'd bring ye up to be a responsible man. And I plan on keepin' my word to my beloved sister. So, all ye are gonna do right now is march yerself to the stable, drop yer britches to yer knees, and bend over for a birchin' ye will never forget."

Oliver blushed with embarrassment. "I told ye, Auntie, I'm too old for you to be doing that."

"Nay, ye're just a boy and a bothersome one at that," Addie scolded.

Gabriel sympathized with the young man standing humiliated beside him. At Oliver's age, he was embarking on learning to be a warrior. If his mother had made such a declaration in the presence of others, and actually carried out the punishment, it would have shamed him to the roots of his hair.

He held up a hand to silence Addie. "I mean no disrespect, Addie, or to come between you and what you feel you must do to correct your household. But who and what Oliver knows can be of great use to us in finding both Riley and Lady Wellington."

"I understand yer way o' thinkin', sir, but 'tis my duty to my dead sister to make sure 'er son grows up right," Addie said.

Time was of the essence. Taking a deep breath, he calmed his frustrations before he spoke. "And I believe you have so far done her proud. But I also think she would want Oliver to do all he could to rescue the women these men have captured."

"Aye, I know she would want 'im to do all 'e could to 'elp," Addie agreed.

"And you have my word, as soon as our mission is complete and we bring Riley safely back to Collins Stead, you can bare his backside anywhere it pleases you for that thrashing he will never forget."

"Nay, that's not fair," Oliver chimed in, his neck and ears now turning as red as his face.

He put a hand over the boy's mouth and whispered in his ear. "You must learn when to keep quiet." Then he forced a smile Addie's way. "I ask you to please postpone his punishment because right now I need him with me."

"Aye, sir, I'll spare his 'ide for the cause," Addie agreed. Then narrowing her eyes at her nephew, she added, "And God 'elp ye if ye don't do exactly as Mr. Eagle and Captain Cavendish tell ye."

****

Riley thought the blond-haired man, who introduced himself as Captain Marshall Langley, examined her like a horse put up for sale at an auction. First he raised her skirt to her thighs, causing her such humiliation she thought for sure she'd be sick again.

"Get your hands off me!" She pushed him away.

Langley slapped her hard across the face, making her head spin. "You will cooperate if you want those at Collins Stead to live."

For the duration of his inspection, she remained quiet, biting her bottom lip until she tasted blood and bearing the humiliation in order to save those she loved.

Throughout his duties the captain commented to the second man, Lieutenant Martin Beck, emphasizing the condition of her limbs. "She has *good bone* and *excellent form*, along with *strong muscle* and lastly, but most important, *soft skin*. My findings please me greatly, and no doubt will do the same for the client."

Next she was made to open her mouth wide while he looked at her teeth. Again he was pleased at what he saw. Then he moved on to scrutinize her breasts, cupping each one in the palm of his hand as he evaluated their size. She swallowed hard, the tears of disgrace stinging the back of her throat. No matter what, she would not cry or look weak and frightened in front of these men.

Lastly, Langley forcibly turned her around. Beck placed a hand at the back of her neck and pushed her face down onto the table. Its ridge stuck into her stomach. Beck then held her shoulders down so her bum was elevated for Langley to properly observe.

As he squeezed and pinched her rounded derrière, he chuckled with pleasure. "It's a perfect size and shape, not too large, but curvy enough to give a man pleasure."

She did her best to control the shame and rage coursing through her body, reminding herself all the while Langley continued his examination that she needed to stay quiet for the sake of her family.

"I think we should remove her skirt and bloomers for a better look, Captain," Beck suggested. "After all, how can we sell merchandise we know nothing about?"

Silence enveloped the chamber as Langley

considered Beck's remarks. And then, her heart sank completely when he said, "You might have a point there, Lieutenant."

"Nay, please don't do this," she begged, trying to twist from Beck's grasp.

Langley slapped her hard on the bum. "Do you want your family killed?"

She stilled her body, fighting back the urge to do a bit of killing herself. She always wondered what drove a person to take another's life. But right here and now, if she had a gun, she'd shoot these two men in cold blood.

"Besides," Beck added, "we aren't going to hurt you. We just want to have a bit of a look, is all."

Langley placed a booted foot between her own feet. Then he pushed her legs aside so she was made to stand with them spread wide.

God, please make them stop.

But when she felt his fingers begin to unfasten the buttons at her waist, she could remain passive no longer and exploded into action.

She threw her head back, clipping Langley in the forehead. He stumbled back. Beck, somewhat shocked by her exploit, released his grip on her shoulders. That's when she ran at him with full force. She heard her neck crack when her head met his chest. He, after all, was a large man. Pain rioted down her spine, but she kept going. Normally such an impact probably wouldn't have fazed him in the least, but she had caught him off guard.

Beck ended up flat on his back upon the floor, and she lay on top of him. He laughed in her face. "If I knew removing your skirt would get you on top of me like this, I would have suggested it sooner."

"You are a pig," she whispered, lowering her mouth to sink her teeth into the tip of his nose.

He threw her off him and jumped to his feet, shouting, "She nearly bit my nose off!" He raised a booted foot to kick her in the stomach, but the captain intervened.

"After the client has had her, you can do whatever you want with her." He pushed Beck aside.

Blood poured from the tip of Beck's nose. "Little bitch," he repeated with a scowl, reaching for a handkerchief in his jacket pocket. Holding the cloth to his nose, he bent down on one knee to look her level in the eyes. "You just wait and see what I've got in store for you," he growled. Then his wicked laugh filled the chamber. "In your case being desired will be a mixed blessing."

"Enough!" Langley yelled. "We haven't the time for this." He marched out of the chamber and returned with a large trunk. After opening the lid, Langley pulled her to her feet. "Get in," he demanded.

She hesitated as she looked down at the faded floral lining, stained with blood. The large crate wreaked with a mixture of urine and another horrible stench...death. She covered her nose with her bound hands, fighting the waves of nausea washing over her.

"So sorry, sweetie," Langley sarcastically apologized. "I didn't get a chance to fumigate it since it was used last."

"Why do you need to put me in there?"

"Your departure will be less conspicuous this way, my sweet. Can't have others seeing you walk out of here with your hands tied and dried blood upon your face, now can we? Besides, this way there's nay a chance of you trying to escape," Langley explained.

"But I won't—don't dare to or else you'll kill my family," she bargained. If she could leave on her own two feet, perhaps she'd have a chance to catch the eye of someone she knew. Maybe even Oliver would come looking around town for her when she didn't meet him as she was scheduled to do at the ally. It was a slim prospect, but a slim chance is better than no chance at all.

"I said, get in!" Langley grabbed her by the hair and threw her head first into the trunk. Again he slapped her on her upturned bottom, harder this time, and laughed. "A good spanking now and then never hurt anyone, my mum would always say."

Beck joined in with his sinister cackle. "My mum would say it builds character."

Which did nothing for you. She rolled away from his abusive hand and onto her side. As she curled her body into a ball, she glanced up at her kidnappers.

"Rest nicely, my sweet." Langley shut and locked the lid.

The darkness and the stench surrounded her. It was like being buried alive. A chill ran down her spine at the thought that indeed this trunk might have been someone's coffin. The panic rose to choke her, as did the rancid stench, and she gulped for air.

Air, where am I getting air from?

As her gaze darted around the dark, tiny cubicle, she spotted light coming from a hole. Maneuvering her face nearer, she stretched her neck to get an eye even with the small opening.

Pain again ran down her spine, but she persevered in spite of it. If she were able to look out, see where they were taking her, then should a chance come for her to escape, she'd know where to run for help.

There wasn't enough room to bend her head in position, so she did the next best thing. She stuck her nose out the hole and took a cleansing breath. If she could inhale fresh air, instead of the stink that confined her, she wouldn't vomit all over herself.

Besides, there was always the hope someone would see two men carrying a trunk with a nose sticking out of a hole. And perhaps they would question them, force them to open the trunk, and she'd be saved.

Perhaps that would happen.

Perhaps it will happen...there's always a chance.

Chapter Nine

As Gabriel—along with Simon and Oliver—
watched two Sea Patrol officers carry a trunk
through the back door of the old hotel, he spotted a
hole that marred one side of the large chest. And
poking out from that hole was the tip of a nose.
Although he could not see if the nostrils were of a
delicate shape or if a spray of freckles dotted the
bridge, he had a hunch the nose belonged to Riley
and no other. When he pointed it out to his
companions, Oliver stood and tried to break from
where they now crouched behind several trees.

He caught the younger man by the scruff of his
neck before he had a chance to give away their
observation point and pulled him back into hiding.
"You want to destroy any chance of rescuing Riley?"

"She's in that trunk, right there in front o' us.
All we need to do is take on the two in the red
jackets, which shouldn't be 'ard since there's three o'
us and only two o' them, and set 'er free." Oliver
tried to rid himself from Gabriel's grasp.

"Have you heard nothing being said?" He
released the young man so quickly he landed on the
ground. Just his luck he had to rely on this boy for
help in order to save Riley.

"I've 'eard everythin'," Oliver claimed, coming to
his feet and brushing the dirt from his britches.

"If that were true, then you would have learned
the key to getting these men arrested is finding
where they keep the women at Lands End. We must
find Suzanna Wellington and rescue her as well as
Riley and any other women who are imprisoned

there," Gabriel explained.

Simon added, "Lady Wellington's word, and that of her rich and influential father, is the only thing that will stand up to put the scoundrels away."

"So, I would say, marching out and getting into a brawl with these men is not a very wise idea," Gabriel concluded.

Oliver straightened his collar. "I don't know 'ow ye do it...'ow ye can just stay back and watch 'er being 'eld captive in that trunk." He inhaled sharply. "Can't ye just imagine 'ow scared she must be? Aren't ye worried she's 'urt, or that those men might 'ave already..."

He seized Oliver by his jacket's lapel. "Do not say another word." The thought of Riley being compromised was something he could not bear and still remain sane enough to complete the mission.

Oliver's glare locked with Gabriel's.

"Of course I am worried. Do you think your thoughts have not run through my mind as well?" He pushed Oliver's back against a tree trunk and held him there. "From the moment I learned of Riley's abduction, I have been tortured by such possibilities," he ground out with gritted teeth. "But if I make myself insane with such ideas, then I cannot do what I must do to release her from their clutches. And the longer they have her, the longer they can hurt and frighten her."

Simon placed a hand on Gabriel's shoulder. "Calm yourself, mate. If we fight amongst ourselves, we can't be united to help Riley."

Gabriel paused a moment before he released Oliver, then stepping back, he ran his fingers through his hair. "You are right, my friend. Our focus must be on what lies ahead for us to do."

"I'm sorry," Oliver apologized. "It's just that Miss Riley 'as been good to me." His dark eyes softened. "She's the only one who doesn't think I'm a stupid mite who doesn't deserve any respect."

"Me thinks I detect a bit of fondness in your voice for the lady," Simon teased.

Oliver blushed. "Ye need to stop thinkin', then, Captain."

Simon laughed. "Aye, my brother, Rafe has often told me the same thing."

"Perhaps you should listen," he grumbled.

For some strange reason, Simon's words sent a wave of jealousy through Gabriel. Although Oliver was only a young man, his feelings could not be disputed. A young man's heart could hold love just as dear as an older man's. He fell in love with his wife when he was around Oliver's age and stayed true to his feelings until the time came for them to marry. Gabriel shook his head to clear it from such thoughts and turned toward the wagon into which the Sea Patrol officers were now loading the trunk. "Enough talk. It is time we follow them to the river."

Simon nodded. "I will have my carriage drop you and Oliver a few feet away from where the Sea Patrol's craft is docked. While you find a way to sneak on board, I will head back to Wade's Landing. Whereby I will incorporate my father-in-law's help in securing a small, worthy vessel to make the journey to Lands End, staffed with adequately armed men to stand with us upon meeting you there."

Gabriel patted the small pocket pistol in his coat. Not as powerful a weapon as the Colt Peacemaker or Winchester Colt .45—preferred by the cowboys in Arizona—it packed light, along with the dagger in his boot. Both weapons would suffice, although he favored a bow and arrow or a spear.

"I know the *mud-larks* that work that end o' the river. I can get them to cause some sort o' uproar so we can board the ship without bein' noticed," Oliver offered.

He arched a brow. "You mean so I can board unnoticed."

"But I thought I..."

"Well, you thought wrong," Gabriel corrected. "I have enough on my mind without worrying about you. Besides, if anything happens to you, Addie will be out for my hide as well. So you will do exactly as you are told." He narrowed his eyes at Oliver like Proud Eagle often did to him when driving home a point. "Do I make myself clear?"

"Perfectly," Oliver grumbled.

The three of them then walked through the trees to the waiting carriage and followed the kidnapper's wagon at a safe distance.

****

Riley shut her eyes, trying her best to remove herself from her closed quarters. The idea helped a bit for her to catch her breath...along with pressing her nose through a hole at one side of the trunk. She felt the men lift the crate off the floor and carry it away.

Away to where, and what fate awaits me then?

She fought to keep her calm. Panicking wouldn't help the situation, but it could sure make it worse.

Anita always told her there is something to be said for showing others your strength. If anyone knew that to be true, it would be her grandmother. The woman lived daily by sheer willpower alone. Even in desperate times, which were more the norm than not, Anita Noble Flanders found a way to rally, come through for her, and raise her to be proud, smart, and independent.

Riley would have to use all of those learned resources to the best of her abilities if she wanted to walk away from this situation alive. These men were ruthless. She knew this was true as soon as she'd seen the one called Beck stab Naomi and Tom to death.

Her body jarred when the men dropped the trunk. Then she was moving, slower at first, then faster. The trunk slipped from side to side, and she rattled within it. She could distinguish the sound of a horse running, wagon wheels turning. They were taking her away...far away from London.

Tears filled her eyes. When she left Collins Stead this morning, she had no idea she wouldn't be returning. She wasn't going to share the evening meal with Gabriel, ask Jane how her day with Charles transpired, or read to Lucinda a few of the forty love poems in Elizabeth Barrett Browning's *Sonnets of the Portuguese* before she retired. How, in the blink of an eye, could her life be so changed?

Riley pressed her nose further out the hole and inhaled sharply.

Right now she needed to concentrate on keeping her wits about her, and breathe...breathe...breathe.

Chapter Ten

Gabriel spotted the Sea Patrol's steamer docked on the River Thames about fifty feet to the left from where the carriage he shared with Simon and Oliver came to a halt. Another fifty feet ahead of them was the wagon that housed the trunk where Riley was being held captive.

The unceasing *clip-clop* of horses' hooves and carriage wheels making their way down the busy boulevard, the constant clang of the muffin-man's bell, the cries from street peddlers selling their wares, and river workers bustling with the usual day's activities carried on, unaware of the two patrol officers unloading the large chest from their wagon and making their way with it to the waiting craft.

As Oliver opened the carriage door, Gabriel placed a hand on the boy's shoulder. "Remember, your only job is to create a diversion so I can slip unnoticed aboard the steamer. Then you are to leave the area and take yourself back to Collins Stead," he said.

"I thought I might stay on with the captain, see what sort o' 'elp I can be to 'im," Oliver said.

Simon arched a brow. "Did you now?"

Oliver nodded. "I know most of the steamer captains, the deck 'ands and *mud-larks*. I could be o' great use to ye."

"Or is it you're just trying to prolong the birching your auntie has waiting for you at Collins Stead?" Simon teased.

Oliver's face reddened. "I'm wantin' to 'elp Miss Riley, but surely ye can't blame me for 'opin' to get out o' that sentence, Captain."

Simon stifled a smile. "Nay, I can't, but you need to take your punishment like a man."

"Nay, not by 'er. I am too old for that," Oliver protested.

"Then tell Addie I will beat your backside instead, when I return," Gabriel said, annoyed so much time was being wasted. One thing he had learned about the English is they could discuss, debate, and dissect a subject to death and still never arrive at a conclusion. "But you go back to Collins Stead where it is safe."

Oliver nodded, seemingly satisfied with this new arrangement, and jumped down from the carriage step. Both Simon and Gabriel watched him walk over to another boy, about his age, that was working on a tangled rope not far from the Sea Patrol's steamer. The two young men held a short conversation before making their way to the officer's wagon.

The other boy picked up a stick from the ground and poked around a pile of trash, then scooped something into his hand before he and Oliver made their way to the horse.

"What in blue blazes are these two plotting?" Simon wondered.

"I do not care what scheme they come up with," he confessed. "As long as it gives me enough time to slip unnoticed aboard the steamer."

Then Oliver steadied the horse and nodded to the other boy.

The other boy then held up what he had been holding...a mouse by the tail.

"By Jove, I don't believe my eyes," Simon hissed. "They're going to..." but before he could finish his sentence, the other boy dropped the mouse on the horse's head. The horse reared, throwing its head back. The scream issuing forth from the animal was one Gabriel would never forget, nor ever believed a horse could make. Then it bolted, leaving the roadway and racing down the causeway to the dock.

The two Sea Patrol officers and five other men ran from the steamer. The boy and Oliver motioned for Gabriel to follow them.

"God speed, mate," Simon called after him, as he raced from the carriage, following the two younger men to the far side of the steamer.

"Alls ye gotta do is climb this 'ere ladder." The river boy pointed to a row of steps mounted to the side of the steamer. "Once ye're over the side and onto the deck, ye'll see a portal to yer left. That's a storage 'old. Since everythin' for this voyage 'as already been loaded, there's a good chance nay a soul will bother to go in there 'til after the boat docks."

"What is your name, boy?" Gabriel inquired.

"Joseph, sir," the river boy said.

He extended a hand to the younger man. "I thank you for your help."

Joseph wiped the palm of his hand down his britches before he accepted Gabriel's handshake. "I 'ope ye save them all, sir."

"Then Oliver has explained to you why I need to get on this steamer unnoticed?"

"Aye, sir," Joseph said. "I've seen the men bringin' the trunk aboard many times. I know what's locked in it, and I know what's goin' on. But for the fact nay a soul would listen to a poor river boy without proper means, I'd 'ave gone for 'elp myself."

The frightened horse continued to run in circles, hampered by the small wagon to which it was harnessed. A wheel flew from its axle, the back of the wagon shattered...the whole episode making quite a commotion and continuing to occupy the five men trying to bring it all to bay.

Simon's carriage had departed, and help would soon be rallied. All that was left was for him to climb aboard the steamer and hide in the storage room until the vessel docked at Lands End.

He gave Joseph a pat on the back, then turned to Oliver with a farewell glance before making his way up the steamer's ladder. Once his feet hit the wooden deck, he sought the storage room's door and slipped inside.

If not for the light coming from a very small outside portal, the room would be as black as coal. Once the sun went down, which it was soon to do, he would not be able to see his own hand before his eyes. Taking advantage of what observation time he had left, Gabriel studied his surroundings.

Crates of all sizes were stacked against the walls, as well as rolled carpets and sheets of lumber. He walked over to a crate and pushing aside a loose slat, discovered bottles of whiskey and rum inside. At another crate he did the same. That one carried weapons, hand guns and small daggers. It seemed selling women was not the only business venture the Sea Patrol dabbled in.

Just as he was about to investigate another crate, the inside portal's latch moved. Gabriel hid behind a stack of larger crates in a far corner. He hated being so trapped. The only way to exit the small chamber was either out the portal, which he could never fit through, or the door, which would be blocked by whomever entered.

He crouched low and removed the knife from his boot. Though the pistol in his pocket would most definitely put down the intruder faster, it would also create enough noise to call attention to his whereabouts. Staying hidden throughout the duration of this voyage and being able to follow the officers to where they held the woman was essential at all costs.

The door opened. Someone stepped into the room. A raspy whisper filled the tiny space. "Mr.

Eagle, are ye in 'ere?"

He raised his head and glared over the crate at the younger man standing with his back to him. The shabby coat, the shaggy haircut, there was no mistaking who looked for him. Gabriel stood and crept behind the boy with panther-like steps. Then grabbing him by the hair and bending his head back, Gabriel brought the blade of his knife beneath the boy's throat.

Oliver stiffened with a strangled gasp.

He brought his mouth to the boy's right ear and whispered, "I thought I told you to go back to Collins Stead."

Oliver relaxed against him. "Thank God 'tis ye. I almost soiled my britches."

"You did not answer my question," he said, pushing the blade of the dagger against Oliver's throat.

The dagger, pressed hard against his flesh, made Oliver stiffen again. "I thought I could be o' better use to Miss Riley by yer side."

"And again you thought wrong." He shoved the boy from him.

Oliver fell to his knees but quickly spun around to face him. "I feel real bad about leavin' Miss Riley alone in that ally, and fully realize because I did, 'tis all my fault she's been captured. Now, I need to set things right. I 'ave to 'elp ye save 'er."

"Well, you got that right, you should have stayed with her," he spat, narrowing his eyes. "But now I will have to watch out for you, when I need all my focus to save Riley."

Oliver stood. "I'm not a babe in nappies, ye know. I can watch out for myself. Always 'ave. Nay a soul 'as ever coddled me. I'm smart, quite fast, know 'ow to fight, and I'm..."

"As stubborn as a mule. And you continue to make unwise decisions." He shook his head. "No wonder Addie is inclined to beat you."

Oliver raised a defiant chin. "Let's get this beatin' over and done with now so I won't 'ave to 'ear another word." He walked over to a stack of lumber and turned his back to Gabriel. Then he undid his britches and slipped them down to his ankles. "Take one o' those small boards and do what ye must," he said, bending over the wood.

"I will not do this now," he said, replacing the dagger in his boot.

"Aye, ye will," Oliver challenged.

Gabriel stifled a smile as he looked down upon the bare, pale, and pimpled backside before him. "Dress yourself, boy," he said, making his tone far angrier than he really felt. "I think anticipating your punishment will be far more deserving for your actions."

Oliver straightened himself to a standing position and pulled up his britches. "I was afraid ye were goin' say that."

They caught their balance as the steamer lurched forward. He arched a brow. "Well, obviously I am stuck with you now."

Oliver smiled. "Aye, sir, that ye are."

Gabriel motioned to his surroundings. "Well, help me see what we have here while there's still a bit of light from that window."

Oliver investigated the chamber. "I found a lanthorn that might be o' some 'elp when it gets dark."

"You mean a lantern," he said.

"Nay, sir," Oliver protested, raising the lighting device for Gabriel to see. "This is a lanthorn. The side panels are made o' animal horn rather than glass."

He took the odd lantern. "I have never seen this type of light."

"Ye don't much anymore," Oliver explained.

"They were used long ago. I remember my grandpapa 'ad one like it once." He smiled. "If ye 'ave a way to light it, we wouldn't 'ave to sit in the dark."

"The light shining beneath the door would draw attention to us," he warned. "So acquaint yourself with what is here now, while we still can see what lies around us."

"I've found a bucket, and a rather large one at that. Should be good for usin' as a privy when the need comes," Oliver said. His stomach rumbled, and he placed a hand on his abdomen. "Sure 'ave a hunger."

"Well, it is your fault you will be missing the pea soup and roasted fowl Addie plans to prepare for dinner," he said.

Oliver swallowed hard. "Aye, 'tis a shame we'll be missin' such a delicious meal." He glanced around at the room's boxed inventory. "Think there's somethin' to eat in any o' these crates?"

"So far I've only found them filled with firewater and weapons," Gabriel said.

Oliver frowned. "Are ye speakin' o' spirits?"

He nodded, then narrowed his eyes when Oliver's face brightened. "And do not be getting any ideas. Drinking the firewater will fill an empty night, but not a hungry stomach. Besides, I thought you were here to help?"

Oliver squared his shoulders. "I am, just thought it wouldn't 'urt to warm our innards a bit, is all."

"A man cannot think or act with any real usefulness under such influence. So, our innards will have to stay cold."

"Perhaps then I might secure a weapon?" Oliver queried. "If I'm to be of any real 'elp, I'll need at least a dagger."

"You might be right on that account." He walked over to a crate and pushed aside a loose slat, then reached into the storage bin for a slim, stout-handled dagger. Handing the blade to Oliver, he said, "Keep it in your boot, sharp-edge to the back of your heel, and handle within easy grasp."

Oliver hid the blade as he was instructed. "What do ye think they're goin' to do with the rest o' them?"

"Sell them, trade them, whatever brings them a heftier profit," he explained.

"What would serve these scoundrels right is if we threw all o' these weapons overboard," Oliver commented. "What a commotion that would cause findin' the crates empty." Then his brows rose. "But it could be the ruckus we need in order to escape the boat."

"That would only cause them to search for the culprit who rid them of their stash, and instead of a diversion, they would form a hunt." Gabriel paced in thought. "But I think your idea has merit, Oliver." He gazed up at the portal. "If we pile a few crates atop each other, I will be able to reach the window. One by one, you could hand me a weapon, and we could empty the contents of only two crates."

Oliver frowned. "And wouldn't two empty crates still 'ave them 'unting us down?"

"Not if they did not find them empty," he said.

Oliver's frown deepened. "And what would fill them if we rid the crates o' the weapons?"

"We would," he said.

Oliver scratched his head. "It seems I've missed somethin' 'ere."

"Have you never heard the story of the Trojan horse?" He took a seat upon one of the crates.

"The Trojan what?" Oliver said.

"The Trojan horse," he repeated.

"Nay, I've not 'eard it told," Oliver said, taking a seat upon the floor.

Gabriel could not help but compare Oliver's eager attention to that of his own. His people were excellent storytellers. Telling a tale or recounting an event around a fire pit was the main source of entertainment after a meal or just before bedtime. He would sit beside his father, looking at him just as Oliver was doing now, and waited with anticipation for the story to unfold. His mother, flanked by both his sisters, would add a word here or a comment there to make the story more exciting and meaningful. How he missed seeing their faces, hearing their voices, or the wide-eyed looks and laughter shared around the wickiup after the conclusion of a good story.

And then suddenly his thoughts shifted from the days that were to a scene that confused him, as he saw himself with a child upon his knee. He was telling a story to the youngster, who sprouted a crown of dark hair resembling his own. The boy's eyes were emerald in color, round and inquisitive, like Riley's. And then, as he peered into his thoughts further, he saw her sitting beside him, her slim waist now swollen with child...his child. She was smiling as she watched him and the boy, her gaze tender and content. The connection felt as strong as the one he shared with Riley at the morning meal.

He swallowed hard. Never did his mind send him such an image, not even when he was about to marry Fire Star. Could the vision be something he received from the spirits of his ancestors? Many times warriors in his tribe spoke of such things, vision quests they were called, guiding the warrior down the path he should take. But his path was not meant to tread beside Riley. He was needed home...where the Apache people lived. He had to release them from the white agents clutches and influence, make them once more an independent nation.

"Will ye tell it, then, this Trojan horse story, or leave me to always wonder?" Oliver complained, bringing him back from his ponderings.

He shook his head to clear it from the intuition that unexpectedly autographed itself on his heart and started the tale. "It was a story my mother learned from her mother and passed it down to me and my sisters, about a war, fought thousands of years ago, between the Greeks and the citizens of a place called Troy."

"What were the two sides warrin' over?"

"The same reasons most wars are fought, out of greed for wealth, land, and power," he said, thinking of how the white agents stole and plundered all the Apache owned or held dear...their traditions and pride as well. "The Greek's leader, a man named Odysseus, wanted to conquer the city of Troy, but the Trojans had built such a mighty fortress for protection, infiltrating the walls became impossible. So, Odysseus came up with a plan."

Oliver crossed his arms across his chest. "And how is a plan made by men thousands o' years ago goin' to 'elp us today?"

Gabriel frowned. "Well if you sit quietly and listen, you will learn." He cleared his throat and continued. "Odysseus ordered a large wooden horse to be built with its belly hollowed out. Then a number of Greek warriors, Odysseus included, climbed into the horse. The rest of the Greek fleet sailed away to make the Trojans believe they had retreated, and the citizens of Troy were victorious."

"So the Trojans let their guard down?"

"Well, not at first, but then they met up with Sinon," Gabriel explained further. "Sinon was the one man the Greeks purposely left behind. So when the Trojans came out to marvel at such a large creation, Sinon pretended to be at odds with the Greeks. He led the Trojans to believe he had been deserted. Then he assured them the large wooden horse was safe and would bring them good luck."

Oliver snickered. "What gullible chaps these Trojans were."

"Well, keep in mind, they believed the Greeks had sailed away."

"Aye, 'tis the truth," Oliver agreed.

"The Trojans dragged the wooden horse inside the gates of Troy and celebrated their victory over the Greeks," he went on. "But later that night after most of the Trojans were asleep or drunk, Sinon let the Greek warriors hiding in the horse's belly out, and they slaughtered all the citizens of Troy."

"'Twas a clever ploy the Greek warriors came up with."

He smiled. "And there is no reason why we cannot do the same."

Oliver's face brightened. "Do ye mean to say, after we empty two crates, we will each climb into one?"

He nodded. "That is exactly the plan."

"Then we'll be carried right into the Sea Patrol's camp by their very own men," Oliver concluded.

Gabriel chuckled lightly. "And they will be none the wiser, my friend...none whatsoever."

Chapter Eleven

The storage cabin was dark. The wooden floor beneath them creaked as the steamer rocked to and fro over the rough river waters. Gabriel could hear Oliver's breath becoming labored as he lay beside him. While they worked, throwing the contents of two crates overboard, Oliver was occupied enough not to grow sick from the rise and fall of the voyage. But now as they rested and waited for the time to come when they would each have to hide in an empty crate, things were much different.

If only Lady Abbott were on board, as she was when he and his sister traveled by ocean to England from America, to give out peppermint sticks or brew a cup of ginger tea. Both remedies helped Sunny endure a journey on the waters. He was sure it could help Oliver as well. But since such a hope was not available, Gabriel thought of another way to ease the sick stomach of the boy gasping beside him.

"Detach your brain from what ails your body, Oliver," he offered.

Oliver gagged and then choked out, "Oh, aye, and 'ow is that possible?"

"More possible then you would believe," Gabriel said. "I have done it many times, as well as other warriors in my tribe. It is part of our training, and it serves us well."

"Then tell me quickly what I must do before I lose what little I 'ave in my stomach," Oliver moaned.

Bad enough the shipmates would find the bucket full, but finding the contents of Oliver's stomach all over the cabin floor could really cause suspicion. Besides, smelling such a stench would get his stomach heaving as well. "Focus your thoughts on a time or place that made you happy...perhaps something you did that you enjoyed," he explained. "Then bring the scene into the center of your vision. Now listen for the sounds and inhale the smells you experienced while you were there, and try to experience them again."

"Aye, I know of one...'twas when my mum was still alive, and she baked dumplin's just for me, for my tenth birthday. She 'ad them ready and waitin' for me on the kitchen's table, the room delicious with the smells o' 'er cookin, mingled with the scent o' lavender she always wore. I got a whiff o' the sweet aroma when Mum bent down to kiss my forehead. 'Twas a happy moment, with Mum singin' as she worked."

Gabriel smiled. "And how many dumplings did you eat?"

"The lot o' them, I believe," Oliver remembered. "Never could I get enough, as they'd melt in my mouth before I could begin to chew."

"What did your kitchen look like?"

"'Twas just a simple room, actually. A large fireplace covered one wall, and Mum's large, cast iron pot 'ung on a 'ook over the flames." Oliver's breathing eased as he explained. "Mum always kept a clean 'ouse, well-scrubbed and orderly. She worked from sun up 'til sun down makin' sure all was right. We didn't 'ave a lot, but she made curtains for the windows and always 'ad a vase o' flowers on the table. 'Twas a good time; one I regularly miss."

"It sounds wonderful, as being with those you love so often is," he said.

"Aye, but then it 'urts something fierce when ye lose it all," Oliver said. "When all ye 'ad is just in yer 'ead."

"Would you sooner not have those memories," Gabriel said.

"Nay, I am glad for them, even if sometimes they 'urt to think about. There's still somethin' about bein' able to call upon them when ye need comfortin' that makes them worth knowin'."

"Like now," he said.

"Aye, like now," Oliver agreed.

"So, how is your stomach feeling?"

" 'Tis feelin' much better. Yer mind trainin' 'as really worked."

Gabriel chuckled lightly. "Did you doubt me?"

"Nay, I can see ye are a wise man, and I trust ye, but I 'ave wondered about one thing."

"What would that be?"

Oliver cleared his throat. "I understand why it wouldn't 'ave been a good plan to storm out and attack the scoundrels as they loaded the trunk into the wagon. And I know we 'ave to bide our time, find where they're 'oldin' Lady Wellington so we can put an end to all this."

"But..."

Oliver finished Gabriel's refrain. "But what 'arm can it do to find where Miss Riley's being kept and let 'er know we're 'ere to 'elp 'er?"

"More harm than any good could come out of such a move, I am afraid," he cautioned.

"Why do ye say that, sir?"

He turned to face Oliver, although in the dark he could not see the boy's face. "Do you know the lay of the ship like the back of your hand so you could duck out of view should a ship mate appear?"

"Nay, never 'ave I been on this ship, or any other in my life," Oliver confessed.

"Well, then, there lies the first problem. The second lies in the fact we have absolutely no idea where the trunk has been placed. For all we know, it could be in the captain's quarters."

"Aye, it could be at that," Oliver agreed. He then took an audible breath. "I just feel sittin' 'ere in the dark, ready to lose whatever's still in my stomach, is a sorry way to be 'elping Miss Riley."

"Did you ever hear of the Chiricahau Apaches, Oliver?"

"Nay, sir."

"They were a ruthless bunch, robbing other tribes of their food and women, as well as the white man. We were blamed and persecuted for the many things this tribe did. One day, when I was just a baby, the Chiricahua captured my mother," he said.

"Blimy, mate, what did yer people do?"

"It was my father, Proud Eagle, who headed the rescue, coming upon their camp a mile away from our village. He found her stripped and staked out." He remembered the pain in his father's eyes while he told the story. Even decades later, the fear and rage Proud Eagle experienced had not calmed. Gabriel cleared his throat of his emotion and continued. "You can imagine how my father felt...how any man would feel, seeing his woman humiliated and frightened in such a way."

"Aye, 'tis a madman I'd be for sure," Oliver whispered.

"But being a madman would have only gotten my father, the men who fought beside him, and my mother tortured and killed. The instant he lost his mind, made an unwise move, would be the end of them all, forever," he explained.

"Aye, but 'twould be so 'ard not to want to just run in fightin'," Oliver said.

"Better to sneak in with a plan, Oliver, and come out walking."

"So, 'ow did yer father save yer mum?" Oliver probed.

"Proud Eagle and his men hid in the brush until the Chiricahua bedded down on their blankets for the night, then they crept in and slit the enemy's throats as they slept," he said. "If a plan had not been hatched and carried out, the time to strike done at the most opportune moment, the night would not have ended with my father as the victor."

Oliver swallowed hard. "I see now what ye're sayin', but do ye think we'll 'ave to do the same, then?"

"In a real sense we are at war with these men, Oliver. There may not be an army of men against the ranks of another troop or big guns and other such weapons, but these men are the enemy and have taken what is ours. It is our right to fight them to get it back. If it comes to fatal blows, I can do it. For Riley's sake, I *will* do it." He sharpened his voice. "Can you?"

Oliver's voice trembled. "I can, if need be...for Miss Riley."

"Then we cannot be reckless in any way. What we think, how we move, what action we take must be thought out and carried through," he said, sounding like the men in his tribe who trained the warriors. Calling upon all his training, he went on to instruct Oliver.

The boy had forgotten all about his sick stomach. As Gabriel talked and tutored, he had a feeling Oliver's nausea was the last thing to be a bother. He hoped Oliver would be up to the mission that lay ahead of them. He also prayed Captain Cavendish and his men arrived in time to help, because Gabriel was not all that pleased to have an inexperienced, seventeen-year-old boy as his only alliance.

"Ye need not worry, sir," Oliver said, as if he read Gabriel's thoughts. "I will stand beside ye and fight, 'ave yer back 'til the end."

"Let us hope it is not our end," he said.

"What I mean is whatever needs done, I will do.

I'm not a coward," he swore with conviction. "You can count on me. I will not let ye down. You 'ave my word."

"That is all any man can ask of another," Gabriel assured him.

"But I can't guarantee that this time," Oliver hesitated, and then lowered his tone, "my britches won't be soiled when we're through."

He chuckled. "That will make two of us, Oliver."

****

Riley squeezed her eyes shut against the smothering darkness, the thirst parching her throat, the pain coursing down her spine, and the strain of trying to hold a very full bladder. She knew she was sailing on the water, could feel the floor beneath her sway to and fro. Thankfully she was not one prone to seasickness, having traveled once across the ocean to visit a friend of Lucinda's living in Paris, or else she'd have one more discomfort to battle.

Then there was the ever-present and frightening thought of unspeakable things to come. The fear of the unknown was often times worse to handle. What would she be made to endure at the hands of her kidnappers and the clients they served? Where was she being taken? Would she ever live to see her home again?

She silently prayed for strength, clutching desperately to her sanity. The last thing she needed to do was lose what little resolve she had. Taking a deep breath, she cast away the horrible images of what was to come and held on to any prospect of hope. But how could she not worry for her predicament? Would this be her demise? Or worse still, what lay ahead of her from this point on? Truth was, she'd rather be dead then suffer the humiliation and degradation these men could inflict upon her body and soul.

She heard the portal open. Light steps entered

the cabin, making their way across the creaky floorboards and stopping beside the trunk. A light filled the tiny air hole at the side of the large chest and shone in on her bound hands.

Then the trunk's lid opened, and the lantern's beam was flashed into her gaze. She shielded her eyes from the brightness.

"And 'ow do ye fare, miss?" a soft voice asked.

She blinked to focus her gaze, then squinted up at a young girl. A head full of matted, golden curls framed a round, pale face, and down the side of her left cheek, a pink and raised scar marred her delicate features. Her dress was faded and too large for her tiny frame, and a tattered, thin shawl was draped over her shoulders.

"Thought ye'd like to stretch yer legs a bit, make use o' the privy...although 'tis just a bucket," the girl added, large blue eyes locking with hers, "then 'ave a bite o' bread and a draught o' ale." Timidly her lips curved into a smile. "My name is Leah Kent."

Riley sat up in the trunk and opened her mouth to speak, but no voice came forth.

"Ah, ye are truly parched," Leah said.

She nodded and cleared her throat.

"Well, coome then, and let's get ye feelin' better." Leah placed a hand beneath her elbow to help her stand.

As Riley straightened her knees, pain shot from her spine, down her thighs, and into her feet. She groaned.

"Oh, aye, stiff as a board ye are," Leah commented as she braced her frail body against Riley's.

"I don't want to take us both down," she said, struggling to compose her balance.

"I'm a 'ardy one, much 'ardier than I look," Leah said. "I won't let ye fall."

Leah helped Riley climb out of the trunk and

make use of the bucket. Trying to manage on her own was too difficult with bound wrists, and the younger woman was not allowed to break those binds. Riley forced a smile. "I thank you, Leah."

Leah's gaze moistened. "And I thank ye, miss, for yer appreciation. 'Tis not somethin' I often get."

Leah, unwrapping bread and cheese from a cloth, placed the food and a mug of ale upon a crate, then sat beside Riley on the floor as she ate. While taking a sip of the ale, she surveyed her surroundings. The cabin was small, dark, and cluttered with wooden crates piled against the walls.

"There's nay a way to escape, miss, with a guard at yer door and the deep, cold river beyond that portal," Leah said, pointing to the cabin's only window. "'Tis best to do whatever they tell ye."

"Is that how you've managed?"

"Aye. 'Twill be in yer best interest to do the same. They like quiet and obedient women," Leah advised.

"Do they, now?" Riley quipped, anger suddenly rising within her.

"Please, miss, if ye give them trouble, 'twill be bad for us both," Leah pleaded.

She reached out with her bound hands to gently trace with a finger the scar down Leah's cheek. "And is this what happens when you aren't compliant?"

Leah cast her eyes to the hands she held clasped in her lap. "It only happened once."

"Once is enough," she said, caressing the girl's cheek. "Look at me, Leah," she urged. The younger woman's gaze reluctantly met Riley's, and in her eyes was something familiar. Where had she seen the same frustration, sadness, and sense of hopelessness? How did she have empathy for the fear, the strife, and daily exhaustion of living in such a hard circumstance? And then her heart was snared with the fact her childhood world somehow seeped into the cracks of Leah's. This younger woman's eyes mirrored her own. Riley once owned the very same visage while she cared for Anita. During her grandmother's last year of life, she was the adult...feeding, cleaning, and caring for the woman who once did all that for her. Her job was to find food, keep the stove burning, and fend for their safety. What would she have done without Top Hat? How would she have been able to cope all on her own, like this poor mite? "How old are you, Leah?"

"I am ten and seven coome next month," Leah said.

"And how long have you been with these derelicts?"

Leah shot a wary look at the portal. "'Tis large ears they 'ave."

She lowered her voice. "Tell me how it is you've come to be with these horrible men."

"My own sweet mother died when I was but nine and not long after Papa married the widow Clairmont," Leah replied in a hushed tone.

Just nine, the age I was when I had to be an adult. But after Anita's death, she had been saved by Lady Collins. Poor Leah has remained abandoned.

"Before they wed, Augusta Clairmont doted on me," Leah continued. "She was kind and carin'. Both Papa and I thought she'd teach me things a mother taught a daughter. But as soon as she moved into our 'ome in Dover, she didn't want me, said I was too much for 'er to care for along with 'er own two boys. Whatever I did, Augusta found fault with, and her sons were always gettin' me in trouble with there lies. My punishment was either a long, 'ard birchin' or takin' away meals. Soon, the daily discipline left my bum so raw and welted I couldn't sit. One time I could barely walk. I grew thin and weak from lack o' food. My father couldn't stand my sufferin' any longer, but 'e didn't want to endure 'is wife's wrath either...besides, 'e 'ad nowhere else to send me. Then Augusta said she knew o' a well-to-do family livin' in London needin' 'elp with infant twins. My father agreed, and the next morn what little belongin's I 'ad were packed in a satchel, and me and Augusta set out for London. When we arrived, I soon learned there was never a family needin' my 'elp. Instead, I was sold to a man named Lieutenant Beck and brought 'ere." She shrugged. "In some ways I am treated better than I was in my own 'ome. As long as I don't ask questions and ready the women brought on board, I am not beaten or starved."

Riley's eyes moistened with pity and concern. "Has your father ever tried to find you?"

"Papa's but a poor farmer who reads poorly and wasn't much for writin' letters, and since I can't do either, 'twouldn't 'ave done 'im much good." Her eyes filled with tears. "'Tis better 'e believes I am livin' with a wealthy family and well takin' care o' anyway. Augusta is 'is wife now, and I'm only 'is daughter. 'Twould be 'er wishes 'e should abide by first. And to cause 'im further trouble would break my 'eart worse."

"Have any of these men touched you, Leah?"

"Nay, not as yet, but I 'eard the captain talkin' not long ago. Since I am gettin' older," she said, glancing down at her budding bosom, "'twon't be long until I'm sold to one o' their clients as well."

"I won't let that happen. Somehow we'll get away from these men, the two of us, and I will take you back to Collins Stead with me."

"Is that the name o' yer 'ome, miss?"

"Aye," she said, picturing the comforts and security of the old mansion. "Lady Lucinda Collins took me in when I was orphaned at nine years of age."

"The same age I was when I left my 'ome," Leah

reflected.

"Aye, an age a girl should not have to worry about adult matters. Lady Lucinda is kind, generous. She made me her ward, and I know you will be welcomed as well," Riley assured her.

Leah's face brightened with hope. "Can you really promise me this, miss?"

She nodded, repeating to Leah the last phrase Gabriel said to her. "You have my word."

Chapter Twelve

As soon as the steamer stopped, Gabriel nudged a sleeping Oliver. "It is time to get into the empty crates." He placed a reassuring hand upon the boy's shoulder. "Remain as still as you can, take shallow breaths, and hold on to your dagger," he advised. Not long after they were settled into their boxes, the footsteps of many men entered the cabin, and the crates were lifted and carried off the steamer. Gabriel could hear the complaints of the two moving the crate he occupied.

"Bluddy hell, me back is about to break," one shipmate complained.

"Aye, me own 'tisn't feelin' so strong either," his companion agreed. "Do ye know what's in 'ere?"

"I've 'eard some talk o' them packed with liquor and weapons," the first man said.

"This one must be filled with bricks," the second man joked. "Mayhap we should take a look-see at what we've got 'ere, lighten the load...'elp ourselves to a bit o' the spoils."

Gabriel held his breath, sent a silent prayer to the heavens above, and tightened his grip on the dagger. Could he fell two men without being noticed? He concocted a plan of survival, should the lid be opened.

"Nay, the captain would find out, and I need this job," the other man said.

In the end, to Gabriel's great relief, the pair decided to incorporate the hands of a third man, and the crate was brought to its destination, which he calculated to be the back of a wagon. The men lifted, with great difficulty and several cuss words, the crate high enough to be placed on the platform. Then the wheels turned, and horses' hooves clopped along an uneven path.

He worried if Oliver's crate had also been placed upon the same wagon, or if it remained aboard the steamer. When the wagon stopped, his crate was again lifted. The men walked only a few feet from the wagon before placing him down. As they unloaded the other crates, his calculations brought him to reason he was still out of doors since the cool night air bled through the wooden slats.

Was Oliver nearby? He peered through one of the spaced planks to scope out his circumstance, but his efforts were met with only the site of another crate beside his. In spite of the back and leg cramps he endured from being confined in such a small space, he waited with forced patience while the men worked in close proximity to unload the wagon. Hopefully, if a guard was not stationed to watch the cargo, when the shipmates left he would be able to scout through the merchandise to find Oliver.

While he waited, his thoughts turned to Riley. Where was she now? Still in the trunk aboard the steamer? And how was she holding up? Had these men hurt her? Compromised her? His questions tormented him, causing his stomach to clench, along with his fist at the thought of her alone and scared, suffering the worst sort of humiliation a woman could. The white agents who had taken over his village pillaged their women as well as their belongings and traditions. He knew of the maidens forced to do their bidding, their innocence ruined, their pride destroyed. And it broke his people, shamed the men who loved those women, left them powerless. Spirits were dashed of any hope to come.

I am that hope. I am their only hope.

He had to survive this ordeal, not just for Riley

and the other women captured, not for Oliver's sake or even himself, but for all those of his tribe who needed him.

Taking a calming breath, he switched his concerns to his younger ally, just seventeen and impulsive. Would Oliver, tall and with a solid build, be able to suffer the cramped quarters without giving away his station?

As time droned on, the shipmates' voices and laughter faded into the distance. When the right moment finally arrived, he used his dagger to pry open the lid from within and peeked over the crate's ledge.

By this time a full moon afforded him a bit of light, allowing his surveillance to take in the row of crates stacked alongside his. Further scrutiny proved the haul had been placed at the edge of a forest.

Gabriel stood with caution, climbed out of the crate, and replaced the lid. Then he crept around to the other wooden boxes, knocking on their lids and whispering Oliver's name.

The fourth one he came upon knocked back and answered with, "'Tis about time."

He smiled to himself and sighed with great relief as he helped Oliver from the crate. While he replaced the lid, the younger man stretched life back into his legs and surveyed their surroundings. "I don't see Miss Riley's trunk amongst the cargo."

"My guess she is still on the steamer," he said. He gestured to the crates littering the ground. "It is much wiser of them to remove the merchandise cargo first, have it secured and ready for wherever it is to be shipped, before transporting the human cargo."

"Aye, I see...better to keep 'er locked away and silent while their mind is on other business," Oliver concluded.

Gabriel nodded. "And though we cannot see civilization from where we now stand, I am sure Lands End is inhabited to some extent. There must be a town or village nearby that these men do not want alerted to their activities."

"Do ye think, should the townspeople discover what these rogues are doin', they'd do somethin' to stop them?" Oliver moved to stand nearer to Gabriel.

"That is hard to say." He took an audible breath. "You must remember these men *are* the authorities. Many have grown accustomed to their dealings, have come to trust them, and believe they are enforcing law and order to the land. And then there are those who might fear them and turn a blind eye to save their own hides," he explained.

"So, it is doubtful we can expect any kind o' 'elp from the locals," Oliver said.

He combed his fingers through his hair. "I would not count on so many, if any at all, coming to our aid."

"Then I pray Captain Cavendish coomes with 'elp real soon."

"He is a good and honorable man, and I believe his word is worth much. I just worry he will not make it in time." He glanced south to where he believed the waters flowed. "The ship from the Isle of Wight could arrive soon or even be docked now, for all we know. Since we do not have the schedule they follow, Riley and Lady Wellington could be made ready to sail to the island as we speak. Then from there, they will be sent to the Indies, as Top Hat Tom suspected."

Oliver's dark eyes grew fearfully wide. "Once out o' our sight, we chance never findin' them again."

He nodded. "That is why we will have to find a route back to the river, discover a way to board the larger ship, and sail with them."

Oliver, clasping a hand over his mouth, groaned.

****

To Riley's relief, neither Captain Langley nor Lieutenant Beck interrupted the small meal Leah provided, but another officer did. He introduced himself as Lieutenant Addison Gray. She recognized the name, having heard it earlier when Beck referred to this man as Naomi's lover.

Gray's visage was pleasant. Dark, golden curls falling to the nape of his neck, framed an arresting face. She could understand why Naomi would be taken with this man. Casting a timid smile, Gray, with his light brown eyes bordering on a shade of honey, assessed her with efficiency.

The warmth of a blush crept into her cheeks. She rose to her feet as dignified as one could under the circumstances and challenged his gaze with her own.

Gray cleared his throat and removed a knife from the sheath attached to his belt. Nearing her, he cut the rope that bound her wrists. "I'm sorry, Miss Flanders, for your inconvenience." His tone was even. "Has Leah brought you enough to eat and drink?"

"Aye, she has," she said, rubbing the circulation back into her fingers. Under such duress it was hard for her to swallow even a tiny morsel, but she knew she had to keep up her strength if she was to best these men. Now it wasn't just her welfare she had to look out for, but Leah's as well.

"Then I will give you a moment to collect yourself before I take you ashore," he said, glancing down at her hands.

After studying him briefly, she decided he was not as crude as Beck, nor as diabolical as Langley. Still, he worked with the other two, helping them kidnap women, so he wasn't exactly upstanding. Yet, if she were able to turn him against his companions, perhaps he'd be more likely to look to her favor. She started to hatch a plan.

"You are the one Naomi knows," she said.

"Aye," he said, his smile deepening.

Her heart raced as she took from his expression the distinct feeling something more existed in his heart for Naomi then just the pleasures of a night between the sheets. He may have bragged about his lusty conquests to Beck, but clearly his reaction proved to be genuinely meaningful. If this was the case, then her plan just might work.

Gray's smile faded. "How do you know this?"

"I heard Beck and Langley talking," she said.

"Sometimes they talk too much." Then he added, "You must know she asked that no harm come to you."

Riley arched a brow. "How could she have expected anything differently?"

Gray shrugged. "I would say to Naomi anything other than death is manageable."

"And what was she promised for my capture?"

"She would receive a sum of money large enough to take her to France where we plan to start a new life."

"And is that where she is to meet you?"

"Aye, when my part here is done," he said.

She took an audible breath. "She will not be in France, Lieutenant."

He frowned. "If you are trying to make me believe Naomi will betray me, you are wasting your breath. I know she wants a new chance, a better life, and she's decided to share it all with me."

"It isn't Naomi who has betrayed you," she said.

His frown deepened. "And what would you know about anything?"

"As you said, Beck and Langley talk too much...and I listened." She raised a defiant chin.

"And what did you hear this time, Miss Flanders?"

"Captain Langley's instructions to Lieutenant Beck."

He smirked. "And what would that be?"

"He ordered him to kill Naomi. And that is exactly what Beck did."

Gray's eyes widened as he grabbed her by the arm. "You lie."

Leah moved between them. "Do ye remember she is not to be 'armed?'"

Gray glared at Leah with venom in his eyes. She was a tiny girl, only came to his shoulders, yet she stood bravely between them.

Riley's heart went out to the young woman standing in her defense. She had to get Leah away from these men, but getting Gray angry wasn't the way to win him over. She put a protective arm around Leah's shoulders. "I swear to you. I speak the truth." Then she softened her tone. "I am so sorry."

Gray removed his grip from her arm and stepped back. "Nay, that cannot be. We had a deal."

"You give your companions way too much credit, Lieutenant. In the line of business they are in, didn't it ever occur to you they'd not care about honoring any sort of deal?"

Gray, his demeanor rattled, combed his fingers threw his hair. "Are you sure it was Naomi?"

"Aye, I saw it all with my own two eyes. Beck ended her life with the blade of his knife." She swallowed hard as the scene of Naomi and Tom lying in a pool of blood came rushing back to haunt her. "I'm so sorry, Lieutenant," she apologized again. "But she isn't going to meet you in France...or anywhere ever again, because Naomi is most definitely dead."

Chapter Thirteen

Lieutenant Gray didn't bind Riley's hands with the rope, but instead tied it around her waist, and then attached the other end around Leah's. In this way he could control where they trod, and like a pair of dogs, he walked them onto shore and out into the damp night. The only light afforded them was from the lantern Leah had brought to the cabin earlier. Gray held it now, but with him walking on ahead, she had a hard time navigating over the uneven terrain, laced with rocks. When her toe hit an unseen obstacle, she stumbled, causing Leah to become off balance with her.

The shoes I wear are not fit for such a trek. My riding boots would have sufficed far better.

In an instant her thoughts disgusted her. Had she come, living with convenience and luxury, so far removed from any discomfort that she only cared for her own plight? When had she become so selfish? Leah's footwear was not even as well made as the pair she wore, and the younger woman's shawl and worn dress were threadbare, yet she never complained. Despite stumbling when Riley did, Leah never cursed or whined.

Instead, she whispered encouragements. "We are almost there. Just stay quiet, and all will be fine."

She had the distinct feeling if she weren't compliant, Leah would be made to answer for it. And she wanted no repercussions against the younger girl because of her actions. Leah looked as though she had endured enough, lest she make her life worse. Even at the most destitute time of her life, she was never abused. Granted, Anita disciplined Riley when the need arose. But her backside was met with a loving hand. The blows stung but were dealt fairly and with control. She was sure Leah would receive a much harder punishment, one quite harsh and humiliating. A birching at the hands of these men would be nothing less than torturous.

Leah helped her stand, but she had a distinct feeling someone watched her. She glanced at a copse of trees, searching for the one who observed her, but the dark forest hid the watcher well.

Not long into the journey, a storm threatened. The rain, vicious and embittered by a chill, pelted her shoulders, drenched her hair, and stung her cheeks like needles of ice. Her teeth chattered in unison with Leah's. Placing an arm over the other woman's shoulders, she draped the end of her cape around her bony visage and drew her close.

"I thank ye, miss," Leah said, soaking in whatever warmth their two bodies could afford them. And in that moment, she felt a bond growing between them.

Neither woman would be in the predicament they shared if it weren't for their paternal parent. Leah's father trusted his wife more than he worried for his daughter's welfare. He allowed a woman, too cruel to care for a child that wasn't hers, to decide Leah's fate. As a result she was sold into bondage. And Riley had hoped to meet her father, to finally set eyes on the man who she believed was her only living kin. Both she and Leah had been tricked and deceived. Their journey brought them to a wrong destiny, and now they'd pay the price all alone.

Except, they weren't alone any longer, they had each other. "You are not alone," she whispered to Leah. "Not anymore. We will survive this and escape from these men."

Leah's large blue eyes glistened with tears. "Do I dare to remain 'opeful, miss?"

"Aye, Leah. For without hope we cannot stay strong, nor do what needs to be done to find ourselves back at Collins Stead," she said.

The path turned into a steep incline, and Riley spotted the mouth of a cave ahead. As they approached the entrance, she heard Langley taunting and threatening to kill someone else's family members if they didn't comply. She had no doubt, even sight unseen, that the person was yet another woman. Wall torches lining the entrance illuminated the large opening as they made their way around a sharp corner.

Gray pulled his two charges behind him, coming to a halt as they stepped into a second chamber. "I've brought the other one," he said, scowling with venom at Langley and then glancing with menace at Beck.

Would he let on to the other two officers he knew of Naomi's death, or would he bide his time? She prayed for the latter. If Gray planned on revenge, and she was sure he felt enough for Naomi to vindicate her death, Riley's chances to sway him to her favor might be possible. She held her breath, waiting for him to reveal his news, throw her further to the dogs, but he remained silent. Handing his end of the rope to Beck, he stepped aside, wiped his face with a kerchief he pulled from his pocket, and then walked out of the cave.

"What's with him?" Beck said.

"I haven't time to play nurse maid now." Langley tied the hands of the person he intimidated, another woman Riley suspected, to a metal ring hanging from the stone wall. The ring was placed low enough to allow a prisoner to sit.

The other female was about Riley's age, fair-skinned and dark-eyed. One long chestnut-colored braid hung over her left shoulder. Strands had come loose from the tie, as well as tiny wisps curling at her temples and forehead. She appeared hauntingly exhausted and wore only nightwear, a cream-colored sleeping gown with long sleeves and a high collar. The flimsy material was streaked with dirt, its hem caked with mud. The woman's bared, muddy feet were scraped and bloody.

Good Lord, the poor girl must have been snatched from her bed.

Langley glanced at Leah tied to Riley, and his voice sharpened. "Set the little twit free and tie the other to a wall ring," he ordered Beck.

Beck nodded and did as he was commanded, tugging harshly on the rope still fastened around her waist. She tripped, coming down hard upon the cave's floor. Her right kneecap landed on a jagged piece of rock, splitting the flesh. Warm blood trickled down her leg. Beck reached for the hood of her cape and roughly pulled her to her feet.

She limped in pain to a wall loop, standing on one leg as Beck tied her wrists together, and then secured them to the metal ring.

"I told you not to mark the merchandise!" Langley shouted at Beck. "You've got this one's feet bleeding, and that one falling on her knee."

"It was her own fault she fell, not watching where she was going," Beck defended.

"Now, raise her skirt and see what harm has been done," Langley demanded.

Beck's leering smile proved he had no problem with that order and promptly lifted her skirt much higher than required.

Upon seeing her torn hose and bloodied knee, Langley growled. "Leah, fetch the items you will need to clean and dress that knee and the wounds on this other's feet. I don't need the threat of infection to ruin a business deal."

Leah nodded and made her way quickly from

the cave.

"You are all swines," the other woman shrieked, her gray-green eyes glaring with hate at Langley.

Langley knotted a fist full of the woman's hair in his large hand. "I have no problem reddening that lily-white arse of yours again, if need be. So think twice before you decide to trouble me further."

The other woman's face burned. Riley felt her own countenance heat, as she remembered Langley threatening to beat her in the same fashion. And most likely he would have, if at that moment, he wasn't pressed for time. Her virtue may not be in immediate danger of being compromised, for she well-realized the client ordered the services of a virgin. And Langley most definitely wanted to comply with his client's wishes. But that didn't mean her modesty was safe from the hands or the eyes of these men. The humiliation of her bum bared and receiving a beaten obviously would quickly heal and nay a soul would be the wiser, except for her.

When Leah returned with the medicinal items, Langley and Beck made ready to leave.

"Leah, after you tend to their injuries, fetch them each a flask of water, a slice of bread, and a bucket for their privy use," Langley ordered.

Leah nodded and bent to the task of cleaning Riley's knee first.

Langley's eyes swept over his bounty with pride. "Not a bad week's work, hey Beck?"

Beck grinned. "Not bad at all, Captain."

"Now, ladies, before I take my leave, I suggest you both rest. Tomorrow we sail early, and I will not tolerate any inconveniences. With that said," Langley added, bowing with mock politeness, "I bid you a good night."

"Sleep well, ladies," Beck concluded before he and the captain left the cave.

Riley shifted the hem of her cape beneath her

backside, to shield her bones against the ground chill, the best she could without using her hands. Then she extended her leg to Leah's administrations.

"Why are you caring for her first?" the other woman complained.

Leah's hands trembled, as gentle and efficient fingers cleaned and dressed the knee. "Because her wound is open, bleeds more," she said, her eyes remaining on her work.

The other woman sat, grimacing with pain as her bottom met the ground. "I hope you all rot in hell," she hissed.

When Leah finished, she made her way to care for the second prisoner and knelt in front of her. The other woman thrust out her legs in such a way her feet kicked Leah in the side.

Leah flinched.

"You need not treat her so. She is only trying to help us."

"She is trying to ready us to be sold," the other woman growled, her hateful gaze fixed on Leah. "Isn't that right, bitch?"

Leah remained silent and continued cleaning the woman's feet.

The other woman glanced at Riley. "Know it now, this little, daft twit does all their bidding."

Annoyed with the other woman's assessment, she came to Leah's defense. "I don't believe she is either daft or a twit, just a scared young woman."

The other woman blinked back tears. "She stood and watched, wide-eyed and silent, while Langley beat and shamed me." She glanced again at Leah. "Was it fun watching someone else being beaten?"

Leah stood, gathered up the medicinal items and said in a soft tone, "I will get the food and drink now."

Tears trickled down the other woman's cheeks.

"Aye, you do that. You do everything they tell you, even if it's wrong and disgusting."

Sympathy filled Riley's heart for the other woman's fear and disgrace. "As I see it, Leah hasn't much choice, for her own fate also hangs in the balance. She might not be tied as we are, but she is still a captive."

"My father will have all of their heads on a platter, including that bitch of a laundress, Naomi," the other woman vowed, choking on a sob.

Riley held her tongue, keeping silent the fact Naomi was already dead. Though she was also one of Naomi's victims, she didn't think it was a good idea for their background to be revealed.

"She tricked me, said my father lay stricken in the garden," the other woman continued. "I had just awakened. My head was still a bit foggy, and when I heard my father was in need, I thought nothing of just following her without question. Once in the garden, the man Beck leapt from a bush, put a cloth over my nose, and the next thing I know, I am lying with my hands tied in the basement of an old building." She raised her chin defiantly. "I am Lady Suzanna Wellington, and I will not be treated with such disrespect."

Riley placed the name immediately to the tear-stained face. Lady Wellington, known for her very rich ancestors and their prestigious titles, was a spoiled and inconsiderate young woman with no concept for other's feelings. She robbed other women of their beaus just for sport and severely punished her servants. "And I am Riley Flanders, ward of Lady Lucinda Collins of Collins Stead in Glenshire Sussex," she said.

"And so, what point does that matter?"

"My point is," Riley retorted, annoyed, "I don't think right now it would matter if you were the Queen of England."

Chapter Fourteen

"Help me fill the crates we occupied," Gabriel said to Olivier. "When the Sea Patrol officers come back for the cargo and discover two of the crates empty, their suspicions will be raised."

"Aye, I agree, but what will we fill them with?" Oliver said.

"Some of what is in the other crates," he said, prying off the lid of a nearby wooden container and removing from it several guns and knives. "If we take a little from about five other crates, we can make up some of the contents of the two we hid in. It will take a while before the officers realize their bounty has dwindled, and hopefully they will just think they have been swindled by their providers."

"Or that the shipmates have been dippin' their 'ands in the loot."

He nodded. "At any rate they will never suspect that two men infiltrate their camp."

Oliver smiled at Gabriel's *two men* reference, his adolescent shoulders squaring with pride. "Aye, 'tis a good plan ye 'ave," he agreed, setting to work unloading and loading the crates until all the wooden containers appeared to be equally filled.

When the task was complete, they made their way through the forest, toward the direction of the river. The large trees and overgrown brush made travel slow but afforded them coverage from being spotted. All Gabriel had learned about scouting and tracking came in handy at this point, and he was thankful he had listened to his instructors.

About a mile into their hike, voices could be

heard. Ducking behind a large bush, they spotted a small ray of light coming into view. A Sea Patrol officer led Riley, who was tied to a younger woman.

"This one is not one o' the two who carried out the trunk," Oliver noticed.

"No, he is not," he agreed. "But the woman tied to Riley must be Lady Wellington."

"Nay," Oliver said. "I'm not thinkin' that's 'er."

He frowned. "And why is that?"

"I remember Lady Wellington's time to coome out was the same year as Miss Riley's. The girl there," he said, pointing a finger, "'tisn't much older than I am, and she's dressed poorly."

He cast a sideways glance at Oliver. "You have a keen eye, my friend."

Oliver's chin rose with pride, but he answered modestly, "Nay, 'tis more like a keen memory."

"Then if she is not Lady Wellington, she must be another girl they have kidnapped."

Oliver took an audible breath. "I wonder 'ow many others there are?"

"I could not even begin to guess," he said. "But if they have been at this trade a while, there could be several women on this trip alone."

"And just 'ow is the two o' us going to rescue them all?" Oliver said.

"We will not," he said.

Oliver's eyes widened. "But we must."

Gabriel placed a hand on the younger man's shoulder. "If we are to save any of the women and stop this trade, we have to stay focused on the plan of action that will accomplish the mission." He wondered if any woman is safe anywhere. Had he not traveled with his sisters to England to keep them safe from the white agents that took over their village? It seems he has brought Sunny to a place where a woman still was not safe in her own land. "The priority is to rescue Riley and Lady Wellington and get them away from these men. Then, when Captain Cavendish arrives with reinforcements, we can go forth to free the others."

Oliver's tone was agitated. "What if they coome too late, and the others are sent to the island?"

He took a deep breath to clear his own mind and spoke calmly. "Without Lady Wellington's testimony, these men will continue to get away with the marketing of women. Do you not see," he added, "she is the key to saving them all."

Oliver gritted his teeth. "Aye, I see, 'tis because she's born of proud blood that 'er safety counts. And a poor girl's plight means nothin'."

"No, it is because she has a title and an influential father the authorities cannot ignore." He frowned. "You of all people should understand that."

"Title, money, proud blood, 'tis all the same," Oliver grumbled.

"It is not the same at all," he said. "I have known many proud men, my father included, who have not the financial wealth or the title of a lord or duke. Yet they have riches beyond compare because they are honest, loyal, and brave. Men would die for them, their families love them, and they will not cower in shame when it is time to meet their maker. That is proud blood, Oliver."

At that moment Riley draped her arm around the other girl's shoulder, shielding her from the cold with a part of her cape.

"See 'ow she worries for the sake o' others," Oliver pointed out. "She would never 'urt anyone and truly cares for all folks. She is a tender soul, beautiful and kind."

Though he felt a twinge of jealousy hearing Oliver's declaration of admiration and high esteem for Riley, he agreed with the younger man's assessment. And his heart warmed toward the woman he had come to save, yearning to hold her close and kiss her full lips. He was sure they would be soft and sweet.

"I was but ten when I came to live at Collins Stead with my auntie," Oliver continued. "Miss Riley took care o' me sometimes, 'elped me learn to read." He glanced at Gabriel. "Did ye know she could sing and play the piano?"

He shook his head. "I had no idea."

Oliver smirked. "That's because ye don't stay around long enough when ye coome to Collins Stead."

Oliver was right. Whenever Gabriel came into London, it was to spend time with Collette Halston. How many trips had he wasted getting to know the wrong woman?

"Well, she is quite remarkable, actually," Oliver went on. "She has the voice o' an angel...or o' what I think an angel's voice might sound like. And she sings all the time while tendin' the garden or 'elping my auntie in the kitchen."

"You seem to have her always in your view," he commented, his tone coming out sarcastic.

"There's nay a need to get yerself riled," Oliver said, arching a brow. "She sees me as nothin' more than a little brother." He chuckled mischievously. "Though 'tis easy for me to see 'er as much more."

He cleared his throat. "What leads you to believe I am in the least bit riled?"

"Besides the tone o' ye voice, this time 'tis my keen eye," Oliver quipped.

He frowned. "I do not know what you mean."

"Don't ye?" Oliver challenged. "Since ye 'ave rid yerself o' the wrong woman and opened yer eyes to the right woman, ye 'ave suddenly set yer claims upon 'er."

His frown deepened. "I have done nothing whatsoever to lay any claims to Riley Flanders. I just want to see her safely returned to Collins Stead and these men stopped."

"Uh-hum, keep tellin' yerself that's *all* ye're 'ere for, and perhaps in a 'undred years, ye might really begin to believe it," Oliver teased. "But ye aren't the only one bitten by fate and tryin' to ignore it."

He chuckled. "Ah, now fate is involved...and being ignored, no less."

"Fate is always involved, and I've been watchin' Miss Riley tryin' to ignore it, but the way she looks at ye gives 'er away."

His heart skipped a beat. "And how does she look at me?"

Oliver smirked. "Like ye alone could fill 'er world. And she's the sort o' woman who would fill a man's world quite nicely as well."

He arched a brow. "And what would you know about how a woman could fill a man's world?"

"I'm young, not daft." Oliver shook his head and chuckled. "The pair o' ye are 'opeless."

Oliver was right. He might be young, but he certainly had good insight, and the words he spoke were not only true but held much wisdom. The elders in his tribe would say Oliver was a young man with an *old soul*.

He thought deeply of how his actions and Riley's feelings would change the course of his life. He still wished to return to America to help his people, yet this new and wonderful feeling he had for Riley could not be overlooked either. He shook his head to clear it, realizing such a dilemma did not have to be figured out right now. His immediate attention must be served on the situation at hand. With that first and foremost on his mind, he turned his gaze back to the small band marching over the incline,

At that exact moment, Riley stumbled, lost her balance, and fell to her knees. She took the younger girl, who was tied to her, down with her. The fall startled Gabriel, jerked his senses into action, and he had to force himself to remain still. His stomach tightened as he fought the impulse to run to her aid.

Oliver, however, was not able to practice the same control and jumped to his feet, fists clenched at his side.

He could not blame his companion for giving in to such a reaction, yet Gabriel shot out a restraining hand, stopping the younger man from moving another inch. Riley was helped to her feet by the younger woman and upon standing turned to search the woods. Her gaze wondered over her surroundings and rested for a moment in Oliver's direction before she moved on.

He pulled Oliver down beside him, keeping a grip on his arm.

Oliver swallowed hard. "Do ye think she saw me?"

He shook his head. "Though the moon is bright, it is still too dark for her to see you from this far away."

"But she looked right at me," Oliver said, his voice cracking with emotion. "I'm sure of it. 'er eyes went right to mine, and I'm sure she saw me."

"She could not have, Oliver. But I do believe she felt someone watching her." He knew the way people can sense things, be drawn by instinct. "And this is a good thing. If she has an inclination someone nearby might be watching and may decide to help, it will sustain her hope. And that little bit of optimism just might give her the courage to stay brave until we can make a move."

Oliver chuckled sardonically. "Brave, 'ow can she possible be the least bit brave, tied like a dog and at the mercy o' these scoundrels?" He shook his head. "I've got a weapon, and I'm still afraid. Fact is I'm shakin' in my boots and could piss myself at any moment."

"It is not shameful to be afraid, Oliver. Every

man going into battle has his fears. But what is shameful is not doing anything about that fear, not standing up for what is right."

"Ye say such things so calmly." Oliver took an audible breath. "I don't understand 'ow ye can be so calm...just sit by and watch Miss Riley, and that other poor girl, being dragged along like a pair o' animals."

"Inside, calm is the last thing I am," he confessed, trying to control the emotion growing in his voice. "But if we give up our cover, there will be no chance to end this hell for her and the others."

Oliver locked eyes with Gabriel. "I want to kill every one o' those bastards."

"If you do not keep your head, set your eye on what is most important for us to do right now, all will be lost. Do you want that to happen?"

"Nay, never," Oliver admitted.

He released his grip on his companion's arm. "Then clear your mind of what your heart is feeling. It will not be easy, but it is the only way a warrior can approach a battle."

"Then what, once I've done as ye say?" Oliver said, this time raising a defiant chin.

"Then, my friend, you must ready yourself to win."

Chapter Fifteen

Riley, her head resting against a smooth niche she found carved out in the damp and jagged cave wall, closed her eyes and silently prayed for the pain to cease from the injury. She felt so daft, tripping like a helpless twit and wounding her knee. Now the hot and vicious ache left her entire right leg in agony, and she feared she would not be able to stand again if she tried. With this new complication, she had no idea how she was to get herself, Leah, and Lady Wellington out of the mess they were in. Wasn't it always her way to believe she should be the one to make a move, set something right, and be in control of a situation? Perhaps this sort of thinking stemmed from the last years she cared for Anita. The poor woman depended upon her like an infant. A baby caring for a baby was what the situation had been, for Riley was only nine years of age. So much responsibility for someone so young, and yet she did what needed to be done and lived to tell it.

Will I live to tell it again?

Leah dispelled her thoughts by returning with food, water, and a relief bucket. When handed her hunk of cheese and bread, she graciously accepted, but Lady Wellington was not so polite.

"This is it? One stale piece of bread and a crusty slab of cheese," Lady Wellington complained, narrowing her eyes. Her dark gaze impaled Leah as she threw the food. The bread hit the younger woman in the face, and she flinched but remained silent as she gathered the food from where it landed on the cave floor.

"Have you eaten, Leah?" Riley said.

"Nay, miss," Leah said, sitting beside her with Lady Wellington's share of food in her hands.

"Then take mine," she offered. "That food has been dirtied."

"Nay, miss, I cannot."

"Let the little twit eat what she retrieved from the ground," Lady Wellington hissed. "It is only fitting for her kind."

She glared over at the other prisoner. "None of this is her fault. Why do you treat her so cruelly?"

"Because she helps them," Suzanna Wellington retorted. "The very men who ripped me from my home, humiliated, and demeaned me with their crude behavior. And now...now they will sell me like a piece of merchandise." She choked back a sob. "She walks around free, this little nothing, and I, Lady Suzanna Wellington, am tied to a post like an animal waiting for the slaughter."

"I am far from free, my lady," Leah murmured. She lowered her tear-filled eyes and hesitated before speaking further. Then, taking a deep breath and squaring her thin shoulders, she stood. Turning her back to them, she lifted her skirt, lowered her bloomers and bent over.

Both Riley and Suzanna gasped. Leah's round bum was marred with pink, raised whiplash marks, and down her thighs she was scarred with cigar burns.

"If this is freedom, then I want nay a part o' it," the younger girl said, pulling up her bloomers and adjusting her skirt. For a moment she remained facing the cave wall, no doubt gathering her wits before glancing into their eyes again.

Riley's heart bleed for the poor girl. The hurt and humiliation she had endured made it all the more evident she had to find a way to get them free from these men.

"I had no idea," Suzanna said, her tone thick with emotion.

"How could you believe differently?" Riley said. "Certainly this young girl didn't choose to be here either."

"Did they...have they," Suzanna stammered. She cleared her throat and continued with a softer and more sympathetic tone. "Have they indulged in sexual congress with you, Leah?"

Leah then turned to face them, her flushed cheeks wet with tears. "Nay, the captain has instructed them I am to remain a virgin for a better first sale, though that does not mean my flesh cannot be marked," she said, touching the scar along her left cheek. "After, it does not matter, as I will be used again and again, but for a lesser price, until the chance I become with child happens."

"Then what will they do?" Suzanna said.

"They will take me to see Miss Inez, who lives down a dank ally," Leah explained. "For a price Miss Inez can rid any woman o' the child within her." She shivered. "I went with my friend, Gloria, when she was in trouble. The stench was worse inside than it was outside the house, filth and trash litterin' the hallways."

"And what became of Gloria?" Suzanna asked, her pale face stricken with horror.

"She died four days later," Leah said. "They all die, from either a fever or bleedin' to death."

Riley shivered with the thought of so many women suffering and dying unnecessary deaths. She searched Leah's tired and sad gaze. "When do they abuse you?"

"Sometimes when the men drink the rum," she hesitated, swallowing hard. "When they are drunk, they like to 'urt me, do things to me that will make me scream and cry." She took an audible breath. "At first I tried my best not to break down, as I know 'tis what gives them pleasure. I think, I still 'ave my pride...and perhaps if they aren't 'avin' fun, they will stop. But instead, they keep it up 'til they 'ear my screams o' pain. So now I cry quickly so they will stop, and 'tis not so 'ard to endure."

"Good God. What are these people?"

"Leah you must...we all must get away from them. They're sick, sick men," she said.

"But 'ow can that be possible? There are so many o' them, and there is always one watchin' my every move," Leah said.

"Is there not ever a time when they are less watchful, or a place you go where they don't know about?" she probed.

Leah bit her bottom lip. "There is perhaps one."

"Then free us and take us there, you little twit, before we're all sold into bondage."

Riley turned sharply on Suzanna. "Your ridicule will get us nowhere."

"Oh, on the contrary, Miss Flanders. I have a staff of many, and it is that kind of treatment that gets them moving every time. If you allow the servants to walk all over you, nothing gets done."

"Such tactics never come to any good," she argued. "A well-oiled household is one staffed with loyal help, not with those that fear and hate their employer. If we do not stick together, work in unity, then none of us is going to get away from these scoundrels." Riley turned back to Leah. "If you know of a place where we can hide from these men, then we all need to go there, and quickly."

Leah nodded. "Soon their stomachs will be full, and they will bed down for the night. Perhaps then I can coome back 'ere to 'elp ye escape."

Riley offered her bread to Suzanna. "Eat, we must all eat," she said. "And drink, for we need to keep up our strength. It is the only way we're going to survive this situation."

Lady Wellington nodded and took the bread.

At least there was a plan of action, somewhere to hide from their kidnappers. But where they go from there, Riley hadn't a clue.

Sitting tied to a wall in a dark, dank cave made the hours drag. When Leah didn't return, she feared the poor girl had been found out and lay beaten and bound somewhere. But Leah prevailed, finally entering the cave with an old knapsack over her shoulder.

Riley's eyes filled with tears of relief. "I feared something happened to you. If you were hurt because of me, I'd never forgive myself."

"Nay, the lout o' them asked me to dance for them tonight," Leah explained. "'Twas my good fortune they were too drunk to want nay a thing more." Laying the knapsack on the ground, she gestured to it with a finger. "I brought these clothes for ye to wear. 'Tis much easier to make it to the safe place with ye two lookin' like ye are just a few o' the chaps walkin' about the island." She pulled a knife from her apron pocket. "Took one o' the cook's blades, the one 'e uses to scale and clean fish. 'Twas all I could get my 'ands on in a 'urry." Taking the knife in trembling hands, Leah cut Suzanna and Riley free. "Now dress quickly and put yer own clothes in the sack. I don't want them left in the cave. That way the men will believe ye both are still wearin' them. 'urry now," she urged them. "We don't 'ave much time before someone discovers I've left camp, and we've got quite a walk to where 'tis safe." She pulled from the bottom of the sack a pair of boots, scuffed and worn, but wearable. "Ain't yer size, my lady, or yer fashion, I'm sure. But I figured ye can't be traipsin' all over in yer bare feet, with the ground so full o' rocks and all."

Lady Wellington curled up her nose at the sight

and smell of her new footwear. "And what happens if their owner goes looking for the wretched things?"

"I don't think 'e's about to do that, my lady, since 'e died o' food poisonin' last week," Leah said.

Suzanna took the boots using only a thumb and forefinger and holding them out far from her person. "God save the Queen and all her children."

"Worry about the Queen and 'er mites later, my lady," Leah said. "I'm sure she's got more folks 'elpin' 'er than we do."

As Riley dressed, she stifled a smile. At least Suzanna was remaining civil, no matter how completely forced her actions were. If she continued to work united for a common cause, then they just might be able to save themselves from their troubles.

Leah cast a glance at Riley's knee. "The wound's seepin', miss. I should've brought bandages and salve as well."

"You did fine, Leah." She tried not to wince as she pulled the trousers up and over her pain-filled knee. Putting pressure on the limb was even more agonizing, but there was no other choice.

She braced herself against the cave while she stuffed her curls into a cap Leah had provided. It took no time for Suzanna to wind her braid atop her head and slip the cap over. But Riley wore her hair free, curls flowing about her shoulders, so it took longer to wad the thick mass in place.

"We dare not take a torch," Leah advised. "Don't wanna take a chance anyone will spot us."

"Then how will we see our way across these God forsaken grounds?" Suzanna complained.

"I've been down the path so many times, I could walk it blindfolded," Leah said. She reached for the cut rope, handing them each a long section. "We will all 'old an end. I will go first, then Miss Riley, and last Lady Wellington."

"Why must I be last?" Suzanna whined.

"Because Miss Riley is injured, and should she fall, we will both be aware o' it. In that way we will not get separated, and I will be able to lead ye both to the safe place."

"Nay a soul should ever call you daft again," Riley said, glaring in Suzanna's direction.

"Aye, I have to admit you have thought out our escape quite carefully," Suzanna acknowledged. Then she narrowed her gaze and added, "Now we'll see just how successful your plan actually is."

The three of them, Leah leading with the knapsack over her shoulder, exited the cave. Each step brought a shooting pain up Riley's injured leg. But she bit her lip and choked back her moans, trying her best to keep a grip on the rope she held before and behind her, without losing her balance. All she needed was to fall a second time, landing on the same knee, and she was sure she'd never be able to stand again.

"Go slow 'ere," Leah instructed. "The land dips and then quickly rises."

She sucked in her breath and stepped carefully down, then immediately up. All the while her knee throbbed in searing agony. Though there was a chilling night breeze, perspiration formed upon her brow. If she didn't think of something other than the pain, she would not be able to carry on. She was sure Lady Wellington would have nay a problem leaving her behind, but she had a strong feeling Leah wouldn't agree. To see her punished for helping them seemed worse than anything she might be doled out. And to believe the women could carry her was far-fetched. Nay, she must be able to walk the terrain on her own validation.

Squaring her shoulders, she brought to mind a game she played as a child. Though she never starved, she did go to bed many a night hungry. As her stomach rumbled with the raw pains of emptiness, she'd think of something pleasant. The pain seemed to cease when she thought of warm summer days by a cool lake, a doll dressed in velvet for her to cuddle, a puppy of her very own, or shiny shoes upon her feet that actually fit her well. Unfortunately her taste for such pleasantries changed and conjuring up the things that worked before, left her lacking now.

So what will I summon to help me through this journey?

It wasn't a specific thing that came to mind, but a special person...Gabriel Eagle. If she hadn't gone looking to meet her father, she'd be enjoying a quiet evening with him, getting to know him better, and having the opportunity to gaze into his sapphire eyes. With Collette Halston out of the scene, one never knew what might transpire. She smiled as she brought to mind his broad shoulders and muscular chest, bared and ready for her touch.

How would his full lips feel on mine...his hands caressing my neck, shoulders, moving down to cup my...

A flash of light broke her thoughts, followed by a force. It struck Leah, knocking her down. "Now I've got ye, ye sneaky little bitch."

In unison she and Suzanna fell as well, the injured knee coming down hard upon the ground. Riley felt the already torn flesh break further. She cried out in pain and let go of the ropes.

The force continued to tackle Leah.

"Get off o' me! Leave me alone!" Leah's slaps and punches could be heard hitting flesh.

"Ye little traitor, when I get ye back to the ship, I'm beatin' every inch of ye 'til ye are nothin' but a bluddy mess," the voice threatened. "And that goes for the rest of ye."

The lantern, which was the flash of light she'd seen, still burned, laying a foot away. And though the fog bubbled up from the ground like steam from a boiling kettle, mist so thick it appeared the earth took a deep breath and then exhaled it all in one blast; the lantern served its purpose. Enough light was cast upon the situation for her to glimpse the figure of a burly, unshaven man wearing a stained apron. His stubby arms were well-muscled beneath his dirty shirt as his fists came down upon Leah's back, beating her frail body over and over again.

"I'll teach ye to steal my best cookin' knife," he growled. Then he ceased the punches and hoisted Leah up by the scruff of her neck.

"Get yer filthy 'ands off me!" Leah kicked his shins with her feet.

Suzanna moved forward. "Leave her alone, you bloody bastard!" She clawed at the man's back.

His backward punch slammed Suzanna in the face, and she fell to the ground. There she remained, with her eyes closed and lying very still.

Good God, was she dead? And how long would it take for this man to kill Leah, then me?

With such horror-filled thoughts racing through her, Riley forced herself to stand. Putting weight upon her leg brought tears to her eyes, but she moved forward in spite of the agony. Hobbling over to where the lantern lay, she reached for it, trembling fingers finding the handle. Just as she was about to raise the lamp and smash it hard against the man's head, a dagger whizzed through the air. It pierced the man's throat. He released his hold on Leah to grip the dagger's handle.

Blood spurt from the puncture, and the man gurgled and choked as he tried to pull the blade free, but his efforts were in vain. Gasping for breath, he fell to his knees, his blood-shot eyes bulged from their sockets and his thick tongue hung out from the side of his mouth. In seconds he keeled over dead.

The odor of blood and death filled the air.

Nausea swelled, bile rising to clog her throat. But she gulped it down, moving to brace herself against the trunk of a nearby tree. Her hands shook, and the lantern slipped from her fingers, rolling a few inches from her feet. Her vision swam, her heart raced, and she fought to stay conscious.

I cannot faint. I cannot faint. Not now. Not now.

A rustling came from the bushes. Through blurred vision she could distinguish two more figures emerging, one large, the other slightly smaller. The larger one pulled the dagger from the dead man's throat, wiping the bloody blade on the victim's trousers before sheathing it in his boot. Then silently, the two, one taking the dead man by the feet, and the other grabbing his shoulders, moved him to lie concealed beneath a clump of brush.

By this time her vision swirled into sickening proportions. Weak and nauseated, she rested her head back against the tree's massive trunk. What would happen now?

When the men emerged from the brush, she watched helplessly as Leah pulled from her skirt pocket the cook's knife and ran at the larger shape, screaming like a banshee in the night.

"Halt, woman, I am not here to hurt you," came the larger figure's stern, deep tone, as he easily wrestled Leah gently to the ground, removed the knife from her clutches, and threw it aside.

The man's rich baritone brought tears of relief welling in her eyes.

I know that voice.

Leah continued to kick and scream.

By now the larger man had her lying flat upon her stomach so the smaller man could sit on her legs.

"Ugh, this is a feisty one," the second man remarked.

I know that voice too, but how could it be?

"Stop, Leah," she choked out. "These men will not harm you." She tried to control her sobs of liberation, but they overcame her.

He caught her, just as her legs gave out and embraced her within his strong arms, holding her tight to his chest. She could hear his heart racing, smell the musk and spice of his flesh.

"How did you know where to find me?" she whispered.

"From Top Hat Tom," he said.

"Thank heaven, then he's alive," she sobbed, laying her head upon his shoulder.

"He was when I left Collins Stead, though he suffered greatly from a knife wound," he said.

"I saw it all, both he and Naomi cut down right before my eyes," she said.

He lifted her chin with a finger, and she met his gaze, looking deeply into Gabriel Eagle's eyes.

"All that matters is for us to get somewhere safe, a place to hide until more help arrives," he said, wiping her tears away with a gentle swipe of his thumb. Shifting her body's weight, he stood holding her. He moved like she weighed no more than a feather.

Riley looked at Oliver, who was checking on Suzanna Wellington.

"How does that one do?" Gabriel said.

"She'll 'ave a 'eadache when she coomes around, but otherwise nay a thing more that I can see," Oliver said.

"We must move quickly," Gabriel said.

"She was taking us to a safe place," she offered, glancing down at Leah who remained upon the ground, her eyes dazed. "You were so very brave and clever," she praised the younger woman in a soft tone. "And now we will not have to escape on our own. We have help."

Chapter Sixteen

The twigs snapped beneath Gabriel's boots, dried leaves and coarse sand crunched as he walked across the un-even terrain. Leah, at the head of the small band of travelers, the lantern she held void of light, issued warnings from time to time concerning the condition of the land.

"There's a drop 'ere," she would say, as she slowed her pace. Or alert them to the land rising, a right turn, then a left turn, and so on.

"I pray, miss, we arrive soon at our destination," Oliver said, quite out of breath.

Gabriel snickered. "Is Lady Wellington getting a bit heavy for you?"

"I think she'd be 'eavy for anyone," was his retort. "The woman must enjoy devourin' 'er sweets upon every occasion she can."

Leah giggled. "'Tisn't much farther, sir."

"Oliver, miss. Call me Oliver."

Gabriel smiled. Oliver seemed a bit smitten with young Leah. Perhaps he could help things along a bit, put the poor girl in an even better light. "I admire your tracking abilities, Leah," he said.

"I thank ye, sir," she responded.

"Especially void of light," he added. "Right now I am relying upon my scouting experience not to lose track of you." Of course, he would be hard pressed to admit or let on his keen instincts were somewhat distracted by the woman he held in his arms as he trekked to the safe place waiting them.

I believe I have become somewhat smitten, myself.

In view of the current situation, smitten was rather mild for how he felt. Riley's warm curvy form, held tight against his chest, did little to enhance his wilderness training and a lot to fuel his imagination. Unlike the petticoats and skirts usually worn, the men's clothes she donned concealed nothing of her shapely body. His right hand, supporting her back, and his left hand, familiarly placed beneath her thighs, burned with the feel of her.

As the ground beneath his feet descended and ascended, she snuggled closer, wrapping her arms tighter around his neck. Her full breasts, pressed close against his chest, sent shivers of desire through his loins. The round, hard peaks of her ample pair could be felt through the shirt's flimsy material, rising and falling with each intake of her breath. He felt her heart beating...racing...matching his. He forced himself to concentrate on the situation at hand, instead of imagining how her breasts would look bared and cupped in the palms of his hands.

Flushed and bothered, he was grateful for the darkness, as it hid his need now growing hard beneath his britches. Inhaling sharply, he raised his face to the heavens, taking in the stars that painted the sky, welcoming the night breeze rustling the bushes and gossiping through the trees. It cooled his face and neck, gave him enough pause to begin controlling his yearnings so he would not embarrass himself in front of the women.

"Am I heavy as well?" Riley whispered. Her face was nestled beneath his chin, and when she spoke, her warm breath and soft lips caressed his neck.

"No, you are nothing to carry," he said, his breath compromised by his rising condition.

She raised her head, and even in the dark, he felt the gaze of those beautiful emerald orbs on him. "But you can scarcely..."

"All is fine...will be fine." He cleared his throat.

"I just need a moment."

"A moment? A moment for what?"

"Just trust I need one," he mumbled.

"Oh—oh my word," she whispered, finally catching on to the real reason for his rapid breathing. She stiffened slightly in his arms and loosened her grip around his neck. "I didn't even stop to think...I am so sorry."

"Please, do not be," he said softly.

I am not.

Now it was her turn to clear her throat. "I can't imagine this safe place being much farther, can you?" she said, shifting ground to another subject.

"No," he said, glad she did not know what he was really imagining.

"Perhaps you could tell me how it is you were able to find me," she said, obviously giving him the moment he requested.

"Top Hat Tom helped us," he explained what they had learned from the elder man. By the time he finished his story, all conditions at his nether regions were under control.

"We're only ten feet from my 'aven," Leah notified them.

He scoped his surroundings. Monuments of stone angels and Christian crosses stood silhouetted in the darkness. Leah was taking them through a burial ground.

Upon the same recognition, Riley shuddered in his arms.

"Do you fear the land we enter?" He tightened his embrace to comfort her.

"Aye, I do," she whispered. "More so at night than by day, but it is still unsettling."

"It is only a place where ancestral spirits rest. Not a one of those who have passed wishes us any harm," he reassured her. "My people believe those who have gone on from this life guide those of us

142

who are still here. They are called Spirit Guides and are not meant to bring us fear or harm."

At his words she seemed to relax but also muttered, "That may be true, but superstitions in England die hard. Besides, what happens when a soul who meant to harm you in life comes beckoning again?"

He had no time to answer. Leah had stopped and after rummaging in her pockets for a match, lit the lantern to reveal an old church. The windows, with remnants of broken stained glass stuck in the frames, were nearly overgrown with vines. The doors hung crooked on their hinges. Pushing aside one of the broken panels, Leah made her way over the threshold. The lantern's swelling yellow light illuminated a long, narrow corridor. Various religious paintings covered the walls, as well as statues secluded in corners. White sheets draped over some of the statues created an illusion of phantoms from another realm.

Riley shuddered again and must have read his mind because with a slant look she said, "This place is even more unsettling."

Unsettling, for sure, but what I feel has nothing to do with where we are.

Leah stopped at a door at the end of the hallway. "I believe this was once the sanctuary." Coming to a large bookcase filled with old books of every shape and size, she pulled on a wall sconce. The bookcase opened like a door. "This stairway will take us to my safe place," Leah said, angling the lantern to shine its best on what lay ahead. "Watch yer step, the stairs are steep, narrow, and in bad need o' repair."

Oliver grunted and groaned as they descended the old staircase. Hard enough to carry Lady Wellington altogether, but down a narrow stairway was an even riskier feat. He did not envy the younger man.

Once at the bottom, Leah set her lantern upon an old wooden table, freed Oliver from the rope connecting them, then rushed around the chamber to light two more lamps. A dog barked, and a cat jumped from a wooden beam.

"Have nay a concern over them," Leah said. "They're my family. I rescued Rufus," she said, pointing to the cream and russet colored cat crouched in a corner, "from a hunter's trap. And Nellie", she said, turning her attention upon a scruffy looking white dog lying on an old blanket with one leg bandaged, "after his owner thought he had put him down."

Gabriel smiled at the younger woman. "You remind me of my sister Sunny. Back home, in America, she healed all sorts of critters, saved many from death as well."

As he walked further into the large chamber, he sized up his surroundings, something a warrior was trained to do and comes as second nature. Musty-smelling and laced with cobwebs, the underground room was in a strong state of dilapidation. Green mold clung to sections of the walls, and fungi gathered on the rotted boards supporting the wooden beams. The fireplace's stonework had dangerously decayed. Yellow, tattered drapery half-hung from a rotted frame over small windows set high on the walls. Leah removed the knapsack from her shoulders and gazed around the place with pride.

"Well, this is it." She knelt beside the dog to scratch him behind an ear. "Make yerselves at 'ome."

Gabriel's spirit ached with pity for the poor girl. For someone to be so proud and thankful to have only a dog and cat as family, or a dank, moldy chamber beneath an old, forgotten church to call her own, was truly heart wrenching. Yet, many of his people did not have much more since the white agents arrived.

Leah indicated two cots covered with faded quilts. "Best ye men place the ladies to rest."

Oliver sighed, relieved to be rid of his charge. Gabriel, on the other hand, was not so eager to release Riley. She fit well in his embrace, like she belonged there. As he gently placed her upon one of the mattresses, its musty smell rose to greet him.

Leah cast a glance at the stone fireplace. "I dare not light it for warmth as someone would see the smoke. 'Twould probably smoke us out anyway, since it 'asn't been fired up in years."

Lady Wellington stirred and opened her eyes.

"Good day to ye, my lady," Oliver said, inclining his head politely.

The other woman only stared, her dark, round eyes wide with confusion.

"All is well, my lady," Leah chimed in. "These 'ere chaps are friends o' Miss Riley, and they've coome to 'elp us."

"Friends?" Lady Wellington repeated.

"Aye," Riley said, scooting herself up to lean her back against the wall. "This is Mr. Gabriel Eagle," she introduced, "heir to Collins Stead. And this is Oliver Mills, who is much like a brother to me."

Oliver smiled broadly and inclined his head again.

"Friends?" Lady Wellington repeated, placing a hand to her forehead as she tried to sit up.

"Best ye stay still a bit, my lady," Oliver warned. "Ye've 'ad quite a punch to the 'ead."

Leah stood, reached for the knapsack, and placed it beneath Lady Wellington's head. "This will 'elp ye some, and I've a jug o' wine in the cupboard. I'll fetch it and will pour ye a cup."

"If there is enough, Leah, we could all use some of that wine," Gabriel said.

"Aye, sir, right away." Leah hurried off to

accomplish the task.

Lady Wellington surveyed Oliver with a rake of her eyes, then she turned to Gabriel and did the same. "I fail to understand how you knew where to find us...I mean, Miss Riley."

"Top Hat Tom told us." In a far corner, Oliver sat on an old wooden church pew, covered with a dirty sheet and a few tattered pillows.

Gabriel joined him, pushing aside one of the pillows. A pang of remorse knotted his stomach for the way Leah had tried to make such a dismal place look homey.

Lady Wellington took an audible breath. "And who the bloody hell is Top Hat Tom?"

Oliver smiled. "Tom's our friend. The bugger that captured ye two ladies tried to kill 'im, but 'e's a tough ol' bird. Lived to tell about it all and where 'e 'ad an idea Miss Riley might be." He shook his head. "Naomi wasn't so lucky, though."

"Naomi!" Lady Wellington shouted, turning to glare at Riley. "You were a friend to that bitch?"

Something deeply sensual appeared in the way Riley raised a delicate brow and defiantly tilted a dimpled chin. He shifted in his seat, for such an action stirred him to his very core and teased again his manly desires.

"Aye, I was her friend, as was my mother at one time," Riley admitted. "But she was never a friend to me, as you can obviously see."

Lady Wellington screwed her lips into a sneer. "Aye, now I remember the scandalous talk about you. The gossip was that you grew up on the streets, was born from scum, a beggar's child, the reason no reputable chap would have anything to do with you," she spat. "Except, it wasn't gossip at all, but the blatant truth."

Oliver stood with clenched fists. "'Twould seem I should 'ave left yer fat bum where it fell, instead o' 'aulin' it to safety."

An overwhelming sense of pride filled Gabriel's heart for his young companion. Oliver was loyal to those he loved, even though he lacked the proper way to speak to a lady. Then again, right now Lady Suzanna Wellington did not really stand up to her title. He stifled a smile. *Perhaps she deserves what she gets.*

Riley held up a hand to quiet Oliver. "Please, sit down. I will handle this."

Reluctantly Oliver obeyed, but his face resembled a thundercloud ready to burst at a moment's notice.

"You are correct, my lady," Riley kept her voice calm, the words precise. "I didn't grow up a child of society. I didn't have a pair of shoes that fit until I became Lady Lucinda Collins' ward." She motioned to the large, dirty boots upon Lady Wellington's feet. "It is very uncomfortable wearing another's footwear, don't you agree?"

Lady Wellington's face reddened as she curled her knees so the ugly boots would not be so clearly viewed. "I had no other choice."

"Aye, so you didn't, as was my case. And yet when you have nothing else to wear, you find yourself grateful for whatever you get." Riley went on. "There was nothing scandalous about the way I grew up. Being poor hardly means you're bad or daft or scum. My mother, the good and decent woman that she was, wasn't scum. She wasn't a drunken wench who warmed any man's bed. Nor did she steal, cheat, or lie. She was a hard-working woman who merely fell upon hard times but did the best she could with what she had and was proud of her efforts. And I am also proud of her, for she loved me well and taught me right. I might not have a title, but I am an honorable person who was born of proud blood. And not you or anyone else will look down

147

your nose at me, or at Oliver, or Leah, or anyone else who has to work for their wages."

Gabriel fought the urge to walk over to Riley, gather her in his arms, and kiss her fully on the luscious lips that were now defiantly pressed together. Suzanna Wellington's malice-laced words and the precision in which she wielded them were obviously murderous to Riley's most vulnerable spot, yet she kept her calm and answered intelligently. She was a woman after his own heart. Why had he not seen this before?

"Did you not agree, my lady, to stand united with us?" Riley continued.

Lady Wellington crossed her arms over her chest and glared in silence. Though she was an arresting woman, Gabriel did not see a pure and natural splendor in her facial features, as he did in Riley. Even Collette, with her exotic features, was not as striking as the spirited woman he gazed upon now with much respect and admiration.

With a pout like a stubborn child, Lady Wellington finally relented. "Aye, that I did, and I suppose you'll hold me to it."

He could not help but believe, even if Suzanna Wellington was to grow a second heart, she would still be too selfish, self-centered, and spoiled to understand about or have empathy for the plight of others. Or even to know the true meaning of loyalty and teamwork.

"It is the only way, you must realize, that we will all get out of this situation alive," Leah added.

Lady Wellington gave a taut nod in agreement.

"Then I ask that we call a truce between us," Riley offered. "After we leave this place, and I pray with all my heart that is very soon, you won't have to ever set your eyes upon me again. Nor I, you," she added.

Lady Wellington raised her aristocratic nose in

the air. "That settles with me just fine..." She stopped when Rufus jumped upon the bed. He stared with round, amber eyes. "God save the Queen and all her children. What on earth is this dreadful animal doing here?"

"I told ye once before, not to worry so for the Queen," Leah said.

Gabriel caught Riley suppressing a smile and wondered about the inside joke.

"And Rufus is not dreadful. 'e is part o' my family and treats me better than most folks." Leah went on. "'e lives 'ere along with my dog, Nellie," she said, gesturing with a nod in the dog's direction.

Lady Wellington curled up her nose in disdain as Rufus snuggled comfortably against her thigh. "Well isn't this just cozy." She scooted away from the feline.

"Aye, 'tis," Leah said with a giggle. "'e must find ye pleasin'."

Oliver nudged him and leaned in to whisper, "Can't imagine why."

Gabriel chuckled lightly. "Perhaps Rufus is not quite himself yet, due to his injuries."

Oliver nodded. "That must be the reason."

He narrowed his gaze in Lady Wellington's direction. "I am thinking it might be wise for us to keep silent the fact Suzanna Wellington's rescue and testimony is important in putting these scoundrels behind bars. With such knowledge beneath her cap, she just might act all the worse toward us commoners as your people call us, then she already is accustomed to." He took a deep breath. "And I do not know how much I will be able to take before I do something I will regret."

Oliver nodded in agreement, Oliver's mouth twisting into a smirk. "Well, I know exactly what my auntie would do. She'd 'ave this twit's bum bared and thrashed in nay a time it takes to blink an eye."

149

Gabriel smiled and whispered. "Where is dear Addie when we need her?"

Oliver scowled. "At this point my own bum's pleased she's in London," he said.

He patted the younger man on the shoulder. "All will be well, my friend. In any case it will do you no good to fret about such things, not when we have much more pressing things to deal with."

"Now, my dear, kind, Leah," Riley said, a smile of genuine care spreading across her tired, yet beautiful face. "Please, may we have that wine?"

"Aye, miss. I 'ave it ready and waitin'," Leah said, moving to serve them each a cup.

Riley raised her mug. "To our victory," she saluted.

Her pale complexion reminded him of piano keys...the white ones made of ivory...come from the tusks of elephants, he was told, all smoothened and pearled. Her laugh lifted light upon the air, like the wings of a bird. And her ginger hair, the locks of curls escaping the man's cap she wore, were highlighted with gold and auburn tones, reminding him of the flames glowing in the fire pit he sat around in the wickiup, or like the red birds he loved to watch soar in the sky.

She is an ivory flame...or better yet, a red bird. Ah yes, that is what my people would call her, Redbird. And how enchanting she would look wearing just the buckskin.

The others repeated the cheer, their voices bringing him from his thoughts. He raised his cup in agreement before taking a sip. As the sour brew graced the back of his throat, he raised another salutation, a silent one all his own.

To the proud and beautiful, Redbird, my sort of woman.

Chapter Seventeen

Riley finished her wine and placed the cup on the floor beside the cot where she lay. Fatigue and hunger made her head throb, along with her injured knee. The pain inched its way into every fiber of her body. Leaning her head back against the wall, she closed her eyes.

"Are you ill, Riley?" Gabriel probed, his deep voice filled with concern.

"Nay, just tired," she responded, keeping her eyes shut. Suzanna Wellington's words cut her to the core, humiliated her in front of Gabriel. Least he think no man would ever be interested in her was a blow to her pride and vanity.

How foolish I am being. There are more urgent matters to worry over at present then my past accomplishments at securing a husband. Besides those Suzanna spoke of, and there were only a few, were all incredibly boring and superficial. I would have never accepted a proposal even if asked.

She shook the haunting words from her thoughts and opened her eyes to search better her surroundings. As she turned her injured limb to rest comfortably upon the other, she glanced in Gabriel's direction. His eyes widened when he spotted the blood staining the knee of her britches.

In an instant he was beside her, looking down at her with a concerned frown creasing his brow. "In the dark and with all the commotion, I had assumed you favored your leg from a twisted ankle. I did not realize you were hurt and bleeding."

"I fell when I was first brought to the cave and

split my knee on a jagged rock. The second fall, during the skirmish with the cook, did not help matters," she explained.

"I've salve and bandages 'ere, miss," Leah offered. "Clean water and rags, as well as a bit o' brandy for keepin' out infection."

"And how is it you are so medically stocked?" Suzanna droned.

Riley almost wished she hadn't called a truce with the snotty bitch, because pulling her hair from its roots would sure do wonders for her morale right about now.

"This is where I care for Rufus and Nellie," Leah said. "So I've made sure to 'ave what is needed to 'eal their injuries and wounds."

"Aye, that's right, they're your family," Suzanna mocked, raising a smug face.

"There is nay a thing wrong with God's beasts being loved well." Oliver came to Leah's defense.

"I agree. My people understand and respect the creatures that roam the earth. And right now I am very pleased you are well-prepared because I will need all those things to care for Riley's wound," Gabriel said, removing a dagger from his boot. It was the same blade that had felled the cook.

"Aye, sir," Leah gathered the items together.

Kneeling beside the cot, Gabriel slit the leg of her britches and then gently pulled the soaked material away from the old bandage, which was drenched even worse with blood. "I wish I had the wisdom of a medicine man, but the Shaman of my tribe guarded his remedies well. Only he knew the language of the plants, herbs, and roots the land gifted him to use."

"And he never once divulged his garden secrets?" She clenched her teeth as he removed the old binding.

"No, and I never asked," he said.

She held her breath while he cleaned the wound and applied the salve.

"I wish I had paid more attention to what the women ground in their bowls, what poultice to use when, and how to apply it where," he said.

"You are doing just fine," she praised. And in truth his administrations were considerate as he cared for the injured area, which was boldly displayed before him, her leg naked from the thigh down.

For a moment, while wrapping the new dressing around her knee, he hesitated. His gaze deepened and roamed the length of her. His fingers, touching now the place just above her knee, heated her flesh. No one, especially a man, had ever taken such liberties with her body in such a fashion.

She swallowed hard. *He only means to help, so I must keep my wits about me.*

But then he lowered his voice for only her ears to hear. "The other men Lady Wellington spoke of..." he paused and raised his gaze to lock with hers. "I am most fortunate they were fools."

A surge of desire flowed through her. Strange and pleasing sensations momentarily quieted her pain and heightened every other facet of her being as he affectionately squeezed the fatty part of her thigh.

"I thank you for that," she whispered.

"I only speak the truth," he said, turning his attention back to wrapping her wound.

If they had been alone, would he have attempted to lean in to kiss her? It appeared for a moment he contemplated the idea. Would she have let him?

Gazing at his full lips, she smiled to herself.

Aye, I would have welcomed his kiss.

Then she grimaced inside at the thought of her appearance. Here, at such a tender and wonderfully personal moment between them, she is dressed in dirty men's clothes, an old cap covering her hair. Could she look more disheveled and pathetic?

"What the bloody hell is this place?" Suzanna pulled Riley from her thoughts. She now wished Oliver had left Lady Wellington's fat bum where it fell.

"I've 'eard it called Saint Isaac's Church," Leah said.

"And we're below it?" Suzanna glanced around the chamber, her nose wrinkling with disgust.

"Aye, we are," Leah confirmed.

Suzanna glared at Leah. "And what is so secret about this place?"

"Nay a thing, 'tis just my secret place," Leah said, her hands clenched into fists beside her. "'Tis a secret that I coome 'ere."

"Is mocking and tormenting Leah your way of being united?" Riley said, trying her best to keep the rage mounting deep within her under control.

Suzanna arched a brow. "I am merely trying to understand why Leah would think this place was safe when obviously it is well known?"

"Because nay a soul dares to step through the doors,"

"And why is that?"

"They are afraid o' Father Gillian 'erman's ghost," Leah explained.

Suzanna's face paled. "Are you saying the place is haunted?"

"Aye," Leah said. "Most truly and definitely."

The blood drained from Riley's face, as the hairs on the back of her neck stood on end. She hated the supernatural and had slept with the covers pulled over her head whenever Top Hat Tom told her a ghost tale.

Suzanna swallowed hard, her expression mirroring how Riley felt. "And how did you come to that brilliant deduction?"

"I've seen Father 'erman's spirit myself, standin' right over there by those wooden pews." Leah pointed to the right corner of the room.

She glanced at the pews, almost fearing she'd spot Father Herman's apparition there and then.

"'Twas the night I rescued poor Nellie," Leah went on. "I didn't think she'd live, and I was cryin' and prayin', and then I saw 'im...Father 'erman. 'e wore a long black coat and hat. 'e looked at me with the most sad and kind expression, then marked off a blessin' with 'is 'and before vanishin' right in front o' my eyes."

"Blimey, did 'e speak to ye?" Oliver questioned with wide, terror-filled eyes.

Truth be told, her own eyes, as well as Suzanna's, were just as wide.

"I've 'eard many a ghost tale, and it is quite a well-known fact that a ghost is 'onor bound to remain silent until spoken to," Leah said.

"And ye remained silent?" Oliver scrutinized further, the tone of his voice piquing.

"Aye," Leah said. "But I didn't get the feelin' the priest would 'arm me. I felt a bit at peace with the whole episode because soon after Nellie started to 'eal. So I figured maybe Father 'erman was lookin' out for us."

"Blimey," Oliver said again. "I would've definitely said somethin' to the chap."

"And why is that?" Leah cocked her head with interest.

"I should think, that if such a sightin' ever 'appened my way, after I wet my britches, that is, the best thing to do would be to speak to it, ask it why it could not go forth to enter the light o' its reward," Oliver explained. "And if nothin' much else came o' it, the sound o' my own voice would at least reassure me I was fully awake. And perhaps with a show o' kindness toward the poor thing's restlessness, the whole o' the matter wouldn't render me insane."

"I do see yer point," Leah agreed.

Suzanna cleared her throat. "Do you know why he still remains here?"

Leah nodded. "I've 'eard it told a long, long time ago there was a young woman in the parish, a farmer's daughter. She would bring daily a bouquet o' flowers to the church and place them at the feet o' the Blessed Mother statue. 'er gift pleased the priest so much 'e taught the young woman 'ow to read and write, as this was 'er 'eart's desire. It seems she 'ad a love away at war and 'e'd send 'er letters. She wished to read them with 'er own eyes and write one in return, by 'er own 'and." She let out an audible breath. "But spendin' so much time with the priest, who I 'eard was quite young as well, caused suspicion in the town. Soon gossip spread and Father 'erman was accused o' wrong doings. Anger mounted and the townspeople became out o' control. An angry mob beat the priest to death, and the young woman was shamed and dishonored. 'er betrothed's family forbid 'im from marryin' the poor girl, as they believed she was unfaithful to 'er promise. She was sent to a nunnery where she lived 'er life out doing penance."

Suzanna let out the breath she was holding. "Aye, I have heard a few of our servants talking about the returning spirit of someone who has long been dead. If the deceased's past is not closed because of previous sins or regrets, a promise not met or an attachment to one still living at the time of death, the unsettled soul becomes a disturbed entity whose plight is leftover, even in death. It then is terribly transformed, possibly even vindictive. Therefore, their resurrection is a potential for terror, a horror which could threaten the lives of the living."

Riley cast a horrified look in Gabriel's direction.

"It is a horrid thought to be sure."

"And I am sure that sort of thinking is what keeps the rest of the folks from entering this place," Gabriel said, standing and placing the dagger back into his boot. "Fortunately for us, at this point, what they believe happens to be in our favor."

"And what if it is true?"

Gabriel chuckled lightly. "I have never heard yet of a spirit harming the living."

Leah raised a defiant chin. "Ye can scoff or credit the tale as it pleases ye, sir. But I speak the truth."

"And I am not thinking otherwise, Leah," Gabriel reassured her. "But obviously Father Herman is harmless, or else he would have hurt you."

"I see your point," Leah stated.

"I do have to ask. Why is it you are not intimidated by the spirit of this holy man?" Gabriel inquired.

Leah shrugged. "It might be because o' somethin' my mum said to me when I was just a little mite. I was fearful o' the dark, thought the dead would come to get me, snatch me away, and torture me. And Mum said 'twasn't the dead I 'ad to fear, but the livin'." Her eyes welled with unshed tears. "She spoke the truth, as 'twas only those still alive that 'ave 'urt me."

Oliver went to her, placing a hand upon her arm. He then raised it to trace, with the tip of his finger, the scar that marked one side of Leah's face. "They won't hurt ye anymore, Miss Leah, because I won't let them."

"And that brings us to what point of action we must take to prevent any of us from falling victim to these scoundrels," Gabriel said.

Oliver turned to look at Gabriel. "What strategy 'ave ye coome up with?"

"Until the others arrive..." he began.

"Others? What others?" Suzanna asked.

"Captain Simon Cavendish, a relative by my sister's marriage to his brother, is helping us in this matter as well. He is the son-in-law to Lord Morgan Wade. The two of them will go see your father, my lady, and hopefully soon reinforcements should be on the way."

Suzanne's smile belied her smug tone. "Oh, you can be sure, Mr. Eagle, my father will send his men. And when they do arrive, there will be hell to pay."

"I am pleased to hear this, my lady," Gabriel said. "But we cannot just sit around and wait."

Riley's own voice sounded dry to her when she spoke. "What can we do in the meantime?"

Gabriel considered her words a moment. "I am sure, when the time comes for us to rid ourselves of these troublesome gnats and make a move in our defense, we will have only precious moments to act wisely and swiftly." He turned his attention to Leah. "For us to do this, your help is greatly needed."

Leah's brows rose in surprise. "And what, sir, can I do?"

"You have lived amongst them, have you not?"

Leah nodded. "For longer than I would ever 'ave wished."

"Then we will first begin with their total," he said.

Leah counted them off on her fingers before she spoke. "With cook dead and a chap dyin' o' food poisonin' last month, I'd say there's ten o' them still."

"We are sorely outnumbered."

Gabriel nodded, his frown thoughtful. "It would appear that way on the surface, but a warrior with a plan can handle many foes. Especially if those he is up against are not as skilled as he in battle."

"And just how well of a warrior are you, Mr. Eagle?" Suzanna snickered.

Rage boiled within Riley. For a moment she was prepared to rebuke Suzanna for her cheeky remark. But Gabriel leveled his gaze upon the other woman with a look so deadly it brought them all up short. Lady Wellington's stunned look strongly indicated no one had ever dared to glare at her in such a fashion. Riley feared the tirade that would follow, but Gabriel's actions seemed to stifle any further contradictions Suzanna might have.

Returning his attention to Leah, he softened his expression. "Can you tell me about the officers?"

"Aye," Leah said with a shaky voice, casting her eyes to the floor.

It was evident to Riley the younger woman now feared Gabriel after the silent reprimand he used to deal with Suzanna. In all truth, if she did not know the man better, she might feel the same. He was formidable, big, confident, and skilled. She almost pitied his enemies.

"Look at me, Leah," Gabriel said, his tone firm yet kind.

Reluctantly, Leah raised her gaze to meet his.

"You have nothing to fear from me, and everything to fear from them," he said then added, "But I have a feeling you already know this."

Leah nodded, eyes welling with tears.

An unexpected pang of pity shot through Riley, and she swallowed back her tears on the girl's behalf.

"Then help me to help you," he concluded.

Leah took an audible breath. "Amongst the ten, there are only three officers. One is Captain Marshal Langley and the other two are Lieutenants Martin Beck and Addison Gray." She cleared her throat nervously. "I'd say the captain is the one to be most concerned with. I 'ave seen 'im in action, and 'e's sneaky. Fights dirty."

"This Captain Langley is the one who gives the

orders, makes the decisions, and handles the deals?" Gabriel probed further.

"Aye, all the men do as 'e tells them, and the clients do business with 'im only," Leah said. Her lips thinned. "Langley is the one who punishes as well." She crossed her arms over her chest. "And 'e 'as nay a shred o' mercy or shame for what 'e inflicts upon others."

Suzanna's face turned crimson, fury so visible, it rose off her like the steam from a boiling kettle. "Bloody bastard, dying would be too good for him. I won't rest until I see him publicly stripped to the bone, beaten, and castrated."

Riley, aware of the humiliation Suzanna suffered at the hands of Captain Langley, thought the other woman's words and attitude were most disturbing. Yet she understood and even empathized with such thoughts of revenge. It seems there was more to Lady Wellington than just spoiled stubbornness. For certain she possessed a measure of toughness as well. Riley hated to admit it, but it somewhat impressed her. A fighting mad woman, in this instance, could turn out to be a good cohort.

If Suzanna's words impressed Gabriel, he didn't let on, ignoring the outburst and continuing to prod Leah for facts. "Where do the officers sleep at night?"

"In the cold weather, like now, they take their rest on the steamer," Leah said.

"And what about the other men?" Gabriel continued.

"Some stay on the steamer, and a few lodge in a small hut on shore, beside the crates," Leah explained.

"Where are the women kept?" Gabriel said.

"All the women are kept in the cave. But there aren't any 'ere now, except for Miss Riley and Lady Wellington." Leah bit her bottom lip. "A ship coome by sea a few days ago and took five o' them away to be sold."

"Lord 'elp us," Oliver whispered.

"I'm especially going to need that 'elp when they discover these two gone," Leah said, indicating Riley and Suzanna. "I'm the one who tends to the women while they're 'ere, so 'tis only sure to believe they'll accuse me o' freein' them."

"Where would you be, and what would you be doing at this time if you did not free them and bring them here?" Gabriel asked.

Leah's cheeks reddened. "That would depend on what condition the men are in after they've eaten their evenin' meal and drank their ale. Tonight all fell asleep after I danced a bit for them. But sometimes they will...they want to..." she stammered, her blush deepening.

"Where do you usually sleep?" Gabriel broke in, sparing her the explanation. He managed to keep his expression impassive, in spite of the fact his hands fisted by his side. Tendons thickened in his wrists, the cartilage pulling taut beneath his flesh as he fought to keep calm, stay in control.

"Sometimes 'ere, with Nellie and Rufus, but most times on the steamer where the captain can keep an eye on me," Leah said. She glanced at the window. "I should be there now, before 'e discovers I'm not."

"Then that is where Oliver and I will follow you," Gabriel concluded.

Leah's eyes rounded. "Nay, sir, ye cannot. 'Tis way too dangerous."

"Have you gone daft?"

Gabriel spun around to face Lady Wellington, shooting her another sharp gaze. The muscles in his jaw throbbed as he spoke. "If all does not appear the same, the men will get suspicious, go to the cave, and learn of your escape."

Suzanna laughed harshly. "And what are we

161

supposed to do while you are gone?"

"Stay put where you are safe, and keep quiet if you think that is possible." Then Gabriel smirked. "Perhaps you will get to visit with the holy man."

Riley shuddered.

Suzanna gasped.

"Not to worry, my lady," Leah called over her shoulder. "Rufus will keep you safe from the rats and mice. 'e's quite a good hunter."

Suzanna shrieked and pulled her knees to her chest.

Gabriel and Oliver stifled a smile as they followed Leah up the stairs.

"Gabriel, I beg of you to be careful," Riley called to him.

He glanced at her over his shoulder. "All will be well if you remember to stay put," he advised again.

"My foreboding is not for myself, but for you. These men are positively uncivil. They have blood in their eyes and morbid delusions," she said, remembering the stench of the bloodstained trunk she had been forced into. "Decayed rakes, all of them, and they will stop at nothing."

A frown indented his brows. "I have, for a long time, been aware of what the Sea Patrol is all about."

"Then you will take great care in how you proceed," she noted.

He nodded, his features softening. "You have my word all caution will be used."

Once the three disappeared, Suzanna curled herself against the wall, looking around the chamber. "I don't know which is worse, the thought of rats and mice or the dead priest."

"Perhaps it would be best if we thought of something else," she suggested.

Suzanna nodded, taking an audible breath before she spoke. "Very well...suppose you tell me how good of a friend Naomi was to you, then."

She spoke with a hollow tone. "I choose not to talk of her or fall out with you in this fashion again, my lady."

"Nay, I don't imagine it being a pleasant memory, living as you did," Suzanna said. "I would certainly be prickly over such memories. Perhaps it was wrong of me to sit in judgment of you." She shrugged. "I suppose, just being a mite yourself at the time, you had not a voice in the choices made for your life and later obliged to survive from your own wit."

She inclined her head politely, knowing full well this was probably the only form of an apology she'd ever receive from Lady Wellington, and swung her legs off the mattress.

"What are you doing?" Suzanna said.

"Seeing if I can put pressure on my leg," she explained. "It will slow us down if I can't walk on my own."

Suzanna smirked. "Oh, I don't think Mr. Eagle would mind very much if he had to carry you."

She clamped down on the impatience mounting within her. "Well, I would mind. The last thing I need or want is to be a burden to anyone, especially to..."

"...to the man who finds you fetching?" Suzanna finished for her.

She forced herself to walk around the chamber, in spite of the pain. "He does not find me fetching, and I would thank you not to remark so again."

"Oh come now, certainly you are aware of his interest in you?" Suzanna cocked her head sideways. "Are you too daft to see it in his eyes, in the way he cared for your knee?"

"All I see is a good person concerned for another," she speculated. "He is here to help us both."

"Then perhaps I should rephrase my inquiry," Suzanna said, her dark eyes gleaming mischievously. "How long have *you* been interested in him?"

"I beg your pardon, my lady, but that is none of your business," she politely remarked, in spite of how she really wished to respond, and continued her walk around the chamber.

Chapter Eighteen

A cloak of stars was thrown over what remained of the night, the moon illuminating their way as they walked through a ghostly breath of fog floating above the earth. Mud layered the path, and by the time they came upon the gravestones, Gabriel's boots were ankle-deep in the mire. It seemed it did nothing other than rain in England, temperatures damp, the atmosphere stale. The gloom settled right to the very core of his bones. What a contrast it was here from his homeland, his Mother country, where even the air tasted different, and one was able to take larger breaths of it, feel the spaciousness of land and sky.

In Arizona, somewhere in between the buzz of the summer insects and the brisk chill of a winter's night, the weeks of autumn arrived with its splendor of radiant hues of gold and reds. It was a time to nest at sundown and eat a bowl of warm soup or stew by the fire-pit. The longer nights were greeted with warmer blankets made of animal fur. They no longer kept the beast that originally owned it in comfort, but heated the new occupant quite nicely.

I am completely saturated with the atmosphere I have so long lived in. Yet tonight, he welcomed the chill night breeze, thankful for it cooling more than his face. It was almost as though he had been holding his breath all this time and now could finally release it. Riley Flanders invoked disturbing and pleasant changes in him, when first in his arms, then her bare leg assessable to his touch. When she gazed up at him from beneath the dark wings of her long lashes, he was held spellbound.

He shook his head to clear it. This was not the time or place to have his thoughts besotted by a female. In the next hours, he needed to be alert and cautious, or else he would get them all killed. He turned to Leah. "Take us to the men's camp before you make your way on board."

"Aye, sir," Leah agreed, walking close to Oliver. In such a short time, the two had bonded well together.

"What are ye thinkin' our next plan o' action must be?" Oliver inquired.

"We would be wise to create a distraction that will move our enemies gaze to the thing that does not matter, so they will forget to notice the thing that does," he explained.

"That fact being Miss Riley and Lady Wellington are no longer in the cave," Oliver concluded.

"Exactly," he said. "Such a strategy will buy us more time."

Oliver's tone was a bit shaky. "And how will just the two o' us accomplish this distraction?"

"I will know that once I have a look at the men's camp and the men," he said.

When they came to a fork in the path, Leah pointed to the trail going left. "That is the way to the men's camp. About twenty feet and to the right you'll see the clearin'." Reluctantly, she glanced to the pathway going in the opposite direction. "This is where I will part from ye, as this trail to the right leads to the river."

"Ye can't go alone. 'Tis way too dangerous," Oliver protested.

"'Tis more dangerous to be caught walkin' with ye by my side."

"She is right on that matter, Oliver," he said. "No one knows we are here, and if we are to accomplish this mission, it needs to stay that way."

Leah placed a hand on Oliver's arm. "I walk these grounds alone every night and day. Nothin' more can 'appen to me that I've not already survived. Nothin' is different from before."

"But there is a difference, Leah," Oliver said.

Leah frowned. "What might that be?"

"I know o' ye now, promised nay a thing more will 'urt ye." Oliver ran his fingers through his hair. "Blimey, miss, do ye take me for a man who doesn't keep 'is word?"

"Nay, nay," she answered quickly. "But neither do I take ye for a fool." Her mouth softened into a smile. "Ye 'ave coome all this way to save Miss Riley and Lady Wellington, and that's what ye must do."

"And now to save ye too," Oliver said.

"Ye will if ye listen to Mr. Eagle, 'ere," Leah said, motioning to Gabriel.

"Leah, do you carry in your pocket anymore fire-sticks?" Gabriel asked. Though he was quite capable of conjuring up fire without such an aid, he was not sure a dry piece of bark was to be found and had not the time for an extensive search.

She nodded, handing him a few of the matches. Then she stood on tiptoe and placed a small kiss upon Oliver's cheek. "God speed," she said, before running down the path to the steamer.

Oliver stood frozen, eyes wide, his fingers gently touching where Leah's lips met his cheek.

Gabriel stifled a smile. "She is a spirited little thing, would you not agree?"

"Aye, that she is," Oliver said, shaking his head to clear it. "I don't want to even imagine what she's been through, but still and all I can't 'elp but wonder about some things. Do ye think..." He paused, his brows knitting together. "Do ye think she's been *rogered* by these prigs?"

Within the few years he has lived in England, Gabriel managed to pick up certain lingo. *Rogered* was the British word meaning to *compromise a woman.* "Does it matter greatly if that be the case?"

Oliver shrugged. "The thought is disturbin'."

"Is it your manly pride that is disturbed, should you decide to win her heart, or the thought Leah has been abused?" he asked.

Oliver cleared his throat. "I would say a bit o' both."

For a moment his thoughts flashed to the women in his tribe who were *rogered* by the white agents. Desperately they kept such exploitation from the men, for fear they would retaliate, fight with the white agents, and end up dead. But also in part their silence was out of worry their men would feel ashamed and offended by their situation, much like Oliver. It was Golden Lady who spoke to the tribe, calmed the men's anger, and returned respect and honor to the women. Gabriel now relayed his mother's wise words to his young companion. "If Leah has been taken against her will, it is not her shame or yours, but that of those who took what did not belong to them. Why should she suffer, live without the love and respect of a good man or that of her family and friends, when the fault of her situation is not hers?"

Often he had the suspicion his sister Raven had been one of the maidens in his tribe to be compromised. He always felt it was the main reason Golden Lady implored Proud Eagle to make arrangements for their daughters to leave Arizona. Then she insisted he escort his sisters to England, adding the hope that he could one day return a man of wealth and means to help his people. He did not question his mother's true motive, not because he was a coward, but because he did not want to see his father die for their honor. And Proud Eagle would have done just that. So would he, leaving the women grief-stricken and vulnerable to further abuse. And so with that in mind he complied, brought them far from America where they would be safe. But it seems a woman is not safe anywhere, especially one without means, like Leah.

Oliver frowned. "When ye put it that way, I see things differently."

He arched a brow. "Differently or clearly?"

"Again I would 'ave to say a bit o' both," Oliver admitted.

"Then keep your new revelation first and foremost in your mind so it will never intrude upon your feelings for that young woman again. And if you cannot do that, then distance yourself from her right now because once she begins to care in return, all you will do is hurt her," he warned. "And I think Leah has been hurt far too much already."

Oliver's frown deepened. "I would never 'urt 'er."

"Then see her for who she is and not what she has been made to endure," he said. "We have all accepted things we do not like in order to survive."

"Aye, that's the truth o' it," Oliver agreed.

He placed a hand on the younger man's shoulder. "Now, clear your thoughts from all things female and come. We must assess the enemy before they discover us."

Gabriel and Oliver crept into the brush to the back of the enemy's encampment, which was nothing more than a small wood-framed hut. The makeshift dwelling, less than a bowshot away, appeared spacious enough to only accommodate a couple of men. Fortunately, those with living arrangements on shore fell right into his plan. It was much easier to create a diversion on land than on the steamer, and much more effectively as well.

Even if Leah had not set the scene for him earlier, the enemy's plan was obvious. With the crates of contraband stacked behind the small compound, it was plain to see these men were instructed to guard the illegal shipment until another vessel arrived to take them to their destiny. And Gabriel had no doubts that the same ship would also include the transport of the kidnapped women.

A lone man, thin as a withered stick, sat on a stool beside the fire, whittling a piece of wood. After yawning and stretching, he placed his creation aside, pocketed the knife, and stood with slumped shoulders to stoke the campfire with a stick.

A moment later a second man emerged from the hut. His large, rounded belly hung over his pants and out from beneath a soiled shirt. Yawning and scratching his crotch, he moved slowly to the other side of the camp, where he stood in front of a clump of bushes. There he opened his britches and relieved himself, while burping and passing a loud and long rumble of gas.

"Well, ain't ye just the refined one," the man by the fire teased.

"Hey, when ye gotta fart, ye gotta fart," the other man boasted, making his point clear by expelling a second stream of bodily wind.

The first man chuckled. "Next time ye might think twice about takin' such a big 'elpin' o' beans."

The second man secured his britches and moved to the fire. "Speakin' o' food, where's Cook?"

The first man shrugged. "Ain't seen the prig since dinner. Most likely he's got that little blonde twit dancin' without 'er bloomers again."

Oliver stiffened, but this time remained hidden behind the brush. "In the name o' decency," he muttered in a tone of deep disgust.

Gabriel placed a hand on the younger man's shoulder, feeling the rage trembling within him. "There will be time enough for revenge, my friend," he whispered, feeling confident he and Oliver could overpower these two in a matter of moments.

The second man cast a glance to the sky. "'Twill

be dawn in an hour, so he better be sendin' the twit down with somethin' to eat soon. I ain't loadin' all this cargo without food in my gut."

Gabriel quickly summed up the situation playing out before him. One man was frail; the other appeared fat, lazy, and complacent. The obvious fact that both men believed they were safe at the moment from any altercations was in his favor. If the others in this band of scoundrels were like these two buffoons, and the dead cook whose husk was now rotting in the bushes, it might not matter so that they were outnumbered.

He leaned closer to Oliver. "These men are only hardened by their circumstance, not honed warriors of strategy for battle. Their cleverness comes in who they can con more so than actually winning a fight. Unless, of course, you were female," he added.

"Aye, it doesn't take great physical ability to overcome a woman," Oliver whispered.

The thinner man made his way to the hut's door, entered the dwelling, and moments later returned holding a carafe of spirits. After gulping down a swig of the white man's firewater, he handed the flask to the other man. "Lace yer gullet with some o' this, and ye will feel better."

"If Langley catches ye stealin' 'is whiskey, 'e'll skin ye alive," the second man warned, before taking his own guzzle.

"Well, 'e ain't gonna know if ye don't tell 'im." The first man chuckled. "And by the time anyone finds out some o' those bottles are filled with tea instead o' spirits, they'll be too far away to do anythin' about it."

"And so will we," the heavier man agreed.

Both men broke out in hardy laughter and finished off the bottle of whiskey.

Gabriel was sure any fighting ability they had was dulled when he decided to strike their camp and cripple whatever power remained. In one fluid motion, he sprung like a feline from where he hid, dropping into a crouch within the clearing.

Oliver followed, not with as much grace and speed, but still ever-ready to take his stand.

Stunned by the unexpected intruders, the heavier man stepped back and lost his balance over uneven ground. The thinner man's reflexes were better, as he reached for the whittling knife. But they were not as quick as Gabriel's. Before the enemy's hand could pull free from his pocket with the weapon, Gabriel tackled him to the ground. Knuckle bones met jaw bone as he landed a hard blow to the frail man's jowl. Blood and spittle flew from his mouth, and a grunt of air escaped his lungs before he was rendered unconscious.

From the corner of his eye, he saw Oliver lunge for the whiskey bottle and break it over the heavy man's head, also knocking the second scoundrel out cold before he ever managed to regain his footing.

"Find something to bind them with," he instructed Oliver.

His young companion rushed into the wooden hut and returned in seconds with rope. Together they bound the two villain's hands and feet, gagged them, dragged them thirty feet into the woods, and tied them to separate trees.

"This should hold them until Simon arrives with help," he said, flexing the hand he used to throw a punch...knuckles now sore and bloody, his flesh stinging.

"Aye, they should stand trial for their crimes," Oliver added.

"Come, now we create the diversion," he said, walking back into the clearing. He made his way to the fire, stirred the dying ambers, but had no luck resurrecting the flame in the pre-dawn dampness. "This fire has gone out." He then reached into his pocket for Leah's matches, handed one to Oliver and scanned his surroundings. "Help to find something to use as a torch."

The younger man frowned. "Why do ye waste time rebuldin' the fire?"

"I am not rebuilding this one, but starting another," he said.

Oliver's frown deepened. "And what do ye plan on settin' ablaze now?"

Gabriel started over to the where the cargo was stacked. "These crates, Oliver," he said, running a hand over one piece of cargo. "We are going to burn them all. Every last one of them."

Chapter Nineteen

Riley sniffed...smelled smoke. Halting her attempt to put pressure on her injured leg, she turned to face Suzanna. "The fighting has commenced."

"God save the Queen and all her children." Suzanna also sniffed the air. Her blue eyes rounded with fright. "What do you think burns?"

She shook her head. "I haven't a clue, but I know it can't be the steamer because Leah was instructed to return to it."

"Aye, that's the truth of it," Suzanna agreed.

"A diversion. Gabriel's set something ablaze to divert these rogues from finding us gone."

"Well, whoever this Gabriel is, he didn't do a very good job, because I found you," a voice came from behind.

Riley spun around to find Lieutenant Martin Beck's pear-shaped form standing in the doorframe, his nose still bandaged from where she bit him. She cast a glance Suzanna's way. The other woman's features were stark, as though she'd been awakened to face a real nightmare.

"The fact that little twit thought she could get you two away from me is a laugh I intend to enjoy well into my golden years," Beck said, stepping closer.

"So much for secret places," Suzanna mumbled.

Beck cackled, moving even nearer. "Though there's not much between the bitch's ears, her hindquarters are perfect for a birching now and then." He shrugged. "All women are brainless, only understand their place after getting a good beaten."

Riley's gaze darted around the room for something to use as a weapon. She might not cause the lieutenant great harm, but perhaps she could injure him enough to stop his advances or knock insensible long enough so the two of them could bind, gag, and secure him to a wooden column until Gabriel returned. In her quick surveillance, she noticed Suzanna moving slowly off the cot. Could it be she shared the same idea?

"Soon you'll be lacking brains of your own, Beck," another voice rasped.

Beck's lips curved into a cocky sneer. "Well now, Lieutenant Gray, have you been following me?" he retorted, turning slowly to face Gray then stepping back in surprise when he met with a gun aimed at his head.

Gray's eyes, filled with raw hatred, bore into Beck's, his expression hard and unyielding like it was chiseled out of granite. "This is for Naomi," he ground out with gritted teeth before he pulled the trigger.

The blast echoed through the underground chamber.

Beck's face exploded, flesh and blood splattering the wall. His body fell to the floor with a thud. Suzanna screamed. Riley's vision swam as she fought the urge to retch.

Gray kicked the dead man in the side as he fully entered the chamber, the gun he held now aimed at her. "'Tis time for you both to return to the cave."

She swallowed hard the bile rising to choke her. "You said yourself Naomi asked that I not be harmed."

"And you won't as long as you cooperate," he said, near enough now to grab her by the arm.

"Please, let us go," she begged.

Gray shook his head. "I can't do that without

being in harm's way myself."

The blood rushed to her head, heart beating wildly. "Nay a soul needs to know you've found us hiding here."

"I can't take that chance," Gray said, digging his nails deeper into her arm as he pulled her toward him.

She was just about to raise a foot and kick him in the shins when her plan was upset by Suzanna plummeting him in the back with a wine jug. Dazed for seconds, he waivered but didn't fall. Again Suzanna hit him, harder this time, the blow striking him in the back of the head. Riley followed through with a kick to the shins, and then she stomped down hard upon his foot. He hollered with pain and staggered back, falling into the table that held the lantern. The lamp flew from its spot and landed in the center of the mattress she had laid upon, immediately igniting it in flames.

Still gripping his gun, Gray got up on one knee. Before he commenced to regain his footing, Nellie, Leah's injured dog, bounced upon him, sinking her teeth deep into his throat. When Gray tossed the dog from him, she yelped, lying motionless where she landed.

Dropping the gun, Gray clutched his throat. Blood seeped through his fingers, streamed down his arms, staining his red jacket with a darker shade. He stumbled toward the doorframe and tripped over Beck's body. That move sent him crashing into a cloth-covered statue that stood in the corner. It toppled over, crushing Gray between it and Beck's body.

The chamber filled with smoke, flames dancing high and fierce burning books, wall-hangings, and cloth-covered pews in its fury. Between the two slain men's bodies, the felled statue, and the roaring fire, the doorway was blocked.

"We're trapped," Suzanna choked out, hands shielding her mouth and nose.

Frantically, Riley's gaze darted around the chamber as smoke filled the air. "There has to be another way out of here."

Suzanna's voice spiked the chaos, her eyes watering. "I don't see one."

A hopeless panic seized her as her own throat constricted. Scorched wood and floating ash swelled her nostrils. Is this how her life will end? Will she never know the love of a man? Nay, she only cared to know one man—Gabriel. If she lived through this, she would somehow taste his lips, feel the warmth of his kiss, even if it were for only a moment and just one time. This was a vow she made to herself, and one she intended on keeping.

Rufus, Leah's cat, chose that moment to make his own escape. Jumping from his perch upon a beam, he ran to the west side of the chamber and squeezed himself through a broken plank at the base of a bookcase.

"There," she pointed with a shaking hand. "That must be a doorway, like the one we used to enter this chamber."

The two women hurried to that end of the underground room, Riley feeling around for a latch. To her good fortune she found the handle, camouflaged as the arrow of a carved cherub, and pulled it. The bookcase slid aside, revealing a tunnel.

"Let's get out of here," Suzanna said, reaching for Riley's hand.

She pulled back. "I must get Nellie."

"Leave her!" Suzanna gripped her hand tighter.

"Nay, she saved our lives," she said, pushing Suzanna and breaking free.

"If you want to risk your own life for a sick, mangy dog that's not worth the air she breaths, then carry on, but I'm getting out of here."

177

"That sick, mangy dog is all the family Leah has. But I don't expect you to understand, my dear Lady Wellington," she ground out sardonically. "You who have had everything you've always wanted and more."

Limping, Riley made her way to where Nellie lay. Fear stabbed beneath the joining of her ribs, as the dog lay very still. It had to have taken every last bit of Nellie's strength to attack Gray. Had his backhand of abuse killed her?

"And how will you carry her with that gimpy leg of yours?" Suzanna called out to her.

"I will manage somehow," she stated plainly, pulling off the covering of another statue that hadn't yet gone up in flames. Gently, she rolled Nellie onto the sheet. The dog whimpered. Relief washed over her. Nellie lived, but not for long if she didn't make a move. "All is well, girl," she whispered, her eyes stinging with smoke. Putting full pressure upon her injured leg brought her great pain. Biting her bottom lip until she tasted blood, she bore the agony as she dragged Nellie to the tunnel entrance.

"She will slow us down," Suzanna argued, lines of worry cutting deep into her delicate features.

"Go then, save yourself as you want, but I refuse to leave this animal behind," she said, struggling to get through the passageway.

"Then you will die," Suzanna screeched.

Riley's lungs ached, her leg throbbed, and she fought to balance her footing. "Then I will die, but it will be while trying to save a life worth saving, a life someone good and kind loves. A life I love as well," she added.

"God save the Queen and all her children," Suzanna grumbled. "Now that you've said that, I shan't be able to live with myself."

"Then help me," she pleaded, raising a prompting brow. "Between us both, we can do this."

With a huff Suzanna took the other end of the sheet. "There, does this set with you better?"

"Much," she said, able now to lift the makeshift stretcher.

"Bloody hell. Let's get out of here," Suzanna said, pulling Nellie along behind her as she led the way down the tunnel.

Riley welcomed the cool causeway, her lungs clearing the farther and farther they walked from the raging inferno. A damp, musty order filled her senses as she stepped with caution through the pitch darkness.

"I'm walking as a blind man," Suzanna griped. "Anything, anything at all could be ahead of us...a deep descent, rats, mice," she said, her voice rising with the panic that obviously welled within her.

"The rats and mice are the least of our worries," she said, thinking back to the time she once lived with such rodents. Their droppings in the cupboards and the scampering at night beneath the bed she shared with Anita were everyday happenings. She shivered at the thought.

Suzanna responded. "I would say if anyone knew about such deplorable creatures, it would be you."

"Aye, as well as head lice, scabs in my ears, fungus between my toes, and infected eyes. These are only a few of the maladies London's poorer class endures."

"You needn't be so graphic."

"And just because you've been brought up to entertain frivolous notions, dispelling a care in the world for anything or anyone else, you needn't be so bloody snobbish." The second her harsh words left her mouth, she regretted them. Her attitude was not exactly unified, and wasn't that what she had asked of Suzanna through this ordeal? She sighed with frustration. "I am sorry for snapping so."

179

"It's just that I've always hated the dark. As a child it frightened me dreadfully," Suzanna admitted. "And what if we run into that dead priest? Leah did say she once saw him."

"If you remember, Leah also said he didn't hurt her. She actually felt he helped her," she said reassuringly. "And right now, wouldn't you agree his ghostly illumination guiding us through this tunnel would be a blessing?"

Suzanna halted.

"Why have you stopped?" Riley probed.

"The toe of my boot hit something. I think it's a step," Suzanna said.

"Can you feel around with your foot?"

"Aye, I can...I am...and it is a step...it *is* a step!" Suzanna resounded with joy. "And where there is a staircase, there is an opening."

Carefully, holding Nellie between them in the hammock-strung sheet, they climbed the narrow, winding staircase. With each step, Riley prayed her knee would hold, that she not trip, causing them to fall.

The opening at the top brought them out into another cave, and beyond that loomed an archway leading to the outdoors where the first light of day was just brightening the sky.

Suzanna hesitated. "I can only imagine what waits for us beyond this point."

She took an audible breath. "Since we cannot stay here, I would say we'll soon find out." They emerged out into a clearing, the stillness sending an eerie chill down her spine. "The quiet before the storm," she whispered, as they both plopped down beneath a tree where Rufus sat preening himself like he hadn't a care in the world. And Riley suspected he hadn't.

"Stupid cat," Suzanna muttered.

"Aye, well, if not for him we'd have never found

passage out of that underground chamber." She leaned her head back against the huge trunk and closed her burning eyes. Exhaustion set deep into the very core of her being. Nellie stirred beside her, moving to place a paw in her lap. She put a hand atop the dog's furry white head. "We're safe now, Nellie girl."

"The bloody hell we are," Suzanna gabbled beneath her breath.

Opening her eyes, Riley affixed them on a man sitting atop a large, black stallion. Within seconds many horses' hooves shook the earth, the thundering sound vibrating through her hind-quarters. Rufus hissed and ran up the tree. Nellie growled, and Riley sat forward, drawing the dog protectively to her.

"Good morning, Miss Flanders," the man said, removing his hat. He inclined his head politely. "It is a welcomed sight to feast my eyes upon you."

She smiled, tears welling in her eyes. "And on you as well, Captain."

Simon Cavendish, replacing his hat atop his head, returned the smile. "Rest assured now, ladies. Your allies have arrived."

Chapter Twenty

From the distance where Gabriel stood, both sky and water seemed to meet, their intense blue matching as the first morning sun blazed into the sky, warming the earth. Its reflection glittering upon the water's majestic curves reminded him of the fire flies he caught as a child. Their sparkle against the night had always amused him. Why was he thinking of childhood fancies when he stood, readying himself for a pending battle? Perhaps it was how all warriors resigned themselves for what came next, thinking back at what once was and holding it dear to the end. And where war resulted, so did death as the two went side by side.

It would not be long before the fighting would ensue, as those on the steamer had caught sight of the burning cargo. They leapt down ladders to reach the shore and hurried across the land to the burning shipment. There were more than Leah said, more than he could handle. Death was only a leg's length away. But he was in it now, and there would be no turning back.

"Mother o' God," Oliver gasped as the band of men coming their way grew in number.

Yet the younger man stood beside him, loyal and steadfast as he had been throughout this ordeal. Gabriel sent up a silent prayer to the heavens that the two would remain standing after this day ended.

Then the ground shook. The glorious sound of horses' hooves growing louder and louder with each second. And bursting upon the scene came the reinforcements they waited for. Their allies swarmed, charging down the hill and heading straight for those men that marched from the steamer. Not expecting such opposition, the enemy was stunned. Many turned and ran back to the docked vessel. Those who chose to stay and fight were sorely outnumbered.

Ahead of them the clamor heightened with the sounds of men warring, guns blasting, shouting, running, screaming, falling, the earth drinking the blood of those slain.

"Come," he said to Oliver. "We must help our men."

"If you move one muscle, I will blow her head off," a voice threatened from behind.

They turned to find Captain Langley holding Leah in front of him, a gun pointed at her head.

"Ah, I see you have struck out of nowhere like the poisonous snake that you are," he said, exchanging venomous glances with the black-guard Sea Patrol officer. The two of them came to the same conclusion without muttering a word. Today one of them would die, and Leah as well, if he made a wrong move.

The captain's face was tense, skin flushed. "Down on the ground. Both of you, or I will pull this trigger."

Though the morning was cool, hot sweat gathered on the back of Gabriel's neck and trickled down between his shoulder blades.

"Don't do it, sir," Leah said, raising her glance to meet his, fear dawning in her blue gaze. "Cut 'im down instead."

Gabriel set his jaw, muscles throbbing at the temples. He ignored Leah's words and spoke directly to Langley. "The girl is not a part of this. Let her go."

Langley sliced the notion aside with a cutting motion of the gun. "Nay, I'm afraid I can't oblige with your request." His next reply was curt. "She's my passage out of here."

He stepped smoothly into the opened area between them. "Then she is no good to you dead."

Langley pressed the gun's barrel to Leah's temple. "I suggest you keep a prudent distance."

"I'm nay afraid o' leavin' this world if it means seein' this prig dead," Leah beseeched again. "And if 'e's shootin' me, 'e can't be shootin' ye too, so do what ye need to rid us o' this rogue and be quick about it."

"Silence!" Langley jerked Leah's frail form hard against him. "Now, both of you, down on the ground," he demanded again, his quick glance surveying his surroundings, looking for Oliver. He frowned and absently said, "Bloody hell, where's the boy?"

"I'm right behind ye, *guvnor*," Oliver noted, stabbing Langley in the back before he had a chance to turn around.

Just as Leah escaped from the enemy's clutches, Gabriel sprang into action, reaching for a rock and clubbing Langley full in the face. The impact knocked out several of the captain's front teeth and broke the bridge of his nose. Blood pumped from each orifice as he collapsed to the ground, his gun flying from his hand. But in spite of his wounds, he managed to pull himself to his knees and reach for a knife in his jacket pocket, raising it against Gabriel.

Then a shot rang out, the bullet hitting Langley dead center in the heart. The captain fell forward, dead.

Gabriel turned to find Leah holding Langley's gun, arms straight out and locked with her aim. She clutched the gun in a death-grip, her knuckles as white as her face.

"Is 'e dead? Is 'e dead? Please tell me 'e's dead!" Leah broke out in hysterical sobs.

Oliver reached for the young woman, pried the gun from her hands, and embraced her.

Gabriel felt for a pulse, and when he found none, he faced the younger woman. "He is very much dead, Leah."

"And is that the scalawag who threatened your sister?" Simon Cavendish said as he entered the clearing on horseback.

"One in the same," he said, glancing up at his friend with relief. "I see you finally made it."

"Aye, I wouldn't have missed it for the world," Simon pointed out, staring down at Langley. "This is the first good look I've had at this revolting man."

"There's two more like 'im," Oliver said, gesturing to Langley, "tied to trees thirty feet into the woods."

Simon confirmed with a nod. "They can join the others we've taken prisoner until the Royal Navy arrives."

Gabriel put hands on hips. "The Royal Navy, is it?"

"Aye, thanks to Lord Wellington," Simon confirmed. "He was once an admiral. He's taking nay a chance of any of them getting away. These rogues won't be capable of creating any further ruses."

"And where are ye keepin' the prisoners until the navy arrives, Captain?" Oliver asked.

Simon smiled. "Why, on their beloved steamer, Oliver, my boy."

"Nay, 'e is a man, sir," Leah corrected, her gaze adoringly locked with Oliver's.

Simon cleared his throat. "Well, his auntie might beg to differ that point with you."

Oliver's cheeks reddened. "I say nay to speakin' further on that matter."

Gabriel stifled a smile as he wiped his sweaty forehead with the back of his sleeve. "I will leave the transporting of the prisoners and the burying of the dead to your men, Simon." He arched a brow. "There is a certain lady waiting for me in an underground

185

chamber."

"Nay, that's burnt as well," Simon informed him.

Gabriel's heart thrashed against his ribs, the blood deafening him as it roared through his veins. Could it be true, that while he fought for her freedom, she was dying in a fire? Again had he lost his woman without even having a chance this time to claim her, tell her how he felt? He slumped against a tree, suddenly bone tired and feeling as though he had lived many lifetimes.

"But bear-up, chap, as I see you must believe the worst by your desolate and pale face," Simon rejoined, jousting Gabriel from his catacomb of sorrow. "All is not lost. The ladies made their way to safety. I saw them sitting on the hill east of here, resting beneath a large tree. They are dressed in men's clothing and could use a bath," he added with a chuckle, "but they're very much alive."

The weariness, so unearthly heavy a second ago, suddenly lifted from his spirit. "Are you certain of this, Captain?"

"Aye, most certain, Mr. Eagle," Simon replied. "And they've taken down the rest of the Sea Patrol. Lieutenants Beck and Gray perished in the fire."

Leah stood, stepping from Oliver's embrace and wrapping her thin arms around herself. She shivered. "I hope all o' their souls rot in 'ell."

Simon nodded. "We're of the same mind on that matter."

"And my Nellie, my sweet Nellie and little Rufus," Leah cried. "Were they by any chance with Miss Riley and Lady Wellington as well, sir?"

Simon frowned. "Nay, miss, nay a soul more caught my eye but the two women, a cantankerous cat, and a dog...a bandaged up, mangy, white, dog. All of them sit there now, as I instructed them, beneath a large tree up on that hill," he said, pointing east from where they stood.

Leah's eyes welled with tears. "Then they live still...they all live and this murderin' spawn o' the devil and his men," she said, glancing with disgust and hatred at Langley, "will not be able to 'urt me, or anyone else, ever again."

Gabriel did not stick around to join the conversation further. As fast as his legs could carry him, he made his way to where Riley waited.

At the top of the hill he spotted her, pacing with a limp beneath the tree.

"Riley," he called, waiting for her to turn and face him. In spite of her injured knee, she ran to him, meeting him half way.

Long, ginger curls spilled from the man's hat she wore, flowing over her shoulders and waving behind her in the chilled morning breeze. Tears of relief welled in her eyes as he caught her in his embrace, lifting her from the ground with a hand beneath her knees and one on her back. He drew her close, tight against his heart where his beat in unison to hers.

"I feared for you," she whispered against his throat, as she buried her face beneath his chin and wrapped her arms around his neck.

"I am here now," he reassured her, his member chafing from the nearness of her...for the want of her.

Pulling back to look at him, she searched his face. Tears trickled down her soot-stained cheeks, streaking her flesh. "Never worry me so again."

His eyes focused on her lips, lush and moist, so near to his own. Did he dare kiss her? Did he have the right?

And then she decided for him. "I would welcome your kiss," she boldly stated.

He arched a brow and smiled, strangely flattered by her declaration. "Then I will not have to steal one of my own?"

187

"Nay, never," she answered breathlessly. "I vowed to myself, while searching for a way to escape that burning chamber, that if I lived through this ordeal, I would taste your lips. Whether it was for only a moment and just once, I would kiss you." She moved her lips closer to his. "I want to taste your lips, Gabriel, feel their warmth on mine. Life is too fleeting to be left wondering."

"Hush, woman," he whispered against her mouth before he captured its fullness. There was no turning back. Their closeness was like a drug, lulling his senses into euphoria. His chest tingled against her full breasts hidden from his view beneath the fabric of her shirt, and the thought of their bared splendor drove him insane with passion.

She heaved a delighted sigh as he deepened the kiss, swelling his loins underneath his breeches, and causing a fervent flutter to rise from the pit of his stomach. When his tongue explored the soft recesses of her mouth, he knew kissing her would always leave him burning with desire, hungry for more of the delicious, heady sensation.

And he realized he would have to come to grips with the fact that kissing Riley Flanders for only a moment, or just once in his lifetime, was definitely not going to be an option.

Chapter Twenty-One

Riley rested her bones with Leah in Widow Frumkee's small, but clean and warm, cottage, sipping a cup of after-dinner tea. The kind, elderly woman, wearing a thick, white bun atop her head, had a smile that brightened her entire round and pink-toned face.

Elma Frumkee, a longtime resident of Lands End, bestowed a motherly concern for Leah who visited her whenever she could break away from Captain Langley's clutches. They'd enjoy tea together and shared stories of the widow's youth and Leah's happier days.

"Another one of your secrets, Leah," Suzanna had quipped sardonically before stepping foot on the Royal Naval ship. It had arrived mid-day, along with another vessel, to barricade the waters and confiscate the ship Langley waited on from the Indies. Lord Wellington was aboard to make sure the smugglers were transported to Newgate Prison and to escort Suzanna home.

"Aye, I wished for nay a soul to cause the poor woman retribution for knowin' me," Leah defended herself one last time against Lady Wellington's snide remarks.

"Though you have a cutting edge about you, I shall miss you to a degree," Riley admitted. "And if ever you're in need, I shall comply my help most readily, my lady."

For the most part, in spite of her snobbish exterior, Lady Suzanna Wellington had come through when she was needed most. If not for her assistance, both she and Nellie would be dead now.

Suzanna smiled. "I will extend the same civility to you, Miss Flanders."

Suzanna would not be a woman she would befriend or even ring up for a visit to share an afternoon of tea. But in a pinch they had vowed their assistance to one another, and that wasn't a bad thing.

And Lord Wellington rewarded Gabriel, Oliver, Simon, and the twenty-man garrison allied with him, a handsome sum.

The Naval ship sailed at dusk, and since Captain Cavendish felt it was too late and his men too spent to set sail aboard the steamer for London, staying another night at Lands End was decided. Thus lodging was needed for all that remained.

Elma Frumkee's offer to share her cottage with Riley and Leah was acknowledged; else the two women would have had to sleep on board the steamer with the men. And since neither of them wished to endure a night of such crude accommodations, Widow Frumkee's hospitality was accepted. It afforded Riley a chance to nurse her knee, using an herbal poultice the elder woman supplied and swore by.

Just before the women turned in for the night, Simon stopped by the cottage to inform them of the morrow's departure time.

Leah announced, "I won't be travelin' with ye, Captain. I can't bring myself to ever board that steamer again." She shrugged. "Besides I won't leave Nellie and Rufus, and there's nothin' in London for us anyway."

Simon arched a brow. "Don't let Oliver hear you say that. He has some notion he's to take care of you, the three of you, from this point on. And since his stomach isn't fond of traveling by way of water, I planned for him to deploy on land with a few of my men. He can help bring the horses back to London." Simon smirked. "I believe he also wishes to delay facing his auntie."

Mrs. Frumkee's frown was more than a little uneasy. "Nay, it is not appropriate for such a young woman to travel without a chaperone, least she be made to practice for marriage before her journey's end."

The elderly woman had no inclination the shifty fashion Leah had lived and dealt with these many years. Only because Langley could get a better price for Leah untouched had her virginity not been comprised.

"Nay a need to worry, Elma dear," Leah reassured. "Oliver would never allow any 'arm to threaten me." She squared her thin shoulders. "Besides, I am not a novice at takin' care o' myself."

The widow nodded reluctantly, her frown deepening. "And then what will become of you, mite?"

"When Leah arrives in London, she will be able to accompany Oliver to Glenshire Sussex. She will have a home at Collins Stead where I live with Lady Lucinda Collins," Riley added to ease the elder woman's mind, as well as her own.

With her knee injured, accompanying Leah on the ride to London by horseback wasn't an option for her. She turned to Leah. "Auntie Cinda will welcome you with open arms, Nellie and Rufus as well. Of this I am positive."

"Are ye sure, miss?" Leah replied with a hopeful gaze.

"Absolutely," she answered.

Simon's face brightened. "Splendid, then we will all be neighbors."

She frowned. "I don't quite understand."

"My family and I are moving into the smaller dwelling on the premises," Simon informed her.

She arched a brow. "I was always under the impression Lady Collins meant that piece of property for me."

"And she still does," Simon reassured her. "But until her demise, which was the time you are to take possession, Gabriel asked I occupy the smaller manor in order to keep an eye on Collins Stead in his absence."

Her heart sank to her toes. "Other than Brighton, which is only a few hours journey by train, where else would he be?" she said, her voice shakier than she liked.

"America, Miss Riley," was Simon's reply. "He plans on returning to his people as soon as his sister has her baby."

She closed her eyes and took an audible breath. Gabriel would leave England, then...and her.

I am ashamed for being so bold, for kissing him, for thinking he...

Simon neared her, his voice interrupting her thoughts. "Are you all right, miss?"

She nodded and glanced up at him. "I apologize, Captain. I am more exhausted than I thought."

"As is understandable," he said. "Then I shall leave you ladies to your rest."

Within an hour's time, she was sharing a room and a bed with Leah, snuggled wearily beneath the worn quilt keeping them warm. And while the younger woman was in a deep slumber, Riley thought further of the kiss she had coaxed from Gabriel. How could she have acted so wanton? Had she not been taught it was the man that made the first advance, and a woman must always decline? It was the way of a lady.

She grimaced. *Exactly what kind of impression did Gabriel now have of me?*

Not a very respectable one, she was sure, though Gabriel seemed to be thoroughly enjoying the whole incident as much as she.

Of course he enjoyed it...he's a man...but such a fleeting pleasure would hardly compel him to stay in England. Obviously, if he had planned to leave for America all along, his intentions were not to court me...especially now that I have appeared so indecent.

Her brows furrowed.

Though I never understood why a woman is considered indecent simply because she acts upon her heart's desire, and a man in the same position is considered suave?

Perhaps it was the severe consequences that followed an impulsive woman. Her grandmother acted upon her desires when she ran off with the gardener. In so doing, she found herself disinherited from her family's wealth and with child. She was made to live in poverty, raise her own daughter under unsafe conditions and amongst those with shady notions. In turn that child, when grown, gave herself over freely to her desires. She became with child without the bands of matrimony and died in childbirth. This was her linage, the stock from which she came. Top Hat Tom always told her she was born of proud blood, but how proud could one be if they gave in so easily to impulsive decisions?

Nay...it was love that my grandmother and mother gave in to...not sin, not debauchery, neither of them was indecent...just totally in love. But love didn't turn out so convenient for them.

She bit her bottom lip.

I understand their hearts now, because I'm in love with Gabriel. I've loved him from the moment I gazed upon his handsome face. Yet he didn't see me, his glances were set upon Collette Halston.

Just thinking of the other woman's name made her ill. She squeezed shut her eyes and pulled the quilt over her head.

Lord, help me. Even with Collette gone, he still

doesn't see my heart.

What she learned from Simon this evening made it all so very clear. Falling in love was not convenient for her as well.

And what will be my destiny now that I have given my heart to someone who will never love me in return?

****

Gabriel occupied a bunk on the steamer, the darkness closing over him like the night sky that took over for the light of day. His body cried out for release, to be able to sink into the depths of a long-needed sleep. His flesh bruised and sore, begged for the delicious unconsciousness awaiting him in slumber.

Yet his mind raced.

The kiss he shared with Riley, the wonderful and oh-so-brief uniting of their lips, had turned his outlook into another whole perspective.

For a long time, he had listened to the wind calling him home to America's shores. It summoned him now, cried for him to save his people. For many moons the doors of their homes have been too easy for the white man to enter and take what pleases them. It is time they are stopped. And now he has the financial means to put the hellish nightmare to an end.

The pale-faced intruders have awakened the sleeping spirits of his ancestors. They have mocked the legacies handed down to his people, and such disrespect has disturbed their grandfather's bones from their eternal rest. The old gray-hairs are angered at the fact the agents have encroached upon their territory, robbed and humiliated their people. Now they call out to him on the wind, beseeching his help.

He cannot...he will not...turn a deaf ear.

Yet, he cannot leave Riley either. Not now, not

after he tasted the promise of a true and honest heart.

But to ask her to come with him, leave all she knows and loves just for him, would only have her resenting such a decision put upon her over time.

He grunted and turned onto his side.

"What disturbs you, Gabriel?" Simon inquired from his bunk.

"Her kiss," he stated flatly.

"Aye, I heard about that kiss from Oliver, who heard it from Leah, who in turn heard it from Lady Wellington, who claims to have actually witnessed it," Simon teased.

"Have none of you anything better to do than gossip?"

Simon chuckled again. "It appears not." He cleared his throat. "And was it not to your liking?"

"What?" he muttered.

"The kiss," Simon probed.

"It was very much to my liking. It just does not fit well into my plans," he grumbled.

Simon chuckled. "Now you sound like my brother, Rafe. His gripe was much the same as yours when he realized he was falling in love with your sister. His jawing over the dilemma set us up talking an entire night."

"And what words of wisdom did you offer him?"

Simon spoke quietly. "I don't remember the exact words, but I do have some advice for you."

Tiredness blurred the edges of reason, but Gabriel would hear his friend's counsel anyway. "I am listening."

"I believe honesty still remains the best option, for both you and Riley. Sometimes being direct is the only way to learn what you seek. And following your heart is always the best policy." Then Simon added, "Of course, when all else fails and you see it best to just *bugger off*, giving the situation up to luck isn't a

195

bad idea. Luck is sometimes the best friend a chap can have."

Gabriel suddenly felt very old and worn, like he had crammed several lifetimes into the span of just one. In many ways he had done exactly that. "I think you have simplified things, my friend. If love were that easy, no one would have to try so hard to make it work out."

"I see exhaustion has made you more stubborn and disagreeable than usual." Simon snorted. Then the tone of his voice piqued with concern. "Don't do anything you'll regret, old chap. Love, true love, as you've just said, is hard to come by. Rare, even, I'd say as finding a convent's nun in a brothel. That's exactly why, if you believe you have found it, you must go against all odds to preserve it. Of this you must trust me. Before I fell in love with Fiona, married her and became a father, I was nothing but a shell of a man. Life...true living comes within a loving relationship, two hearts beating as one," Simon offered, rising from his bunk and lighting a lantern.

"Where do you go at this hour?" He turned to catch a glimpse of the other man's face.

"To evacuate my bowels." He rubbed a hand over his abdomen. "The day-old beans I ate for dinner is having a jolly time with my stomach."

Gabriel snickered. "A good cleaning out never hurts anyone."

Simon looked taken aback. "Are you insinuating I'm full of..."

"Not insinuating, stating a fact. It is all the tea you Brits drink. The stuff is binding, clogs me tight, right up to the ears."

Simon reached for the lantern. "Try a bit of claret, old chap. If it doesn't help that problem, it will do wonders for anything else that ails you."

"I will pass on that advice, as you must

remember how I lose my sensibility and outlook when the drink is in me," he grumbled.

"Aye, I've seen firsthand what you're about when you've got several sheets in the wind, quite embarrassing," Simon recollected. "And now, if you'll excuse my quick departure, I am in need of finding a make-shift privy, preferably an empty bucket somewhere private and out of the way from any unsuspecting noses, before I embarrass myself." With that said, he hurried, knees slightly pinched together, out the portal.

Chapter Twenty-Two

Riley's homecoming was bittersweet.

Sweet it was, upon entering Collins Stead's doors. Here she always felt safe, bathed in the warmth and love she came to rely on since Lucinda had taken her to live there. The sounds, the smells, the familiar surroundings were just what she needed after her horrendous ordeal.

Rafe and Sunny, her belly swollen with child, awaited her and Gabriel. In spite of her husband's disapproval of traveling from home when she was ready to give birth, Sunny would not remain at Bentwood once she got word of Riley's kidnapping. Their hugs and kisses reassured her of the goodness the world still held. She was a part of a family, made up of kind and trustworthy people, and within this clan she desperately wanted to always belong.

But bitter, it became, upon learning Top Hat Tom had succumbed to his injury. Elderly, and not generally in good health, the wound he suffered put an end to him.

She sat on the edge of Lucinda's bed, freshly bathed and garbed in her own clothes instead of the cotton floral dress Elma Frumkee had given her to wear when she left Lands End, and listened to her aunt's account of Tom's last moments upon the earth.

"He called for Anita a few times in his feverish haze. I know now, with the tenderness he said her name, he loved her deeply. And I have no doubts at all he summoned her to guide him to the afterlife, because he passed with a smile upon his weathered face. With a soft sigh, Tom left us peacefully," Lucinda said, taking Riley's hand and cradling it between the two of hers. "He just smiled and slipped away, moving on to somewhere much grander than anything he'd ever known here."

"I am so thankful you were with him at the end," she said.

"Aye, I would not leave his side." Lucinda sighed. "I believe no one should have to die alone."

She swallowed the tears burning the back of her throat. "He has nay a soul to worry where he rests."

Lucinda's thin lips curved into a thoughtful smile. "You need not concern yourself further on that matter, my dear. A man such as Tom, kind as he was to Anita and you, will not rest in a pauper's grave. I have arranged for him to be interred in my family's plot, beside Anita, for as you know she had nay a soul to lay her to rest as well. Services will be in a few days, after you've had time to collect yourself."

She leaned forward and hugged the elder woman. "Thank you so much, Auntie Cinda."

"And now tell me more about this young woman who helped you escape," Lucinda said, stroking Riley's hair as she'd done when she was a child.

She pulled back and told Lucinda all about Leah, what she had endured, her strength and bravery, her dog and cat. "I took the liberty of offering her a home at Collins Stead," she concluded. "I hope you won't mind too terribly. And if in time things don't work out here, I'm sure we can recommend her to another family. I believe her to be an honest and hard worker, so I wouldn't hesitate to help her have a better life than the one she presently has."

"Nonsense," Lucinda said. "We will make sure all works out, and she will stay here, be my ward as you were."

"That would be too much to ask."

"Well, you didn't ask, I offered," Lucinda stated firmly. "A young woman like your Leah sounds to me just the sort I need around here to stir these old bones of mine into living life again." She wrinkled her nose. "It seems to me it's been rather quiet as of late, everyone settled in their ways, doing the same thing over and over again. A bit of variety, noise, a dog and cat, might be just what I need, maybe what we all need, to get our circulations going again."

Riley frowned, concerned. "Just promise me you won't overdo."

"If you promise me, no matter how things might appear, you won't let Gabriel Eagle slip away," Lucinda said, raising a devilish brow. Then the elder woman cast a mischievous smile. "And with the way he kept his eyes on you throughout dinner, I'd say he's thinking of keeping you near as well."

"I wouldn't place a wager on that notion."

"Why is that child?" Lucinda asked softly.

"Mr. Eagle plans to return to America, as you must already know, since you allowed Captain Cavendish to move into the smaller manor house to keep an eye on Collins Stead during his absence."

Lucinda waved a casual hand in the air. "Oh, is that all that troubles you?"

She frowned. "I would say that is quite enough. What's more, I have it on good authority Gabriel plans on leaving England as soon as Sunny gives birth," she explained.

Before Lucinda could return a remark, a knock came at the chamber door.

"Enter," Lucinda said.

Regis peeked into the room. "Permit me if you will, my lady, for intruding upon you at such an inopportune moment, but there seems to be a bit of a commotion in the guest wing."

Lucinda frowned. "What sort of a commotion do

you speak of, Regis?"

"It concerns Mr. Cavendish and Mr. Eagle," Regis said. "Mrs. Cavendish has gone into labor, and Mr. Eagle insists upon entering her chamber." He arched a brow. "Mr. Cavendish believes this to be a preposterous request and refuses Mr. Eagle admission."

Riley stood, turning her attention to Regis. "Is Mr. Cavendish the only one tending his wife?"

"Nay, miss. Jane, Betsy, and Mrs. Cavendish's own handmaiden, Cirie, are with her as well," Regis explained.

"If you wouldn't mind instructing Addie to boil water and gather clean towels, and then send Charles for the doctor, I will address Mr. Eagle," she said.

"Very good, miss." Regis closed the door.

She cast a glance back at Lucinda. "It looks like Gabriel will be leaving a lot sooner than I realized."

Lucinda gave her a reassuring smile. "Go to *your* Mr. Eagle, Riley. Be there for him now, and I guarantee you he won't be able to forget it later."

Gabriel was far from *her* Mr. Eagle, but this was not the time to debate the issue.

"I'm sure you're right, Auntie Cinda," she said, forcing a smile of her own before she left the room.

Riley took the stairs to the guest's quarters as quickly as her injured knee would allow. Reaching the top of the steps, she paused. Gabriel, with head in hands, sat on a bench outside of Sunny's chamber. His hair, dark and shining, was unbound and fell in thick strands about his shoulders. His shirt was unbuttoned to the waist, his bronzed, muscular chest in full view, and his feet were bared.

Poor chap. He looks like he was readying himself to take his slumber.

Throughout their journey back to Collins Stead, he was quiet, preoccupied, and appeared exhausted.

Dark pockets beneath his eyes, evidence of a sleepless night, mirrored her own. They hadn't spoken of the kiss, to her relief. She had enough wits about her to recognize a fool's errand when she spotted one, that being capturing Gabriel Eagle's affections. And enough pride not to rehash her unwise decision to place her heart upon her sleeve in such a bold, unladylike manner.

He lifted his head when he heard her approach. Large, sapphire orbs, red-rimmed with fatigue and worry, locked with her concerned gaze.

"I've sent for the doctor." She moved closer.

He reached for her hand and pulled her down to sit beside him. "When I heard her scream, I tried to enter the room." His grip tightened. "Cirie, Betsy, and Jane are with her. I should be as well. But Rafe will not allow it."

"Surely you can understand, except for the doctor, the only other man present beside Sunny at such a time, should be Rafe," she whispered.

"But I am her brother, her only family," he choked out hoarsely.

"And he is her husband, the baby's father."

The muscles at his jaw throbbed. "Woman can die on their child-bed."

"Sunny isn't going to die," she reassured him, in spite of her emotions rising with the thought of her own mother dying in childbirth. But to confess her fears or agree with Gabriel's notion would only feed into his anxiety. And adding fuel to an already smoldering fire was a very unwise move. Especially since his nerves appeared tightly wound and ready to snap at any given second.

"She could, you know...my wife did," he whispered.

She took an audible breath and forced the tone of her voice to remain even. "You must not let this notion stick in your craw. Death can just as quickly come to a rider falling off a horse. Or be the result of any number of acts people perform daily. To be afraid of every move one makes does not allow for a very interesting or productive life. And to believe every woman giving birth will die would never produce the generations to follow."

His gaze upon her was so intent, Riley was sure he was taking an inventory of all the teeth in her mouth, the hairs upon her head, and the bones in her body. "Sunny is all I have here."

His devotion for his sister swelled a twinge of jealousy within her, and though it was fleeting, her actions sickened her. Was she this desperate for his love that she compared his feelings for his sister to what she wished he felt for her? "I'm sorry," she apologized. "I didn't mean to make light of your feelings or your fears. I know they are very real to you, but you must control them. They will do you, nor Sunny, little good."

A cry of pain came from Sunny's chamber.

His glare bore into the door's wood, as though he willed his sight to peer through to the other side. Then he stood, pulling her up with him. For a moment she thought he would burst into the birthing room, but instead he closed his eyes and bowed his head.

The silence now was deafening as she waited for his next move. Could she contain him? Should she even try?

Then he opened his eyes and released her hand. Moving lethargically, like a drunken slug in a garden overrun with brambles, he made his way to the window at the end of the hallway. There he stood, a proud and commanding figure, in spite of the anguish spreading through his body like poison ivy. Gazing out at the coal-hole darkness of night casting a veil over Collins Stead, he looked as though he carried the weight of the world solely upon his broad shoulders.

Her heart went out to him, and nothing at that moment, least of all her pride, mattered. She went to him, placing a hand on his arm. "How can I help you see all is well and as it should be for Sunny?" She swallowed hard the emotion rising to choke her. "After this night she will be a mother, will have the family she wanted, the family every woman hopes for."

He turned toward her, sullen, worn, and searched her face. After a lengthy reflection, he said, "And do you...do you hope for a family as well?"

She moved her hand to rest on his bared chest. His flesh was smooth, muscles rock hard. The rapid beat of his heart vibrated through her palm, as the heat from his body coursed through hers.

"Aye," she said, moistening her lips with a swipe of her tongue.

He pulled her close. "And then I would fear for you."

"Nay, there must not be any more fear or misgivings," she whispered.

He brought his lips to her forehead and placed a tender kiss there. "That is easier said, than done," was his reply.

She closed her eyes. "Then how else can I convince you? What will it take? What possible thing can I do for you to ease your heart?" Her voice broke with emotion. "Just tell me, Gabriel. Just show me and I will gladly..."

As his mouth captured hers, Riley's last words were smothered.

His kiss, slow and thoughtful, drugged her senses. Emotions whirled and skidded as he parted her lips with his tongue. She quivered, drinking in the tender and sweet way he explored her mouth. Thoughts spun, pleasure radiated, and she found herself returning his ardor with reckless abandon.

As her passion roused, his grew stronger. And he took her mouth with a savage intensity, devouring, challenging, and causing the blood to pound in her brain. Her heart leapt, knees trembled, currents of desire robbing her of all resolve.

He pulled her against him, his hands locking against her spine. The intimacy of his bared chest pressing snugly to her breasts teased her nipples. Sensational surges of delight awakened her body, and she surrendered to him, a moan of ecstasy slipping through her lips.

His embrace grew bolder, encompassing more than her waist. Her limbs trembled as she clung to him, moving her hands to his neck, conscious of where his warm flesh met hers as she buried her fingers in his thick hair.

Regis clearing his throat loudly instantly parted them.

Riley, stepping back and away from him, covered her lips with a hand.

Gabriel's face flushed under his reddish-bronzed complexion as he turned his gaze once again out the window.

"The doctor has arrived, miss." Regis tried to act as though he saw nothing.

She moved her hand to rest on her neck and cleared her throat to recover her voice. "Thank you, Regis. You may send him up immediately."

"Very good, miss," Regis said, inclining his head politely as she left.

He broke the silence, a faint tremor in his tone. "I believe you have found it."

She hoped he didn't notice the tremor in her own voice. "And what might that be?"

When he spoke again, his voice was warm. "A way to convince me."

Chapter Twenty-Three

It seemed to Gabriel, that from the time the doctor arrived and well into the night, everyone in the household was engaged in synchronized activity.

Cirie and Betsy, the upstairs maid, could be heard coaxing Sunny to push. Jane encouraged her when she did. Rafe soothed his wife with loving and caring words. Addie made frequent appearances, going to and fro with pots of hot water and armloads of towels. Regis and Lady Lucinda searched the attic for anything resembling a cradle, and when five were found, they proceeded to clean and cover them with fresh bedding for whatever use any of them might serve. Even Riley made her way into Sunny's birthing chamber, taking on the role of main organizer. She kept the others running like the cogs of a well-oiled machine. Everyone was helping in some way, playing a part, except for him, Sunny's only real blood kin.

Feeling useless and disconnected, he took several deep breaths to summon up control, as he watched all the non-stop commotion taking place. Finally, he reclaimed his seat outside his sister's room and sat quietly, silently praying.

Not long after the dark of night unveiled the flush of a pink-dawn sky did a baby's cries sound from the room.

"We've a son, Sunny," Rafe resonated joyfully.

Tears prickled his eyes.

Then all was silent.

Again a baby cried. The wailing this time softer than the first.

"And a daughter," Rafe exclaimed. "By Jove, we've got twins." His brother-in-law laughed. "Can you imagine, Sunny?"

He waited, hands clasped in his lap.

"Sunny?" Rafe said again.

He stood with his heart racing, ready to enter the room no matter what anyone said.

Then he heard his sister's voice. "Good heaven, Rafe. Your mother was right."

He flopped back down upon the bench and closed his eyes.

"She is alive. All of them are alive and well," he whispered to himself, then dropped his head in his hands and wept.

Hours passed before he was permitted to enter Sunny's room. Stiff from sitting the night upon a hard seat, he stood and stretched his spine, pacing the hallway as he waited. When Riley finally did summon him, he quickly buttoned and straightened his crumpled shirt as he followed her over the threshold.

"All is well," she whispered, reaching for his hand and giving it an affectionate squeeze.

He returned her fondness with a warm smile. "I thank you for..."

"There is nay a need," she interrupted.

But there is a need...to do much more than just thank you.

After some time was spent with Sunny and both he and Riley allowed ample rest, he would show her how much more he appreciated her presence.

"I will leave you now to have a bit of private time with your family," Riley added before closing the door behind her.

His gaze found his sister, sitting up in bed, her long golden curls fanned out over the pillows. Her face was lit with pleasant exhaustion as she held in her arms one of the newborns. Rafe, sitting at the end of the bed, his dark hair in disarray, held the other. The morning light flooded past the opened drapes, and warm beams of a new day spread over the bed's coverlet. It seemed to encompass the newly-formed family with its rays.

Sunny reached out a hand to him and smiled. "There you are."

He went to her, entwining his fingers with her delicate digits, as he struggled to control the overwhelming rise of emotions circling within him. She was alive, the babies were alive, and in that instant he felt unfettered. A sense of relief lifted his shoulders from the weight they had carried since the day he learned she was with child.

"Gabriel," she whispered, not to wake her sleeping infants. "Are they not beautiful?"

His loving glance took in the small, pink faces, sleeping peacefully in their parent's arms. "They are more than beautiful."

"Sorry, old chap," Rafe apologized, raising his gaze from the babe he held. "I meant nay an ounce of malice when I stopped you at the door. I just thought, in view of the fact my wife's modesty was in plain sight, your presence would be inappropriate."

Gabriel realized what Rafe spoke of, as he was present at his wife's childbed. He held up his free hand. "I hold no hard feelings, my brother. You made the right decision."

Rafe nodded. "When the doctor arrived, he nearly gave me the boot as well, but Sunny Beth wouldn't hear of it," he added, returning his admirations upon his child.

"Would you like to hold her, Gabriel?" Sunny said, removing her hand gently from his grasp, to caress the cheek of the infant she held.

He nodded, taking a chair from a nearby corner and bringing it beside the bed.

She waited until he sat, then held the babe out

to him.

He took the infant gently from his sister's embrace. While supporting the floppy head, he brought the babe close to his chest. Once he had held his son like this, for only a few moments many years ago. But his darling's body was lifeless, the flesh blue, his eyes shut in death not slumber. He swallowed the tears stinging the back of his throat and leaned forward to place a kiss atop the infant's head. The pale fuzz covering the small girl's skull was soft upon his lips.

"Gabriel Golden Eagle, meet your niece," Sunny announced softly.

"And this handsome gent I'm holding is your nephew," Rafe chimed in. "If I have anything to say, he will definitely not be a foppish youngster."

Gabriel glanced over at the other infant, his head capped with hair as dark as his father. "It appears each of you has a smaller version of yourself."

Sunny giggled. "It does at that, a little girl much like me, and a little boy resembling Rafe." She leaned back against the pillows. "But I understand completely now why giving birth is called labor."

"I should go, leave you to your rest," he offered.

"No, not just yet," Sunny protested with a yawn. "Do you want to hear what we have named them?"

He nodded.

"She will be called Amelia Dove, after her two great-grandmothers, Amelia Bentley Gregory and White Dove," Sunny explained. "And he will be called Peter Jerome, named for his grandfathers, Peter Proud Eagle and Jerome Cavendish."

He nodded again, remembering Peter was his father's Christian name, given to him by his grandfather, Silas Collins.

"I know Apache tradition frowns upon a child being named after the dead, fearful it will bring the child bad luck, but I wanted to honor those no longer with us," she clarified.

"And so history will repeat itself as another Amelia will live now at Bentwood," Rafe concluded.

"And I hope she has just as much of a sense for adventure as her great-grandmother," Sunny said, beaming with pride as she looked over at her tiny daughter. "If it were not for Amelia's spirit, our own dear mother might have been born in England, instead of America. Think about it, my brother. If that had happened, she would not have met and married our father." She frowned. "And although we would be somebody, we would not be the people we are."

"Good heaven, I perish the thought," Rafe teased.

"Well, it is true," Sunny said, raising a defiant chin.

Gabriel chuckled lightly, still seeing in his sister's mannerisms a trace of the little girl she once was. "Ah *dayden*, I can see you as no other then who you are, and the winds of fate realized this fact. All balance, I am sure, would have been disturbed if otherwise happened."

"Aye, I agree. It would have been an atrocious injustice, especially for me," Rafe said, casting his wife a mischievous grin.

Sunny blushed, returning her husband's playfulness with a demure smile. "You need to always keep that in mind my *shikaa*."

Gabriel stifled a smirk. His sister's use of the Apache word meaning *husband* sounded much like his mother. Golden Lady is able to get whatever she wishes from Proud Eagle with a soft smile and a bat of an eyelash. He always admired his parent's marriage, the way they had defied all odds to be together. And now he was happy for the love his sister and Rafe shared. But seeing the joys of such a close bond made his empty heart yearn all the more for the same relationship in his own life. He had it once, but all too quickly, it was snatched from him. Would he ever find it again?

"You are...we all are who we're supposed to be and doing what we're made to do," Rafe philosophized further.

Gabriel looked at little Amelia snuggled in his arms. "And doing the best we can with what we have."

"I wish Mother and Father could see my babies," Sunny said.

He raised his gaze to see her large blue eyes suddenly growing moist.

Rafe, the protective husband that he is and the first to admit he cannot stand to see his wife cry, immediately reached out a comforting hand to her. "When they are older, we will take them to America."

Sunny smiled through her tears. "Do you promise?"

"Aye, *shi'aad*, that I do," Rafe responded softly.

Gabriel liked Rafe's attempt at speaking their family's language. His Apache use of the word for *my wife* pleased Sunny, and she brought his hand to her lips, bestowing a small kiss on his thumb. "*Ashoge,* thank you," she said.

"*A he ya ch*, you are welcome," Rafe replied slowly, careful with the pronunciation of each syllable.

She giggled. "Your British accent makes the Apache language sound strange, but nevertheless, my parents would be proud of your efforts." Then she turned to Gabriel. "I have been dreaming of them more than usual."

He nodded. "I have strongly felt them as well."

She frowned. "Do you think anything is wrong, my brother?"

He hesitated, wanting to speak the right words. The last thing he wanted was to upset his sister. After all she has been through this night, revealing his apprehensions and fears would not be wise. Neither would it be right to announce his departure from England. There was time enough in the days to come to explain his decision. "I think they are just missing us as much as we are missing them," he lied.

"Then we must definitely send them a wire about the births," Rafe said, trying to lighten his wife's spirits. "In that way they can share our happiness."

Sunny's face brightened. "Oh, Rafe, that is a wonderful idea. You always know just what to say, just what to do to ease my heart."

Rafe gazed deep into her eyes. "I pray you always cherish my efforts, Sunny Beth."

"When will you send the wire?" she asked.

"First thing come morning," Rafe vowed.

"It is already morning."

"Then first thing after we've all rested," he returned.

"Which none of us will do if I remain," Gabriel added. He stood, returning Amelia to her mother's arms.

"Wait, Gabriel," she said, reaching for his hand. "What happened when you asked Collette to marry you?"

"Aye, with all that's happened, we never heard," Rafe inquired further.

"She flatly refused me," Gabriel said.

Sunny's eyes softened with pity. "I am so sorry."

He shrugged. "I am better off without her, *dayden*. You were right from the beginning. Collette Halston is not the woman for me." He arched a brow. "I do not believe she is the woman for any man."

"There is a woman for you, Gabriel," Sunny said

212

in a hopeful tone. "It is just a case of you finding her."

He smiled. "I believe I might have already found her."

Sunny returned his smile with a large one of her own. "Could it be Riley that you speak of?"

He tweaked her nose. "It could be."

"Sit and tell me everything," she urged.

"Another time, when we are all more rested," he advised.

Rafe chuckled softly. "And now you realize, of course, she won't sleep a wink for wondering."

"It is true, my brother," Sunny added.

"I need time to figure it all out myself, *dayden*. So, you will just have to wait." He bent down and bestowed a brotherly kiss upon her forehead. "Now, rest," he whispered before turning to leave the room.

Once in his own chamber, he flopped upon the bed. Too exhausted to remove even a stitch of clothing, he raised his arms above his head and closed his eyes. With stillness finally surrounding him, he was able to relive Riley's kiss. Swiping his tongue across his lips, he could still taste her sweetness, feel the warmth and softness of her mouth upon his. Her kiss did more than quench his thirst. It fed his hunger, satisfied his deepest longings and filled an urgent desire for true affection he craved for so long. Though the fusing of their lips took place only in a matter of moments, it expanded to a lifetime in his mind. The sort of lifetime he wanted...needed...prayed for.

The scent of her was caught in the fiber of his clothes, and he could not help but wonder how it would be to have her forever by his side. The soundless empty void he carried around within since his wife's death would finally be filled.

Riley was so much more suited to his spirit and his traditions then he ever dreamed she could be, and it thrilled him. In a true sense, she risked social disapproval by showing her intentions toward him first, much like a maiden would do a man in his tribe. An Apache woman did not stand on the same protocol as English-born women and made the first move in the courting ritual by taking part in the marriage dance.

A maiden would dance around the circle made up of unmarried women and men, and then stop in front of the warrior she loved. With a slight slap upon his cheek, she would make her preference clear. If he accepted, he would set himself back from the circle. Within a week's time, he would structure a path of stones for her to walk down in an area she frequented most, like the place she went to wash her clothes. Then he would hide. When she used the path, he would jump from his hiding place and take her to his wickiup.

At that point she would cook for him, saddle his horse for him, and share his home, but not his bed. Only after her parents accepted his gifts of beads, blankets, and other trinkets he brought them would she be his wife.

Just as he contemplated how and where he would construct a path of stones for Riley, a commotion could be heard downstairs. Reluctantly, he rose from his bed and made his way to the lower floor.

In the foyer he found Addie hugging, kissing, and making an all-around fuss over Oliver. Leah stood quietly beside him, her eyes brimming with tears as she witnessed the family reunion taking place.

He held out a hand in greeting to the younger man. "Good to see you made it home."

Oliver beamed, returning the gesture. "Aye, finally we are 'ere."

"And ye must be Leah that we've 'eard so much

about," Addie said, reaching out to take the younger woman's hand. "I thank ye for 'elping save Miss Riley's life."

Leah blushed, wiping a tear with the back of her free hand. "Ye are most welcome, Mum."

"If yer going to be livin' 'ear, mite, then ye must learn to call me, Addie," the older woman advised.

"Or perhaps I could call ye Auntie," Leah shyly suggested.

Addie giggled. "I can't see the 'arm in it."

"Well, in a sense ye're 'er auntie, now."

Addie's smile faded. "What are ye tryin' to tell me?"

"I married 'er on the way 'ome," Oliver blurted out, his own face beaming.

With mouth agape, Addie's face paled. It was the first time Gabriel ever witnessed the elderly woman stuck for words, and it worried him.

"I am 'onered to be a part of yer fine family, Mum," Leah quickly added, looking concerned for Addie's silence as well.

Addie's shocked gasp and wavering balance brought Gabriel closer.

"Aren't ye going to congratulate us, Auntie?" Oliver continued, "I'm a married man now."

Bracing himself, Gabriel reached around behind Addie and caught her just before she hit the floor. "Ah, yes, I had a feeling this was coming."

Leah's hand went to her throat. "Oh, mercy, Oliver, what 'ave ye done to the poor woman?"

Gabriel gathered Addie's limp, plump form into his arms. "I would say, Oliver, you might have finally found a way to get out of a beating."

"Or get us both one," Leah groaned, as she and Oliver followed Gabriel to the library.

Chapter Twenty-Four

Riley watched Tom's coffin being lowered into the grave. With the slight breeze of the cool autumn day veering her way, she caught the scent of the white carnations placed around the site. Up until now she hadn't cried. Tom would not have liked her to grieve for him in such a way. And so her heart ached with the pain of unshed tears.

Reverend Holmes traveled from Brighton to give a final blessing, his words comforting. Tom was a good and decent man, loving and kind. She had nay a doubt in her mind his soul would find it difficult to enter heaven, a much happier home than he ever had on earth.

Oliver, standing to her right with an arm around his new bride, was the only other person who knew Top Hat as she did. The two were good friends, and the pain on Oliver's face proved just how much Tom would be missed.

Gabriel stood to her left, his warm, muscular arm drawing her close. She leaned against him, resting her head on his shoulder. A clean, citrus scent crept from the folds of his shirt, engulfing her senses. Her thoughts swirled with excitement, as though a tempest had gone through it. In spite of her heart grieving for the death of Tom, it was also very much aware of the living, breathing man standing beside her. She squeezed shut her eyes to clear her head of anything other than the situation at hand.

I must stop being so selfishly oblivious to what matters now.

"Riley, did you wish to say a few words?"

Reverend Holmes inquired, interrupting her thoughts.

She opened her eyes to find Oliver, Leah, Addie, Jane, and Charles staring her way. All of them waited for her to speak.

She raised her head from Gabriel's solid, brawny shoulder and glanced down at the casket that held her friend's remains. Tom's death was her fault. Had she not tried to meet the man claiming to be her father, none of what happened would have taken place. Naomi would still be alive as well. Those unshed tears now trickled down her wind-chilled cheeks, trailing a hot path into her flesh.

"I am sure Tom will understand if it pains you too much to speak," Gabriel whispered.

She gazed up into the sapphire blue of his eyes. "Nay, I need...I want to say something."

He nodded in agreement.

Glancing back at the grave, she began, "It is with a heavy heart I say farewell to a dear and loyal friend. If it weren't for his bravery, I would not be here today with my friends and family. Neither would Lady Wellington or Leah. It is only because Tom fought death long enough to send help our way that we were all saved. And yet, it pains me greatly to realize I am the cause for his demise. If it weren't for my foolish notion,"—her voice caught on a sob— "the hope that I would finally meet my father, Tom would still be here with us."

"Nay, 'e would never blame ye," Oliver said softly, reaching out to briefly grip her arm.

"Ye 'ad nay a way o' knowin', Miss Riley," Leah added, tears streaking down her pale, thin face.

Riley pulled a hanky from the cuff of her sleeve and dabbed at her eyes with it. "I am so very sorry, Tom. I ask for your forgiveness and pray you rest happily at the bosom of the Lord."

"Amen," Reverend Holmes said.

"Amen," the others repeated simultaneously.

Riley bent to retrieve two carnations from the bouquet nearest her. She tossed the first flower into Tom's grave and placed the other beside Anita's headstone.

"Amen," she whispered, as she glanced down at the resting places where the only parents she'd ever known would sleep for eternity.

****

Gabriel found Joshua Holmes, alone, standing at the library's hearth and warming himself by the fire. He turned to face Gabriel, upon hearing his approach, and smiled. "There's nothing like the heat of a fire to bring comfort to the bones."

He nodded and took a seat nearby. "The fire pit at home is a welcomed place."

"I remember it well." Josh claimed a seat. "You must miss its warmth."

He nodded again. "I do, and all those who sit around it."

"I am no stranger to knowing how it feels to be so far from home," Josh empathized. "At least you have your sister with you." He smiled. "And a niece and nephew as well."

"Sunny and Rafe have a beautiful family, as do Raven and Lord Shannon." Gabriel sat back in the chair. "I expect any day to receive word of their new babe."

"Aye, Proud Eagle and Amanda's family is growing," Josh reflected.

"At least by way of Raven and Sunny."

The reverend searched his face. "I am sorry for your loss, for all you endured. I have never been blessed with a wife and children, but if I had, and then lost them..."

"It is a sorrow, a pain no one can begin to imagine unless he has lived through it."

"I don't doubt that for a moment," Josh agreed.

"Forgive me if it sounded as though I was making light of the situation."

A stony silence enveloped the room as Gabriel gathered his thoughts. "I have deliberately sought you out today because I need your counsel. There is an answer to a question I believe only a man of your calling can supply."

Josh crossed his arms over his chest. "I will give it my best try."

"I am very happy for my sisters and the love they have found. I know well how wonderful it is to have your heart swell with such feelings for another." He leaned forward in his seat. "I experienced those same feelings once, and when it was gone, I thought I would never find it again."

"And were you ready to settle for never finding love again?" Josh probed.

"I believe I was, at first, because no woman could ever be to me as my wife was," he explained. "No one could ever replace her."

The reverend took an audible breath. "I understand your feelings completely."

"And then I felt falling in love again was dishonorable, a disloyal thing to do," he went on. "But life is..."

"Too long and too lonesome to live it alone." Josh's empathy obviously stemmed from a similar experience.

Gabriel hesitated before speaking further, remembering the reverend once loved Golden Lady. *Or did he still?*

Many times he and Sunny discussed the matter, as the holy man's past affections for their mother was not a secret. His sister believed Josh's love had never died, and that he still carried Golden Lady in his heart. Gabriel refused to entertain such notion at the time, and now that prospect caused him to shift uneasily in his seat. His mother belonged to his father, and that fact was a solid conclusion that would never change. Knowing another man loved her as well was disturbing.

"What was the question you thought I could answer?" Josh asked, bringing Gabriel from his thoughts.

He stifled the bothersome feelings he conjured within and cleared his throat. "My mother often read to us before bed from the holy book, so we were well schooled in her beliefs as well as the traditional Apache spiritualisms. She painted a very clear picture of heaven for us; one whereby we fully understood how our spirit would live on after it left our body. And we marveled over the thought that we would be able to see again all those souls that had departed from this plain, to live eternally with them in the afterlife."

"Aye, that is the way of it," Josh agreed.

"Then, I will one day meet up with my wife and son?"

"Well, it is a bit more complicated, I'm afraid."

He frowned. "What complicates it?"

"Obviously, to enter Christ's Kingdom, you must believe in Christ and that He is the Son of God sent to die for our sins," Josh enlightened. "Otherwise, what would be the point of you being in heaven?"

"My wife did believe in my mother's God. She was baptized by Reverend Ben six months before she gave birth to our child. And before my son died, the holy man baptized him as well," he said.

"Then both of them wait now for the day when you will join them. They've gone on ahead to make a place for you in Paradise," the reverend explained with a happy assurance.

Gabriel's frown deepened. "But what if I should at some point in my life decide to remarry and have children?"

"If your new family believes in Christ, they will

also follow you into Paradise," Josh said.

Gabriel arched a brow. "Oh, I cannot imagine my afterlife being much of a Paradise, then."

Josh cocked his head sideways. "Why is that?"

"If you knew my wife, you would not need to ask. She would never share me with another woman."

The reverend threw his head back and burst into hardy laughter.

Agitated, Gabriel combed his fingers through his hair. "I see nothing amusing about this, Reverend."

"On the contrary, this is the best laugh I've had in quite some time," Josh relayed through his mirth.

He stood and paced the room, his brow creasing in a thunderous frown. "That is because you will not be the one standing between two angry women."

Josh pulled a handkerchief from his pocket and struggled to speak the words, "Neither will you," while he wiped the tears of hilarity streaming down his cheeks.

He stopped pacing and gazed at the reverend quizzically. "What...you think my soul too sullied to make it into Paradise?"

Josh struggled a moment for composure. "I haven't a clue as to how sullied your soul is. And whether or not you enter into heaven is between you and your Maker. But the fact that the Lord's Kingdom is referred to as Paradise, don't you think all will be fine once you're there...whether with two wives or not?"

"You are the expert in this matter, so you tell me," he relied curtly.

"Dwelling in heaven will not be like life here on earth," Josh explained. "There will be no jealousy, hate, vengeance, or anger. Affairs with other souls will be different than the ones we have with each other now."

"Are you saying we will all get along?" he said.

"Aye, that we will," Josh concurred. "Like one

big, happy family, our mission only to love Christ and share the many rooms of His home."

Gabriel smiled, relieved. "Then I do not have to remain alone forever."

"Nay, you are free to love again, thus why the marriage vow only binds until death doth do part the couple wed," the reverend expounded. "So you'd better not tarry any longer in asking the lady to marry you."

He crossed his arms over his chest. "And what lady do you speak of, Reverend?"

Josh stifled a smile. "Why, Miss Riley Flanders, of course."

Chapter Twenty-Five

The last month found Collins Stead anything but in its normal, tranquil state. Where before, the halls of the old mansion were quiet and calm; now they bustled with constant activity. And it seemed all the visitors were of one family circle.

There was Lady Kaylena Bentley-Wade, Gabriel and Sunny's aunt, who came by at least three times to see her new great-great niece and nephew. Along with Kaylena came her husband, Lord Morgan Wade, who was Fiona Cavendish's father. So, their visit was two-fold, as they also made a stop at Collins Stead's smaller mansion, where Lord Wade's daughter and family now lived.

Rafe's parents, Jerome and Marietta Cavendish, couldn't be outdone. As new grandparents, they too stopped by frequently to enjoy the two tiny additions to their family. And since their eldest son, Simon and his family, also dwelled on the estate, they'd pay a visit to them as well.

Reverend Joshua Holmes, brother to Marietta, uncle to Simon and Rafe, and an old friend of Sunny and Gabriel's family, came to perform Top Hat Tom's burial, and stayed on for a few days in case an emergency baptism needed to be performed. Though the infants were of low birth weight, which was not unusual for twins, they remained in good health and survived the first crucial weeks of their lives. Therefore, a baptismal ceremony would be officially performed, with family present and a large dinner to follow, in a month.

And then there was Lord and Lady Abbott. The

Abbots were friends of Sunny and Gabriel. All four met while traveling aboard the ship bound to England from America. Lady Eugenia Abbott was also Lord Morgan Wade's sister.

Nay, life was certainly not as it usually was at Collins Stead. With all the company, and the servants they brought along to tend them, the mansion's staff was pulled quite thin with their new duties.

Thus the very reason Riley took to dressing herself and doing up her own hair, since Jane was busy most mornings with other responsibilities. It wasn't really an issue, as she'd not been brought up in the genteel manner and could tend to her own needs sufficiently. She did what she could to help lighten the load for others as well.

On this bright morning, Riley quickly performed her usual toilet so she could spend the early hours, as she'd done every morning for several weeks, helping a very frustrated Sunny with the newborn twins.

Sunny had griped, only after the third day of her labors, about remaining in bed. "I do not understand the sense of staying bed-bound for this amount of time. An Apache woman never lingers this long. The next day she is up and about, taking her duties lightly, but nevertheless, not confined to bed."

"Where I grew up women were up and about shortly after giving birth as well," she'd confided. "But it is the fashion of the wealthy to remain at rest for a number of days, sometimes longer."

Sunny's lower lip protruded out into a pout. "Well, I am perfectly fine and do not want to be bathed, fed, and use a basin to relieve myself, all while lying in bed." She took an audible breath. "Though I love being at Collins Stead and appreciate the kind and caring hospitality my family has been shown, I want to be in my own home, be able to put my babies to bed in the room that awaits them there, and start living life again."

Riley couldn't blame her friend and sympathized with her predicament. "I understand your feelings, but a few more days will only benefit your health as well as the infant's, which will allow all of you to travel much better." She smiled. "Besides, I love holding them."

It was the truth. Every time she held little Peter or Amelia, her heart was filled with such a loving warmth, she was sure she'd burst with joy. And when she'd place one in Sunny's arms to feed, she yearned for a child of her own to suckle at her breasts.

Bringing her thoughts back to the present, she finished buttoning her blouse and tackled the tangled mess of her wild, ginger-colored hair. As her reflection peered back at her from her vanity mirror, she couldn't help but think how much she wanted Gabriel's child.

And, oh that he would look upon me while I nursed his babe with the same admiration and love that Rafe holds in his eyes, when he gazes upon Sunny.

She sighed, as she pulled the comb through her thick tresses and reached for a few pins to secure a bun at the nape of her neck. To be a part of a family and share such love and closeness was all that circled her thoughts as of late. It seemed to Riley every young woman at Collins Stead experienced the pleasure she sought.

Fiona Cavendish was fully and completely doted upon by her husband, Simon. Riley, one morning standing at her bedroom window, caught a glimpse of the captain's affection toward his wife as the couple made their way to the main house. Beneath the purpling-blue of a sky laced with fluffy white clouds, Simon held his wife's hand, shared a secret with her that brought on a fit of the giggles, and even gave her a peck upon the cheek. The news, a few days ago, that Fiona was expecting a second child in six months made for an excuse to have a celebration dinner. The dining room table was set with Lucinda's best china, and an array of delicious food and wine graced each plate and goblet.

Leah and Oliver, the resident newlyweds, had also been given a celebration dinner. Leah's thin, pale cheeks blushed with delight at Oliver's display of affection. With a kiss upon her hand, an arm around her waist and the center of her new husband's admiring and appreciative gaze, Leah seemed to be floating on a cloud.

Jane was also in love. Charles had finally proposed, and the two planned to be married in the spring. When Riley came downstairs late one night to fetch a warm mug of milk, she caught the two sitting at the kitchen table, heads together and smiles bright as they shared their day.

Even Rufus, Leah's cat, found a mate. Lulu, the stable-dwelling feline, caught Rufus's eye, and Riley had no doubt the place would soon be swarming with kittens.

Though she was happy love was in the air at Collins Stead, Riley couldn't help feeling a twinge of envy. She had shared two wonderful and extraordinary kisses with Gabriel, experiencing his favorable response in return. Yet in spite of this and the fact his eyes were constantly watching her, he never declared a single word for a future together.

His silence on such matters stemmed from the fact he planned to leave England...return to America and his people. No doubt his departure would be soon, since he was only waiting for his sisters to have their babies.

Sunny's children were born weeks ago without complications, and only three days prior word came from Limerick, Ireland. Raven gave birth to a daughter, naming the child Amanda Maureen. Mother and baby were doing fine. So, Gabriel had no reason to stick around.

And yet he did.

What could she take from that? Was he biding his time, or did he believe she would not want to leave England?

She rose from the dressing table chair and stepped to the window. Looking out to the grounds below, she remembered the first night she spent at Collins Stead. Scared, missing Anita, she curled up on the window seat and gazed out at the same scene that met her glances now. What would she have done if Lucinda hadn't taken her in?

She closed her eyes, not wanting to even imagine what would have become of her; a nine year old girl, alone on London's streets. But as grateful as Riley was for Lucinda, loving the elder woman with all her heart, she was not a blood relative. All her real kinfolk were dead. And now that the Cavendish's took over the smaller mansion meant for her, and Leah was there to fuss over Lucinda, would she really be missed all that much at Collins Stead?

She sighed.

Nay, I think not.

Her heart leapt at the prospect of a new adventure, a new life with someone she loved.

Oh, Gabriel, I would go to the end of the earth with you. If you would just ask, you'll see how agreeable I can be. Just try and see, Gabriel, just try and see.

She opened her eyes and returned to the mirror, smoothing aside one stray tendril of hair before she made her way to Sunny's chamber.

She found Sunny out of bed, standing by the window. Her long blonde curls fell to her waist, and her arms were crossed over her chest, as she gazed up at the morning sky.

Riley reached for the robe at the foot of the bed and draped it over her friend's shoulders. "You're sure to catch a chill standing like this, barefoot and in just a nightgown, by this drafty window."

"I am fine," Sunny said, turning to face Riley. "I knew you would be here soon, so I sent Cirie off for our breakfast, and I quickly snuck away to the bathing room." She frowned. "I refuse to do my business any longer sitting on a bed pot." Her eyes moistened. "It is so frustrating the way everyone is treating me like I was made out of glass, like those crystal goblets of Lucinda's, and I cannot stand much more."

"Come, love," Riley coaxed, escorting Sunny to the edge of the bed. "They only have your best interest at heart."

"I know, and I do not mean to sound ungrateful," Sunny whispered.

She found the other woman's slippers and knelt to slide each one upon a delicate foot. "Why, your feet are like ice bricks," she noticed, standing to take Sunny by the hand and leading her to a chair by the fire.

Sunny sat back in the armchair and allowed Riley to cover her legs with a throw. "You are way too good to me, my friend."

She smiled, giving Sunny's hand an affectionate squeeze before moving to stand beside the two cradles. "And how are our little angels today?"

"You would not think them angels if you heard how they scream for food at all hours of the night," Sunny quipped in an exhausted tone. "When one is done, the other begins."

Looking down at each sleeping babe, Riley smiled adoringly. "Well, they seem content enough at present."

"They have nothing to be discontented about. Well, not for at least two hours, that is," Sunny added. "They have been fed, burped, changed, and fussed over by both of their parents since the sun came up, as well as coddled and cherished by Cirie, Betsy, Jane, and now you." She laughed softly. "You are looking at a pair of much-pampered infants."

"Aye, we're going to make spoiled mites of them for sure," she teased.

Sunny bit her bottom lip. "How am I ever to take care of them when I get home?"

Riley took a seat in a nearby chair. "Well, you will not be alone. There will be Cirie to help, and of course a nurse will be hired, along with a nanny."

Sunny's eyes widened with horror. "No, I will never hire a nanny. My children will not be subject to such cruelty."

Leaning forward in her seat, she reached for Sunny's hand. "What frightens you so about hiring a nanny?"

"I heard what a nanny is like from Aunt Kaylena," Sunny said. "They are dreadful to children. Aunt Kaylena's nanny punished her severely for the slightest mistake. She told me all about how she was dragged to her room and after her bloomers were removed, made to bend over a chair. Then she was whipped until her bare-backside was welted and raw." She shivered. "I would never allow anyone to unleash such a humiliating and harsh punishment upon my children."

"Not all nannies are so vile," she said. "My own was a sweet-faced young woman who never laid a mean hand upon me. She taught me songs, took me shopping, and read me stories before bed."

"You were fortunate to have a nice nanny." Sunny frowned. "But how can you tell which ones are nice, and which are not?"

"First you hire the service of a reputable

company. Then you and Rafe will conduct a lengthy interview to each applicant, go over their credentials, and talk to all their references before either of you make a decision," she explained.

Sunny's frown deepened. "I know absolutely nothing about what you speak."

"Trust me when I say you will learn fast enough. But if you like, I can help," she offered.

Sunny's face brightened. "Would you really, Riley?"

"Aye, of course I would," she said, looking again over the side of a cradle closest to her seat. "I would never stand for Peter and Amelia to be abused or frightened in any way."

Sunny searched Riley's face. "That is good to hear, especially since I have a very important favor to ask."

She smiled reassuringly. "You know I would do most anything I could for you and your family."

Sunny nodded. "You have been like a sister to me, and I am so blessed to have you in my life."

Riley's eyes welled with emotion. "I feel the same toward you."

"I have already asked Simon and Fiona to be little Peter's godparents at the baptism in a few days. And graciously they have agreed," Sunny added. "But I would like you and Gabriel to be godparents to Amelia."

Her heart filled with joy. "Really, Sunny?"

Sunny giggled. "Yes, really. There is no one else I would consider."

She stood and embraced the other woman. "Never fear. I will be the best godmother to Amelia."

Sunny giggled again, returning the affection. "I have no doubts about it. And my brother will also be pleased to share this honor with you."

Riley pulled back to look at Sunny. "I am the one to be honored. If not for Gabriel, I could be somewhere far away, being made to do..."

"Do not speak of such things," Sunny interrupted. "You are here where you belong...with Lucinda, with me, and with Gabriel."

She reclaimed her seat and looked down at the hands she now clasped in her lap. "Well, with you and Lucinda, at least."

"And with Gabriel as well," Sunny insisted.

"Nay, I think not," she whispered.

"Well, you think wrong then."

She raised her gaze to meet Sunny's. "What are you saying?"

"My brother has spoken to me about his feelings for you. He marvels over the way you have shown your affection for him, made your heart known as the women in our tribe do to the men." She cocked her head sideways. "Do you not remember me telling you of the Apache courting tradition?"

"Aye, I remember very well," she said, a twinge of hope filling her heart. "The maiden chooses her mate at a ceremonial dance, lightly taps his face, and if he sits apart from the circle, he has accepted."

Sunny nodded. "Then a few days later, he will go to a place she frequents and places a path of stones. If she walks down the path then she has agreed to go with him to his home, where she will cook his meals and saddle his horse, but not sleep in his bed." She smiled. "Not, that is, until he brings gifts to her family. And when they accept those gifts, then she is his wife."

Riley's face warmed. "Surely not all of that exact ritual is appropriate here."

"Maybe not, but you have made the first step when you kissed my brother after your rescue," Sunny reminded.

She cleared her throat. "He told you about that?"

Sunny nodded again, arching a mischievous brow. "And now, all I can say is watch for the stone path."

Riley stood and made her way to the window. Her heart raced as she looked out onto the grounds. "I don't think that stone path is mine to walk, Sunny."

"Do you think this way because Gabriel plans on returning to America?" Sunny said.

She turned to face her. "Then he's told you?"

"Yes, he has told me," Sunny said.

"And how does that set with you?" she probed.

"Although I will miss him with every inch of my heart, I do know Gabriel has to do what he believes is right." Sunny took an audible breath. "I also know that if Rafe had to leave England to do something he believed in, I would not hesitate to go with him. I love him beyond words." She shrugged. "Where else is there that I would want to be, or that I would belong, if it were not beside him?"

Riley whispered, "Where else would you be, indeed."

"Then you will go with him when he asks for your hand?" Sunny asked with a hopeful tone.

"He has not asked," she said, afraid to allow such a magnificent hope to fill her own heart. "And I don't think he..."

"But when he does ask, will you go?" Sunny ignored the protest and insisted further.

She frowned. "You only guess he will ask."

"But when he does ask, will you go?" Sunny repeated more firmly this time.

"Aye," she said with a sigh. "I will go." Her eyes filled with tears. "Most definitely, I will go."

Chapter Twenty-Six

The morning dawned in fog. As the thick and gloomy mist enveloped Collins Stead, a cold wind blew in from the north. But in spite of the bleak weather brewing outside, Sunny was in high spirits inside. She beamed as she sat across from her brother at the breakfast table.

"Do you realize this is the first day in a month I am wearing clothes?" Sunny smoothed down her skirt with a gentle stroke.

"And for once you do not look like you mind all that goes on beneath," Gabriel teased.

"I was referring to the day clothes," she corrected, a light blush washing her cheeks.

"Ah, yes. You were beginning to remind me of the little girl I used to know who fought with her mother to get out of her bedclothes each day," he playfully reminisced.

"That was different," she said, taking a sip of tea from a blue china cup.

He supposed it was, and so long ago. Yet, at times he felt it was only yesterday the golden-haired young woman before him was a small girl.

He could see her so clearly, lilting to and fro on tiny bared feet, and could almost hear his parent's exasperated tone as they admonished her for touching other's belongings. She was overly curious, inquisitive at every turn and had the energy of five more like her all stored up in one. She would climb into his bed when she was frightened, cuddling in the crook of his arm. In those moments he knew he would die protecting her if need be.

I still would.

She begged him to tell her stories, told on him to his parents, looked up to him, bossed him, manipulated him, idolized him, stood by him, and loved him with the fierce loyalty only blood kin could.

"And I cannot tell you how good it is to actually be out of that bed," she said, breaking through his thoughts.

"Oh, I am sure being pampered day and night, having your slightest whim answered, was pure torture," he teased.

"Being pampered and being treated like an invalid are two entirely different things," she said, raising a defiant chin. "Do not tell me it would not drive you crazy."

Gabriel chuckled again. "When sick, I have never been a good patient."

"But I was not sick. I was just having a baby...well, two babies."

He grew serious. "A woman giving birth is no light matter, *dayden.*"

She searched his face in silence, then stood and made her way beside him. With child-like affection she wrapped her arms around his neck and rested her cheek upon his forehead. "I did not mean to sound so callous, my brother."

Gabriel placed a hand on her arm. "If I lost you too..."

"But you did not lose me, or Raven, who has two children. So, you need to stop worrying," she consoled. "You need to make your peace and find acceptance in what happened in the past, or else you will never discover true happiness."

He took an audible breath. "I suppose you speak the truth, but it is easier said than done."

Sunny kissed his forehead. "You must try, or how else will you ever be able to have a family of your own one day?"

"Perhaps I will not," he said softly.

"Well, you certainly will not unless you get to work placing the stones," she warned.

He pulled back to gaze up into the delicate features of her face. She was so much like his mother, with the high cheekbones and slanted sapphire eyes. "None of this is any of your business."

"Your happiness is very much my business," she said, a small frown creasing her brow.

"I am going to find your husband and tell him he needs to properly keep you occupied so you will stop bothering me," he quipped.

Sunny folded her arms across her chest. "You are a pig-head."

At that moment Cirie came into the room. "Excuse me, mum, but Master Peter is awake."

Sunny pointed a finger at him. "This conversation is not finished."

"I say it is." He stifled a smile.

As she made her way out of the room, she called over her shoulder, "And I say it is not."

He shook his head and whispered to himself, "Sometimes little sisters never change."

****

Riley found Gabriel at the dining table, sitting in thoughtful silence and sipping from a mug. She knew the brew was coffee because other than a good brandy, he shied away from drinking much else. She filled a cup of tea for herself from the pot atop the sideboard before joining him. Making a gesture to the empty chairs around the table, she said, "And so what have you said to clear away the others?"

He smiled, his large sapphire eyes locking with hers. "It seems other than you and Sunny, everyone else is too busy to join me."

She looked around. "And where is Sunny?"

"She just left to feed her son," he explained.

"Aye, the duties of motherhood," she said with a sigh.

He nodded. "One babe can be demanding enough. I cannot imagine the responsibility of having two infants at the same time. Sunny will be spending most of her time just feeding them."

"Aye," she agreed. "But I've had a talk with her about hiring a nurse and a nanny."

Gabriel arched a brow. "You might as well have saved your breath on the matter of hiring a nanny."

Riley took a sip of tea. "Sunny's already expressed her fears to me, due to the horror stories your Aunt Kaylena shared on nanny-tactics. Sunny believes all nannies dole out harsh and humiliating discipline."

"And did you set her fears straight?" He reached for the plate of scones and offered her one.

She accepted with a gracious nod and filled her own plate with two of the pastries. "I have tried, but Sunny is a...well, she's a bit..."

"Stubborn."

She frowned. "I was going to say willful."

He chuckled. "Then you would have been overly kind."

"You mustn't think such about your sister," she scolded.

"You have not seen Sunny with the eyes I have. She was a mischievous child, cunning as well as she was cute. Being the youngest, she got away with much more than Raven or I ever did." He smiled. "She had my father wrapped around her little finger. He would always try his best to please her, to please us all."

"How wonderful for her to have been so loved by her father, and for you to have all those family memories," she said softly.

"And do you have none of Anita?" He sat back in his chair.

"Aye, I do, but the happy times were few and far between." She held up a finger. "Now, mind you, it wasn't because Anita treated me harshly that the good times were scarce. She gave me everything that was humanly possible to give. It was just that we were so terribly poor and so horribly caught up in a circumstance that was too difficult to escape from. I was always cold, and hungry, and afraid of my surroundings, and Anita hated that, but there was not much she could do about it." She paused. "I often think how sad she must have felt to know her very best was not anything much at all."

He reached out and covered her hand with his. "I promise you, you will never be cold, hungry, or afraid again." He squeezed her hand lightly. "I am here for you now."

The warmth of his touch circulated through her entire body. In spite of the fact that at any second she'd turn into the consistency of butter, melting in a puddle at his feet, she had to have clarification for his declaration. "And how will you be here for me, Gabriel?"

Her bold question momentarily stunned him. "Do you doubt my words to you?"

"Nay, I would never doubt anything you say, for I know you and Sunny to be as truthful and honorable as the day is long." She squared her shoulders. "But I need you to make your intentions clearer." She cast her gaze aside. "I know I was not born a genteel woman, but I still deserve a man's respect."

He brought her hand up to his lips, kissed her knuckles and then placed her palm over his heart. Beneath her touch, it raced.

"Look at me, Riley," he said.

She shifted her gaze and met his, the heat of his glance penetrating to her core.

"I never want you out of my sight," he confessed,

his tone as soft as velvet. "And by that I mean I want always for us to be together. But I need you to be patient with me." He took an audible breath. "First, I must get my own thoughts straightened out, know what is right for me to do, before I can make the proper decision for the future."

The long silence between them was drowned out by the sound of her blood rushing to her brain. How she longed to kiss him, to run her fingers through his thick, dark hair, to feel his flesh naked against hers. Every fiber of her being cried out to be caressed by him, kissed, and loved, and...

"Will you...can you be patient?" He broke the silence and pulled her thoughts to the moment.

"Aye," she whispered, an unwanted blush heating her face. "That, I can."

He stood, pulling her up with him and drawing her into his embrace. Placing a light kiss upon her forehead, he whispered, "I hold much respect for you." He sighed, his warm breath washing over her temple. "If you only knew how I have restrained myself, fought to keep my lips from tasting every inch of you, forced my hands to be still, you would understand the honor I feel for you."

Aye, honorable. He is being honorable toward me, not indifferent, not uninterested, but honorable.

Her heart sang.

He raised her chin with the tip of a finger, and their eyes locked. "My people believe there must be honor between a couple as well as love. But such righteousness cannot be rushed. Integrity and trust must have time to grow." He arched a brow. "I know you would not want it any other way between us."

"Nay, I would not," she managed to mutter, her senses whirling at hearing him speak the words *between us.* If her knees didn't stop trembling, she was sure she'd soon find herself collapsed upon the floor.

As he lowered his head, his one lock of pale hair fell across his forehead. A sigh escaped her, and she rested her hands upon his muscular chest as she lifted her lips to meet his. Just as he was about to capture her mouth, Regis cleared his throat in the doorway.

She quickly stepped aside, cringing with embarrassment. This was the second time Regis had caught them in such a familiar position.

"I beg your pardons," Regis droned. Except for one raised brow, his expression was as stoic as always while going about his duties. He held a bouquet of pink, long-stemmed roses in a milk-glass vase.

"What is it, Regis?" Gabriel asked with an annoyed tone. His agitation was evident at being interrupted, and that made her smile from within.

"There is a message for you, sir, from Mrs. Halston," Regis said, handing Gabriel an envelope. "Her driver waits now for an answer."

Gabriel arched a brow. "And who are the flowers for?"

"Mrs. Cavendish," Regis said. "I suspect they are a congratulatory gift for the new arrivals."

He nodded. "Have Addie take them up to Sunny, then return for my answer."

Regis inclined his head politely. "Very good, sir."

"Gabriel," she began, her voice shakier then she liked.

"I do not plan on leaving Collins Stead, Riley," he reassured her as he tore open the wrapper and pulled out a delicate piece of stationery. A whiff of jasmine filled the room and a wash of jealousy consumed her. As he swept over the words written with a critical eye, Riley held her breath. It seemed like an eternity to her, standing there in the dining room, waiting for his next move.

He replaced the notepaper into the envelope and

slipped it in his breast pocket. "Would you give me a moment?"

"Aye," she muttered. "I will be in the library."

He nodded, forcing a smile.

She forced a smile of her own before taking herself to the library.

From the window there, she could see Collette Halston's carriage parked on the circular drive. She waited for Regis to bring him Gabriel's decision. The clock on the desk clicked away the minutes...one, five, ten, and still Regis didn't bring Gabriel's answer. Then from the front door, Gabriel emerged. With his long strides, he made his way down the path toward the elegant vehicle and climbed in.

Her heart sank as she watched the carriage disappear at the end of the drive, swallowed by the morning fog. If Gabriel truly felt something for her, how could he even think of going to Collette?

She frowned. What happened to his promise to stay at Collins Stead? What was in Collette's note that made him change his mind?

A sudden chill filled her being. She walked to the fire, stoked it, and remained to soak up its warmth. But no matter how it blazed, a cold, heavy dread weighted down upon her chest. Was it not only moments ago he spoke of how he restrained his affections toward her out of honor and respect? With such a confession, he was admitting his feelings for her. And yet now he was heading into Collette Halston's arms.

She squeezed her temples with her fingers, totally at a loss for Gabriel's actions. None of it made any sense whatsoever. And then a sudden realization made her gasp.

Is Collette with child?

It was common knowledge the two partook in intimate romps outside the bonds of matrimony, thus the reason Gabriel felt he should propose to

Collette. But she had refused, and Simon brought him back to Collins Stead, drunk and humiliated as a result. While Collette escaped to Egypt.

But could Collette have now returned carrying Gabriel's child and changed her mind about his proposal?

Knowing Gabriel to be the honorable man that he is, he would be compelled to do the right thing...marry Collette and claim the child.

Oh, why...why did it have to be this way? Why did Gabriel even take up with such a woman?

At one time Lucinda explained to her certain needs men desired, and the things genteel women should never lower themselves to do. For this reason, men were permitted to seek out the women who would do those unspeakable acts, leaving the woman of worth to only bear their heirs. Riley knew the women these men sought. They walked the streets of London's dark side, performing the unmentionable wants and needs for money. It was the very life Lucinda kept her from by taking her in. And the life Gabriel saved her from when he rescued her from the Sea Patrol.

But Collette Halston was different. She didn't need to sell herself for money. She wasn't dirty, destitute, and stuck in a bad situation. She didn't please a man in an ally while standing up against a wall, nor did she wear tattered clothes, or sleep in the gutter. Nay, Collette was rich, beautiful, and could travel anywhere she wanted. She was everything Riley was not, could not be...will not be, because Lucinda had raised her to play by society's rules.

And yet she was sure Sunny pleased her husband to fulfillment, not giving a care or worry to what society thought she should or shouldn't do. Behind closed doors, between a husband and his wife, who had to know what went on? Different things Sunny confided in her was enough to assume she kept her husband satisfied, as well as enjoying the freedom to express her own desires. Riley felt those same desires, every time Gabriel kissed her. And she wanted more than just bearing her husband's heirs. But now her chance to wed Gabriel was over. She'd never be able show him the unbridled passion that burned within her. Her eyes filled with tears as she thought of him as Collette's husband, lying beside her naked, touching her, kissing her, having a family with her.

She groaned. "Oh, Gabriel, why couldn't you have just waited for me?"

Chapter Twenty-Seven

A knock at her chamber door awakened Riley. Startled, she sat up in bed, wiping her moist eyes with the backs of her hands.

Why have I fallen asleep crying?

As the second knock came, she remembered what drove her in tears to her room.

"One moment," she called out, swinging her legs off the bed and straightening her clothes. She hurried to the dressing table to look in the mirror and was horrified at her reflection. "Mercy," she whispered. Peering back at her was a red-nosed, swollen-eyed young woman with hair in disarray.

"Riley," came Sunny's voice from the other side of the door. "I have lunch waiting for you in my room."

"I am not hungry, Sunny," she responded.

"Are you ill?" Sunny questioned with a concerned tone.

"Nay, I am fine," she called back, trying to smooth aside the wayward wisps of hair clinging to her face.

"Please let me in," Sunny insisted.

Reluctantly, she went to the door, took a deep breath to calm the fluttering within her stomach, and turned the knob.

Sunny sized her up in one glance. "You are not fine."

"Aye, I am," she softly protested. "Just a bit tired."

"You are not fine," Sunny repeated, entering the room and shutting the door behind her. "And I know

243

why."

She stepped aside and walked to the window. "I'd rather not discuss it."

"You have every right to feel betrayed," Sunny said.

Her emotions broke like water bursting through a broken dam. Covering her face with her hands, she sobbed, "Oh, Sunny, I am such a fool."

Sunny ran to her, cradling Riley in her arms. "No, my friend, you are not a fool, just a woman in love. And my brother's choice to visit Collette today has hurt you deeply, made you feel betrayed."

She pulled back to gaze into the other woman's large, sympathetic eyes. The last thing she wanted was to have anyone take pity upon her. Nay, she would not be poor Riley, left with a broken heart because the man she loved was bound to another. She stepped out of Sunny's embrace, wiped her tears with the back of her hands, and squared her shoulders. "There is no betrayal, because nothing was promised."

"But there was, and we both know it," Sunny said. "I know Gabriel's feelings for you are true. We have talked about it." She frowned. "Something else drove my brother to Collette Halston's side today." Her frown deepened. "I know he would not go unless there was good reason."

Riley squeezed her throbbing temples. "Please, Sunny, I can't bear another moment talking about him and Collette. Whatever reason he had, it doesn't alter the fact he went to her. That is something I can't forget nor can anyone change."

"Come," Sunny said, taking Riley by the hand and leading her to the guest quarters. "You need nourishment, or you will make yourself ill."

She reluctantly followed her friend, sure she couldn't swallow a thing.

Once in the other woman's chamber, Sunny

handed her a finger sandwich of cream cheese and cucumber. "Now, eat. I am sure there is an explanation for my brother's actions today, and when he returns, we will both be there to hear what they are."

She numbly chewed her food, not tasting a thing, her gaze wandering over to the flowers that Collette sent Sunny. They sat atop a small corner dresser, blooming pink and lush.

"Your flowers are lovely," she mentioned.

Sunny nodded. "I think the pink shade is so soft."

"Much more appropriate, I'd wager, for a baby gift," she reflected, rising from her chair to smell the unusual blooms. The card lay beside the vase, and Riley scanned the message. But then she took a closer look at the script. The curls and lines of Collette's handwriting had been one she'd seen before. "The writing is familiar."

"Has Collette not sent many messages to my brother here in the past?" Sunny said.

"Aye, but I never saw them. Regis would take them from the messenger and bring them directly to Gabriel," she said, turning to look at Sunny.

Sunny frowned. "And yet you know the handwriting?"

"Aye, I do...but I don't know how," she said.

Sunny shrugged. "That sort of thing happens to me often, and I find that in time the answer always comes to me."

She scrutinized the script once again before she turned to place the card where she found it.

Sunny continued. "You will be doing something and all of a sudden," she snapped her fingers, "just like that, you will remember."

And just like that, Riley did. The handwriting on the card she held was that of her father's, which in truth turned out to be from her kidnappers, the dreaded Sea Patrol.

Riley frowned.

But they are all dead.

Panic seized her.

Unless one more still lives...someone nay a soul would suspect.

Her eyes widened.

Collette Halston!

Then another horrid thought struck her. Gabriel never saw the note from the kidnappers. After she read it, she stuck it in her skirt pocket. And that skirt burned in a fire at Lands End. Right now Gabriel could be walking into a trap.

"Are you all right, my friend?" Sunny asked.

"Aye," she managed to choke out past the lump in her throat. Gabriel's reasons for leaving Collins Stead now didn't matter, only that he was safe, and Riley didn't believe he was.

"Then come and finish your lunch," Sunny suggested.

She took a deep breath to control the terror rising to smother her. Explaining her findings to Sunny would only frighten the new mother, and such a trauma after childbirth could cause disastrous results. Composing herself as best she could, she turned to face her friend.

"And where is Rafe today?" she calmly inquired. If she went to him with what she suspected, he would not hesitate to help Gabriel.

"He has gone off with Simon and Oliver to run some errands. They left not long after Gabriel," Sunny said.

Hearing this news foiled the idea of incorporating Rafe's help. And by the time she sent for a constable, waited for his arrival, explained the trouble, and then sent him to Collette's estate, it could be too late to help Gabriel.

Then she thought of a quicker way to come to

Gabriel's aid. "Where is Charles?"

"I think he is in the dining room, helping Jane polish the silver for my babies' baptism on Sunday." Sunny cocked her head sideways. "Why all the questions?"

Riley didn't answer. Rushing out of Sunny's chamber, she took the stairs two at time to the dining room.

When she hurried into the room, Charles looked up from his task. "What is it Miss Riley?"

"You must make ready the carriage immediately, Charles," she said. "I must pay an urgent call."

"Aye, miss," Charles agreed without further question, taking off for the stables.

"What is it, miss?" Jane inquired.

"I haven't the time to explain. But for right now, I need you to quickly fetch my cape."

"Aye," Jane said, leaving the room just as fast as Charles did.

Once at the carriage, Charles opened the door. "Where to, miss?"

"To the Wellington mansion, please Charles, and quickly," she said.

The Wellington estate was much closer to Collins Stead than Scotland Yard and on the way to Collette's mansion. Suzanna's father could send his men to aid Gabriel much faster than the authorities could arrive. And from what she witnessed at Lands End, they'd be far more effective. Riley had nay a doubt in her mind that Lady Wellington would refuse to do as she asked. Suzanna would be most happy to oblige.

"Aye," she whispered to herself, remembering the humiliation the other woman endured by the kidnapper's hands. "She will be most happy indeed."

Chapter Twenty-Eight

As Gabriel strode the familiar path to Collette's door, he found himself in a much different state of being than his previous walks. Times before filled him with anticipation, knowing the night held erotic passion from a woman uninhibited by society's protocol. Collette Halston could please a man in ways far beyond the imagination. He dared never to question as to how and by whom such skills were learned, for such information would have had even him blushing. It was one thing for a man to cultivate a woman in such matters, show her, teach her how to fulfill his yearnings, but quite another for a woman to take the lead, and such an erogenous one at that. Unless the woman worked in a house of ill-repute, and Collette was never of this kind, some actions performed were considered unthinkable.

Now, after tasting Riley's innocence and sincerity, he was ashamed to have partaken in Collette's taboo. The memory of the things she requested, and in turn those he allowed her to do to him, were acts he would bring silently to his grave. What they shared was tainted and dirty, not something he would ever want to build his life on. He was glad Collette refused his proposal, as it opened his eyes to the sort of woman he should stay away from in comparison to the kind he really wanted.

Riley was precious and sweet, pure and true. She would love him in a genuine and tender way. And although he had much to teach her when they were able to come together as one, he had a feeling

Riley could be just as sensual as Collette, minus the depravity. There was not a doubt in his mind, after the kisses they shared, that loving Riley would be anything but wonderful.

No, it will be much better than wonderful, because Riley will be only mine.

He frowned.

That is, if she will still have me after this visit to Collette.

Though the thought sickened him to the core, it was a chance he had to take.

"You look as though you swallowed a frog," Collette said, meeting him at the door.

He frowned. Usually it was Veronica who greeted him. "Where is Veronica today?"

"I gave her and the rest of my staff the day off," Collette said, rising on tiptoes to plant a deep kiss upon his lips. Normally this news, coupled with such a kiss, would entice him to scoop her up into his arms and carry her to her chamber. Once behind closed doors, he would remove her quickly from her clothes, like a long-awaited present, all along a fire burning in his loins. But now he was left cold, disgusted. When he did not respond, she stepped back to search his face. "Ah, so you're going to be that way."

Gabriel arched a brow. "How could you expect anything different?"

Collette took an audible breath. "I just thought by now you'd be missing me." She reached up to caress his face and whispered, "I find it hard to believe you've forgotten the warmth between my thighs and the scent of our bodies as we..."

"Enough." He gripped her by the wrist and cast her hand aside.

She laughed sardonically. "Oh, but you could never get enough, love."

He glared at her with an inevitable look of

disgust.

"Methinks you have found a bit of warmth elsewhere." Cocking her head sideways, she glowered up at him. "Perhaps Miss Flanders has a set of warm thighs as well."

His lips thinned. "If you were a man, I would punch you for that remark."

Collette stared him down. "Tell me truthfully now, Gabriel. Beneath that pure and innocent demeanor, Riley Flanders is not as prudish as we all think."

He seethed. "Riley is a lady in every sense of the word, and you are never to forget it."

"I also haven't forgotten it wasn't a lady you've craved all this time."

"What was once between us is wrong. I want something different. And so do you, or you would have accepted my proposal," he said, the muscles at his jaw twitching with the anger he fought to control.

Collette smirked. "Oh, is this what this is all about, your wounded pride?" She rolled her eyes. "And men have the nerve to say women are sensitive."

"Why have you asked me here, Collette?" he asked through gritted teeth.

She motioned to the parlor. "Shall we?"

He followed her into the large room, decorated in blue and gold. The plush drapes that hung from the floor-to-ceiling windows were pulled tightly shut. And only one small lamp lit the dimness.

"I would offer you tea, but I know how much you despise the brew. And I am fresh out of coffee." She made her way to the serving board, the aroma of jasmine floating from her swishing skirt. Reaching for the liquor decanter, she raised it in the air. "Under the circumstances I don't believe it's too early for a brandy."

"And of what circumstance do you refer?"

She turned away to prepare them each a drink, taking her time to fill each glass. "We shall discuss that over our brandies, like civilized people."

"I do not have anything to discuss with you," he said, moving to the hearth.

Collette turned, holding a glass in each hand, and made her way to him. "Well, I say we do," was her curt reply as she handed him a goblet. "Besides, if that were the truth, you wouldn't have come." In a further act of defiance, she turned her back on him and sauntered over to the far side of the spacious room. "Now, drink the brandy. Drink it all," she demanded, leaning against the piano in the corner and taking a sip from her own glass.

The air in the room grew heavy, almost smothering, the silence broken only by a ticking clock.

When she finally turned to face him, her glass was as empty as his. He placed the cut crystal goblet he held upon the mantel and seated himself in a nearby chair. "I am listening."

Placing her glass upon the piano, she made her way to him. Animosity seeped from her gaze and soaked her words. "Aye, you listen, and listen well." Her nostrils flared. "For it shall be the last time you will hear my voice."

Gabriel's muscles tensed. Every nerve and tendon was on edge. Yet he forced himself to appear calm. It was a warrior's way of tricking the enemy, and at this point, Collette was looking more and more like she fit the part. A measure of fear coursed through him, but to fear was a good thing. When afraid, a warrior's instincts were heightened, sharp and ready to act upon whatever it took for survival. He refrained from answering with words, not trusting his tone to remain as calm as he held his body, so he merely gave a taut nod.

She quirked her lips and continued in a bemused tone. "I didn't think this would be so easy." She leaned toward him, giving him an ample eyeful of her plunging neckline, and smiled sardonically, her cool fingers tracing the outline of his lips. "He worried I could capture you with just my charm."

He arched a brow, recoiling from her touch. "Who do you speak of?"

Collette's tone was mockingly apologetic. "Oh, now love, there's not a need to look so irritated. I will tell you soon enough all about my consort. But you see, darling, everything must unfold just at the right time or the rich effect of it will be unappreciated." She straightened, waving a hand in the air. "Besides, getting ahead of ourselves will completely ruin the story."

He could feel his stomach tying in knots as he fought to keep his facial expression impassive. "And you should never ruin a good story."

"Now, I just knew you'd agree with me on that," she said, taking a seat opposite him.

He crossed his arms over his chest. "But I have not all day to sit here and wait for you to tell your little tale, so suppose you get on with it."

"All in good time, Gabriel." She stood, collected his glass from the mantel and her own from atop the piano. "Can I interest you in another brandy?"

"No," he said flatly.

"Very well, then," she said. "But I think I shall indulge, in spite of the early hour."

He shifted in his seat while he waited for her to fix herself another drink.

She stayed standing by the sideboard, her back to him, as she downed her drink. Then she turned and with slow steps neared him, reclaiming her seat. Raising the hem of her skirt above her ankles, she crossed one long, shapely limb over the other before beginning her story.

"I believe I have shared a morsel of my childhood with you before." Collette shrugged. "Enough, at least, for you to realize I had a wretched home life," she said, folding her hands neatly in her lap.

His tone was curt. "Yes, I remember well the little you shared."

"Aye, it was the afternoon you came to propose, and I was leaving to have lunch with Jackson Hodge."

He nodded, the humiliation of that day mounting his face with heat.

"I probably should have allowed you much more than a glimpse of those horrendous days," she said. "But the memories are painful, you see, and I'm not one to rehash what cannot be changed."

He remained silent as he studied her, the ebony hair curling perfectly around a beautifully sculpted face, which now appeared hard and cold, as did the rich, dark eyes that stared back at him. They burned into him like live coals, an underlying evil penetrating him straight to the back of his skull.

"Then why rehash it now, Collette?"

Her lip curled in a sardonic grin. "So you will understand better the reason I did what I did."

He arched a brow. "Why is it so important to you that I understand anything?"

Collette took an audible breath. "I suppose because I've genuinely grown fond of you and Sunny." For a moment her expression softened. "You two are the first real and sincere friends I've ever had, and to a small degree, I care what sort you see me as." Then in the next instant, her face hardened. "But getting sentimental is not my forte, as it weakens the resolve, hinders survival. So, I will get on with my story." She sat back in her chair. "I've already told you my marriage was a deal my father made with Alistair Halston, a man thirty years my

Roberta C. M. DeCaprio

senior, in order to pay off his gambling debts and supply him with enough alcohol to drink him into his grave."

"Yes, that much I already know," he admitted.

She cast her eyes down to her hands, now clasped tightly. "Before that deal, my father used me in other ways to pay his arrears. As it happened, by the time I turned fourteen, I was quite skilled in pleasing the many chaps Father brought home for dinner."

"Collette, there is no need for you to..."

"Aye, there is, Gabriel." She raised her gaze to meet his. "The evening went something like this," she expanded further. "Mum would serve us all dinner, Papa would moan and groan over his poor financial situation, and then a trade for some monetary compensation would be discussed. Once the deal was agreed upon, Mum would take me upstairs to my room and ready me for my performance. She remained silent through my protests, forcing herself to carry on her duties in spite of my pleas. She refused eye contact as she fixed my hair, dabbed my neck with lemon verbena, stripped me of my girl's clothes and dressed me in...in..."

Inside, he cringed as he waited for her to continue, the memories contorting her beautiful face into a mask of hatred.

Collette cleared her throat. "When all was done and over with, I would wash my flesh until it was raw." She arched a brow. "But I never felt clean regardless of how much I bathed. Eventually I realized I'd never feel clean again." She hesitated a moment. "Then I'd lay awake 'til late, listening to my mother in the next bedchamber, crying herself to sleep. I worried for her health. She was already a fragile being, pale to look at, sick more than not, and I feared she'd die and leave me alone with my father.

If Mum was gone, how long would it be 'til Papa visited *my* bed? As it was, he would look at me with hunger in his eyes. So, after the first few times, I shut something off inside, made Mum think it didn't bother me, hoping it wouldn't bother her so much. I did whatever I was told with whomever, and learned well what was expected of me."

"I am sorry," he whispered, genuinely sad for her lost innocence.

Collette frowned. "I don't need or want your pity, or anyone's pity. I did just fine for myself in the end."

"You were just a child, a frightened little girl," he said. "What could you know, how could you make the right decisions for yourself?"

"Nay, I was never a child, and I made many wise decisions. It wasn't long before I rose above the fear as well. I became fearless. It was the only way I could keep from hating myself, hating what I had been made to do. By the time I married Alistair, I was a strong woman, skilled in the bedchamber. I left his old hide gasping for breath and needing medication. I used him instead of him using me. I took all he owned, all he worked for, and then some. And when he died, after the three long years I endured being his wife, it all belonged to me. So I continued with his business dealings, though they were tainted and vile, because I vowed never to be poor and submissive to any man's whims again." She took a deep breath. "With that said, it brings us to the reason I summoned you here today and the present state of affairs."

"Which is?" he muttered.

Collette's voice held a bored tone. "Why, your latest adventure. It complicated things for me, my current consort, and the clients."

"And I suspect your past consorts were once the Sea Patrol," he stated firmly.

"You catch on fast," she said, standing to make her way to the closed drapery. Pulling a panel aside, she gazed out the window. Rain pelted the panes of glass.

"You of all people, knowing as you did the horrors of being taken against your will, should have put a stop to such depravity. How could you destine any woman to such a fate?"

The heavy material slipped from her grasp as she turned to face him. "London's prostitutes were destined to a far worse fate then what my well-oiled operation offered. Homeless and full of disease, they walked the streets in the cold, the rain, the heat, and the fog. They were subjected to being murdered or left to die somewhere alone. They were dirty, hungry, and drunk."

He arched a brow. "And how did you better their situation?"

"My clients were willing to offer them a permanent position. As a concubine a woman is well clothed and fed, would have a place to dwell, be watched over by guards. It was all such a perfect plan. Even the Queen approved, was pleased the streetwalkers were no longer a problem. Her royal head didn't worry or question for a moment what happened to them or where they were brought, just as long as they didn't continue to infest London with their sort."

Anger swelled in his chest. "My sister, Raven was not of that sort, and if Lord Shannon had not come to her rescue and married her to save her from the Sea Patrol's clutches, right now she would be...she could be..."

"Aside from your sister's situation, it was a winning outcome for all involved, until Captain Langley stepped beyond his orders." She sneered. "He became too sure of himself, over calculated the authority of his position. His confidence turned into arrogance, which eventually blinded him like a bat to the original mission. He became overzealous by taking from higher means, offering well-bred virgins, instead of from our usual source."

"Which were women whose disappearance would hardly be noticed," he concluded.

"Aye, Captain Langley made a paramount mistake in kidnapping Lady Wellington and Riley Flanders. Their disappearance drew too much attention." She studied him with disdain. "But then again, greed is the way of all men."

"Not all," he said.

She shot him a black glare. "Perhaps my plans would have paid off better if I had hired a warrior to do my bidding."

"A warrior would not have done your bidding," he said.

"Ah, aye, the very concept a warrior holds breathes nothing but honor, isn't that correct, Gabriel?"

He nodded, silent wrath gripping his insides.

"You are a magnificent specimen. And I am not ashamed to admit you've given me more pleasure than any man I've known, but you've also caused me tremendous trouble." Collette sauntered closer, leaning down to gaze levelly into his eyes. "If I were just involved, I'd ignore what you did, pack my belongings, and move to Australia. It would be hard to prove I was a part of any wrong doing, as I've stayed relatively in the shadows. But my partner hasn't been as indirect as I've managed to remain. I believe you've already met him. Jackson Hodge?"

He remembered clearly the name she mentioned. Hodge was found with Collette the day Gabriel came to propose.

"Because he isn't able to disappear as easily as I can, this causes him concern. So I'm sure you can understand why he sees things much differently than I do. Besides, he tends to be the type who likes to tie up loose ends," she added.

With that said, Collette stood and walked to the double doors at the far end of the parlor that led to the mansion's library. Upon opening the door, three men appeared.

"I believe we've already established the fact you've met Jackson Hodge," Collette said as politely as though she were being a hostess at a gala. "And these are his assistants, Lionel Tubbs and his brother, Horace." She indicated the other two men.

Hodge, decked out in a fine black suite, top hat, and walking stick strutted into the room. "So again we meet, Mr. Eagle. A pity it has to be under such awkward circumstances as I've admitted to Collette you sound like an interesting chap. Truly an individual I'd enjoy getting to know."

Lionel and Horace Tubbs, both much larger in build and very tall, wore worn gray trousers and a black shirt. They remained silent as they took a place beside Hodge. Both brothers' dark, beady eyes glared down at Gabriel.

"Lionel and Horace are quite efficient at what they do," Hodge said. "So if you cooperate, Mr. Eagle, we can all go about this in a quick and easy manner."

Gabriel knew that if he stood, both the Tubbs men would be on him in an instant. And since he suspected what sort of thing they were efficient in doing, he refrained from making any fast moves. "And what if I do not cooperate, Mr. Hodge?"

Hodge smiled, large lips pulling over uneven, stained teeth. "The truth is, old chap, you haven't much of a choice in the matter. The brandy you consumed was laced with a relaxing agent, and at any moment, you should be feeling very weak."

"I would say, then, you have me at a disadvantage," Gabriel said.

"The very way I like my adversary, Mr. Eagle," Hodge boasted. "I find it much easier to remain the victor that way."

He leaned back in his chair, seeming to his audience his strength was waning.

"You'll feel nothing in a bit, love," Collette said, her voice slightly shaking. "They promised me it would all be painless."

"And it shall be, my dear, it shall," Hodge reassured her with a gentle pat upon her arm. "Once he's unconscious, Lionel and Horace will take him to their carriage and dispose of him in the river." He chuckled lightly. "To London's finest it will just appear Mr. Eagle had the misfortune of drowning."

"Those at Collins Stead know I have been summoned by Collette this morning. Do you truly believe they will not become curious at my disappearance and come here asking questions?"

Hodge smiled sardonically. "And don't you think I've thought of that myself?"

Gabriel raised a defiant chin. "So, what do you plan on telling them?"

"I plan on not saying a word because I was never present at this little morning meeting, but our lovely Collette, here," Hodge said, tilting his head in Collette's direction, "will simply say you proposed once more, and she again refused. You left in a rage, getting a ride into town by her driver. From that point your actions are a mystery...until, that is, someone fishes your body out of the river." He arched a brow. "I am most assured it won't be hard for all to surmise you were so distraught over a second rejection, you decided to end your life."

"I'm so sorry everything turned out this way," Collette said, her apology almost sounding genuine.

"So am I," he said, his arms flopping down to his sides as he slipped lower in his seat.

"There, you see my dear, the relaxant has begun

to work." Hodge beamed. "All this will be over momentarily, and we shall be free to take our leave for lunch."

Gabriel slipped off the chair, his eyes locking with Collette's dark orbs as he rolled onto his stomach. He landed face down by the hearth, feeling the warmth of the fire at his side. His fall knocked over a small shovel used for removing the ashes. The iron implement fell beside him, its length being hidden by his frame. Quickly he gripped the handle and lay very still.

"There, it is over. Now remove him," Hodge ordered.

Gabriel felt a hand grip him by the back of his collar. Just as he was turned face up, his eyes shot open. Letting loose with a blood-curdling war-cry a warrior would yell as he went into battle, he struck a stunned Lionel Tubbs in the face with the shovel. He heard the other man's nose bone crack. Tubbs stumbled back, blood pouring from his nostrils as he fell into Hodge. The two, knocked off balance, landed in a heap on the floor. Hodge cussed and sputtered his profound annoyance at the inconvenience while trying to quickly push Lionel off him.

Gabriel sprung to his feet, glimpsing the astonished look upon Collette's face. "This cannot be; I dropped a dose and then some of the relaxant into your brandy."

He did not bother to respond, his warrior reflexes fueling into fighting mode. Again he swung the shovel, dropping a heavy blow upon Lionel's head before his adversary was able to regain his footing. Hodge, still trapped beneath the thug, shouted a command to Horace. In an instant the other Tubbs brute was on him, pushing Gabriel against a wall and fighting to wrench the shovel from his grasp. But he held firm to the only weapon he had, pushing himself away from the wall with a knee-jerk to Horace's gut, and then a head-butt to the enemy's forehead.

Horace, larger and more solid than Lionel, was quick to recover from the blows and came back with a vengeance. The other man's meaty fist slammed into Gabriel's jawbone. Pain shot through his jowls, his vision blurred, and he fell to one knee. Shaking his head to clear it, he fought to remain conscious and struggled to stand.

But by this time, Lionel was back on his feet and hurried to join in on the beating. He came from the rear, wrenching the shovel from Gabriel's grasp and pinning his arms behind him. Sandwiched between the two Tubbs brothers, Gabriel was vulnerable now to whatever brutal punches Horace threw.

Horace Tubbs sneered, his large lips curling up to reveal a toothless grin. Reaching into his hip pocket, he pulled out a small knife. Spit formed at the corners of his mouth as he brought the blade up to Gabriel's throat. Drool spilled over his bottom lip and trickled down the left side of his unshaven chin as he pricked Gabriel's flesh with the tip of the blade.

"Nay, Horace, you cannot spill a drop of his blood here," Hodge warned.

The derelict hesitated before he reluctantly replaced the knife into his pocket. Once more he doubled his large hand into a fist and pulled his arm back to pack a wallop. But before Horace could plunge his knuckles into Gabriel's throat, a shot rang out, and Horace went down with a bullet in his back. Just as Collette screamed, another shot followed, and behind Gabriel, Lionel fell atop him, landing them both onto the floor.

Gabriel struggled to free himself from Lionel's weight. A quick inventory of the other man's condition proved the bullet entered Lionel's skull, just between his beady little orbs. He now stared up at Gabriel with vacant eyes, blood smeared across his face from the broken nose, and another puddle forming on the floor from the fatal wound in his head. Horace also lay dead.

Across the room another skirmish ensued as his rescuers, Simon and Rafe, wrestled Jackson Hodge to the floor. They hog tied him with rope and gagged him with his own neck-scarf.

"You won't be getting free from these binds, old chap," Rafe remarked to Hodge, who was squirming like a worm on a hook. "My nautical knots are more than secure."

"It took you two long enough," he said, stepping over Lionel's body as he flexed and rubbed his sore jaw.

"We were a bit detained," Rafe said, replacing his gun in its holder.

"Sorry mate," Simon added, also stashing away his weapon. "But all is well, as it seems we got here in the nick of time."

"She tried to drug me with a relaxing agent so the Tubbs brothers could dump my body in the river," Gabriel said, gesturing to the empty glass of brandy. "But when she turned her back, I emptied my glass into the plant sitting nearby."

Simon frowned. "How did you know the drink was drugged?"

"Collette grew up with a drunken father, so she hates for men to drink, especially this early in the day. When she offered me a brandy, insisted I drink it all, and then offered me another, my suspicions took hold," he explained. He frowned, looking around at the wreckage of the room. "Where is Collette?"

Simon arched a brow. "She was here a moment ago."

"Not to worry," Rafe said. "She isn't going to get too far on foot and in the pouring rain, dressed in all that satin finery and clad only in a pair of linen pumps."

Gabriel arched a brow. "You noticed what she was wearing during all this."

"It comes with being married," Rafe said. "My wife has educated me to fashion whether I like it or not."

He stifled a grin.

"The reason we were slightly detained was because we were helping Oliver," Simon explained. "He was trying to take on a couple of drivers by himself."

"But now the pair are tied up as secure as this chap," Rafe added, indicating Hodge with a wave of his hand. "Without their drivers, the carriages aren't going anywhere and neither is Collette."

A woman's agonizing scream brought them all into motion, the three hurrying out of the mansion and down the front lawn's path to where the commotion was taking place. There they found Collette face down in a puddle, clothes soaked from the deluge rained upon them. Straddling her back was Suzanna Wellington, also looking as drenched as a drowned rat, with her dark hair pasted flat to her to face and eyes wide with wild rage. She was striking Collette about the head and shoulders with her fists.

"What the hell is Lady Wellington doing here?" he said.

Rafe shrugged. "I haven't a clue." He turned to Simon. "Did you call for reinforcements again?"

Simon frowned. "Nay, it wasn't me."

"You will pay for the humiliation you caused me!" Lady Wellington entwined her wet fingers around a long curl and tore it free from Collette's scalp.

Collette screamed in agony, "Get her off of me!" Coughing and sputtering each time her head was pushed into the puddle, she choked out, "Someone, I beg, have mercy."

"You deserve nay a shred of mercy!" Lady Wellington pulled from Collette's bloody scalp another large hunk of hair.

"Please, help me! Someone help me!" Collette screeched.

It took two of Lady Wellington's men to pull her free, and she kicked and cursed all the way to the carriage she came in, "I want the bitch stripped and beaten, do you hear me? Stripped and beaten!"

Collette remained on the ground, too hurt and dazed to move. Simon and Rafe pulled her to her feet. Scotland Yard's men arrived at this point and bound Collette's hands before they asked questions and demanded to see the crime scene. Simon and Rafe led them inside, where they could conduct a full investigation. Collette was arrested and taken away. By this time she practically needed to be carried. Along with her went the drivers and Hodge. All would be spending the first night of many in Newgate Prison.

Turning to make his own way into the mansion and out of the pouring rain, Gabriel spotted her, standing beneath a large tree. He smiled. "Ah, so it was you who brought the extra men?"

"Aye," Riley said, folding her arms in front of her.

"You are truly a brave woman, coming to my aid as you did," he said, making his way nearer.

"You once did the same for me." Her large, green eyes locked with his. Her voice quivered. "Thank God you're all right."

Closer now to her, he was better able to take in her appearance. Riley's cape hung wet over her shoulders, soaking through to the blouse she wore. Her ginger tresses clung in limp ringlets about her shoulders. Her full lips, purplish-blue in color, trembled as she shivered uncontrollably. "But you won't be if you stay out in the cold, soaked to the bone in those clothes," he said, gathering her into his arms and carrying her into the mansion. With everyone busy in the parlor, arguing over whom should remove the dead men, no one noticed him making his way up the stairs to Collette's chamber.

"Nay, don't take me in there," Riley protested through chattering teeth. "I don't want to see where the two of you laid, where you...you and her..." she stammered, her words clipped by irrepressible sobs.

He ignored her objections, kicking the door shut behind them with a booted foot. He sat her on the bed and removed her wet cape. Her blouse was just as saturated. "I need to get you out of these clothes immediately, Riley." He fumbled with the buttons as he unfastened the first three at her collar.

"Nay, you can't do this, Gabriel," she pleaded. "Not to me, not to me."

"I am not doing anything but trying to help you," he said, unfastening two more buttons.

Her cold fingers clamped over his. "Nay, I am not like her, do not treat me like you do her."

Her words froze him. He blinked, stepped back, and looked down at the beautiful and frightened young woman who was gazing up at him. "I did not mean...I only wanted..." He lowered himself to a kneeling position. "Forgive me, Riley. I honestly had no dishonorable intentions in mind." Reaching out to her, he caressed her porcelain complexion, tenderly running the tip of his finger down her cheek, to her neck. Her delicate and pale splendor was soft to the touch, too soft, too tempting. Abruptly he pulled his hand away and cleared his throat. "But if you do not get free from these wet garments, you will certainly catch your death." He combed his fingers through his own wet hair. "And I could not bear that, Riley...not again...not ever again, I already have lost one I love."

She slid off the bed and into his arms. Burying

her face under his neck, she wept. Her tears undid him, and he ached for her deep within his being.

There was nothing now he would not do for her. There was no way he could ever leave her. At this moment his heart claimed her, she was his, and he knew he could not...did not want to be without her. As he held her cold, trembling body close to his, he whispered, "I must get you out of these wet clothes, Riley." He felt her nod, and together they stood. He then reached for a quilt draped at the foot of the bed and wrapped it around her. Reaching beneath the quilt, once again he tried to unfasten the rest of the buttons. It was even harder to accomplish without looking.

"To hell with all these damn buttons," he muttered, ripping the blouse away from her cold, wet, flesh. Then he tore the camisole and threw it aside.

She burrowed against him, her naked breasts now firmly against his own drenched shirt.

He did not look down, though every fiber in his being yearned to glimpse her full, round bosom. His passion mounted as he desired to cup each one in the palm of his hand, warm and suckle a hard peak with his lips. Swallowing hard, he picked her up and placed her on the bed. Before joining her he stripped off his waistcoat and shirt. Then he climbed in beside her and gathered her once again into his embrace, heating her flesh with his own.

"This morning you promised to join me in the library, and I believed you. You said you would not go to her," she said softly.

"I did not go to *her*," he said, tightening his grasp.

"And yet you are *here*."

"As you might have noticed, Simon, Rafe, and Oliver are here as well," he pointed out.

She pulled back to look at him. "If you knew you

were walking into a trap, why did you come? Why not just call the authorities?"

"It would have taken too long. I needed to catch the rogues while they believed they were catching me," he explained. "I wanted it to be over so they could never hurt anyone again."

"And how did you figure out Collette's summoning you was a ruse?"

He smiled. "I have Addie to thank for that."

She frowned. "Addie? What does she have to do with anything?"

"After you left the dining room, Addie entered holding the card that accompanied Collette's flowers. Marked on the front of the envelope were the words, *Congratulations Sunny and Captain Cavendish.* Addie recognized the writing as the same hand that scripted the note sent from your so-called father, which she brought to you the morning you were abducted."

Her frown deepened. "But Addie has never really learned to read."

"I would say that fact alone was to her favor in this case, and probably why she detected the similarity so quickly. She views words like we do pictures, since she cannot make out their meaning." He chuckled lightly. "Of course, the way she loves to stick her nose in other people's business also helped."

She joined in on his mirth. "I would say, for once, Addie's prattling in other folk's affairs has worked out well. I have nay a doubt she found someone to fetch the authorities as well, else why would they be here?"

"Now, suppose you tell me how you knew I was walking into a trap," he said.

"Much the same as Addie, I'd say. When I joined Sunny for lunch in her chamber, I admired the pink blooms Collette sent and spotted the card beside them. After reading her note the first time, I remembered such a script from before but could not place where I'd seen it. Whenever you received word from Collette in the past, Regis would bring the message to you, or to your chamber. So, I hadn't ever seen her handwriting. Yet I believed somehow I had, so I searched my brain for the answer." She widened her eyes. "And then it came to me with startling clarity. Collette's script and Kevin Delaney's were one in the same. That meant Collette was in on the kidnappings and hoped to sink her clutches into you for breaking up the operation." She sighed. "I realized with a sickening fear you were in grave danger. I didn't want to frighten Sunny, so I kept my findings quiet. But I did inquire on Simon, Rafe, and Oliver's whereabouts, knowing it would take too much time to get the authorities involved. However, when Sunny informed me they had all departed Collins Stead shortly after you, I went to Lady Wellington for help."

"It was a wise move, since Lord Wellington supplied reinforcements before when they were needed," he said.

She nodded. "That was my thought exactly. Besides Susanna and I agreed, even though we don't move in the same circles, that if either of us needed help, the other would oblige." She giggled. "It didn't take much to persuade her, once she knew Collette was part of her abduction and humiliation. Lady Wellington couldn't wait to get her hands on Collette."

He laughed. "Yes, I saw that for myself."

Riley's face grew somber. "Did it hurt you awfully much to learn of her actions?"

"Only because any betrayal from someone you know stings," he said. "But that hurt had nothing at all to do with me still having any feelings for Collette." He took an audible breath. "If anything, I ached for all the women who have been taken from their homes, abused, or killed because of Collette's actions."

"Are you positively sure, Gabriel?"

"I am more than positively sure, Riley," he said, planting a tiny kiss upon the tip of her nose. "And, my little half-naked beauty, if I do not release you and leave the room while you dress yourself in something dry, I am afraid I will be moved to show you just how much feeling I have for you."

Riley bit her bottom lip. "And what shall I dress in?"

He pointed to a large wardrobe at the far end of the chamber. "Take your pick."

Her eyes widened. "Oh, Gabriel, I couldn't."

He arched a brow. "Why not?"

"Well, because...because I shouldn't...it wouldn't be proper to..."

"It is not like she will know." He chuckled. "And in truth she is not going to need any of her clothes where she is going." He shrugged. "Besides, you just need something to wear long enough to see you to Collins Stead."

She smiled, giving him a slight push with the palm of a hand. "Then go. Get yourself out of here, so we can go home."

He returned her smile. "Going home sounds mighty good to me."

Chapter Twenty-Nine

Gabriel had counted the days until he returned to Collins Stead. After the horrible take-down of Collette Halston and the rest of her rogues, he was even more cautious for the women in his life. Collette's rampage might be over, but other diabolical people could easily take her place. That was the very reason, after the twins had their baptismal celebration, he helped escort Sunny and her family back to Brighton. Though Rafe would sooner die before he would allow any harm to come to Sunny and the babies and could rightly hold his own in dangerous times, Gabriel thought an extra pair of hands and eyes would not hurt. But the few weeks he remained at Bentwood became agonizing, until his sister, with hands on hips and sounding an awful lot like his mother, demanded he leave Brighton and return to the woman he belonged beside. The truth was he worried for Riley's safety as well, for she once had been a target for Collette's dealings. Precisely why he left Simon and Oliver, as well as Charles, in charge of making sure all the women at Collins Stead were well watched over.

Now, traveling on Christmas Eve to Glenshire Sussex and Riley was something he had anticipated for weeks. It was time to prepare a path of stones for her to walk down and proclaim his intentions. And he did not want a drawn out affair after his declaration was made public. Waiting another year to wed her was something he did not wish to do. He wanted to visit Raven in Limerick with his new bride, as well as gift Riley with another surprise while in Ireland...that being meeting her father's people. His brother-in-law, Lord Braiton Shannon found the Delaney family and arranged a reunion. Then he planned to journey onto America, all within a span of a few months. Besides, he was sure if he had to wait any longer to make Riley completely his, the very core beneath his bones would explode.

Charles brought the carriage around to the back of the mansion, as Gabriel instructed when he was picked up at the train station. Together the two of them outlined the path that led from the solarium door to the stable.

"And ye say, sir, this tactic works with the ladies back in yer 'omeland?" Charles inquired.

"Not in the entire land, Charles. But the idea has been an Apache marriage tradition for centuries."

Charles frowned. "Wonder if by chance it would work on Jane?"

He arched a brow. "I was under the impression, from what Riley tells me, that Jane has already agreed to wed you."

"Aye, to wed me, but she has yet to set a date," Charles said. "And I'm needin' it to be soon, if ye know what I mean, sir?"

He chuckled. "I know only too well, Charles."

Charles's frowned deepened. "Do ye think all this will get Jane movin' in the right direction?" He indicated the stones with his hand.

"I can only say the women in my tribe are completely flattered by the attention." He gave Charles a pat on the back. "But, my friend, you will not know anything until you try." Gabriel bent to put the last stone in place. "And since Jane has been made aware of this tradition, it just might do the trick. You are more than welcome to use the path when I am through with it."

Charles returned the smile with a large one of

his own, his eyes beaming with excitement. "Aye, sir, I believe I will take ye up on that offer. The whole idea just might give my Jane an immense thrill enough, perhaps, to finally set a date."

After brushing his hands together to clean them, he straightened his waistcoat and made his way around to the front of the mansion. "Good luck to you, Charles," he said over his shoulder.

"And to ye as well, sir," Charles called out.

Regis met him at the front door. "Good cheer to you, sir," he said, taking Gabriel's coat. "I assume your trip from Brighton was satisfactory."

He smiled down at the efficient little man. "All went well, thank you, Regis." He looked around the gaily-decorated foyer. Small wreaths lined the staircase banister, and candles of all sizes and colors set upon the hall tables illuminated the room with a warm glow. "Everything looks so festive," he commented.

"Aye, Lady Collins loves the holidays and spares no expense to make Collins Stead inviting to all who grace her doors," Regis replied.

"Well, she has done a fine job," he said, taking another glance at the splendor before him. "And where might I find Riley this evening?"

"She is engaged in the parlor, sir, with Lady Collins, Leah, and Oliver," Regis supplied.

When he entered the parlor, his breath was taken away at the beautiful picture Riley made, standing by the large, decorated Christmas tree. The red and gold balls reflected against their shiny orbs the light from the many candles placed upon the mantel, end tables, and the grand piano. But Riley was the real vision of beauty, the mere sight of her made his spirits come strongly alive. She was dressed in a cranberry-colored velvet gown, trimmed with ivory lace at the dipping neckline and cuffs. And her ginger hair was pulled atop her head, large curls cascading to the middle of her back.

She smiled when she saw him and ran into his embrace. He held her tight, inhaling the scent of lavender and musk that met his senses.

"I've missed you so much," she whispered in his ear.

"As I have you," he said, meeting her mouth with his own and placing upon her lips a long, deep kiss. She was so sweet to the taste, and his heart raced at the nearness of their bodies.

Lady Collins, sitting in a chair by the fire, cleared her throat. It was a discreet warning, and immediately Riley broke the kiss.

As she stepped from his embrace, color mounted her face. "You've come just in time."

He chuckled. "Do I dare ask in time for what?"

"For placing the angel atop the tree," she said, making her way to a box sitting on a nearby table. "It is the last of the decorations to go on the tree, and only you are tall enough to reach the highest bough," she explained as her dreamy gaze held his. "Would you do us the honor?" She handed him the white satin and feather clad ornament.

"I would be proud to," he said, reaching up with little effort to place the angel where she belonged.

"Do help yourself to a bit of eggnog, Gabriel," Lucinda said in a jovial manner, gesturing to a serving cart beside the sofa.

"It's spiked with brandy," Leah chimed in. "And it makes ye feel all warm inside."

"I'd say, love, ye best not be drinkin' anymore, or else I'll be carryin' ye to bed before dinner," Oliver's loving tone warned.

Leah giggled, batting her lashes at her young husband. "And would that be so wrong?"

Gabriel stifled a smile as he caught Oliver's face warming to Leah's words. He had the distinct impression Oliver was thinking there might not be anything wrong with such an idea after all.

Lucinda cleared her throat again. "Hush, all of you now, as I am about to tell you the legend of the Christmas tree."

Riley neared him. "It is tradition for Auntie Cinda to tell this story each year on Christmas Eve. In view of the fact your people love storytelling, I'm sure you'll enjoy listening to this one since the Christmas tree has come to play such an important part in celebrating the holidays."

Lady Collins waited until everyone was comfortably settled. "The legend of the Christmas tree has been handed down to us from the early days of Christianity in England. It has been said that in those beginning times the one who helped spread the word of Christ among the Druids was a monk by the name of Wilfred, later to become, Saint Wilfred. One day the young monk, encircled by his many converts, struck down a tree, a huge oak tree to be exact." Lucinda dramatically paused for effect, as a good storyteller often does. "Now, the oak tree is an object of worship in the Druid religion," she further explained. "So as it fell to the earth, the tree divided into four sections. And lo and behold, from the center a young fir tree miraculously raised."

Leah gasped, her eyes wide with surprise.

Oliver swallowed hard as he draped an arm around his young wife's shoulders.

"The converts gazed amazed as the tree pointed a green pinnacle toward the heavens," Lucinda continued. "Dropping his axe, Wilfred proclaimed the tree to be a Holy Tree. He told the converts a fir tree's timber is the wood of peace, for their homes were all built from fir lumber. And the evergreen leaves, pointing heavenward, were a sign of infinite life. Wilfred called the fir, the tree of the Christ Child and encouraged all to gather about it, not out in the wilderness, but instead inside the warmth of their homes. Once within each dwelling, the tree would be the center of all the festivity, surrounded by gifts of love. And to this very day, the fir tree remains our loveliest symbol of the Christmas holiday," Lucinda concluded. "In some homes it is topped with a star, in others an angel, and decorated with ornaments of all shapes and sizes."

"Such a beautiful legend," Gabriel commented. "I am so pleased to have been a part of you telling it, my lady. My father would say you are an excellent storyteller, worthy of tribal honor." Lucinda, sitting back in her chair, beamed with satisfaction at his praise. Gabriel took advantage of her good spirit and spoke further. "I would ask your permission, now to steal Riley away for just a few moments before the evening meal is served."

"Permission granted," Lucinda agreed.

Taking Riley by the hand, he led her out of the parlor, through the foyer, past the library, and into the solarium. Once at the back entrance, he stopped, turned toward her, and smiled. "Wait here."

Completely baffled, she spoke not a word but nodded.

Gabriel opened the kitchen door and walked down the path to the end, then disappeared behind a tree. His smile grew as he heard Riley's squeal of delight once she realized what was happening. Her slipper-clad feet ran down the path, halting at the end.

That was when he jumped out from behind the tree, neared her, and knelt upon one knee. "Riley Flanders, would you do me the honor of becoming my wife?"

"Oh, aye, Gabriel, that I will," was her breathless response, tears of joy glistening in her eyes.

Her agreement sparked bliss throughout his body, such happiness and contentment he had not felt in a very long time. Standing, he gathered her into his arms, carried her from the winter's night cold, and back into the warmth of the solarium. With the tip of a booted toe, he kicked shut the door. Then he placed her down upon her own two feet and recaptured her into his hold. He kissed each of her eyes, her nose, and her chin. She threw her head back and willingly offered him the creamy expanse of her neck.

Without hesitation he complied. Down her neckline his lips traveled, past her throat, to the plunging décolletage of her gown. She gasped but did not protest. Instead, she trembled with desire. His heart raced, his loins swelled, as he tasted the soft mound of a breast with the tip of his tongue.

"Gabriel, oh Gabriel," she whispered, leaning into him.

Encouraged, excited, completely enticed, he pulled her against his swollen member. She gasped again at the feel of his erection but still did not object. However, just as he was about to be so bold as to caress her firm, rounded backside with the palm of his hand, Regis cleared his throat behind them.

"Begging your pardon, but dinner is now ready to be served," Regis droned.

Riley jumped from his embrace, her face scarlet. Covering her neck with a hand, as if that would hide the kisses he just rained upon her flesh, she flew past Regis and out of the solarium without a word said.

Gabriel ran a hand threw his hair. "Thank you, Regis," he managed in a shaky tone.

"Sir, it is my personal rule not to meddle," Regis began, his face pinched in the usual constipated expression. "Keeping one's mouth shut and turning a blind eye has kept me employed for two decades at Collins Stead."

Gabriel acknowledged the other man's words with a taut nod while he straightened his waistcoat.

"But I wish to break my rule for just this once, if you would allow?"

He nodded again. "Feel free to speak your mind, Regis."

Regis inclined his head politely. "Thank you, sir." He cleared his throat again, but this time his esophagus cleansing sounded more like a reaction someone would do before giving a speech. "I have watched Miss Riley grow from a scared, shy mite to a strong and beautiful young woman, and now to an intelligent and independent lady. Lucinda Collins has done right by showing Miss Riley the virtues of respectability. I am proud of the many accomplishments Miss Riley has made, in spite of all the challenges she's had to face. And in these years that have past, I have grown to care about her as though she were one of my own."

"That is admirable of you, Regis," he said, suddenly realizing a protector does not always have to be a man of warrior status or one who wields a weapon. Regis, by the standards of brawny men, would probably be looked upon as somewhat of a dandy fellow, though his preference for the delights afforded by his own kind was not a fact anyone could attest to. And yet, no matter what his liking may be or his puny physical attributes, Regis had the fortitude to stand by a young woman of his household. Much like Gabriel did for his sister when he confronted Rafe's intentions before they became happily wed.

"Thank you, sir." Regis squared his shoulders. "And within these few years, I have also become quite fond of you as well. It is for this reason I am compelled to speak from my heart."

"I am listening," he said.

"I fear you will bring disgraceful ruin upon Miss

Riley's reputation."

He frowned. "I would never allow anyone or anything to smear Riley's good name."

Regis arched a brow. "And yet I have caught you thrice, to be exact, in the act of taking advantage of her virtue."

"I was not...I did not mean to..." he stammered, the guilt and shame of his insensitive behavior rising to gag him.

"Riley is not, at this point, comparable to the likes of Collette Halston. However, if you do not make an honest woman of her soon, that is exactly the type of individual she will become, and how all of society will see her," Regis warned.

Gabriel pondered the elder man's words before he spoke. "This is a delicate subject we tread upon, my friend. And I want you to know I hear your concerns loud and clear. I could not agree with you more. That is why I have asked Riley to be my wife."

Regis's stone-faced expression broke into a relieved smile. "Oh, very good, sir. Very, very good indeed. I am truly pleased to hear this news. And if you don't mind me inquiring, sir, what was the lady's response?"

"She has accepted my proposal. She clearly and most definitely said, *yes*."

It was the first time he ever heard Regis laugh; in truth, it sounded more like a mix between a chuckle and a grunt. "That's very good, sir. Very good indeed," he repeated.

"I think so as well," Gabriel agreed. "Now, if there is nothing else troubling you, I believe my dinner is waiting."

Regis inclined his head politely. "After you, sir."

"Thank you, Regis. And I would like to take this time to thank you again for caring so much about Miss Riley...about all of us," he added warmly, as he made his way to the dining room.

Chapter Thirty

Glenshire Sussex, England
February 1895

Riley's wedding day had finally arrived. It was the moment she'd dreamed of since she was old enough to wish upon a star, admire a beautiful gown, and fancy herself in love with a handsome prince. Though Gabriel Golden Eagle was not a prince, he was a handsome warrior, and she was very much in love with him.

As she smoothed the cream-colored silk and satin skirt of her gown, she smiled at her reflection she presented in Lucinda's full-length mirror.

"You are a vision of loveliness." Lucinda rose from her seat at the foot of her bed. "I am so pleased you agreed to wear my mother's gown." The elder woman sighed. "Since I was never able to make use of it, I'm sure Mum would be happy you are."

"I am honored beyond words, Auntie Cinda," she said, gently stroking the gown's beautiful laced sleeves. "And so very thankful for all you've done for me these past twelve years." She turned from the mirror to face the elder woman, giving her a big hug. "None of what I have or this day would have ever been possible for me, if it weren't for you taking me in when Anita passed."

"It is I who should be thanking you," Lucinda whispered.

Riley pulled back to look into the soft, aged eyes of the woman who saved her life. "Thank me for what?"

279

"For being the daughter I never had," Lucinda said, eyes welling with unshed tears. "I don't know what I shall do now without you."

She smiled in spite of the tears filling her own eyes. "You have plenty to do, my lady. With Simon and Fiona Cavendish and their growing family nearby and Leah's announcement just last week that she's with child, you will be up to your ears with newborn babies, and all the commotion that accompanies them."

Lucinda sighed again. "Though all of them are splendid in their own way, none of them is you, my dear." She forced a smile and affectionately patted Riley's cheek. "And you must always know whenever you and Gabriel wish to return, a place waits for you at Collins Stead. When I am dead and gone, this mansion will be left to Gabriel and his sisters. He promised me it would stay in the family. And the smaller mansion, though the Cavendish's dwell there now, still belongs to you."

"We shan't speak of your passing, for you have many good years ahead. Besides, it is bad luck to talk of such sorrow on a happy day," she said, squeezing Lucinda's arm affectionately.

"So true, my dear, but I wanted you to know my wishes, if and when you and Gabriel come back to England."

"And until we decide to return, the Cavendish family will take care of the main mansion for us, leaving the smaller mansion empty again. So, I would like for your barrister to make a provision whereby Oliver and Leah would mind it in my absence," she said.

"Aye, first thing on Monday I will do just as you asked," Lucinda promised. "Enough with such sentimental nonsense, or else you'll not be ready when your attendants arrive. And Jane," she added, glancing around the bedchamber with a frown.

"Where in God's name is that woman?"

She giggled. "You've sent her to fetch us tea."

Lucinda's frown deepened. "So I did. Well, she needn't be taking so long. There's your hair yet to arrange," she said, reaching out to gently touch a lock of Riley's hair.

"I believe I shall leave it down, falling around my shoulders," she said.

"But, my dear, all the fashion is those lovely, large curls atop the head," Lucinda advised.

"I know, but Gabriel likes my hair down. And besides, all the married women in his tribe wear their hair in such a way, so I will be honoring one of his traditions," she added.

The elder woman's eyes glistened again. "You will be a good wife to him." She pushed aside a curl from Riley's forehead. "Already you are considerate of his ways, doing your best to please him. And I have nay a doubt he will be just as attentive and caring to your needs as well."

"I agree," she said, her heart swelling with happiness. "I see love in his eyes when he looks at me and respect toward me in all his actions."

"Love and respect are very important in a marriage, but so is honesty and trust. Without these other two essentials, a relationship cannot survive," Lucinda explained. "Above all, my dear, remember to be honest with Gabriel about the things you're feeling, then trust him to consider and understand them. And by the same token, you must oblige him in such matters as well."

"I will, Auntie Cinda. I promise you, I will."

It wasn't long after she shared a quiet sip of tea with Lady Lucinda that her attendants arrived. Sunny Cavendish served as her matron of honor, dressed in a burgundy gown of silk and organza. The deep plum shade against her pale curls and sapphire blue eyes was charming. Fiona Cavendish and Leah

Mills served as her bridesmaids. Both of the women, toting bellies in different stages of gestation, looked lovely in gowns of forest green. Against Fiona's auburn tresses and Leah's golden locks, the deep green color took on a rich tone.

"Who would've believed I'd be wearin' somethin' as grand as this?" Leah gushed, admiring herself in the mirror.

Riley hugged the younger woman. "You are absolutely beautiful."

"Oh, nay, miss, 'tis ye who are the beauty," Leah corrected.

"You all are visions," Lucinda commented. "However, my dear ladies, I must declare you've all had quite enough of this preening."

"You are right, my lady," Sunny agreed. "If Riley wishes to make a stop at Tom and Anita's grave before we reach Wade's Landing, we must get going real soon."

"How generous of your father and Kaylena to offer their home for my nuptials and reception," Riley said to Fiona.

Fiona smiled. "They were pleased to be of service. Wade's Landing couldn't be more perfect, since it is built like a tiny castle. There's more then plenty of room for a chapel-set-up in the solarium and a reception in the banquet hall, not to mention room to dance in the ballroom. Besides, Kaylena is Gabriel's aunt, and she felt strongly about making his wedding one to remember."

"Not to mention she is utterly and completely controlling and would not take *no* for an answer," Sunny chimed in.

They all laughed, even Lucinda.

"Well, in this case I appreciate her persistence. Wade's Landing is one of the most well-designed, sophisticated, and stylish mansions in London, so I shan't complain," she admitted.

"Now, for the final touch," Jane said, making her way to Riley and placing the veil upon her head.

Riley smiled warmly at her handmaiden. "Come the spring, you will wed next."

Jane's eyes grew moist. "And ye won't be 'ere to share it with me, miss."

"But I shall keep you in my thoughts that entire day and be with you in spirit, Jane." She gave the other woman a quick hug. "Nevertheless, it shall be a glorious day, and you will be absolutely enchanting."

"I thank ye," Jane whispered. "Now, 'urry on with ye cloak, least ye be late for yer own weddin'."

Two carriages awaited them. The smaller vehicle, owned by Lucinda and driven by Charles as always, transported Lady Collins, Jane, Addie, and Regis. The second coach, much larger, more elegant, and owned by Lord Morgan Wade, held Riley and her three attendants.

At the family burial plot, Riley asked for a moment of privacy. Her veil and cloak billowed in the wind as she stood alone over the two graves of those she considered her parents. With tears in her eyes, she said a quick prayer and her final goodbyes.

In two days she and Gabriel will be leaving for a three week stay in Ireland. Once in Limerick she will meet the Delaney's. Word from Gabriel's sister, Lady Raven Shannon also living in Limerick, explained Lord Shannon made some inquiries and discovered Riley has an uncle, her father's brother, and three grown cousins still in residence there. They are very anxious to meet her, as is Raven and her family. From Ireland they will travel to America, which will become her new home. Though she knew Gabriel planned on returning to England in time for an extended visit, that opportunity might not be for years to come.

So on this most anticipated day of her life,

happiness was bittersweet. In marrying her one true love, she also had to say farewell to the others she loved as well.

"It will be a long time before I am able to stand here again," she whispered. "But deep within my heart, I will remember you both. And when the time arrives, I shall speak with love about you to my children." Then, pulling two roses from the bridal bouquet she held in trembling hands, she placed a bloom upon each grave before walking back to the waiting carriage.

Wade's Landing was decorated to receive a queen. All of them gasped upon entering the solarium. The romantic glow of tall, white candles lit the large room, and bouquets of red roses were placed all about. Rows upon rows of chairs were filled with people. At a glance she spotted Lord Wellington, his wife, and Suzanna present, as was Lord and Lady Abbott. Jerome and Marietta Cavendish were in attendance, along with a countless number of Lucinda's friends and business acquaintances.

At the end of the aisle, Reverend Joshua Holmes stood ready to officiate. Gabriel, looking dashing and handsome, broad shoulders filling out the black jacket he wore also stood on the podium. Rafe, his best man, stood beside him, also dressed in a tux with tails. Both men wore top hats. She smiled to herself. *Top Hat Tom would have fit right in.*

Sunny was the first to walk down the aisle. Simon escorted his wife, Fiona, and Oliver paired with his wife, Leah. Both men dressed in gray tuxedos and top hats to match. Then it was Riley's turn. It was customary for a father or a male member of the family to give away the bride, but since none was available in her case, she bent the rules. Lady Lucinda Collins was the most likely candidate and the nearest to any living family Riley had. So, the two women walked arm and arm down the aisle to meet Gabriel, Lucinda giving her permission when asked, before taking a seat in the front row.

Her heart raced through the vows, every fiber of her being sang with joy when Gabriel placed a gold divinity band encrusted with diamond chips upon her finger and kissed her. She barely tasted the roast chicken and almond stuffing, baby peas, potato casserole steeped in cheddar cheese, green beans with sausage, plum pudding, or the apple cobbler served. The wedding cake, decorated with creamy white frosting and sprigs of mint, melted upon her tongue. She danced, wrapped in her husband's strong arms, gazing into his mesmerizing, sapphire eyes. People congratulated her, kissed her, and tears were shed. Then Jane handed Gabriel an overnight bag containing the garments she'd need for the night, and Regis supplied a satchel for Gabriel before they said their goodbyes and climbed into the coach provided again by Lord Wade.

Off they went...just the two of them, no chaperone needed, to a quaint little one room cottage gifted to them for a night by Lady Wellington. It was a whirlwind of a day, and now came nightfall...their first as husband and wife.

Gabriel carried her over the threshold, into the tiny enchanted-looking dwelling that would be their love nest for a time. Champagne waited for them, as did a large, canopy bed. Only one lantern, placed on a bedside table, was lit, and a fire burned in the fireplace. She removed her cloak and veil, while her husband downed his own hat and jacket. Then she watched him stoke the fire and uncork the bottle of champagne, pouring them each a portion of the bubbly drink into crystal goblets.

"I must remember to thank Lady Wellington profusely for such a magnificent gift," she said, taking the goblet Gabriel handed her.

He smiled, looking around the room, his gaze resting long upon the huge, soft-looking bed steeped with pillows. The coverlet's corners were already turned down for their use. "It does serve a perfect purpose."

Her face heated. "Aye, it does at that," she murmured, as she also took in her surroundings. The large room housed an eating and sitting area, as well as sleeping quarters. There was only one other outlet, a small water closet, which also served as a privy.

They sipped their drinks in silence, and when he took her glass, he rubbed his finger over the long, jagged scar atop her hand. "How did you come by that?"

"Anita sent me out for a couple of apples one afternoon after she was paid for doing a chap's laundry, and on the way home, a couple of boys chased me. All they wanted was my apples, but such a treat was hard to come by, and I wasn't about to give them over so easily." She took an audible breath. "But they were big fellas, and at the time I was only a thin, small, six-year-old girl. I put up a good fight, got in a few slugs before I was cut with a piece of broken glass by one of the boys. In the end they managed to rob me of my apples. And I remember just sitting on the ground, holding my bleeding hand, and vowing that one day I would have as many apples as I'd wanted and not be afraid someone would take then from me."

"You never have to be afraid of anything again. I am here now, and I will protect you with my life," he said, taking her glass from her and placing them both upon a table. "Would you prefer I step outside while you undress?"

"I cannot—it is rather difficult, you see, to get out of this gown on my own," she said. The thought of him helping her to undress made her cheeks burn as though they were on fire. "I am so sorry to have to ask."

"No apology needed," he said, his eyes twinkling as he neared her. Then, turning her around by the shoulders, he commenced unhooking the trail of small, pearled fasteners down her back. She bit her bottom lip, remembering how frustrated buttons made him. She prayed he would not rip Lucinda's cherished heirloom off her, as he once did her blouse in Collette's chamber.

Thankfully, his patience held, but his comment showed the effort of his restraint. "Why do women's clothes have so many damn buttons?"

His remark somehow broke the tension, and she giggled. From behind her, he joined in on her mirth, as he continued, one by one, to unhook each button. Then he slid the gown off her shoulders, and in one quick sweep, down past her hips, to around her ankles, where she quickly stepped out of it. Spinning around, she retrieved the gown from the floor and held it against her breasts, shielding herself from his eyes.

His smile was a quirky, mischievous sort of grin that excited her. "Now might be a good time for me to step outside."

"Perhaps it would," she managed to choke out, knowing what would take place once he returned.

He nodded and reached for his jacket. Hesitating at the door, he turned to look at her. "Take all the time you need."

Her voice came out shakier than she liked. "Not too long, I promise. I know it's awfully cold outside."

Once the door latched behind him, she placed the gown on a nearby chair and reached for her overnight bag. She rummaged through the toiletries, the fresh undergarments and outer wear for the morrow, but there weren't bedclothes available. Was that an oversight on Jane's part, or did her trusted handmaiden expect her to sleep naked?

She felt herself blush right down to the roots of her hair. "Oh Jane, how could you?" she whispered.

Well, there was little she could do about Jane's error, assumption, or whatever the case may be. In a matter of moments, Gabriel would be coming through the door, expecting her to be ready to...

As quick as she could, she stripped herself of everything but her chemise and climbed into bed, pulling the coverlet up to her chin.

He entered in silence, stepped before the fire, and undressed with his back to her. She watched as he downed his jacket and shirt, his muscular back and arms sending rivets of desire pulsating through her. Off came his shoes and socks, cast aside one by one. And then his trousers, slipped down past his hips, removed from one leg, then the other. The backs of his thighs were hard with muscle. Strong legs supported his perfectly sculpted body. Lastly, he shed his under drawers, pushing them down to pool around his ankles. Kicking the material aside, he walked naked to the table.

Riley swallowed hard as she watched him pour himself another glass of champagne, his firm, rounded backside drawing her eyes like a magnet. Slowly, he sipped the champagne, all the while standing gloriously in the nude before her.

When he finished his drink, he set the goblet down. But before he turned around, he called to her, "Riley, I wish to come to you now."

"Good heavens, Gabriel. I've never been with...I've never done this...never even seen a naked man."

He remained standing with his back to her, his tone gentle and calm. "I am not just a naked man. I am your husband."

"Is there such a big difference?"

"Yes, *shi'aad*, my wife, there is. And if you will allow me to turn around and come to bed, I would be glad to show you," he said softly.

"Aye, but turn slowly, please," she agreed, her heart racing with a mixture of anticipation, curiosity, and a twinge of fear.

He seemed to read the latter emotion. "You have nothing to fear, never from me, anyway. I will never hurt you. I just want to love you with my body, as I do with my heart."

"Then come to bed, for I want to do the same." She pulled aside a piece of the coverlet. "But would you douse the light first?" she whispered.

"No, it will remain lit. I want to see all of you while I love you." As he turned to face her, he added, "And I wish for you to see all of me as well."

Her gaze went immediately to his sex. Try as she might, she could not cast her eyes away from his erect staff, now jutting out long and hard from between his thighs. The mere sight of him caused her already fast pulsing heart to pump passion through all her arteries.

"Oh, my." She sat straight up in the bed. The coverlet fell to her waist, revealing she still wore the chemise.

"You are still dressed," he said.

She raised her gaze to meet his. "Not really," she said, feeling the heat mounting in her face. "I'm not wearing any...there is nothing else but..." she stammered. Then after clearing her throat, she blurted out, "I just could not bring myself to remove everything."

"Will you allow me?"

"Aye," she whispered breathlessly. The flesh at the juncture of her thighs tingled as he neared her.

With one knee he knelt upon the bed, his phallus only inches away as he reached to find the hem of her chemise, working it up over her thighs, hips, and then pulling it up and over her head. Casting the garment aside, his eyes feasted on her naked breasts.

She automatically crossed her arms over her bosom, shielding them from view.

Her actions caused him to raise his gaze, locking with hers. "You need not feel ashamed. There is nothing wrong with what we are about to do in our marriage bed."

"It is just a bit difficult to suddenly think differently. Just yesterday our actions would have been all so scandalous," she said, biting her bottom lip.

"Yesterday is gone and will never come again." He entwined a lock of her hair around a finger. "You have hair as red as fire."

A nervous little giggle escaped from her throat.

He smiled. "And your laugh lifts my spirits like it had the wings of a bird." He arched a brow. "Redbird then, is what I have wished for a long time to call you." His voice softened. "Do you even know, my beautiful Redbird, how perfect you are?"

"Nay," she managed to whisper, captivated by his new name for her.

"Well, you are more wonderful then I could ever have dreamed," he said, his eyes filling with desire. "And I can no longer hold back from wanting to kiss, touch, and taste every part of you." He released her tresses to caress her cheek with the tip of a finger, moving it to tenderly trace the outline of her mouth. "Please, *shi'aad*, let this now be the first time of countless others that we will come together as one."

Riley opened her arms, and in doing so, fully opened her heart. He reached for her hand and placed it on his chest. Beneath her palm, his heart raced. She caressed his smooth, hot skin, marveling over the hard muscles that met her touch. Then in pure abandonment, she gave herself over to her own longings and slid her hand down his abdomen, past his navel, to rest between his thighs.

His intake of breath, as she clasped her fingers around his thickened column, froze her advances. But with his own large, warm hand placed over hers, he encouraged her to continue...moving her grasp to glide up and down along his shaft.

"Your touch pleases me," he said, closing his eyes while she stroked him.

He throbbed, his erection growing harder and slippery with her touch.

Then, ceasing her hand with his, he opened his eyes. "Now, I will please you."

Gently, he pushed her to lie back upon the pillow. With feather like kisses, he favored her neck, moving lower to her breasts. When he suckled a teat, she gasped at the wonderful sensations vibrating through her. His hand moved to caress her abdomen, then the inner thigh, and finally the valley of her own sex. His finger slipped within, finding the fleshy button hidden there, and teasing it with quick, tender strokes. She closed her eyes to the ecstasy, opened her legs, arched her back, and allowed herself to become totally encompassed by the strange, yet thrilling responses her body was experiencing.

He lifted his mouth from her breast. "Open your eyes and look at me," he whispered.

Closed lids fluttered open, her eyes searching deep into his hot gaze.

"I want to see in your eyes the pleasure brought by the first glorious mounting and then release of your passion," he said, the tip of his finger working faster to stimulate her wet nub.

"Gabriel, oh Gabriel," she moaned, raising her arms above her head. She fisted her hands, her fingernails painfully piercing her palms, etching crescent-shapes into her flesh.

"Your passion sets me afire, my beautiful Redbird," he whispered breathlessly, his own excitement gleaming in the sapphire eyes that watched her. Her toes curled as the spasms grew stronger and stronger, dominating her senses until the yearning for release became both agonizing and sensational. Crying out his name once again, her desire crested, then burst, shattering through every nerve ending in her body.

"Now you are ready for me," he said, moving between her thighs. She wrapped her legs around his hips, feeling the tip of his phallus making way for penetration. With one thrust he'd be inside her. But he remained still, posed at her gate.

Searching his face, she saw uncertainty clouding his eyes. He tried to turn his face aside, but she stopped him, resting the palms of her hands on each side of his face. "Enter me, Gabriel. I am ready to please you as you have done me."

"I cannot, Riley," he choked out hoarsely, pulling away from her grasp and rolling off of her. Reaching for the extra throw blanket draped at the foot of the bed, he wrapped it around himself, and took a seat on a nearby chase beside the fireplace.

The wonderful and warm sensations of a moment ago gelled like lumps of ice in her veins. She watched as he curled up on the lounge and stared at the fire. Though he said not a word, his actions spoke volumes. And what they said broke her to the very core. He was unable to make love to her because he still felt something for Collette.

Riley swallowed hard past the lump of shame and sorrow lodged now in her throat. How she wished she could run from the room, leave his sight so she could cry her heart out in privacy. But the cottage was only made up of one room, and spending the night in the privy would be more humiliating then staying in the bed.

"I am sorry. This is not about you," he added, running a hand through his hair.

"Then who is it about?" As if she didn't already know, but would he be honest enough to say the other woman's name? Lucinda said honesty and trust were most important in a marriage. Did Gabriel feel the same? Would he trust her enough to be honest? She waited...and silently prayed.

"It grows late, and Lord Wade's carriage will be here early tomorrow to fetch us," he said, keeping his eyes on the fire burning before him. "So it would be wise for you to get some rest."

Rest! How is that now possible?

She bit her lip until she tasted blood, trying to still the hurt and rage that coursed through her. Having an argument the first night they wed was not her idea of starting out a marriage on a good foot. "Are you coming to bed?"

"In a moment. I need a moment," he muttered.

"Very well," she said. Turning down the dim, flaring light of the lantern, she rolled onto her side and faced away from him. She may not be as skilled in bed as Collette Halston, but she did have a sense of pride. As she pulled the coverlet up to cover her nakedness, tears silently fell from her eyes, wetting the linen pillowcase.

Never...ever would she beg for his love.

Chapter Thirty-One

Gabriel's insides ached. His chest felt tight and his stomach churned. How could he have done what he did? Did he not wait so long, want so much for the moment to come when he could make Riley completely his? Now, instead of feeling the warmth of her body close to his, he was sitting, freezing on a lounge, wrapped in a throw that barely covered his flesh. And she was alone in bed, weeping. As hard as she tried to keep her tears silent, he heard them in the darkness...heart-wrenching, spirit-breaking sobs that he caused, and all he could offer as an explanation was *the problem was not about her*.

He cringed at his behavior. If his father were here, he would be ashamed of Gabriel's actions. Never would Proud Eagle humiliate and hurt Golden Lady in such a way. A man who loved his wife respected her, honored her, was honest with her, and trusted her with his feelings.

It had been a long time since he cried real tears of sorrow and pain, loss and anguish. But now his eyes welled, and he covered his face with his hands. He was in love with Riley and wanted to show her how much he yearned for her, hardly able to contain the rolling desire within him. And yet the paralyzing facts of the past halted him in his tracks. When he was about to enter the passage of her womanhood, he suddenly realized the consequences...on this very night he could get her with child. His seed would fill her with life, a life that could render her death. It happened once before to a woman he loved. He would not allow it to happen again.

He slept fitfully, his dreams tormenting him.

He found himself walking in a darkened land, dense with trees, void of human touch, cold and sad. This was the exact condition of his heart before he met Riley. As he wandered further, he came to an opening in the forest's wall, where the moon could be seen shimmering in the waters of a pond. There is where he found her, the splendor of her delicate visage awash in the moonlight. When she spotted him, she made way to leave the area.

His voice held her as he called her name. She turned to face him. "Do not go," he pleaded.

"I cannot stay where I'm not wanted, Gabriel," she said.

The truth fell out of his mouth unexpectedly. "I do want you, Redbird, but alive, not dead, not dead," he cried.

"Unless you live for today, your heart will forever be locked into a bloody vendetta with the past. Yesterday is gone and will never come again," she said.

"My own words back to haunt me," he moaned, before waking with a start.

When he opened his eyes, it was to the new day. He found her sitting on the window seat cushions, with her chin on her fist, looking out at the forest beyond. Her angelic profile was silhouetted against the pre-dawn light.

His stomach tied itself in knots as he sat up. "I am sorry, *shi'aad.*"

"I know that word," she said curtly. "Sunny taught it to me." She pulled the coverlet that shielded her nakedness tighter around her bared shoulders. "It means, *my wife,* in Apache."

He shifted where he sat. "You speak the truth."

"But you didn't," she said, turning to face him. There was just enough gray light to see the tears prickling her eyes, threatening to spill over. "You

295

said you wanted me, but you don't. You didn't speak the truth."

He shot her an apologetic glance. "I am sorry from the depths of my heart if that is what I made you feel."

Frustration, anger, fatigue, and whatever other nameless emotions she might be feeling shifted across her face. "It is how I feel. And I won't stay married this way...to a man who keeps me as his wife in name only, then fills his primal urges with other women."

He frowned. "I would never do such a thing."

"You will eventually, if you never wish to lie with me. It is authentic human nature for men to fill their carnal needs in such a manner, especially if the man is in love with a woman other than his wife."

He stood, his wrap falling to pool around his ankles. "Is that what you think? That I love another woman?"

"Aye, last night you made it perfectly clear to me that you still had feelings for Collette," she remarked brusquely.

"Collette?"

"Aye, Collette. And so I have decided when we reach Ireland, I will remain there, with my father's folks. They are the only blood kin I have left in this world. Perhaps they will grow to love me...be my family."

He made his way to where she sat and took her by the shoulders, pulling her to her feet. "First of all, I am not the type of man who marries and then disrespects my wife by climbing into another's bed. I have given my word, taken vows, and I will keep my oath until death parts us. And second, I am now your family, and you will only be wherever I am."

"Nay, I will not be second best in your heart," she cried, the tears now slipping down her cheeks.

"You are not second best. You are the only one

true love of my heart," he reassured her.

"Then why did you stop loving me?" she sobbed. "Why did you pull away, after you...you...?"

"Because I feared I would get you with child. And then you would die and leave me alone, cold, sad, and unloved again," he blurted out.

Her rants subsided, and she stared wide-eyed and puzzled. "I thought the day Sunny gave birth you were resolved of such fears."

He shrugged. "When I was about to enter you, the consequences of my actions returned to haunt me. And that is the whole truth of the situation, *shi'aad*," he said in a softer tone. "As I told you last night, it was not about you."

"But it *is* about me. With such a notion as that, you are dooming me to a loveless marriage as well as yourself. Soon there would be a vast distance between us. Oh, we might appear as though we are a couple, because we'd be living in the same household, but the emotional distance would eventually build an invisible wall between us. With you on one side and me on the other, going our separate ways, how can our hearts be anything but empty and lonely? I have seen such unions between a man and woman, and it isn't for me. Not to mention the fact we wouldn't have children or grandchildren. I don't want a life such as that." She searched his face. "Do you?"

"No. I do not want...I *never* want that for either of us," he confessed, true regret for his actions constricting his throat.

"Well, then I'd say there is no further reason to speculate about it," she finally replied. "You must decide now whether you wish to love me to your fullest capacity." She opened her arms, allowing the coverlet to fall to the floor. Standing stark naked before him, she cast him a mischievous smile. "There is still some time left before our carriage arrives to make things right between us."

His only response was an amused grin. Gathering her into his embrace, he carried her to the bed, marveling before he set her down over the warm sensations her nude body felt against his. She lay back against the pillows, long, ginger curls fanning out around her face like a tribal headdress. His grin grew into a full, satisfied smile. "Riley Eagle, should I make you ready for me once again?"

"Oh, aye, Gabriel Golden Eagle," she quickly agreed, spreading her legs to reveal the exquisite scene of her female gender.

He climbed into bed beside her, and this time sought to pleasure her using his mouth. With the tip of his tongue, he gently entered her soft folds, teasing the wet, hot region with feather-like flicks. She squirmed with delight, spreading her thighs even further apart. Then he increased his attention upon her, feeling the slippery nub quake against his tongue. The unique scent, taste, and texture of her flesh swelled his loins. And when she arrived at the pinnacle of passion, her climatic spasms thrilled him to the core of his being.

He raised his head, glimpsing the fulfilled expression upon her sweet countenance. Her contentment filled him with such an overwhelming bliss he thought for sure his heart would burst from happiness. He drew himself up on his knees and looked down at her.

Her green eyes shone with flecks of gold, dreamy now as they gazed up at him adoringly. "Oh, Gabriel, what you do to me is so absolutely amazing," she breathlessly muttered.

"I only pray I can continue to summon such unbridled praise from your lips," he said, positioning himself between her thighs.

She wrapped her legs around his waist, the dainty heels of her feet resting on his lower back.

"I've got you good, now my love."

"I have no intentions of going anywhere this time, *shi'aad*," he whispered, erect with desire. Without further hesitation he entered her pocket, breaking her virginity with one thrust.

She gasped, her thighs tightening momentarily around him.

He kissed her lips, whispering against her mouth. "Do you know what makes this even more wonderful to me?"

"Nay," she said softly, her inner thigh muscles beginning to relax against him.

"The fact that I am the first and will be the only man to ever touch you in this way," he said.

She sought his mouth with her own, deepening the kiss as he moved in and out of her, slowly at first. She was tight and hot, and the feel of her beneath him made him want to savor the pleasure. But then the savoring turned to devouring, as his momentum increased. She matched the rhythm of his motions, the friction of their bodies bringing him to the edge of what he craved for so long. It took every last modicum of control to keep from exploding inside of her, as he yet wanted to relish the experience.

But when she increased the movement of her own hips, arching her back to consume him deeper, he could hold on no longer. With a fervent groan of pure ecstasy, he erupted within her. Every muscle, nerve, and tendon in his body bulged to capacity as he filled her hard and long. Then breathless and spent, he rolled onto his side, pulling her to him.

She nestled her face beneath his chin. "I had no idea it could be this way."

He smiled to himself, completely happy for the first time in many years.

She draped a leg over him, snuggling her perfectly sensuous body closer.

"If you are chilled, I can get the coverlet," he offered, remembering it was left upon the floor.

"Nay," she whispered. "I'm far from feeling cold. In fact," she added, "I don't believe I will ever be cold again."

"Well, not if I can help it," he whispered in return, before drifting into a deep sleep.

Chapter Thirty-Two

Gabriel did not think much about the reason Lord Wade's carriage arrived a few hours later than it was expected. At the time, he was somewhat grateful. The delay afforded him and Riley well needed sleep, plus a chance to discover each other all over again. But once back at Wade's Landing, the gratitude turned into sorrow as Percival, Lord Wade's butler, ignored their wish to freshen-up a bit before greeting the others and instead adamantly directed them with a subdued expression to the oversized parlor. Upon entering the large sitting room, his eyes went around to the saddened faces staring back at them. Sunny, Rafe, Aunt Kaylena, Lucinda Collins, and Reverend Holmes all appeared somber. But amongst them, Sunny appeared the worst. The utter and complete devastation upon her face frightened him. Instantly he assumed something horrible happened to one of the twins.

He shared a puzzled look with Riley, then after taking an audible breath, he inquired, "What is wrong?"

"Oh, my brother," Sunny cried, hurrying from her seat to run straight into his arms.

He held her close as she sobbed uncontrollably against his shoulder. Many times he held his little sister in this fashion, soothing her from a cut knee, or after she had to set one of her critters free. But the tears she shed now, those of a broken heart, scared him through and through. "*Dayden*, what has happened?"

Reverend Holmes answered his question

instead. "I've received word from Reverend Newcomb. The letter was sent to Cavenworth, my sister's home. It's how Benjamin always contacts me."

Dread enclosed around his heart, and he swallowed hard the lump lodged in his throat. "And what did he have to say?"

"It is our father," Sunny managed to gulp out between sobs. "He is dead."

As his sister's words penetrated his senses, the room began to spin. He staggered back against the wall with Sunny still clinging to him.

"Gabriel!" Riley grabbed his arm to steady him. Her eyes were already brimming with tears.

"Whoa, there, old chap," Rafe said, coming to his rescue. After taking Sunny from him and settling her into a nearby chair, Riley helped Gabriel to sit in another.

He was positioned directly opposite the fire, now quite ablaze. Yet the room felt so cold. He shivered and turned his gaze to Joshua Holmes. "How did he die?"

"It was a hunting accident. A few months ago, he decided to go on a hunt, and another hunter accidentally shot him in the leg. Without the proper care, the wound festered, and the infection spread."

Gabriel doubted it was an accident. Proud Eagle was an experienced hunter, knew the dangers and acted accordingly. His father was more than likely purposely shot. He knew the white agent's tricks. For a long time, they had wanted to rid themselves of the tribe's chief. And withholding the proper care was just the way to get the job done.

His hands fisted in his lap, the knuckles gleaming white and the tendons in his neck bulging with rage. But he controlled himself, for Sunny's sake. It would do her no good to entertain his suspicions, though they are well founded. As it was,

Sunny kept sobbing. "I always had hopes of seeing my father again, of him seeing my babies," and her anguish wrenched his heart.

Then another dreadful sadness welled up in him as he remembered Golden Lady. Her grief was probably just as insurmountable, if not more so than either he or Sunny could imagine. And her life, now without the protection of his father, would be in grave danger. "What of my mother?"

Josh held a grim expression. "She is beyond herself with sorrow, as you might well expect, but she is being kept safe, with the Newcombs at the parsonage."

"And the others?" he said.

"According to Benjamin's account of tribal members, there are less than a dozen left. He fails, however, to list who they are," Josh said. "Those that remain are also at the parsonage, sharing quarters in the barn and the stables until other accommodations can be made."

He pinched the bridge of his nose with a thumb and forefinger, as if to ease the pain of a headache brought on by the devastating situation. "You say this all happened a few months ago?"

"Aye," Josh said. "Unfortunately mail travel overseas is slow."

Gabriel inhaled sharply, managing to collect himself before he spoke further. "That is just the time my intuition filled with apprehension, and I felt deep in my bones something was not right with my people. I wanted to return to America but..."

"But you did not want to leave me while I was with child. If it were not for that, you would have gone home. And if you had, perhaps father would still be alive." Sunny glanced hurriedly around the room. "Do you not all see how this is my fault?"

"That is just ludicrous," Kaylena remarked. "How could you...how could any of us have known?"

"For once in my life, I tend to agree with Kaylena," Lucinda added.

"As do I," he agreed.

Sunny's voice was resigned. "You can all believe what you will, but I know this is all my doings. Gabriel stayed in England because of me."

He stood and made his way to where his sister sat. The remorse, etched so intensely upon her face, almost gave her a deathly pallor. Taking her hands, Gabriel spoke softly. "Listen to me well, *dayden*. You had no fault in my decision. It was my own fears that kept me here. I was haunted by a past tragedy. I was so frightened it would happen again, that my judgment was clouded. And I allowed that fear to eat at me clear through to my bones. But now I see through the fog of terror that surrounded me, thanks to the love of my wife, and I will not make the same mistake again. In the future, if I have uncertainties or I am fearful, I will be courageous enough to meet the situation head on."

Sunny glanced past him to Riley. "I am sorry, my new sister, that this sorrow has daunted your spirit, come at a time when you both should be having nothing but happy thoughts."

"You are my family now," Riley said. "I only wish to be of some comfort."

Sunny looked back at Gabriel. "You need to go on with your plans; take Riley to Limerick to meet her kin. We have been blessed to know our relatives. We know from what proud blood we are born. Riley has a right to know hers. And you must bring Raven the news of father's death. She will need your strong shoulders to cry upon, as I did. You, Raven, Mother, and I are the only four people in this whole world who understand completely what Father's passing means."

He nodded, forcing a smile. "You sound just like Mother." He turned his attention to Josh, addressing him directly. "Holy man, if I am to spend three weeks in Ireland, I will need your help."

Josh arched a brow. "Now you sound just like your father."

"Before we speak further, I think Sunny needs to be taken upstairs to rest," Lucinda suggested.

"No, I do not want to rest," Sunny protested.

"Please, Sunny Beth," Rafe pleaded. "It is the best thing for you now."

"But I will not be able to sleep a wink with this headache," she complained, rubbing her temples with the tips of her fingers. "Nor do I want to be alone."

Rafe pushed aside a golden curl. "I promise not to leave your side."

"Rafe, once you two are upstairs, call for my maid, Clara," Kaylena chimed in. "She knows where I keep a bit of Laudanum for an occasional headache of my own. Right now, a small dose will help Sunny's pain as well and allow her to rest."

"Aye, thank you, my lady," Rafe said, escorting Sunny from the parlor.

Josh folded his arms across his chest. "I have a good idea what you are about to ask of me, Gabriel, and I believe I am way ahead of you."

Gabriel made his way to the window. The sun, by now, sat further down in the sky. He reached for the latch and opened one pane a crack. Cool air touched his forehead. "When do you leave for America?"

"In four days," Josh said.

"And what of your duties in Brighton?" Kaylena inquired.

"I will turn them over to Reverend Daniel Kane," he said.

Kaylena frowned. "And who is this Reverend Kane?"

"He is Lord and Lady Abbott's son-in-law, their

daughter, Annabella's husband. The couple and their two-year-old son, Thomas, have returned to England just before Christmas. Daniel was doing missionary work in Texas."

Gabriel remembered Lady Abbott telling him and Sunny about Annabella and her family when they were traveling to England onboard the *Entrenous*.

"Daniel is an ordained minister anxious to settle down and lead a congregation, especially now that Annabella is expecting their second child in a matter of months," Josh continued. "So, I have been counseling him in such matters. I figured he'd be my ideal replacement so I might retire. He's caught on to the dealings quite fast. He's the reason I am able to be in London now. And the parsonage is just big enough to house his little family quite comfortably." Josh arched a brow. "So you have nay a reason for alarm, Kaylena. All will be just as it was for Brighton's chapel, and I can leave in four days for America."

He turned from the window to face the other man. "You have been waiting for this moment for a long time."

Josh appeared momentarily startled by the remark. "I beg your pardon?"

"Gabriel, don't," Riley warned, coming to stand by her husband. Placing a hand upon his arm, she looked deep into his eyes. "Don't let your grief make you say something you might regret."

"Listen to your wife, Gabriel," Lucinda added.

Josh held up a hand. "It's all right, my lady. I have nothing to be ashamed of." He looked over at Gabriel. "Speak your mind."

He moved to stand in front of a nearby table. Leaning over it, he rested his weight on his hands. With brows heavily drawn and lips curved into a scowl, his anger exploded. "It is no secret how you have felt...how you continue to feel about my mother. I would say my father's death has made everything very convenient for you."

Kaylena gasped. "Gabriel, this is entirely not necessary."

"I agree," Lucinda said.

He smirked to himself. In the past Kaylena and Lucinda never got along. How miraculous is it now that they both agree at his expense.

Josh's expression was rigid, his hands curling into white-knuckled fists by his side, yet he spoke calmly. "You are no longer a boy that needs to be shielded from certain facts in life, so I will not deny to you my feelings for Amanda. But by no means have I ever wished for any ill will to befall Proud Eagle. Believe it or not, your father was my friend as well, and his death brings me great sorrow. Though we did not see eye to eye on many things, we respected each other. We agreed a long time ago that we had a common bond, that being your mother. Together we worked to keep her safe and well cared for. That was and still is the main reason for everything said and done between us. And after all these years, your father still held true to this reasoning." He pulled from his pocket a letter and offered it to Gabriel. "Read Benjamin's words yourself, and you will learn that before your father died, he asked for last rites. Then he made Reverend Newcomb promise to contact me. He asked that I return to Arizona and care for Amanda."

He straightened his stand, reached for the letter, and read it for himself. Though he desired to contradict Josh, he truthfully could not. Proof of what he claimed was clearly collaborated in Reverend Newcomb's words.

"I am sorry," he said, placing the letter aside and wearily taking a seat. Riley came to stand behind his chair and very gently lowered her hands to rest on his shoulders. He reached for one of her hands, brought it up to his lips, and kissed the scar etched there. In that instant he realized he would not only protect her, but she would be there for him too. His new wife would be his rock, the foundation he needed to stay sane, focused, and anchored.

"There's something else I need to show you," Josh said, reaching into his vest pocket to retrieve another piece of paper. "This document is the deed to your grandfather, Ethan Gregory's farm."

He frowned. "Why do you have it?"

"Your mother gave it to me after she married your father," Josh explained. "She knew Proud Eagle would never leave the tribe, and she'd never return to the property without him. But she didn't want poachers to set up quarters there either."

His frown deepened. "I have heard her talk of the farm she grew up on, but she never told me you held the deed."

Josh shrugged. "I don't know why your mother withheld that bit of information from you." He smirked. "Amanda is a strong-willed woman who has a way of getting what she wants, when she wants it. Only the good Lord knows the reasons behind the things she does."

"Amen to that," Kaylena ratified.

He nodded. "I know what you mean."

"It is prime property, fifty-seven acres in all," Josh went on. "The soil is rich for farming, and there's a stream and hunting grounds nearby." Josh took a moment before continuing. "It's been my project all these years to preserve the land. Months before I left America, I hired a young chap to keep the grounds for me. His name is Vernon Washburn. My deal with him was that I pay for a cottage in the woods to be built for him, his wife, and two sons, as well as allow him half of the profits the farm produces and a monthly stipend. He's done a remarkable job. Now upon the land there is a barn housing chickens and two cows, plus the stable has a few horses. Washburn also maintains the family burial plot, where your grandparents, Amelia and Ethan Gregory rest in peace. Sadly, Mrs. Washburn passed away about five years ago, and both the sons live in Boston. But Vernon remains steadfast, and I'm sure he would welcome company."

Gabriel's hopes soared. "Are you suggesting what I think you are?"

"Aye," Josh said. "All of these acres have the potential to serve as a new village for you and Riley, your mother, and the tribe's people remaining. Houses can be placed a good distance apart to afford each dweller their privacy."

"And do you wish to remain permanently there as well, Reverend?" Riley asked softly.

"Aye, if Gabriel doesn't hate the idea so much," he said.

Gabriel arched a brow. "In truth, the land is yours. I have no right to keep you from living on your own property."

Josh handed him the deed. "Nay, the land is now yours. I have signed the deed over to you."

He frowned, taking the aged document. "Why would you do this?"

"By all that's holy and right, this is a legacy left by your grandfather." Josh smiled warmly. "You can now lead your people as a chief must do."

"That's right, Gabriel. Now you are the chief," Riley said.

"But I take no happiness in the title, as it comes with a great price."

"I have something for you as well, Gabriel," Kaylena added. "I have set up an account in your mother's name and deposited her share of the inheritance from the Bentley fortune. My barrister has also set up an account for you, whereby the monthly stipend you receive from your own inheritance, plus whatever share of the profits you get from Bentwood's health resort business, will be deposited for your use."

"And a monthly stipend from the Collins fortune will be added into that account as well," Lucinda added. "I've also set up a separate account for Riley so she can continue to receive her own monthly stipend." She smiled. "You will have plenty of capital to support your endeavors, and there is nay a thing the white agents can ever do to your people again."

His heart was overwhelmed with love and respect for all those in the room who stood up to help his people. "I cannot thank you all enough."

"It's what family does for each other," Lucinda said.

"I did not want to come to England, grumbled about being the one chosen to escort my sisters across the sea," he explained. "But my father pointed out my duty to their safety and ignored my arguments. Then my mother spoke, her large, kind eyes seeking mine, and she made me realize the second importance of my travels. She spoke of the financial means, afforded by my inheritance, and what it could accomplish for the Apache people. In truth, she had a vision, over two years ago, of what would transpire here today."

"Your mother is a wise woman," Josh beamed.

"Yes, she is," he said softly.

"And what will become of the current Apache land?" Riley inquired.

"It is no longer Apache ground," he said. "It has not been since the first white agent set foot upon it."

"They can never again set foot on this land, Gabriel," Josh said.

In spite of the sorrow for the loss of his father, he smiled. "No, never again."

Chapter Thirty-Three

Dinner was a quiet meal. Everyone who sat around the table was lost in thought. Sunny and Rafe took their meal in the chamber they occupied. Before he joined Riley in their own chamber, he stopped to comfort his sister again, tell her about their grandfather's land, and the real hope of saving what was left of the tribe.

His words seemed to appease her somewhat, though she would miss him terribly. And come the morning, he would be bound for Ireland, whereby he would break the sad news to another sister.

Once in bed, he pulled Riley close to him and kissed her forehead.

She snuggled beneath his arm, resting a hand upon his chest. "I understand now the grief you must have felt for your first wife, Gabriel, and empathy for your mother as well. If I ever lost you, I couldn't go on."

"The heart is resilient, *shi'aad*," he whispered. "If it was not, I could not have married you. I will always remember Fire Star. But just because I still hold a measure of love for her, it does not mean I love you any less."

"Do you think your mother's heart, in time, will be resilient?"

He frowned. "Are you thinking one day she and the reverend..."

"I am thinking she has the right to do as you have done. Life without someone to love can be so lonely."

"You speak the truth, and since it was by my

311

father's last wish that the holy man return to Willow Creek, there is not much I can say on the matter. Whatever the outcome, the decision must be hers."

"Do you realize you are now a landowner, and soon you will have tenants living on that land? Here in England, you would be considered a lord. And in America you are a chief." She pulled back to look at him. "I love you, my lord and chief."

"I love you as well, Riley Redbird Eagle," he whispered. Then capturing her full lips with his, he decided to show her just how much.

A word about the author...

Roberta C. M. DeCaprio is a freelance writer of romance and woman's mainstream fiction. A prior "sexuality" columnist for *A.B.L.E.D. Women* magazine, and former Assistant Editor for *Independence Today* newspaper, (both publications dedicated to the needs and rights of the disabled), Roberta has insight into the problems other physically challenged people face due to living herself with a walking impairment.

She is the author of *Once Upon a Sonnet*, and has won awards for her poetry, becoming published in several anthologies. Her first paranormal, *Coma Coast* was published in 2006 by Wings Press. Its sequel, *The Vanity*, followed in 2007. *A River of Orange* was published by The Wild Rose Press in 2008, as well as Roberta's historical romance, *The Golden Lady,* (Book One in the *Between The Rifle and The Spear* series) in 2009. Book Two, *One Perfect Flower*, was released in 2010, and Book Three, *A Rose In Amber*, in 2011. Her latest paranormal, *Altered Journey*, was released into second edition printing also in 2010 from The Z Group/ZLS Publishers.

Roberta is a graduate of the Writer's Digest School and Cornell Cooperative Extension. During the years she was a member of the Romance Writers of America, she held office as newsletter editor for her local chapter's monthly publication, interviewing such published authors as Elaine Raco-Chase, Sue-Ellen Welfonder, and the late Kathleen E. Woodiwiss.

A mother and grandmother of two, Roberta shares her upstate NY home with many dearly loved pets and her artist husband.

To view Roberta's backlist and read excerpts from her books log on to: www.robertadecaprio.com.

Thank you for purchasing
this publication of The Wild Rose Press, Inc.
For other wonderful stories of romance,
please visit our on-line bookstore at
www.thewildrosepress.com.

For questions or more information
contact us at
info@thewildrosepress.com.

The Wild Rose Press, Inc.
www.thewildrosepress.com

To visit with authors of
The Wild Rose Press, Inc.
join our yahoo loop at
http://groups.yahoo.com/group/thewildrosepress/